REMEMBER US

REMEMBER US

Jason C. Mavrovitis

GOLDEN FLEECE
PUBLISHING

While *Remember Us* is inspired by oral history, actual events, public records, court transcripts, and newspaper accounts, it is a work of fiction.

ISBN: 978-0-6151-6357-4
LCCN: 2007937158

For Bette, with love.

CHAPTER ONE
1881
SOZÓPOLIS, EASTERN ROMYLIA

A caïque plunged through rolling swells, heeled to starboard, and reached toward the blazing sun. Before it, gilded wave-crests stretched to the eastern horizon. Seaspray showered over its bow. Clinging to the mast and wiping salt water from his eyes, a passenger turned his head astern, laughed, and called to the helmsman, "Bravo, *kapetánios.*" Pointing to the seagulls that swooped low over the caïque's wake, he shouted, "They want fish!"

"They'll be disappointed," the captain answered, pulling down the peak of his cap to wedge it against the wind. "They think every boat is a fishing boat." The gulls squawked their protests and soared into a crystalline blue sky.

The caïque passed a wave-washed point that marked the southern boundary of a great bay, and sailed several kilometers out to sea. "Sit down," the captain commanded. "I'm falling off the wind." He changed course to the southeast, and as the fresh breeze filled the mainsail, he warned, "Watch your head. We are going to jibe." The caïque ran southwest before the wind. Squinting, the

1

passenger made out a distant, low-lying breakwater that was veiled by a swirling mist.

A quarter of an hour later, the captain guided his boat behind the breakwater and into a sheltered harbor. Above the protected anchorage, along the crest of a promontory that thrust out into the sea, homes with red-tiled roofs; and an ancient Byzantine church of patterned red, brown, and ocher stones reflected the morning sun, radiating a golden, shimmering welcome to the passenger. He smiled.

Well into the bay and close to the harbor's stone quay, the captain brought the caïque about. Its sails luffed, and the boat drifted backward, coaxed to shore by the wind. While one of the crewmen dropped sails, the other secured lines to the quay's bollards and prepared to unload the cargo. The passenger jumped over the gunwale onto the landing. Waving farewell, he called, "*Antío, kapetánios.* I'll see you in two days."

"Be here early," the captain advised. "I'll sail one hour after sunrise."

"I'll be here."

Konstantínos Kapidaghlís hurried across the wheel-rutted dirt road that bordered the harbor. He carried his tall frame like a soldier. Blue eyes bracketed the straight, narrow nose on his angular face, and a well-trimmed, waxed mustache advertised his masculinity. Stepping onto a cobblestone path, the energetic twenty-two-year-old followed it up a slope. He stopped at the crest of the hill, took a deep breath, and gazed across the expanse of the sea: south to the Bosphorus, east to far away Georgia, and north toward the Danube and the Crimea. As a child, he had learned that ancient-Greek adventurers — romanticized in the Jason myth — had first sailed this sea. Hellenic, Roman, and Byzantine emperors, Latin merchant princes, Ottoman sultans, and the great powers — Russian, British, and French imperialists —had all dominated it in their time, and engaged in commerce and war. Early maps labeled it the *Pontos Eúxeinos.* "*Pontos Eúxeinos?*" he thought. "*Hospitable?*

Peaceful? Bah! Treacherous storms. Shipwrecks. Mavrothálassa. Beautiful."

The Black Sea surrounded his city, his birthplace; a Greek city, accessible only by boat, or by a narrow neck of land that connected it to the Balkan coastline. It was Sozópolis — the City of Salvation. For two thousand years, it had been the first safe haven ready to shelter merchants' boats from the violent seas that too frequently surprised them on their reach from the Bosphorus to the Danube.

Konstantínos stood silently, taking pleasure in the soft, whistling sounds the wind made as it crossed the taut stays of cargo boats rocking at anchorage. They dotted Sozópolis's harbor. Other boats, *alamánes*, lay on their sides on the pebble-strewn beach. He thought of them with men at their oars, blessed by a priest, and carrying icons of St. Nikoláos as they went to sea to chase schools of fish along the coast. Most often, they all returned home laden with mackerel, anchovy, tuna, mullet, and swordfish. But there were times when the sea engulfed them, swallowing some into its black depths, denying grieving families their husbands and fathers.

Konstantínos hurried on. His feet pounded up the steps of his parents' home and carried him through an open door. He stopped short when he saw his mother's astonished face. "Surprised?" he asked, hugging her and kissing her forehead.

She pushed him away. "What are you doing here? Are you all right?"

"I'm fine," he answered, collapsing on a low divan. He leaned back and watched his mother's eyes smile. Her chest heaved a sigh. "You're thin. Are you hungry? I'll fix you something to eat."

"No. Not now. Just some water."

"Wait." She left the room with the grace of a young woman.

Her face had brightened when he arrived, and her wrinkles — more of them now — seemed to fade as she smiled. *How many of those wrinkles did I cause?* he thought.

"You're going to join the Russians? Fight the Sultan?" she had asked when, under the noses of the Turks, he had joined the secret Bulgarian militia that had been recruited by Russian agents in 1877. "Are you crazy?" And then when he returned from the war and told her that he was going to apprentice to a tailor in Pyrgos, she worried, "And what about Haríklea? Are you going to make her wait forever?"

Theófano Kapidaghlís returned to the parlor with a small tray in her hand. In spite of the anxiety he had caused her, she beamed at her son. "Here, drink your water. And have some quince. I saved a jar for you."

"Thank you, *mána*." He lifted a small spoon with its deep orange-red treasure to his mouth. "Miraculous. The best in Sozópolis." Konstantínos was happy to see the glow his compliment brought to his mother's face. He drank. "Even water is better in this house." Drying his mustache, he twisted its points with his fingers and got up from the divan. "Now, I have things to do."

"What? What do you have to do? We didn't expect you for weeks."

"I have news. The blood we shed at Shipka was worth it, and I..."

"Shipka," she grumbled. "You could have been killed. My prayers to the *Panaghía* saved you."

He knew that his mother had no understanding of the battle of Shipka Pass, nor of the war, nor why he had fought. "The main reason I am here is more important to you," he explained. "I came to see Haríklea, and her mother and father."

"See her? She has waited like a saint."

He remembered Haríklea's sad and gentle face, and how she had fought back tears when he told her that he was going to join the irregulars to fight the Turks. She had asked, "Why? Why do you have to fight? What will I do if you don't come back?"

4

"I have to be part of it," he had answered. "We'll help the Tsar throw out the Turks and take the City."

She waited for him then, and then again when he went off to become an apprentice in Pyrgos.

"No more waiting," Konstantínos told his mother. "I finished my apprenticeship and made some money. And I've found a place for us to live in Pyrgos. Haríklea will like it. We'll set our wedding date today."

"Glory to God. I'll be able to face her mother again in church."

Konstantínos smiled.

"And Haríklea will be able to hold her head up," she continued.

"Where is *babás*?"

"Working in the fields. He'll be back late afternoon."

He thought for a moment. "I'll go to see Hrístos. He'll want to hear the news."

"Good. Vasilikí is in labor. Go. Keep him company."

Konstantínos hurried between the rows of almost identical homes that lined Sozópolis's narrow lanes. Their stone first floors were storage rooms. Above, wood-framed structures that slightly overhung the lower stories served as living quarters. He ran up the stairs to the open door of Hrístos's home, and called to his friend who sat at a small round table in an airy, sunlit parlor. "'*Yiá sou*, Hrístos."

Oblivious to Konstantínos's greeting, Hristodoúlos Zissis picked nervously at a colorful embroidered doily on the table. Konstantínos stepped into the room. "Hrístos. It's me. Konstantínos."

Hristodoúlos looked up, paused for a moment, and then began to scratch together the flower petals that surrounded a small vase in the middle of the table. When an anguished moan filled the room, he looked up at Konstantínos and sighed, fingers to his lips. His hair was uncombed and several days of stubble darkened his

5

face. He twisted his narrow-hipped frame away from the table and peered down a hallway. "Listen."

Unmindful of his friend's state, Konstantínos erupted, "The newspaper reports from Berlin say that the great powers gave Greece Thessaly and part of Epirus..."

"Listen," insisted Hrístos, looking blankly at his visitor. His fingers continued to fidget, and he turned again toward the hallway.

Konstantínos went on. "Crete will rise against the Sultan, and then..."

"Aaaah!"

The piercing cry stopped him in mid-sentence. Hushed, anxious word-sounds carried from the room furthest from the small parlor. Another anguished scream changed Konstantínos's bearing. He forgot about Berlin and Greece for a moment, and looked at his friend sympathetically. "Vasilikí?" he asked.

"It has been hours." Tears came to Hrístos's reddened eyes. He trembled, his head fell forward, and his hands covered his face. "Maybe this time the *Panaghía* will grant us a son."

Konstantínos grasped his friend's shoulder. "I'll stay with you."

Konstantínos sat on the Ottoman divan that stretched along the wall of the small parlor and leaned forward with his elbows on his knees. Through a gap between two worn, dark-wood planks at his feet, he made out shadowy forms in the stone-enclosed storage room below him. From its dark recesses came wisps of pungent smells — musty wine barrels and *toursí*, the mouth-puckering pickled vegetables that helped to sustain the people of Sozópolis through the winter months.

A stream of air from the window behind Konstantínos cooled his neck. But Vasilikí's periodic screams brought a nervous sweat to his brow. In them, he heard the shrieks of flesh-torn men — those who had fought at his side at Shipka Pass. His thoughts raced back to a terror-filled, stifling August day.

6

Waves of Turkish assaults left mangled dead and suffering wounded comrades on the ground around him. He was splattered with blood, and nauseated by the stench of loose bowels and rotting corpses. With his aides, a Russian colonel galloped through an artillery barrage, and on reaching Konstantínos called, "Where are your officers?"

"They're dead," Konstantínos growled.

"What's your name?"

"Kapidaghlís. Konstantínos Kapidaghlís."

"Romiós?"

"Yes."

"You're in command." The colonel turned to the men remaining on their feet and ordered, "This is your commander. Obey him." And to Konstantínos he said, "Hold to the last man," and galloped off.

They fought until their ammunition was gone, and then, desperate, they threw rocks, their equipment, and even body parts of their dead at surges of charging Turks. Finally, they engaged body to body, with knives, fists, and teeth.

Konstantínos and his men held the position, and they rewarded him with an epithet — *Generalis*.

Another cry from Vasilikí brought Konstantínos back to the present. He shuddered at the dread that had seized him in the safety of his friend's home. Minutes passed slowly in the tension-filled parlor. From time to time, one or the other of the men stood, stretched briefly, and then returned to his place. They did not speak. Late morning strained into early afternoon. Vasilikí's moans and cries were constant.

Other cries, those of seagulls, distracted Konstantínos. He got up, looked out the window, and watched gulls high above the town drop shiny black mussels onto rooftops. They retrieved and dropped them repeatedly until one cracked on a hard red tile. Then the closest gull tore out and swallowed the mollusk's substance before another could take the prize.

Konstantínos remembered the legend he had learned as a child.

When the great hero Achilles died, his mother, Thétis transported his soul to the island of Leúke at the mouth of the Ister. She commanded seagulls to guard his tomb, and to wash it clean each day with their sea-wet wings.

Two gulls plummeted from the sky. He heard the flutter of their wings as they landed on Hrístos' roof. Their cries accompanied the cry of a baby.

The men waited. In a few moments Vasilikí's mother, Kyria Sultána appeared. Her eyes sunken with fatigue and her hair disheveled, she seemed older than her sixty years. She saw Konstantínos. "You're a surprise," she exclaimed.

Hrístos pleaded, "Tell me."

"A girl."

Konstantínos saw a flash of disappointment cross his friend's face. Hrístos hesitated for a moment and then asked. "Vasilikí?"

"She'll live."

He crossed himself, saying, "Praise to Him."

Kyria Sultána waved her hand at her son-in-law. "*Haíde*. Bring the girls to see their mother and baby sister. Run." Starting back to supervise the women who were tending her daughter and grandchild, she called over her shoulder, "Go with him, Konstantínos. Or go tell Aleksiev."

Konstantínos said, "*Na sas zísi*," to his friend; the prayerful phrase common in the Balkans, where death often claimed the newborn and the young.

Hrístos did not reply to his friend's prayer for life. Bent, he moved through the door and down the steps to the stone-paved street. Konstantínos followed, calling out, "Where is Aleksiev?"

"At the *kafeneío*, across from the boats. Tell him..." Hrístos paused. "Tell him that Vasilikí and the baby are well."

"I'll tell him."

Konstantínos stopped at the door of the *kafeneío* for a moment to relish the blended smell of wine, coffee, tobacco, and fish that discouraged any but habituated regulars. Facing the harbor, the coffee house was a white-walled room furnished with a few rectangular tables, four times as many straight-backed wood chairs, and a narrow two-meter-long counter. It served the men of Sozópolis as an informal employment agency and a news center. Landowners and boat captains came here to find field workers, or crews for caïques and *alamánes*. They listened to news brought to them by cargo boat crews from as far away as Odessa, the Danube, and the City. Women, excluded from the sanctuary, met in their homes, at the bakery, and at church, and busied themselves constantly with care of homes and children.

A small preparation area behind the counter held an ancient, sand-filled brass brazier. At its center, atop a glowing bed of charcoal, frothy *kafé* bubbled in a mottled brass *ibríki* that had long lost its shiny copper finish. Men sipped cups of *kafé*, or glasses of *krasí* or *rakí* while they talked farming, fishing, and politics, played *távli*, or sat quietly smoking a bubbling *narghilé*.

When Konstantínos stepped into the *kafeneío*, he heard the click-click sounds of *kombolói* passing through the fingers of a daydreaming old man who sat by the door, and thought. *What a good place."*

Covered by a stained white apron, the skinny, stooped, balding owner of the *kafeneío*, Thanási, saw the new arrival and jumped to his feet. "*Generalis.*"

One voice called, "Konstantínos." Another, "*Generalis.*" And others, "Thessaly ... Epirus..."

Konstantínos raised his hand to quell the outburst. "I heard it all in Pyrgos. I went to tell Hrístos before coming here."

A voice from the corner of the *kafeneío* rose above the clamor. "Is my grandson born?" Aleksiev Vserkosov, Vasilikí's father, sucked at his amber *agizlik* making the water in the *narghilé* next to him bubble as he filled his lungs with aromatic tobacco smoke. He

9

exhaled. The smoke swirled about his head. "Is my grandson born?" he asked again.

"Forget the baby," a man shouted. "Will Greece fight?"

"Is my grandson born?" Aleksiev bellowed. He stood up, and removed the *agizlik* from a long tube attached to the *narghilé* and stored it safely in his vest pocket. "I've been waiting for hours, cast out of my home. Do I have a grandson?"

"A granddaughter," Konstantínos reported.

Aleksiev's body sagged for an instant. "And Vasilikí?"

"She's fine."

"Good."

Thanási's eyes squinted at Aleksiev. "Is the birth of a granddaughter more important than news from Greece?"

Aleksiev's eyes turned cold. "Yes. And this is Eastern Romylia, not Greece. I am Bulgarian. You…you'll all become Bulgarians."

Thanási raised a fist toward Aleksiev, shouting, "Never!"

Aleksiev lunged forward and encircled Thanási's upper body in his powerful arms, threatening to crush the scrawny man's chest. While others stood back, not willing to risk his anger, Konstantínos stepped forward and grasped Aleksiev's forearm. "Allow me to buy everyone *rakí* in honor of your grandchild."

Aleksiev hesitated, and then as he realized that his overpowering physical reaction to Thanási's taunting had been excessive, he relaxed his hold and smiled. "Thank you, Konstantínos, but the honor must be mine. *Rakí* for everyone. You too, Thanási."

Thanási hurried behind the counter and filled glasses from a bottle of the clear liquor. Lowering his head submissively, he poured Aleksiev's drink with trembling hands. Tensions eased, and the men drank to the baby. "May she live, Aleksiev."

Aleksiev downed his drink and smiled. "Now I'm going to see my new granddaughter. You can all talk about the news from Berlin — and dream that is good for you."

As Aleksiev moved to the *kafeneío's* door, Konstantínos heard him whisper, "What sin did Hrístos commit to deny me a grandson? How will he marry three daughters?"

Not expecting answers, Aleksiev stepped out into the early evening light. But when he heard Thanási shout "*Zíto Ellás!*" from the safety of the *kafeneío*, he turned and raised a defiant fist. A moment later, he kicked at a cat that crossed his path and disappeared around the corner of a house.

Years before, in 1828, the Tsar had taken advantage of the Sultan's preoccupation with the revolution in Greece and ordered his army to take Ottoman held Balkan territory. In support of its land army, Russian ships had bombarded the Turkish stronghold in Aleksiev's birthplace, the coastal city of Varna. When his father sent him to forage for food outside the city's walls, the boy stumbled on a burned out wagon and discovered a pouch of dried lentils in its charred remains. Returning home with the hoard hidden under his shirt, he found his mother, father, and sister dead — mutilated by a barrage from the Russian ships. As if to blot out what had happened, the stunned twelve-year-old boy covered their torn bodies with rubble and wandered away.

Desolate and frightened, Aleksiev fled Varna, the sound of cannon, and the smell of death and corruption. He trekked inland, and then south, begging food from poor peasants and sleeping on the dirt floors of their huts until, at last, he turned his steps east, back again toward the sea. He reached Sozópolis in time to relive the horror of Varna, for the Tsar's ships bombarded and subdued the small Turkish fortress on the island that protected Sozópolis's harbor, and landed troops and artillery on its shore.

At the harbor, Aleksiev begged for work in exchange for food. In the boy, a Greek boat builder saw an able-bodied replacement for dead and injured workers. Hearing the boy speak Bulgarian, he asked, "Are you friendly with the Russians?"

"No. I hate them."

"Why?"

"They killed my family in Varna."

"The Russians won't stay. You are safe with us. We are mostly Romiói. They will leave. You'll see."

The Russians left, and Aleksiev became an apprentice. He learned the skills that made safe the fishing and merchant vessels Sozópolis's men depended on at sea. In time, he learned Greek and took a Romiá as his wife, became a master boat builder and a valued member of the community.

Aleksiev entered his daughter's home to find his son-in-law and his granddaughters waiting in the parlor. His wife's namesake, Sultána, and her sister Smarágda ran to their grandfather. He smothered them in a massive embrace, and with kisses cautioned, "Shh, shh, korítsia, not too much noise. Your mother and little sister are sleeping."

Approaching two meters in height, Aleksiev was taller than most Bulgarians or Romiói. Broad shoulders supported his thick neck and massive head. While heavy eyelids often gave him the appearance of detachment, his eyes sparkled at his granddaughters. Thick, white-flecked black hair reached to his shoulders, and distinctive white stripes marked his beard at his jowls and chin.

Aleksiev's wife, Kyria Sultána, came into the room and invited them forward. "Haíde, korítsia. Come. Kiss your mother and the baby." She took the girls by their hands and led them down the hallway. The men followed and entered the space where just a few hours before Vasilikí had endured the miraculous agony of labor. Once in the small bedroom, they turned toward the sacred icons that rested on a narrow shelf in the corner of the room. Cradled in Vasilikí's arms, her baby slept in the glow of flickering votive candles that illuminated icons of the Panaghía and Hristós, and of Sozópolis's two patron saints, Zosimos and Nikoláos.

All but Aleksiev bowed their heads toward the icons and made the sign of the cross on their bodies. He went directly to his daughter, took her hand, and bent to kiss her and the baby. Tears glistened in Vasilikí's eyes. He used her pet name and smiled. "Don't cry, Kiki. Your baby girl is beautiful. I love you."

Aleksiev saw the baby's eyes open. She seemed to look into his face, and her mouth puckered into a little smile. He asked Hrístos. "What will you name her?"

Vasilikí answered for her husband. "Eléni."

There were footsteps on the stairs. "Hrístos? Sultána?" two voices cried as one.

Hristodoúlos greeted his parents, Zísos and Sofía, in the hallway, whispering, "Softly. Vasilikí is resting. It's a girl."

Zísos grumbled under his breath. "Another granddaughter."

They entered the room and exchanged wishes for the baby's long life with Aleksiev and Kyria Sultána, their *symbétheri*. They bent to kiss Vasilikí and the newborn. Hrístos lifted Sultána and Smarágda to kiss their mother and to see their baby sister. Sultána whispered, "She's so small."

"What's her name, *babás*?" Smarágda asked her father.

"Eléni," he answered. "*Na mas zísi.*"

In another corner of Sozópolis, Konstantínos smiled at Haríklea's smile and dried her tears with his handkerchief.

"Really?" she asked, looking into his bright blue eyes. "Really? In September?"

"Yes. Really." Konstantínos glanced over his shoulder to be sure that Haríklea's happy mother and father had shut the door of their home behind them. It was dark, Konstantínos and Haríklea were alone, and he chanced a moment of intimacy. He drew her into his arms and kissed her lips gently. She gasped, "Someone will see us." She kissed his cheek, pushed him away, and ran into the house, confused by the feelings that had arisen in her.

Several weeks later, on August 15, the people of Sozópolis commemorated *Tis Panaghías*. Their fast in preparation for the feast day of the Virgin had begun at the peak of the harvest, fifteen days before. Wheat, barley, lentils, and chickpeas had been gathered and stored. Soon, the work of harvesting grapes would begin. Now was a time for rest and social gathering.

At the end of the liturgy, families rushed to their homes. They gathered baskets of food for the celebration and carried them to a place at the shore where trees offered shade, and there was ample space for family groups to gather at tables and to dance. Near them, fat dripped and flared on embers under crisp, spitted lambs.

Sitting in a quiet spot with his friends, Aleksiev opened a jar of marinated *tsíri*, and placed two pieces of the fish on a chunk of bread. Taking a bite, he offered the jar to Zísos. "Have some. Delicious. I love these little dried mackerel with bread soaked in olive oil, vinegar, and dill."

Nodding agreement, Zísos took the jar from Aleksiev and, while preparing a snack for himself, pointed to Konstantínos, who approached them carrying four glasses and a carafe of wine. "Am I welcome?"

Aleksiev smiled at him. "Is the Sultan a Moslem? Pour the wine."

Konstantínos's father, Stéfanos was just a step behind his son. Born Stefan Tsvetkov, he had met and married Theófano, daughter of Aléxandros Kapidaghlís, taken his father-in-law's surname as his own, Hellenized his given name and become Stéfanos Kapidaghlís. But with some pride, he kept Tsvetkov as a middle name and passed it on to his sons.

"Stefan, sit here with Zísos and me," Aleksiev ordered.

"Stefan?" queried Konstantínos. "You don't miss a chance to make the point that my father is not Greek, do you?"

"I don't miss the chance to embrace him as a brother Bulgarian and Slav. Like me, your father is adopted here."

"He's right. I was born a Bulgarian in Serbia and fought with the Russians at Shumla and Silistria in '28, and south to the gates of Constantinople. We could have had it, but the bastard Tsar betrayed us after we took Adrianópolis. As long as he got his trade routes and didn't offend the Franks, he was happy. Our blood meant nothing to him."

Tall and slender, Stéfanos had the same handsome, angular features that he had passed on to his sons Konstantínos and Ménas. However, unlike his sons, there were deep creases at the corners of his eyes and mouth earned by years of squinting at the bright light of the sun reflecting off the sea, and worry. He sat down next to Aleksiev, and leaned back against a tree to enjoy the scene.

Zísos slapped Aleksiev's shoulder exclaiming, "We've done well, *symbétheros*. Count them — eight children and six, no, seven grandchildren with Eléni. We'll fill Sozópolis."

"All I want to fill is my belly," Aleksiev said. "The smell of roasting lamb makes my mouth water. But to serious matters. Konstantínos, in a few weeks you will start a new life. Are you prepared?"

"Prepared? For what?"

"For marriage. For life. Do you have a list?"

"List? No."

"You had better start one. When you get home Konstantínos, write down salt."

"Salt? Why salt?"

"Just write it down."

"What else?"

"Salt," Aleksiev repeated.

Konstantínos frowned. "Salt, again?"

Aleksiev ordered, "And add salt to the list."

"Enough. What is this?" asked Konstantínos.

"Marriage. Year after year, it remains the same," Aleksiev explained. "Saltcellars empty and fill, one day follows another, seasons pass, and years flow on. Always the same."

"There is something else, my son," Stéfanos said.

"What?"

"Don't expect *éros* to survive long in your marriage. It is like dew. It dries before the midday sun. In time, *agápe* takes its place."

Annoyed, Konstantínos took the wine flask and stood up. "Are you trying to discourage me?"

"No. No, my boy," Aleksiev said, reaching after the wine. "Sit down," he urged. "Here, I'll hold the wine."

Konstantínos continued to stand.

Stéfanos changed the subject. "Did you see Prince Alexander's yacht near the south beach? His family and friends went swimming yesterday. There were guards posted on the shore to protect him."

"Our German Prince wants the sea all to himself," Zísos said.

Aleksiev scowled. "He's an autocrat. He's here because he's the nephew of the Tsar."

"No. He earned becoming Prince of Bulgaria," argued Stéfanos. "Like me and my son, he fought with the Russians against the Turks."

"He'll get into trouble when the Bulgarian politicians try to make Eastern Romylia part of Bulgaria."

"Speaking of trouble," Stéfanos said. "Konstantínos told me that there was a fight at the *kafeneío* the day Eléni was born. What happened?"

"Fight? Nonsense," Aleksiev declared. "Your son uses too much oil and vinegar on his salad. The young Romiói had their blood up about Thessaly and Epirus. 'Kill Turks. Take the City. Hellenic Empire' — nonsense."

"Why?" Zísos asked. "Sooner or later we'll be rid of the Turks. Constantinople is our mother."

"Nonsense." Aleksiev was adamant. "Constantinople is your mother, Zísos, not ours," he said, holding out his arm toward Stéfanos as if to gather him in close. "Look to the north. It is Bulgaria. You are in Eastern Romylia, not Greece. And Eastern Romylia will become part of Bulgaria too. The Romiói are on the coast, the Bulgarians hold the heartland. You'll be Bulgarian or they'll push you off the edge and into the sea."

"They'll push me and my children into the sea?" cried Zísos.

Stéfanos put his hand on Zísos's shoulder. "Calm down, Zísos."

"Listen," Aleksiev insisted. "We're surrounded by Bulgarians who want their own country — church — bishops — their own language."

"No," Zísos insisted. "We are Romiói, Orthodox Christians. We fought with the Greeks when they revolted against the Sultan in 1821. The cities on this coast, from the Bosphorus to the Danube belong to Romiói."

"We share grandchildren, and we dance at baptisms and weddings," Stéfanos said. He turned to Konstantínos. "That's all that matters. Right, son?"

"Well, no." Konstantínos, who had been standing, handed his glass to his father and then sat on the ground next to him. The men waited for him to continue. He took back his glass and sipped a little wine. "You are talking about the way we lived one hundred years ago, when we were all governed by the Patriarch — Orthodox subjects of the Sultan. Now Greeks have Greece, and Serbs, Serbia — their own countries, their own churches. Bulgaria became a country with the help of some of the Romiói who live here, including me. The Patriarch no longer rules the Orthodox in Bulgaria for the Sultan. Soon, Eastern Romylia is bound to merge with Bulgaria. Without the rule of the Patriarch and the Sultan, our different languages, customs, and jealousies separate us. And then, there is Macedonia."

"What about Macedonia?" Zísos asked.

"It's about who gets what," Aleksiev answered, his voice betraying his frustration. "Bulgaria wants Romylia. Bulgaria, Greece, and Serbia want Macedonia. The Tsar wants to dominate the region. The Sultan wants to keep it all. And the cursed Franks, who call Romiói and even Hellenes 'Greeks', want to control it all." His voice trailed off as his and Stéfanos's wives walked up. Two girls helped them carry food, and bowls, plates, and forks to the men.

"Are you hungry? Ready to eat?" Stéfanos' wife, Theófano asked.

"Maybe the wise men are too busy with politics to eat?" Kyria Sultána set a heaping platter of sliced lamb in front of them. The women smiled at their men indulgently and served them bread, cheese, olives, and bowls of rice and vegetables.

As they started away Theófano said, "Join us at the beach when you've eaten. The musicians have come."

Zísos, concerned about what Konstantínos and Aleksiev had said, wondered what it all meant for his family. The worry on his face changed to a smile when he heard a voice call, "*Pappoú. Pappoú.*" It was Chrysóula. She let go of her father's, Décimos, hand, and ran to her grandfather's welcoming arms. "Show me the anchor and the ugly woman."

"Again?" Zísos laughed. "We'll wear out the little coin."

Chrysóula, a fair-skinned, blonde-haired, and blue-eyed five-year-old, looked much like her mother, Olga, who had been born in the Crimea. Olga was the child of a Greek ship owner and a Russian woman whose ancestors were from the far north, from the shores of the Baltic Sea. Décimos, Hristodoúlos's seagoing brother, met and married her in Odessa while he waited out winter storms that made passage south past Cape Kalliatra treacherous. Reckless captains who disregarded the danger fouled the shore of the Black Sea with wrecked ships and rotting bodies.

Zísos reached into his vest pocket, took out a small leather bag and untied a thong that held it closed. "Here, here it is." A silver coin fell out of the bag and into his hand. It glistened in the sunlight. On one side were an anchor, a crayfish, and the letter 'A'. On the other — a round, globule-eyed Medusa stared out with her tongue grossly extended from her lips. Snakes danced in her hair.

"Tell me the story, *pappoú*," Chrysóula demanded as she made herself comfortable in Zísos's lap.

"Again?"

"Please, *pappoú*?"

"All right." He began, "Many years ago, long before you were born, I left Anatolia to find a better life."

"Why?"

"My mother and father went to heaven, and I was alone. And I wanted to get away from the Turks."

"But there are Turks here, *pappoú*."

"Yes, there are, but not as many. Besides, here in Romylia we have an Orthodox governor and the Turks leave us alone as long as we pay our taxes."

"What is that?" she asked.

"Well," he thought for a moment. "The Sultan in Constantinople wants a share of all of the grain we grow, and fish we catch, and wine we make. What we give him we call taxes."

"Did you give him taxes before you came here?"

"Yes, but more. There are more Turks in Anatolia and they made our life hard."

"What did you do?" Chrysóula adjusted her position so that she could see her grandfather's face.

"I walked from Ortaköy over high mountains, in deep snow, to Amisos, to the sea. I was hungry. A boat captain fed me, and hired me to load and unload his ship on a trip across the waters to Constantinople, and then to the cities of the Pontos."

She laughed. "And you threw up on the boat."

"You remember that part, eh? Yes, I was sick. But when I saw the Golden Horn, and Constantinople, and Ághia Sofía — it was worth it."

"And now we'll hear all about the City," Stéfanos interjected.

"Again?" asked Aleksiev.

"So don't listen." Zísos shrugged. "Eat. Drink."

Zísos left out a description of Constantinople, and went on. "Our first port after leaving the City was here, Sozópolis. It was hot, and after unloading the boat, I jumped into the water to cool off. My knife fell out of its scabbard and sank to the bottom. I dove down, and when I grabbed the knife my hand took muck from the bottom with it."

Chrysóula squeaked, "Eeeh." Her eyes closed, and her nose and lips puckered in disgust.

"It was just mud," said Zísos. "Besides, in it I found this little old coin."

"Older than you, *pappoú*?"

"Much, much older. The first Hellenes to live here two thousand years ago made this coin to buy things from Constantinople, when the City was called Byzantio. Do you remember what the anchor, crayfish and alpha stand for?"

"Ummm — the anchor is because we have boats. The crayfish is like what we catch and eat. And the alpha is for — aaah — apopollona ponka."

"Apollonia Pontika," he corrected. "It is the ancient name of our city. And Medusa? Who is she?"

"She scares anyone that wants to hurt us."

"Good," he said as he put the coin away in its bag and tucked it into his vest. "*Haíde*. Go. Play with your friends. Later I'll watch you dance."

"Zísos, why didn't you use your name, 'Zissis', instead of Ortakioglis?" asked Aleksiev.

"We like to remember where we came from," said Zísos. "Ortaköy in Anatolia was my birthplace. The people of Sozópolis called me the man from Ortaköy from the day I found the little coin and decided to stay. It's good enough for me. Besides, my sons use 'Zissis'. And remember, Stefan's father-in-law came from

Kapi Daghi in the Sea of Marmara. That's how he got the name Kapidaghlís."

Aleksiev mused, "Stefan, Zísos, and me — we all came from other places. Here, we found wives and made families."

Konstantínos lifted his wine glass high and called out, "Over here, Hrístos."

Hristodoúlos shepherded his daughters, Sultána and Smarágda, toward their grandfathers and his friend. He held a roasting pan full of food. Aleksiev and Zísos hugged and kissed the girls.

"Where is Vasilikí? And Elenítsa?" Aleksiev asked.

"Vasilikí is at home with Eléni. She has been crying all day. Mother came by a few minutes ago looking for us and sent me to bring some food home." He nodded down at the pan he held. "She said that you should go to get her later."

Konstantínos got up and handed the wine bottle to Zísos. "Here, take care of this," he said with a wink at Aleksiev. "I'm going to walk with Hrístos and the girls."

Zísos took the bottle and turned his attention back to his friends.

Aleksiev drained his glass and held it out toward Zísos, while asking Stéfanos, "Why did Konstantínos fight alongside the Bulgarians for Russia?"

"He thought that the Tsar would take Constantinople. Now he thinks that Greece will unite all the Romiói in Bulgaria, Macedonia, Ionia, and the Pontos. He says it's the *Megali Idhea* — a new empire."

"Ha! He's a dreamer," said Aleksiev.

"With a gun," responded Stéfanos. "There are dreamers with guns everywhere."

Zísos crossed himself. "God protect us."

CHAPTER TWO
1885
SOZÓPOLIS, BULGARIA

At eighty-five, Zísos no longer went to sea. Memories of his trek from the high plains of Anatolia over the Pontic Mountains to Amisos, and his arrival at Sozópolis faded. He had stopped telling the story to his granddaughter, and he rarely looked at the ancient little coin that rested safely in his vest pocket. He filled his summer days helping younger men in the fields and vineyards, and when the grape harvest was over, he set about household tasks.

On October afternoons, he opened wide the doors to his storeroom, inviting the slanted, warm rays of the afternoon sun to enter the space where he tended his barrel of fermenting grape juice, crocks of pickled vegetables, and stores of food that Sofía preserved in anticipation of winter. When the sun vanished behind the coastal hills and wind blew in from the sea, stealing warmth from the stones of the storeroom's walls, a chill came over him. He wrapped himself in a warm lambskin cape, closed the doors, and climbed the stairs to dinner and rest.

November found him repairing his farming tools. He was often kept company by four-year-old Eléni, who liked to play with him and his tools. She asked him endless questions while her sisters Sultána and Smarágda looked after their year-old baby sister Sofía and visited with their grandmother on the second floor.

He spent his late afternoons at the *kafeneío* by the harbor, caught up on local news, or when someone arrived from Varna or Pyrgos, or even the City, huddled close to his friends to hear about events beyond the boundaries of his small world.

One evening while climbing up the hill from the harbor, Zísos's ashen face twisted in anguish. He grasped his left arm and gasped for breath. A cold sweat covered his face and upper body. He stopped and sat at the side of the path for a few minutes. Color returned to his face. "I'm old," he whispered. In a moment, he got up and slowly walked home.

A week later Sofía heard knocking and loud voices at her door. "Sofía. Sofía. Quick. It's Zísos." Neighbors carried her husband into the house and to his bed. Sofía sat on the bed, held her husband's head against her breast and rocked back and forth. He was motionless. She looked at his slack face and open mouth and said, "You left me." She looked up to her neighbors, her face in pain. "He's gone."

Sofía's stoicism masked her grief. With a prayerful countenance, she fulfilled her spousal obligations in the ceremonies that accompanied Zísos' death, holding her emotions in check even as she greeted mourners who came to her home after the funeral service. When Stéfanos stepped through the doorway and spoke the traditional words, "May God forgive his sins," she kissed his cheek and accepted a warm hug with a smile.

Theófano, close behind her husband, repeated the incantation, embraced Sofía and added, "We'll miss Zísos."

Aleksiev rose from his chair on seeing Stéfanos and Theófano. "Life to us, Stefan. He died quickly. A blessing."

24

"I didn't see you at the church or the cemetery," Stéfanos said. "Are you all right?"

"You know me. I don't like priests or churches. Zísos knew how I felt. He forgives me."

Stéfanos let the matter drop.

Aleksiev whispered, "Thank God Sofía's blessed with three sons."

Stéfanos' face showed surprise at Aleksiev's reference to God and blessings.

Hristodoúlos arrived leading his daughters, Smarágda and Sultána, and dragging along their sister Eléni, whose arms were wrapped around his leg. The three girls were dressed warmly against the cold November day. Last through the door came Vasilikí, who carried her baby, Sofía.

Sofía Zisova hugged her son and three of her granddaughters before taking little Sofía from Vasilikí. She held her in her arms cooing, "Sofía. *Agápe mou. Hrisó mou.*" She smiled as she said her grandchild's name — "Sofía." When she heard Pater Elefthérios's voice coming from the steps to her home, she nuzzled her grandchild, handed her back to Vasilikí and went to the door to greet the priest, kissing the hand he extended toward her expectantly. His black beard, and *ráso* and *kalimáfion,* the clerical cassock and hat that symbolized both his religious position and his administrative role under the Ottomans, lent him dignity as he waited for those present to attend him.

"Priests," Aleksiev muttered to himself. "Bah!" He ignored the priest's extended hand. "Pater Elefthérios," Aleksiev challenged, "what will happen to the Patriarch's Greek priests now that Eastern Romylia is part of Bulgaria? Prince Alexander entered Plovdid as our sovereign. The Sultan must be trembling. And the Patriarch, too."

Pater Elefthérios greeted a mourner, extending his hand and offering a blessing while trying to hide his terror at the events of the past year behind a confident tone. Revolutionaries had carried out a coup in what had been Romylia's capital, Plovdid, arresting the governor and declaring union with Bulgaria. Bulgaria's monarch, Prince Alexander, accepted the inevitable and entered Plovdid as Romylia's sovereign, just as Aleksiev had foretold.

The priest thought of the new Bulgarian Church. The Sultan had allowed its formation fifteen years before to pacify his Bulgarian flock. Even the idea of a Bulgarian Exarch independent of the Patriarch was schismatic — anathema to the cleric. He knew that with Romylia no longer subservient to the Ottoman Empire, these were dangerous times for Greek priests.

"Well?" Aleksiev taunted. "What will happen to you Greek priests now?"

The priest crossed himself. "The Patriarch will protect us," he said tentatively.

"But we have a Bulgarian Exarch. We don't need a Patriarch."

Pater Elefthérios crossed himself and as if chanting a prayer, said, "God willing — dear Christ — please God, Ellás, King George and Ellás will save us. God will protect us, and Christ will return us to Holy Constantinople."

Hristodoúlos stepped between the priest and Aleksiev, who enjoyed the priest's discomfort, took the cleric's hand and kissed it. He turned to Eléni. "Kiss Pater's hand."

She spun around her father's leg and hid behind her sisters, pushing them forward. "You kiss," she said, and then ran to her grandmother, Kyria Sultána.

"I'm sorry, Pater. Sometimes Eléni has her own mind."

Mourners overflowed the parlor into the hallway and bedrooms of the small home. In its kitchen, women who had brought covered pans and baskets filled with food made ready the traditional funeral meal.

Earlier, Hristodoúlos's brothers, Décimos and Ioánnis, had cleared out the storage space on the ground floor of the house and set planks on frames to provide a makeshift table and benches. Embroidered tablecloths covered the rough planks. The women led a procession of mourners out of the living quarters, down the outdoor steps and into the storeroom, where they placed platters of fried fish and bowls of greens and rice, olives, cheese, and bread on the table. All stood while Pater Elefthérios said a short prayer and led the *Pater Imón*. When the prayer ended with, 'deliver us from evil, amen,' they sat and began to eat. In keeping with tradition, wine was not served at the *makaría*, so the men ate more quickly than usual and with less conversation. But once the women had cleared the dishes, everyone raised a customary glass of brandy and chorused the reminder that life continued in the wake of death, "Life to us."

One by one, mourners left Sofía Zisova with her immediate family and her grief, murmuring reassuring words to her.

"You have your sons and their families — grandchildren."

"You'll never be alone."

"They'll take care of you."

After the door closed behind the last guest, Sofía called to her granddaughter Chrysóula, "Come with me to the kitchen to bring water for the men." Once in the kitchen, Sofía pumped the water handle at the sink, filled a pitcher and handed it to her granddaughter. "Here, my love. Serve the water and come back to me." When the girl returned, Sofía led her into a bedroom and closed the door.

"*Pappoú* left something for you." She took a small leather pouch from her apron pocket. Tears finally ran onto her cheeks. "*Pappoú* loved telling you the story about this little coin. He wanted you to have it."

Chrysóula took the pouch and opened it. She held the ancient coin tightly in her hand for a moment, sobbed, and fell into her grandmother's arms. "I miss *pappoú* so much, *yiayiá*." Sofía stroked her granddaughter's hair and watched her as she returned the coin to its pouch and tied the leather drawstring around her neck.

While Sultána and Theófano helped Sofía put the house in order, Aleksiev and Stéfanos remained seated at the table in the

27

storage room. Décimos and Hristodoúlos joined them just as Konstantínos returned with a bottle of brandy and fresh glasses. He poured the liquor and asked, "What did you say to the priest, Aleksiev? He looked like he'd seen the devil."

"His devils are the new Bulgarian Archbishop, and his sovereign, Prince Alexander."

"They're my devils too," said Konstantínos.

"Drink to all the devils," Stéfanos suggested, "the Greeks, and their King George — the Bulgarians and their Prince Alexander — and to Serbs, and Turks, and the Sultan."

Aleksiev frowned. "Even I'm worried. The Bulgarians are overdoing it. Their schools are teaching children about Bulgaria's ancient empire, and the politicians promise it will return, and include Macedonia, and Salonika."

"What will the Sultan do if Bulgaria fights for land in Macedonia?" asked Stéfanos. "Do you think that the Romiói will fight the Bulgarians to keep their towns and villages under the Sultan and the Patriarch?"

Konstantínos answered his father. "The Sultan will be in the middle, fighting Bulgarians, Greeks, and Serbs, as they fight each other. I think that eventually the Sultan will lose. He is getting weaker. The question is: 'Who will win?'"

Aleksiev changed the subject. "Enough serious talk. *Generalis*, are you starting an army? You've been married barely four years and you already have two sons. When will Haríklea give you another?"

Hristodoúlos mimicked Aleksiev, "'Married barely four years and you already have two sons.' I've been married twelve years and I have four daughters. My father didn't live to see one grandson."

"And I don't have a son or a grandson," complained Aleksiev.

The door opened and a gust of north wind filled the room. When he saw his brother at the door, Konstantínos jumped to his feet, embraced Ménas, and turned away gasping, "You stink like rotten fish."

Ménas waved his brother away. He looked much like his Konstantínos, but shorter and thinner. Stéfanos's features were stamped on both sons.

"We didn't expect you home for another week," Stéfanos said. "What's happening in Varna?"

The men made room for the new arrival. He sat a little apart.

"I heard about Zísos when I arrived. Life to us. We'll miss him."

Konstantínos poured him a brandy.

"What's going on in the world?" Stéfanos persisted.

"The Serbs attacked Bulgaria."

"When?" Konstantínos shouted his question.

"They declared war on the thirteenth," Ménas told them, downing his brandy. "I learned about it in Varna before I boarded a fishing boat to get home. The *kapetánios* had just delivered a catch. That's why I smell so awful. By the time we reached Pyrgos, the war was over. Prince Alexander led troops inland from Romylia and beat the Serbs at Slivnitsa."

"Bravo, another war won," Aleksiev gulped down his brandy. He slouched in his chair. "Victory deserves another toast." He refilled his glass.

"Will there be any more fighting?" asked Décimos.

"No, I don't think so. It's over."

"What is over?" Theófano asked, entering with Kyria Sultána to join the men for a few minutes. She saw her son. "When did you get here, Ménas?" She hugged and kissed him, but then stood back. "By God, you smell. What will people think about the way I brought you up? Bathe and change your cloths."

Ménas answered his mother's question, but ignored her comments. "The war with Serbia is over."

Kyria Sultána clasped the table with both her hands. "What war? Will they conscript our men?"

"Don't worry about Hrístos," Aleksiev said, his speech slurred. "If the Bulgarians need help, they'll ask for Sofía."

Décimos laughed. "You mean *Yiayiá Macháira*. Remember, Hrístos? How many years ago? Thirty?"

"How could I forget? *Mána* took the old saber from the wall and ran, wielding it over her head and screaming at the French and British sailors who were landing at the harbor. We ran after her."

"They thought she was crazy," Décimos added. "I'll bet they couldn't wait to sail for the Crimea to fight the Russians instead of her. When the men came in from the fields, they heard the story and laughed themselves sick. *'Macháira, macháira,'* they called her, and sang, 'You made the British piss their pants.'"

Hristodoúlos shook his head. "She was like Medusa, ready to fight the Franks to protect us."

Aleksiev's chin fell to his chest. He mumbled, "Another war in little Sozópolis. Where is Zísos? Oh, he left us."

Kyria Sultána opened the door to the empty street. "Come, Aleksiev, you've had enough to drink. Let's go home. Tomorrow we'll visit Vasilikí and the girls to remind ourselves that life goes on."

The late afternoon sun gave no warmth. The sea's raw wind encouraged the young men to remove the planks and frames from the storeroom, and to put the farming tools, fishing gear, and nets back into their places. But Zísos no longer needed them.

CHAPTER THREE
1896
SOZÓPOLIS, BULGARIA

Eléni entered the bedroom that she shared with her sisters with a basket of red-dyed eggs in her hands. Sultána jumped out of bed, selected an egg from the basket and held it in her hand with only its point visible. Eléni accepted the challenge. She struck Sultána's egg with her own exclaiming, "*Hristós Anésti.*"

Sultána responded, "*Alithós Anésti,*" as her egg cracked under Eléni's blow.

The girls repeated the ritual they had performed much earlier that morning after the midnight Resurrection service and liturgy. They ended their forty-day fast by choosing an egg to crack against someone else's — large end to large end, or small end to small end, proclaiming: 'Christ is Risen,' and receiving the response 'Truly, He is Risen.' According to folklore, the one holding an unbroken egg, or even an egg with just one end unbroken would have good luck for the rest of the year. After a forty-day fast, the girls found hard-boiled eggs delicious in the predawn hours of Easter Day.

Eléni and Sultána's sisters, Smarágda and Sofía, were huddled together, buried under blankets on one of the two beds in their room. Outside, green-budded trees signaled the coming of spring. It was too early in the year for flowers — nature's colorful celebration of the Resurrection.

Sofía's muffled voice came from under the covers. "Eléni, do you have an egg for me?"

"You and Smarágda can pick one from the basket. Crack your eggs against each other, and whoever wins can try to break mine."

Fragments of Sultána's egg fell on her blanket as she shelled it. Eléni scowled. "Sultána, use the napkin I gave you."

"You're not my mother, Eléni. Stop telling me what to do. Don't forget I'm older than you."

Sofía, crawled out from under the covers, took her egg from Eléni, and shook Smarágda's leg. "Wake up. Pick your egg. Let me hit it. Wake up."

Smarágda moaned. "Leave me alone, it's early."

Vasilikí entered the girl's room, her tiny figure overwhelmed by a long nightdress and a coarse woolen robe. "*Korítsia*, don't argue. *Hristós Anésti*."

The three girls who were awake responded with, "*Alithós Anésti*." Smarágda moaned again and curled up under the blanket, covering her head more securely.

Vasilikí lifted the blanket from Smarágda's feet and pinched her toe. "Get up, Smarágda. Wash and dress, girls. Make your beds and have breakfast. We have a lot to do. No more fighting. We are going to the *Agápe* service later. You must forgive and love each other."

Eléni went to the kitchen with Sofía trailing behind her. Of the four girls, Sofía was the youngest, shortest, and smallest of frame — much like her mother. While her features admitted the mixture of blood that flowed in her veins even more than her sisters, Aleksiev Vserkosov had bestowed the slightly round faced, deep olive complexioned, dark-haired, and brown-eyed characteristics of his Turkic-Bulgar ancestors on all of his grandchildren. Eléni had inherited her grandfather's build. She stood taller and fuller than twelve-year-old Sofía, and at fifteen was a young woman.

Hristodoúlos' relationship with Eléni was unusual for a father and daughter in Sozópolis. Through habit, he had come to treat her more like a son than a third daughter. From the age of five, she got up early in the morning to accompany her father to the fields, or to see him off on a fishing boat at the harbor. As the months and years passed, she continued at her father's side. When she was physically able, she helped him carry his farming tools or fishing gear. Because the men and women of Sozópolis were accustomed to Eléni shadowing her father, they took little notice of her later when she was in her teens. She walked with the men, listened to them talk, and questioned them constantly: "What's it like in Constantinople?" "Where do good wools and silks come from?" "Can we get better cotton material from Varna?" "Is Athens far?"

Eléni set herself apart from other young women, gently breaking the convention that kept them at home within view of their mothers until they married. The independence she had developed gave her confidence. At fifteen, she showed little inclination to master homemaking skills, except for sewing. Her contribution to the household consisted of handmade dresses, skirts, blouses, and accessories for her mother and sisters.

In the kitchen, Sofía set about cutting slices from a large loaf of bread while Eléni arranged pieces of cheese on a plate.

"Will Konstantínos be at the Easter celebration?" Sofía asked.

"**Théo** Konstantínos." Eléni emphasized the respectful 'Théo' as a lesson to Sofía. "Yes. He came from Pyrgos three or four days ago. I heard that little Haríklea might be baptized in June."

"Why is he giving the baby his wife's name?" Sofía asked.

Eléni thought for a moment. "He wants to honor her memory."

"Do you think that he'll marry again?"

"Probably."

"When?"

"How should I know? Anytime. The year of mourning has passed. He is young. And his children need a mother. Zenóvios is the oldest and he's only eleven."

"He is so handsome." Sofía sighed.

"Yes, Zenóvios is a good-looking boy," answered Eléni.

"No. I meant Konstantínos." Sofía looked down.

Eléni saw a pink blush blossom at her sister's throat. "Sofía. Théo Konstantínos is old enough to be your father. Are you crazy? What would people think?"

Sofía ran from the room crying. "You're mean. You don't understand."

A moment later, Smarágda and Sultána hurtled into the room. Smarágda reached around Eléni and took a piece of cheese. "Where's your egg, Eléni? I smashed Sofía's before she ran into the bedroom. What's wrong with her?"

"Nothing." Eléni distracted her sister. "Here, here's my egg. Try to break it. *Hristós Anésti.*"

Smarágda's egg crushed on impact with Eléni's.

Sultána jumped up and down. "Eléni won! Eléni won!"

The girls ate their eggs, cheese and bread, and then hurried to groom and dress themselves.

This, the greatest feast day of the year, celebrated the Resurrection, and the arrival of spring — just as pagan Thracians and Hellenes had celebrated in Apollonia Pontika two thousand years before — with religious ceremony, feasting, drinking, and dancing.

Konstantínos stepped out of his parents' home into the chill Easter morning and walked toward the beach. "Brrrr," he groaned. *Before long,* he thought, *it will be warm; winter grain will be chest high, and Sozópolis's men will pull at the alamánes' oars, hauling in nets heavy with fish.* In his mind's eye, he could see tall poles set along the length of Sozópolis's northern shore. Strung between them in parallel rows, six tiers of slender lines would hold thousands of salted mackerel hanging to dry in the sun and sea air.

He stopped for a moment to look at the home where Haríklea had grown up. His eyes filled with tears. "I kept you waiting for so long, and you were so good. Where did fifteen years go? Why did God take you?"

Walking on, he saw men standing around pits of bright red embers. Dripping fat gave birth to licks of flame. A light breeze carried the smell of sizzling lamb to him and aroused his appetite. He saw someone look toward him and wave. "Over here, Konstantínos," he heard. It was Ioánnis Zissis. His brothers, Hristodoúlos and Décimos were with him.

"*Hristós Anésti*, Konstantínos," cried Hrístos. "Welcome home."

"*Alithós.*" Konstantínos grasped the hand of each of the brothers, and hugged them. "I'm well."

Turning back to his work, Ioánnis teased his brother. "Décimos, turn the spit faster or our lamb will catch fire. It's too close to the coals."

Décimos glowered at his instructor. "And your way, little brother, it will be raw."

Hrístos took Décimos's place at turning the spit and said, "Ioánnis isn't little anymore. He added three mouths to his table already. Three sons. I'm chilled to the bone." He turned his back to the glowing pit for a moment, tending the lamb with one hand. He laughed and said to Décimos, "Between us we have five daughters, and little brother gets all the sons."

Two days before, the brothers had risen early and led a bleating lamb to a tree. They hung it by its rear legs, and in the same way that the ancients had sacrificed to the gods at the time of the earth's renewal, cut its throat. When they finished dressing the lamb, they put its skin on a tree limb to dry, and its carcass in Hristodoúlos's cool storeroom to age, setting aside the organ meats and intestines for their wives to prepare tasty *kokorétsi*.

Early in the morning, the brothers had spitted their lamb and set it over glowing embers. They took turns rotating it over the fire and visiting their friends who were tending their own lambs nearby.

"Do you have an appetite, Konstantínos?" Ioánnis asked, leaning forward, close to the bed of coals. "I'm starving."

"The *kokorétsi* smells good. How soon will it be ready?"

Fat sputtered on the surface of the lamb.

"In a few minutes you'll have a *mezedáki*," Décimos said. He used one hand to pour liquor into a glass held by Ioánnis, and balanced a long spear loaded with *kokorétsi* over the embers with the other. "Come, Konstantínos, take *rakí* to warm you."

The lamb's liver, kidney, heart, and sweetbreads had been bathed in lemon juice and olive oil, sprinkled with mint and oregano, spiced with salt, pepper, cinnamon and cumin, tied into a roll with the lamb's intestines, and skewered on a spit. The aroma of the sizzling *kokorétsi* was irresistible.

Hristodoúlos stood for a moment to stretch his legs and allowed the lamb's underside to sear a bit. "Your children keep your parents busy, Konstantínos. They are happy to have them close."

"I don't see them enough."

Ioánnis stepped back, looked his friend over and whistled softly. "Look at Konstantínos, brothers. What a dandy."

Konstantínos looked down at his shoes. Accustomed to wearing a coat, tie, and polished shoes, he no longer owned the rougher clothing common to Sozópolis.

Décimos saw Konstantínos's embarrassment and changed the subject. "What's the news from Pyrgos?"

Konstantínos looked up with relief. "They're talking about completing the railroad trunk line to Yambol. That will link Sofía and Constantinople and bring more Bulgarians to the coast from inland. There are so many now that they've changed Pyrgos's name to be Bulgarian — Burgas." He sipped his *rakí*, took the glass

36

from his lips and grasped Hrístos' arm. "I forgot to tell you. I found a place for Eléni to apprentice. She can live with my cousin Marieka and her husband in Pyrgos. They have a daughter the same age as Eléni. They'll share her room and apprentice together."

"God protect you." Hristodoúlos hugged him and took both of his hands as if to kiss them. Konstantínos pulled his hands free.

"We'll miss her — and worry about her."

"I'll be there and watch out for her. She'll be fine."

Toward noon, families joined the men and surrounded the roasting lambs. When Vasilikí walked up to Konstantínos with her daughters, she offered him her cheek to for a kiss and said, "*Hristós Anésti.*"

One after another, the sisters greeted Théo Konstantínos with hugs and kisses. Sofía's kiss was as light as a butterfly's touch. She turned away quickly.

"Eléni, you're off to Pyrgos," Hristodoúlos announced. "You're going to apprentice to a seamstress."

Eléni jumped up, her hands flying to her face. "When? How?"

"As soon as the Easter holiday is over. You'll live with Konstantínos's cousin, who has a daughter your age. She'll apprentice with you."

Vasilikí looked stunned. She put her arm around Eléni and pulled her close.

"Théo Konstantínos, is it true?" Eléni clutched her upper body with her arms.

"Yes. Of course. You're off to a new life."

Smarágda pouted. "Why can't I go?"

Sultána whined. "Me too. Eléni shouldn't have all the fun."

"Because you have no reason to go," their mother said. "Eléni wants to be a seamstress. You both want only to get married as soon as you can. You can do that here. That's why."

Sofía said nothing. But Konstantínos noticed her fleeting glances. He smiled at her. She turned her head and ran to her cousin Chrysóula.

Friends and neighbors assembled and filled the communal space by the sea, each family surrounding a makeshift table for the celebration. By early afternoon, the day cooperated by providing a clear sky, a warm sun, and a gentle breeze from the sea. Platters of roast lamb joined golden loaves of *Lambrópsomo*, the sweet bread, crowned with eggs dyed deep red, and baked only at *Páscha*. Olives, cheese, rice, and young, boiled field greens crowded the centers of tables, joining bowls of Easter eggs and flasks of wine.

When the musicians played, Hristodoúlos struck the side of his wine glass with his knife, keeping time with the rhythms that invited young and old to dance. "Dance, girls." His daughters needed little encouragement. The ever-changing surface of the sea complemented the movements of the young women who joined hands and moved in a graceful circle by the shore. On the horizon, streaking clouds looked like lacey, white under-feathers that fall from seagulls skimming above the surf.

Aleksiev called from the next table, "Hrístos, come, sit with us. Konstantínos and Décimos will tell us what's happening in Pyrgos."

Hrístos, Ioánnis, and Stéfanos, joined Aleksiev and filled their glasses. Others gravitated toward the group.

Konstantínos motioned toward a heavyset, awkward young man. "Let's hear about Constantinople first," he insisted. "Halámbros got back yesterday."

Halámbros's speech was hesitant. "Well, just days ago, I was in the middle of an Armenian demonstration. It was … ah … about Turks … ah … killing Armenians in the Pontos. A Turkish mob attacked them. I thought I was going to be killed. Armenians were murdered — there was blood everywhere."

"More trouble," growled Aleksiev.

"The Sultan is collapsing," said Konstantínos. "Armenia, Macedonia, and Crete are screaming for independence."

Décimos stood. "You're right. Cretans want *énosis* with Greece. I heard Cretan sailors at the docks in Pyrgos say that they would revolt soon. And this time King George and the Greeks won't be able to ignore them. They'll have to help the Cretans."

Halámbros put his hand on Konstantínos's shoulder. "Will you fight the Turks again?" he asked with admiration on his face. "I'll go with you."

Stéfanos laughed. "My son is getting a little old to run off with a *tuféki* to fight. He's a tailor now, not a soldier. And he has a family."

"Not too old," said Konstantínos, half rising. "Besides, I have you and mother to watch the children for a while yet."

Stéfanos responded with parental authority. "It's time for you to marry again, and provide a mother for your family, not to run off to fight."

Konstantínos set his jaw and turned toward his friends. "The sooner we get the fight over with, the better." His fist pounded the table. "Greece will be our home when the Bulgarians throw us out of here. And they will. Where else can we find safety for our families?"

"Konstantínos understands," said Aleksiev.

Décimos stood, put his foot on the bench and rested his arm on his knee. "All the sailors I talk to say that Macedonia is the big trouble. The Turks will fight to hold on to it."

"They're already fighting," Konstantínos said. "Bulgarian guerilla bands are terrorizing Greek and Serbian villages in Macedonia. The Bulgarians want the Greeks out. They think Macedonia is part of their country."

"No one is going to throw me out," said Hrístos. "I was born in Sozópolis and my bones will stay here."

"And I'll be with you," said Aleksiev. "And you too, Stefan. Your bones will be in a box next to ours when they pull your skull out of the grave to join Zísos and the rest of us."

All this time Eléni had been close by at the next table listening intently. She felt a hand on her arm and turned to see her cousin Chrysóula. "Come with me, Eléni, I want to talk to you."

They walked until they were alone at the water's edge.

"Sofía told me that you'll leave for Pyrgos soon. I'll miss you."

"Not for long. You'll be busy enough after you marry Ángelos." Eléni laughed. "I'll be here for your wedding. I'll have to call you Kyria Marínos."

"No. Just Chrysóula. I'll be so happy with Ángelos. We love Sozópolis. I don't want anything to change."

"It won't. Not here. Not for you."

"Eléni — I want you to have something from *pappoú* Zísos, something to remind you of Sozópolis and us, and me." Chrysóula's hands moved behind her neck. She untied a thong and held out a small leather pouch to Eléni.

"I'm only going to Pyrgos," said Eléni, "not to Constantinople. I'll be in Sozópolis for holidays, and weddings, and baptisms."

"I know, but I had a dream of you in a boat far away. *Pappoú* and I were calling to you to remember us. Here, take this with you."

"But it's *pappoú's* little coin, isn't it? I can't take it."

"You must. It's a gift."

Eléni untied the pouch, took the ancient drachma into her hand, put it to her lips and kissed it. "Thank you, Chrysóula. I'll keep this always."

Eléni placed the amulet her mother had given to her in the leather pouch with the coin, and tied the leather thong about her neck. She joined a relic of ancient Apollonia Pontika, a city dedicated to the god Apollo, with those of Sozópolis's patron Saints: Zósimos, who protected the city, and Nikoláos, who watched over its men at sea.

"Eléni." She turned toward the voice and saw Konstantínos approaching.

"Can you be ready to leave with me next Monday morning? We'll take a boat if the weather is good."

"Yes," she answered — her heart pounding. "I'll be ready."

CHAPTER FOUR
1897
PYRGOS, BULGARIA

Almost one year had passed from the time that Eléni had left Sozópolis for her new life. Anxious and excited, she missed her father, mother, and sisters even before she boarded the caïque with Konstantínos on that bright Monday morning.

When they arrived in Pyrgos, Konstantínos carried Eléni's two wicker cases from the wharf to the Statev home on Rilska Street. The size of the city and the bustle of its busy streets intimidated her. But her insecurities were eased by Konstantínos's presence and the knowledge that he lived and worked near to her new home.

Marieka Stateva greeted Eléni with a reassuring smile, open arms, and warm words at the door of her second-story apartment. Looking over Marieka's shoulder, Eléni saw a young woman with glistening eyes.

"Eléni, this is my daughter, Maria."

Maria stepped forward and embraced her new friend.

43

Later in the day when he returned from work, Eléni met Maria's soft-spoken father, Georgi Statev. His greeting was formal: "Ah, Miss Zissis. Welcome to our home, I will call you Eléni. I hope that you and Maria will be good friends." He nodded to her, walked into the parlor, sat down, and began to read a newspaper. Eléni learned quickly that while Georgi Statev was quiet and formal, he deeply loved his wife and daughter and was given to teasing and gentle signs of affection. In contrast, Marieka was informal, full of life and lively in conversation. Marieka and her husband soon treated Eléni as a second daughter.

The morning after Eléni arrived, she and Maria followed Marieka into the dress shop of Kyria Anthoula Mavromátis. They smiled at the little bell that rang when Marieka opened the door. Kyria Anthoula looked up from her small desk. "Ah, Madame Stateva. How are you?"

"Good morning, Kyria Anthoula. Here are your new apprentices."

"Come in, girls. Good morning, Maria," Kyria Anthoula said. And then turning to Eléni, she continued, "You must be Eléni Zissis. Konstantínos told me all about you. He says that you have talent." Both girls stood mute.

Marieka walked toward the door. "I'll leave them in your care. My appointment for a fitting is next week, isn't it?"

"Yes. On Monday."

"I'll be here." Marieka hesitated for a moment and then said to the girls, "We'll be waiting for you this evening. Come straight home."

"The apprentices leave at exactly five o'clock, Madame Stateva," Kyria Anthoula said.

Marieka turned and stepped into the street.

"Come *korítsia*, meet the other apprentice in the workroom. Then we'll get started."

Kyria Anthoula Mavromátis, barley thirty, looked like her apprentices' older sister. Nonetheless, they considered her as one of their mothers' generation. She was tall for a Romiá, and had a fair-skinned, smooth-as-porcelain face. From her turban-like hairdo, delicate curls of shiny black hair reached down alongside her ears to her shoulders. Having never carried a child, her figure was trim and perfect for her to wear her own fashions as advertisements of her skill with the needle.

She had lost her husband, *Kapetánios* Anésti, to an unseasonable, violent storm that swamped his ship as he sailed to Constanza. Weeks after he disappeared, beach scavengers discovered the remains of his ship on the rugged coast north of Cape Kalliatra. Kyria Anthoula did not want to return to her village of Vasilikó and the dour life of a sea captain's widow so she opened a small dress shop in Pyrgos. She maintained her friendships with her husband's seafaring friends, and the merchantmen brought her illustrations of the latest fashions in the west and shipments of the best fabrics from Constantinople and from ports in France and Italy.

Within one year of her husband's death, the women of Pyrgos, who sought to emulate European society, had inundated Kyria Anthoula with orders. As her success grew, she needed help, so she took her husband's niece from the town of Agathopolis as an apprentice. In time, other young women apprenticed to her. From them she gained love and respect.

Kyria Anthoula's new apprentices were both almost sixteen. Dark-haired, brown-eyed, and olive-skinned, they looked like sisters. Maria's sculpted features distinguished her from Eléni, whose more oval face showed the influence of Tartar and Slavic ancestors. Maria's vibrant personality reminded Eléni of her sisters, and like them, Maria followed Eléni's lead. From the time that they woke to the sun's ascent from the sea, its rays brightening their room, to when they closed their eyes to sleep, they were constant companions. They quickly became close friends, their intimacy expressed in the way they touched, groomed each other, and communicated with their eyes.

They spent long days at Kyria Anthoula's dress shop, where they learned to design and make clothing for the wives and daughters of a growing number of Pyrgos's prosperous ship owners and merchants. Though Kyria Anthoula challenged them every hour of every day, they felt comfortable and secure in her kind care.

While they worked, Maria and Eléni sometimes overheard Kyria Anthoula's clients gossiping about their personal lives. The hushed comments often perplexed the girls, and they whispered to each other about the implications of what they heard. Occasionally Kyria Anthoula granted them insights into the world of women.

One day, a remark from the wife of a politician to Kyria Anthoula shocked Eléni. "My husband and his friends think that the Romiói don't belong in Bulgaria. Aren't you and your girls Romiá, Kyria?"

Kyria Anthoula defended her apprentices. "They were born here. They speak Bulgarian and Greek. They're Bulgarians, not Greeks," she argued. Alarmed, she said nothing about her own position as Romiá.

No, Eléni thought, pursing her lips and keeping her head down. *I and all my relatives in Sozópolis, well almost all, are Romiói.* Eléni had never considered herself a Bulgarian, although her maternal grandfather, Aleksiev Vserkosov, was one. He had married a Romiá, her grandmother Sultána. He always spoke Greek. And his daughter, her mother Vasilikí, had a Greek first name.

Before they left the house on the morning of March 25, the Day of the Annunciation, Marieka Stateva reminded the girls that they were to visit Evangelía Stateva that evening in honor of her name day. She was the wife of Todor Statev, Georgi's brother.

While they were walking to work Eléni asked Maria, "Do you think of yourself as Romiá or Bulgarian?"

"Bulgarian. But of course I speak Greek too, because my mother is Romiá."

"Why is your mother named Marieka? That's a Bulgarian name."

"Simple. Her father was Romiós and her mother Bulgarian. Her mother gave her a Bulgarian name."

"Well, what's important is that we are all Orthodox," Eléni declared as they entered the small shop and greeted Kyria Anthoula.

A busy day of pattern and cloth, and needle and thread passed swiftly for Eléni. She had lingering thoughts about what it meant to be Romiá or Bulgarian, and wondered how the small Turkish communities inland, west and south of Sozópolis, fit into the picture. She had heard stories of the old days when there was a Turkish garrison in Sozópolis, and when Turks walked the streets of her city as overlords. But that had all changed in the years after her birth.

At the end of the day, Kyria Anthoula announced, "It's time to close the shop, *korítsia*. Finish what you're doing and leave everything neat and ready for tomorrow."

After an early dinner and helping Marieka in the kitchen, Eléni and Maria excused themselves and rushed to their room to primp and dress for the evening.

While he waited for his wife and the girls, Georgi Statev read newspaper reports from Crete and Athens. They were ominous. Turkish soldiers had massacred Cretan civilians in February, street demonstrations in Crete and Athens called for war, and Cretan insurgents declared union with Greece.

Konstantínos was already at the party when the Statev family arrived. Eléni crossed the threshold, hugged him, and kissed his cheek.

"How is my seamstress?" he asked. "Kyria Anthoula is pleased with your progress. I saw your father and mother last week in Sozópolis. They send you kisses."

"Thank you, Théo," she responded. "Are they well?"

"Yes. Yes, they are fine. They can't wait to see you. Your sisters have thousands of questions, and Sultána has special news for you."

"What? What?" Eléni asked excitedly. "Does it have anything to do with Ioánnis Thomá?"

"Aah." He winked at her. "Wait to hear from Sultána or your mother."

A voice called from across the room, "Konstantínos, join us. Have a glass of wine and talk." It was Georgi Statev. Todor, Georgi's brother and business partner, sat next to him.

Todor was short, rumpled, plump around the middle, and peered through thick glasses. His appearance suited his bookkeeping, backroom role in the family business. Georgi, distinguished and always carefully groomed, dealt with foreign merchants, often traveling to distant ports to purchase goods. He met with ship's captains to arrange transportation for cargo, and trans-shipments to buyers in Constanza, Varna, and Odessa, and to cities on the Danube. Todor, meanwhile, surrounded by his ledgers, carefully made entries about purchases, sales, and inventories, receipt of payments, and invoices paid. He conducted routine business at the bank, while Georgi maintained the relationship with the bank's president and gained access to the credit line necessary for their dealings.

As Konstantínos crossed the room, Georgi and Todor shifted their seating to make space for him among the other men, who, typically, had gathered on the opposite side of the room from the women.

"What do you think about what's happening in Athens, Konstantínos?" Georgi asked.

Todor leaned forward. "What is Greece up to?"

Konstantínos hesitated for a moment. "Well, the people want King George to act — to support Crete in joining Greece, and to take Macedonia and Thrace too."

"Are they crazy? The Turks will crush them," declared Todor.

Konstantínos exploded. "Were the Bulgarians crazy when they rose to help the Russians throw the Turks out of Bulgaria in '77? No." He turned to Georgi. "Were they crazy when they annexed Romylia in '85? No. They weren't crazy. They had vision and courage."

Georgi leaned back and raised his hand, palm outward. "Easy, Konstantínos. I'm worried about what might happen here because of what the Greeks do."

Evangelía Statev's nephew, Nikolev, an aquiline-nosed student at home from university in Paris, interjected, "What can happen in Bulgaria just because an Athenian mob yells for war?" Thin wisps of a beard that he nurtured on his chin to give his pronouncements more weight failed miserably. They seemed comical. "How can the Greeks support Crete? They don't have the army or the money."

Konstantínos's grimaced. His voice was uncompromising. "When a Cretan shoots at a Turk in Chanía, the Bulgarians in Monastir, the Serbs in Belgrade, and the Turks in Adrianopolis hear the shot and prepare to fight. The crowds in Athens lust for blood. They've already crossed the frontier in Thessaly to skirmish with the Turks."

Nikolev tried to interrupt. "But..."

"But nothing." Konstantínos ignored the younger man. "Soon, Greeks, Bulgarians, and Serbs will fight for Macedonia."

"*Pappoú* Aleksiev says that too," Eléni exclaimed.

Censuring eyes found Eléni. She had crossed the boundary that separated men and women in Balkan society.

Konstantínos replied in a soft voice. "Yes, Eléni, he does. It's wonderful that you remember your *pappoú's* words. Now, why don't you tell your friends about your sisters in Sozópolis?"

Eléni cringed at Konstantínos's patronizing tone. It was not like him to talk to her that way. Her feelings hurt, she retreated into the center of her circle of friends. The men let pass the momentary infraction of the unwritten rule — one that had not applied to her in Sozópolis.

Georgi renewed the conversation. "What does what's happening in Athens mean for us?"

Konstantínos opened his arms. "Us?" He brought his arms together and folded them across his chest. "I'll fight for Romiói, both here and in Greece. You? We'll see."

"You'll what?" cried Georgi. He raised his voice, asking, "Are you going to become *Generalis* again?" The question silenced the room. Konstantínos paused for a moment. Eléni waited for him to speak. Her lips were parted and her eyes wide open.

"I'll fight for Greece," Konstantínos repeated. His slim body rose from his chair, and his stature grew with his words. "I fought for Bulgaria at Shipka Pass, to rid Romylia of Turks, and I'll fight for Romiói, for Crete, for Greece. We must have a safe place for our families."

"Come now, Konstantínos," Georgi said. "You're a tailor, not a soldier."

"I'm leaving for Athens tomorrow."

Stunned, Georgi rose and took Konstantínos's arm. "You can't, Konstantínos. What about your children? You're a Bulgarian citizen."

"And what will happen if the Macedonian problems spill over to Bulgaria?" asked Todor. "What will you do then?"

Konstantínos's voice filled the room, "What happens to Romiói here if Bulgarians and Greeks fight over Macedonia? Eventually we will have to find a new place for our families. As far as I'm concerned, Sozópolis and the Black Sea should be Greek. But they won't be. And we'll be forced to leave."

For a moment, the men surrounding Konstantínos were silent, shocked at his words.

Evangelía seized the opportunity to change the mood. "That's enough serious talk. Come to the buffet and have something to eat. Georgi, please see to the wine. Todor, let us hear some music. Play your mandolin."

Georgi rose, taking Konstantínos's glass to replenish it. "Come, Konstantínos, fill your plate." He turned to his niece. "Maria, lead the girls in a dance."

In minutes, the music provided by Todor, the gay songs the young women sang, and their dancing prevailed over talk of conflict and war. Todor was visibly proud that he had a parlor large enough to accommodate the party. He shouted, "Rejoice in your name, Evangelía. May you have many years." Others echoed his good wishes.

Later, as the party ended, Eléni went to Konstantínos and in a tremulous voice asked, "Are you really leaving for Athens tomorrow to fight?"

"I have a ticket on the morning steamship to Piraeus. I'm not as young as I was when I fought the Turks in '78, but if they'll have me, I'll volunteer."

"And the children?" she repeated.

"Their *yiayiá* and *pappoú* love them and will take care of them. I have to do this. If anything happens — my brothers and sister will help."

"Eléni, we're leaving," called Maria.

Eléni kissed Konstantínos gently on the cheek. "May God protect you."

"And you, Eléni."

SOZÓPOLIS, BULGARIA

Eléni danced all afternoon in celebration of Sultána's wedding to Ioánnis Thomá. Breathless, she was happy to sit for a moment, enjoy the cool sea breeze, and watch her sister be the center of attention. Ioánnis had not asked for a dowry. In any event, her father could not have provided one. She smiled, remembering how Konstantínos had hinted about Sultána and Ioánnis four month before. Now they were married and Konstantínos was far away, fighting in a war. *Smarágda should marry next,* she thought. *I wonder when Dimitrios will return. I wonder if he'll return. She hasn't talked about him at all.*

Stéfanos, Aleksiev, and Hristodoúlos sat together, shared a bottle of wine and enjoyed the music. They encouraged the young dancers, who reminded them of their youth and of the excitement of their own weddings. Stéfanos called to his son, "Ménas. Come here. I have news about Konstantínos. We've finally heard from him."

"Why didn't you tell us earlier?" Hristodoúlos asked.

"And take attention away from your daughter's wedding?" Stéfanos sat back in his chair and paused, as if gathering his thoughts. "Elenko received a long letter from him yesterday. He wrote to his sister and asked her to tell their mother gently that he was in hospital. She did that this morning."

"Is he badly hurt?" The anxious question came from Sofía. She was sitting at a table behind their father, next to Eléni. Both had left the dance and come close to the men to listen.

Hristodoúlos turned his head toward his daughter. "Sofía, quiet. Don't interrupt."

Ménas moved his head to see behind Hrístos and smiled. "Ah, Sofía. Don't worry. Konstantínos will return to see what a pretty young lady you've become."

Eléni put her arm about Sofía's shoulder and whispered, "Sofía, be careful. Don't be so obvious. People will laugh at you. He has a son your age."

"I can't help it. I just can't, Eléni." Sofía rested her head on her sister's shoulder.

Pater Elefthérios said, "Tell us. Tell us about Konstantínos."

Stéfanos sat forward and put his outstretched arms on the table. "Well, he wrote that he joined the irregulars in Athens in the first days of April — just after he arrived in Piraeus. He says that they were like a mob, not like the volunteers here in '78. He got to the front in mid-April, somewhere in Thessaly called Tirnovo, and dug trenches and built barriers until the Albanians attacked. He was wounded on the second day of the battle. He has a bad tear on the right side of his chest. But the bullet didn't break his ribs or enter his body."

"Praise God," Aleksiev said, crossing himself.

"Aleksiev, I've never seen you cross yourself in all the years I've known you," Stéfanos said.

Eléni heard Sofía quietly pray, "Thank you, Panaghía, for hearing my prayers."

"What else did he write?" Aleksiev asked.

"Only that he saw Queen Olga and Princess Alexandra when they visited the wounded in the hospital. They came every day."

Hristodoúlos lifted his glass. "Drink to the *Generalis.*"

The company drained their glasses.

"When will he return to Sozópolis?" asked Pater Elefthérios.

"I don't know, Pater. He was going back to the front."

Sofía got up from the table and walked toward the shore. Eléni followed, listening to her soft prayers and wondering what to do about her.

Aleksiev moved to make room next to him and said, "Pater Elefthérios, come sit with me and have another a glass of wine."

The invitation from Aleksiev startled the priest. He responded tentatively, "Thank you. A little wine would be good."

Both Stéfanos and Hristodoúlos looked quizzically at Aleksiev.

"The marriage service was beautiful, Pater," said Aleksiev. "I especially liked the way you chanted when you crowned the couple with the *stéfana.*" Aleksiev sang pensively, "The Servant of God, Sultána, is crowned to the Servant of God, Ioánnis, in the name of the Father and the Son and the Holy Spirit..." His voice trailed off to silence.

"Aah, thank you, Aleksiev." Pater Elefthérios sighed, showing pleasure at the compliment.

"Pater Elefthérios, I want you to make me a promise."

"Yes?"

"Promise me that you'll forgive my offenses and chant beautifully at my funeral."

"Chant — at your funeral? What do you mean?"

Aleksiev responded calmly. "Pater, when my time comes, I want to go in peace."

Stéfanos and Hristodoúlos looked at each other incredulously and then at Aleksiev.

"Enough, Aleksiev. You've had too much to drink," said Hristodoúlos.

"Promise, Pater," Aleksiev insisted in a more commanding voice.

"Yes, yes, of course Aleksiev — if I'm still alive."

CHAPTER FIVE
1898
BURGAS BULGARIA

Marieka was preparing breakfast when she heard Eléni and Maria coming down the hallway. She looked up to welcome them into her small kitchen. "*Kali méra*," she said brightly. "Sit down and eat your breakfast." She and the girls exchanged good morning hugs and kisses. "Don't forget, we're going to Elenko's this evening to welcome home Konstantínos."

Eléni needed no reminder. She had prayed for him for months.

"Where did father go this morning?" Maria asked.

Marieka turned to the girls with a little huff. "Where did he go? Where else? To the *kafeneío*. Men can't get enough news they can do nothing about."

"What time will we go to Elenko's?" asked Maria.

"Early evening. She'll serve a buffet. We'll have dinner there. Be sure to tell Kyria Anthoula..." She paused, and then continued, "She'll know. Elenko invited her too."

After eating a breakfast of cheese, olives, and dark bread, the girls hurried out of the house and crossed to the other side of the street to walk to Kyria Anthoula's shop. They lifted their skirts an inch or two above their ankles, carefully side-stepping the mounds left behind by the horses that pulled Burgas's carriages.

In the distance, sailing ships with tall masts and new coal-burning steamships vied for berths to load or unload cargoes. Shipping schedules had once relied on seasonal and unpredictable winds. Now, engine noise and black smoke had replaced the snap of billowing sails, and the new ships left from Burgas's port and returned to it at the will of their captains, independent of the vagaries of the weather.

The girls opened the door to their place of work to the cheery ring of the bell above the door. Kyria Anthoula looked up from the paperwork on her desk and exchanged good morning greetings with the girls before following them back into the crowded workroom. On one table were rolls of cloth, tailor's chalk, thimbles, and pins, and on another, fabric pinned to a pattern, ready for pinking shears to do their work. Two mannequins draped with semi-finished dresses, modern foot-treadle sewing machines, and cabinets holding spools of variously colored thread filled the rest of the space.

Two young apprentices were already at work. One of them came from Agathópolis, a lumber and charcoal-producing village to the south of Sozópolis, and the other from Anchíalos, a small city just to the north of Burgas. Salt from its expansive saltpans had been its source of wealth from ancient times.

Before Eléni was able to say anything about Konstantínos's party, Kyria Anthoula announced, "Now to work, girls. We must finish Madame Zurkov's dress before mid-afternoon." She awarded the French social title to her best clients. "We'll close at four o'clock today to get ready to go to the Stoyanni's home."

"We're going too," Eléni cried, and then contained her excitement and began to cut the fabric that lay under the pattern on the table. While she worked, her mind wandered to Kyria Anthoula's mention of Madame Zurkov, and then to Madame's husband, Monsieur Zurkov, who owned the newest apothecary in

Burgas. Finally, she evoked the image of Andrei Atanasov, the handsome apprentice who worked for Monsieur Zurkov. She sighed deeply, feeling an empty place in her chest, a longing — like being homesick, but different.

Eléni had met Andrei two weeks before when she had run an errand to the apothecary for Kyria Anthoula. While serving her at the counter, Andrei smiled and asked, "How can I help you Kyria, ah, Miss ..."

"Miss Zissis," she said, swallowing her words and looking away from his eyes. "I am here to collect Kyria Mavromátis' order."

"Ah yes, I'll get it for you." He returned to the counter, and asked as he handed her a small package, "Are you from Burgas? I haven't seen you here before."

"No, I'm from Sozópolis. I'm apprenticed to Kyria Mavromátis."

Mr. Zurkov, the apothecary's owner, who was formulating a prescription nearby, witnessed the exchange, glanced over his eyeglasses, puckered his lips and grumbled, "There are more important things to do here than flirt."

Embarrassed, Eléni took the package and hurried out of the shop. *What beautiful brown eyes he has,* she thought.

They met again the following Sunday at the end of the liturgy. Eléni saw Andrei waiting outside of the church; his eyes searched the congregation as it emptied into the sunlit square. When he looked toward Eléni and Maria, his face brightened. He removed his hat and walked up to them, asking whether he might escort them to their home. Just then, Georgi and Marieka Statev appeared.

"Please introduce us, Maria," Statev said pleasantly.

Maria hesitated, looking bewildered.

Andrei saved her. "Sir, my name is Andrei Atanasov."

"Do you always approach young women without the consent of their parents?"

"No, ah, no sir, but…"

"No 'buts'," interrupted Georgi. "You may ask my permission at my place of business to acquaint yourself with these young ladies. Good day." He handed Andrei his card and led his wife and the girls away.

Eléni's heart raced. His face was open and sincere, and his warm, brown eyes seemed to focus on her. But he looked at Maria, too.

Late the next morning Andrei asked Mr. Zurkov for permission to leave work for an hour to conduct some urgent personal business. Zurkov chuckled. "Personal business? What kind of personal business does an apprentice have?"

Andrei could only stammer. "Well…ah…"

Zurkov chuckled again. "Could it have something to do with Mr. Statev?"

Andrei's mouth froze half-open. Beads of sweat glistened on his brow.

His apparent discomfort amused Zurkov. "Don't you think that Mr. Statev would make inquiries about a young man loitering after church to encounter his daughter and her friend?"

"Well, sir, I…I don't…"

Zurkov took pity on the young man. He liked Andrei. He was an intelligent, honest, and hard-working apprentice, and would become a good apothecary. And Madame Zurkov had warmed to Andrei's good nature and told her husband that Andrei was the best of all the apprentices her husband had trained. She thought that his sensitive face and long-fingered, slender hands made him look like an artist. "Perhaps," she had said, "perhaps his gentleness will make him an even better apothecary. He'll care."

Zurkov clapped Andrei on the shoulder. "Yes, take your hour. Tell me the day before your appointment with Mr. Statev. I warn you — be sure of your intentions. Don't waste a young woman's time or damage her reputation. I'll be watching."

"Thank you, Mr. Zurkov. I'll act honorably, I promise." Andrei hesitated for a moment. "Mr. Zurkov, I've been an apprentice for two years. Can you tell me how much longer you think it will take me to complete my training?"

"Two more years, Andrei, perhaps less." He smiled. "If you don't let personal business get in the way."

A day later, after Andrei had visited Mr. Statev's offices to ask his clerk to schedule an appointment for the following Tuesday, the excited young man went directly to a small print shop and placed a minimum order for engraved calling cards. He sacrificed his lunch for several days to pay for them.

A week later, as Andrei prepared to leave Mr. Zurkov's apothecary to visit Georgi Statev's offices, Eléni worked busily in Kyria Anthoula's shop a few streets away, anticipating the evening and seeing Konstantínos.

"Go, go," Zurkov said with some humor, watching Andrei glance in the mirror on the counter, smooth his hair, and groom his mustache. "And good luck to you."

Andrei stepped out of the apothecary and turned down the street with a determined walk. He arrived at Mr. Statev's office exactly at ten and presented his newly engraved card to the clerk. In a moment, he was ushered into an office where the Statev brothers sat at a desk behind a mound of papers with their eyes focused on ledger entries.

Georgi Statev looked up from his work. "Ah, Mr. Atanasov. Come in. Come in."

Andrei walked stiffly to the front of Statev's desk and stood almost at attention. It was several minutes before Statev rose from his chair and extended his hand.

"Relax, young man. This is my brother, Todor Statev."

Todor greeted the Andrei, and then, responding to a signal from his brother, excused himself and left the room.

"Have a seat, Mr. Atanasov."

"Oh…uh…thank you," Andrei said, but he remained standing, his face furrowed with anxiety.

Georgi Statev smiled at the young man's nervousness. "Would you like coffee? Water?"

"Thank you. No, thank you. Nothing, thank you."

Statev sat and motioned at a chair again. Andrei followed Statev's lead, sat down, and made a tentative beginning. "Mr. Statev, I apologize for my behavior when we met. I'm afraid I allowed my…ah, enthusiasm about…admiration for a certain young lady to cause me to behave impulsively. I hope you'll forgive me."

"Well, I may give you the opportunity to prove that you're a gentleman. What can I do for you?"

Andrei moved to the edge of his chair and leaned forward. "I wish to be permitted to call on Miss Eléni Zissis. I understand that she is in your care, living with you. If I understand correctly, she's from Sozópolis."

"Mmm," murmured Statev. "Yes, I see." He drummed the desk with his fingers for a few seconds. Finally he said, "There's a problem. I'm not comfortable with allowing you to call on Eléni without her father's permission."

Andrei sank into his chair.

"Now, don't be disheartened. I asked Mr. Zurkov about you, and, except for your tactless approach to the young women, what I've learned is in your favor. Therefore, this is what I propose. You may meet Eléni, accompanied by my daughter, my wife, and me, after liturgy next Sunday — Palm Sunday. We'll walk to my home together and you may join us at our Palm Sunday dinner."

"Oh yes. Wonderful!" exclaimed Andrei.

Statev held up a hand. "Be more measured, Mr. Atanasov," he cautioned. "After you leave us next Sunday, if Eléni wishes, I'll

write a letter of introduction to her father for you. You can take it
to Sozópolis and ask his permission to pursue Eléni seriously. Do
you understand what seriously means, Mr. Atanasov?"

"Yes, yes I do. I am serious."

Statev smiled. "Yes, I believe you are. Good. Then I'll look for
you outside the church immediately following the liturgy this
coming Sunday. You may greet me there."

"Thank you. Thank you, sir. I'll be there."

That evening, Maria's parents, Maria, and Eléni walked to the
Stoyanni's home, chatting along the way. Eléni asked, "Have you
seen Konstantínos, Théo Georgi?"

"Yes. He looks well enough, but thin and tired — I doubt that
he will ever fill out."

Marieka huffed, "A good wife would be a help."

"Now, now, Marieka. Give Konstantínos time to regain his
health."

"What happened to him, father?" asked Maria. "Does he ever
talk about it? You don't tell us anything."

"When he left the hospital in Athens he was sent back to the
front, and when the fighting was over he was released, and he
came home. He suffered physical wounds, but I believe that his
spirit bears more serious scars." The exchange ended with those
words. They walked on in silence to Nikolai and Elenko Stoyanni's
large home, where Konstantínos lived with his sister, her husband,
and their children.

Nikolai had become a successful merchant in Odessa in the
Ukraine before spending three years establishing an office in
Varna, and then moving to Burgas to expand his business. He and
Konstantínos became fast friends soon after Nikolai had ordered
suits from him.

Seeing an eligible bachelor in his new friend, Konstantínos
invited him to visit Sozópolis for a weekend. Nikolai met
Konstantínos's sister, Eléni, and the match was made. Once

married and living in Burgas, Konstantínos's sister changed her given name to its Slavic form, Elenko.

The Stoyanni's parlor was already full of guests when Eléni and her surrogate family entered it. Konstantínos stood in the center of the room, looking thinner than Eléni had expected, and not exuding the energy that she associated with him. She hugged and kissed him, and after he took a seat close to his friends, she left his side to join the party.

This gathering, celebrating Konstantínos's safe return, was an acceptable exception to the rule that there be no parties during the Great Lent. So the celebrants enjoyed good food, wine, and conversation. But in keeping with the Lenten season, there was neither music nor dancing.

As the last guests were leaving at the end of the evening, Konstantínos asked Georgi to allow Eléni to stay with him for a little while longer. He promised to send her home accompanied by Elenko's teenaged sons.

"Come, sit with me, Eléni. I want to talk to you for a few minutes." She took a chair facing Konstantínos. They waited quietly until Elenko ushered her husband and children out of the room.

"What happened?" Eléni asked. "Why are you weak? Aren't your wounds healed?"

"My body has healed. But the horror is with me. I am sick of war, and the politicians that bring it on. They fed our bodies to Turkish guns without plans, without hope. Just to satisfy the mobs who vote for them. Never again." He paused and looked into Eléni's eyes. "And there's something else."

"What?"

Turning his face from Eléni, Konstantínos stared at the glowing embers in the fireplace and spoke softly. "I can't live here in Pyrgos, or in Bulgaria. I am Romiós to the center of my bones, and I know that we won't be allowed to stay here in peace." He paused for a moment. "But where to go? Constantinople? No. Our place there is gone. The Turks will rid themselves of the Greeks in the City as fast as they can. Perhaps even of the Patriarch."

Eléni listened intently, waiting for his next words.

"Greece?" he went on. "Most of the Greeks in Piraeus and Athens, and those who fought by my side are not like us. Many have made ancient Greece their heritage. Some are Romiói, with their hearts in Constantinople. Others divide their hearts between Athens and the sacred City. They are different from the Romiói of the Black Sea."

"What will you do?"

He was quiet for a moment. Eléni could not think of what to say and was relieved when Konstantínos went on.

"I may move to Athens. After that, I'm not sure. I must take care of my children, and I'm lonely for companionship."

Eléni felt uncomfortable at the implication of Konstantínos's words.

"Eléni, I respect your family. I don't want to do anything to offend them, but Sofía ..."

"Sofía?"

"When I visited Sozópolis, she always followed me about, and I liked seeing her. I thought it was just family affection on my part, but it's more. Eléni, do you think ..."

Eléni jumped to her feet. "Yes. Yes. She adores you."

"I'm much older than she is — twenty-five years. Zenóvios is almost her age. What will your parents think?"

Eléni felt on equal terms with Konstantínos. He was talking to her as a woman and asking her advice. She sat down again and took his hands in hers to reassure him.

"My parents will be happy. They have loved you for as long as I can remember. They know that you'll take care of Sofía."

"And you, what do you think?"

"I will thank the Panaghía for making you and Sofía happy together."

Konstantínos stood and brought Eléni to her feet. He gave her a kiss on her cheek and received one in return.

"Thank you, Eléni. Tomorrow I will go to Sozópolis and speak to your father."

Eléni tossed and turned in her bed for an hour before she fell asleep. She thought about Konstantínos, Sofía, and her family. She thought about Andrei too, and whether or not she would ever see him again, or if it was Maria that he wanted to meet and not her. There was no way for her to know that her questions had already been answered.

The next morning, Eléni walked to work with Maria at her side and imagined the joy her family in Sozópolis would feel when they learned about Sofía and Konstantínos. The wedding would be soon, she was sure.

Maria was puzzled over Eléni's mood. The night before when she had returned home from the party, they had not exchanged their usual banter. Eléni had gone directly to bed, and gave no hint of what Konstantínos had talked to her about.

"Why are you all smiles this morning, Eléni, and so quiet?"

"I'm just cheerful, Maria," Eléni responded, thinking about the incredibly beautiful day it would be for Sofía. She would love to be there to see her sister's surprise and happiness. Eléni would not share her knowledge until she knew that her father and mother agreed to the match, even though she was sure there could be no other outcome. They all loved Konstantínos. *It's not that unusual for a widower to take a much younger wife*, she thought. *Twenty-five years is a lot, but his age won't matter to Sofía or my parents.*

SOZÓPOLIS, BULGARIA

While Eléni and Maria walked to work, Konstantínos boarded the first caïque he found bound for Sozópolis. A brisk north wind from the Ukraine promised a quick voyage across the bay, and then south to his birthplace. His complexion, pale the night before, took on a ruddy glow in the fresh, salt air.

He paid a small fee for his passage to a *kapetánios*, who with his two sullen crewmembers had delivered a cargo of fresh fish to Burgas the evening before. They suffered the residual effects of drinking *rakí* all night in a seamen's tavern. Although they had known him since childhood, Konstantínos' cheerfulness, and his out-of-character, impromptu, and out-of-tune rendition of sea songs irritated them. They lived the hard life of seagoing fishermen; Konstantínos had become a city dweller, a tailor to gentlemen. However, as much as his voice grated on them, his epithet, *Generalis*, reminded them of his heroism fighting the Turks at Shipka, and recently in Thessaly. Acknowledging him as a hero they suffered him.

Konstantínos arrived at Sozópolis mid-morning, walked to the *kafeneío* across from the boats and found Aleksiev seated in his usual corner with a half-empty coffee cup in front of him. The *narghilé*, whose water-filled bottle would normally have been bubbling next to him, sat in the corner, dull and lifeless.

"'*Yiá sou*, Aleksiev."

Aleksiev responded sluggishly, his eyes slow to find and focus on Konstantínos. His shirt was too big for his body, and his neck seemed too thin to support his massive head. He sat slouched, with his arms heavy on the table. In a moment, Aleksiev's mouth smiled weakly. "Konstantínos, I'm so glad to see you." His voice was faint, almost distant. He rose from his chair with obvious effort to embrace the younger man. "You look better than I thought you would. Better than me. Are you fit? Strong?"

"I survived. No more fighting for me. Not for mindless politicians. I am going to look after my family from now on. Sit. Sit down, Aleksiev."

Aleksiev fell back into his chair. Konstantínos was shocked at the old man's appearance. Just the year before, he had been robust, able to walk into a room with authority. Now he was fragile, older than his eighty-two years. "What's wrong?" Konstantínos asked gently.

"You aren't blind." Aleksiev's lips tightened for an instant and a soft groan rose from his throat. His face turned ashen. "I'm dying — slowly — too slowly."

"Have you been to a doctor?"

"It's too late for doctors. I have a cancer. There's nothing they can do." Aleksiev took a sip from a small bottle that he retrieved from his jacket pocket. "He gave me this. Morphine — to deaden the pain. I'll feel better soon."

Konstantínos saw Aleksiev's face relax. His breath came easier.

Aleksiev sighed deeply. "Tell me about yourself."

"I'm on my way to see Hrístos," Konstantínos told him. He grinned boyishly. "I want your advice."

"About what?"

"Your granddaughter."

"Is there a problem?"

"No."

"Well then, why? Which one?"

"Sofía."

"Sofía has a problem?"

"No. Not a problem. I want to marry her."

Aleksiev's eyes widened. "Sofía?"

"Yes, Sofía. I know that she's young. But she has always shown me affection. And many widowers marry younger women. I'm just a little older than usual, that's all. Do you think that Hrístos will approve?"

"Ha!" Aleksiev exploded, coming alive and pointing toward the door. "Let's ask him. Here he is."

Hristodoúlos walked toward them and took Konstantínos in his arms. At sixty, the older man was vigorous and lean, and exhibited the agility required to spend days in a small, rolling fishing boat. He released Konstantínos from his hug and stepped back, saying, "We were happy when we heard that you were in

Pyrgos. The news from Greece worried us." Hristodoúlos turned to Aleksiev. "And how are you, *bétheros*?"

Konstantínos's revelation had transformed Aleksiev's face. He was animated, his eyes as alert as they had once been. "Don't waste time, Hrístos. Konstantínos has something to ask you."

"What?" asked Hristodoúlos. "Would you like *kafé*? Thanási, two *kafés*," he ordered.

"Sit down, Hrístos, and listen." Aleksiev was his old self, taking charge. "Go ahead, Konstantínos. I want to be around for the event."

Hristodoúlos took his accustomed chair and leaned forward, resting his arms on the table. "What event? What do you want to ask?"

"I want to marry Sofía." The words flew out of Konstantínos's mouth.

Aleksiev grinned at Hristodoúlos's stunned face. "Ha! The *Generalis* comes right out with it. Like a commander. Wake up, Hrístos. Did you hear? He wants to marry my granddaughter. What do you say to that?"

"Sofía?"

"Yes, Sofía."

"But…but she is barley older than your son. Zenóvios and she played together. Are you sure?"

"I'm sure. I think she'll accept me. And I want more children. Listen, I love her." Konstantínos's face displayed all the excitement and hope of a man twenty years younger.

"Well, Hrístos, what do you say?" asked Aleksiev. "I haven't felt this good for months."

Thanási came to the table and served their coffee. Hrístos took a sip and looked across the table at Aleksiev's happy face and nodding head. "Konstantínos," Hrístos said finally. "You know the situation. Sofía has no *príeka*, except for what she's made with her own hands."

"That doesn't matter."

"Then come by this evening. I will talk to Vasilikí, and to Sofía. You will have your answer then. As for me, you have my blessing."

Aleksiev was smiling. "Bravo, *symbétheros*. Konstantínos, insist on an early wedding. I want to be there."

The discussion between Hristodoúlos and Vasilikí took two or three minutes. Neither of them was surprised at Sofía's response — she nearly burst with joy. Sofía opened the door when Konstantínos arrived that evening. Her parents stood behind her. All three were smiling. Sofía stepped forward, went up on her toes, and kissed Konstantínos's lips for the first time.

BURGAS, BULGARIA

On Palm Sunday, worshippers filled the church to witness the remembrance of Christ entering Jerusalem. The priest's prayers, the chants of the *psáltis*, flickering candles, clouds of incense, and radiant icons mesmerized Eléni. Her thoughts ran to Konstantínos and his trip to Sozópolis to ask her father's permission to marry Sofía, and then to her own excitement about the afternoon she was about to spend with Andrei Atanasov and her adopted family in Burgas.

Georgi and Marieka Statev had talked to Eléni in the parlor on the Tuesday evening before Palm Sunday. Georgi's face had been serious enough to worry her for a moment. "Eléni," Statev began, "we are going to have company on Palm Sunday."

Marieka smiled. "Stop being coy, Georgi." She adjusted herself on the sofa and turned toward Eléni. "Eléni, your Théo Georgi invited a young man, Andrei Atanasov, to meet us at church on Palm Sunday. He asked permission to meet you formally, and says he is serious. Do you know what that means?"

Eléni clasped her hands as her eyes widened. "I think so."

"I invited Mr. Atanasov to have dinner with us," Statev said. "And then, if you tell me that you want me to, I will write a letter of introduction for him to your father. It will be up to you, entirely up to you. Do you understand?"

"Oh, yes, Théo," Eléni answered. "Do I have the right dress for church, Théa?"

Marieka smiled. "I think she likes the young man," she said to her husband. And then turning to Eléni, "Let's tell Maria. We can both help you get ready."

The Palm Sunday service ended. Eléni did not move. Maria poked her friend in the ribs and took her by the hand. "Eléni, wake up." They followed Georgi and Marieka Statev in the line of faithful moving forward to receive willow branches and *antídoron* from the priest.

Once out of the church Eléni saw Andrei waiting in the bright light of the square. When their eyes met, a timid smile appeared on his face. She thought him handsome. He wore a pressed, conservative suit, and his mustache was perfectly waxed. A winged, white collar embraced his elegant silk cravat. As Andrei approached them, he directed his attention to Georgi Statev and removed his hat. "Good day, Mr. Statev."

"Good day, Mr. Atanasov." Statev smiled. "Allow me to present my wife, Mrs. Statev, my daughter, Maria, and her friend Eléni Zissis."

Andrei greeted them in turn, bowing slightly as he mentioned each name.

Statev grasped Andrei's arm. "Good. Well, let's go on to our Palm Sunday dinner. Perhaps you'd like to walk with the two young ladies, Mr. Atanasov."

Andrei walked between Maria and Eléni, under the watchful eye of Mr. and Mrs. Statev, who followed behind the trio, just out of earshot. But all Andrei did was mumble words about the Palm Sunday service and the beautiful weather. Maria remedied the awkwardness of the situation. "We had a wonderful party at the Stoyanni's home last week. It was in honor of Konstantínos

Kapidaghlís, Elenko Stoyanni's brother. He had just returned from fighting the Turks in Greece."

"Really? Why did he do that?" Andrei asked.

Eléni shot back defensively, "He is a patriot."

"Is he a relative of yours?"

"Well, no, not yet. He's a family friend from Sozópolis."

"Not yet?"

"He is a family friend," she repeated firmly, in an attempt to close the subject.

Maria looked at Eléni with a puzzled and annoyed face. "Yes, he's a friend of our family, too."

"Why did he fight for Greece?" Andrei asked.

Eléni remembered Konstantínos's words. Her voice rose. "For the same reason that he fought for the Russians and Bulgaria in 1877. He fought to rid Bulgaria of Turks, and he volunteered to fight to get the Turks out of Greece too."

"But he lives in Burgas. He's Bulgarian."

"He lives in Burgas, but he's Romiós."

Andrei stopped walking for a moment. "Eléni, you live in Burgas, in Bulgaria. Aren't you Bulgarian?"

"No. Romiá," she answered.

Maria stepped forward, took Eléni's arm, and started to walk briskly, saying "Come, Mr. Atanasov, mother has prepared a wonderful roast fish with vegetables for our dinner."

Once home, Maria pulled Eléni into their bedroom. "Eléni, are you crazy?" she asked. "Why are you arguing politics with Andrei? You'll chase him away."

When she entered the parlor, Eléni took pains to avoid confrontation and to make Andrei feel comfortable. She offered the men *rakí* and an appetizer of *taramasaláta*, and helped Marieka and Maria serve dinner. Andrei had rarely had such delicious food. The life of a bachelor apprentice, even one preparing to become an apothecary, did not include fine home cooking.

Andrei and Eléni sat opposite each other at the table, frequently exchanging glances. She found him sensitive and intelligent. As they were finishing dinner, there was a knock at the front door. Marieka hurried to see who it was and returned in a few moments carrying an envelope in her hand. "It was a boatman from Sozópolis," she reported. "He brought this letter for you, Eléni."

"Thank you, Théa." Eléni took the envelope, examined it briefly, and rose from the table. "May I be excused for a few minutes?"

"Of course. Come back quickly to tell us any news you can share."

"Would you come with me, Théa?"

Mr. Statev got up from the table and motioned to Andrei, saying, "Come, let's sit in the parlor and relax. After the ladies clear the table, they'll serve coffee."

Once they were in her bedroom, Eléni gave the envelope to Marieka. "Please read the letter to me, Théa. You know I never learned how." She did not feel particularly embarrassed by her matter-of-fact admission, for few young women knew how to read. She was able to recognize words that related to her work. Numbers and arithmetic were part of her everyday life. She could measure material, mark off button locations, and calculate costs readily, but not read.

Marieka opened the envelope to find a sheet of paper signed by both Sofía and Konstantínos. Eléni listened while she read aloud.

In the parlor, Mr. Statev was giving Andrei a running commentary on the economic growth of Burgas when the young man interrupted him in the middle of a sentence. "Mr. Statev, may I ask — is it true that Mrs. Statev is Romiá?"

"What? Romiá? Yes, she is Greek, or half Greek. Her father was Romiós. What was I saying?"

"Does she consider herself Romiá now that she is married to you?"

71

Statev stared at Andrei for a moment. "What are you talking about?"

"As we were walking home, Eléni told me about Konstantínos Kapidaghlís, and how he fought for Greece against the Turks. She says that he's not Bulgarian, and makes much about being Romiá."

"I see," said Statev, leaning forward in his chair. "Look, we Bulgarians and Greeks have lived here together for a long time just thinking of ourselves as Orthodox Christians. There are some — Konstantínos is one of them, and perhaps Eléni is one too — who hold fast to their Greek heritage. Many think of themselves as Romiói, and even yearn for the rebirth of an empire at Constantinople. It is a fruitless dream. They live here and are Bulgarian citizens. Once a Bulgarian man marries a Greek, the child is Bulgarian, and the mother becomes Bulgarian too."

Andrei made no comment.

"Look, Andrei — Eléni is proud of Konstantínos."

"I know. I think I understand," Andrei stammered.

Statev resumed his one-sided discussion of the Bulgarian economy.

Meanwhile, Maria had cleared the dinner table without Eléni's help. She was in the kitchen preparing coffee when Eléni and her mother entered the room and told her the happy news. Andrei and Mr. Statev heard an increase in the volume of the women's voices.

Eléni and Maria came into the parlor followed by Marieka, who was carrying a tray with two steaming demitasse cups. "Eléni has news," Marieka announced.

"What is it, Eléni?" asked Statev.

"Konstantínos Kapidaghlís and my sister, Sofía, will be betrothed the day after Páscha."

"That's what all the secret talking was about after the Stoyanni's party," explained Maria. "Konstantínos told Eléni that he was going to ask her father for Sofía's hand."

"Congratulations, Eléni. This calls for a brandy. Join me, Andrei?"

"Yes. Thank you."

"You are leaving next Thursday to spend Páscha at Sozópolis, aren't you, Eléni?" asked Statev. "Will you stay for the betrothal?"

"Yes, if Kyria Anthoula will allow me."

"I'm sure she will."

"Do you like your work as an apprentice?" Andrei asked.

"Very much. I love to design and sew beautiful dresses, and Kyria Anthoula is a wonderful teacher."

Marieka and Maria rose from the sofa when they saw Mr. Statev's head signal for them to follow him. "Excuse us for a few minutes, Andrei. I will fetch some brandy from the storeroom while my wife and Maria prepare the dessert. It's my favorite — custard."

Eléni and Andrei found themselves alone together for what they knew would be only a few minutes. Seconds passed in silence. Finally, Eléni looked at Andrei.

"I'm happy that you are here today, Andrei." She blushed at using his given name.

"I am too — Eléni. May I call you Eléni?"

"Yes."

He stepped toward her and blurted out, "Do you mind that I'm Bulgarian?"

Eléni smiled and said, "No, I don't mind. My grandfather, Aleksiev Vserkosov, is Bulgarian. My feelings about being a Romiá don't preclude a love for Bulgarians."

The word love brought another blush to Eléni's cheeks, and then to Andrei's.

"I mean — like all Bulgarians, I mean …"

Andrei touched her hand. "As long as I am included."

"Yes."

Mr. Statev entered the room carrying a bottle of brandy. Maria brought two glasses on a tray, and Marieka carried another with dessert.

Mr. Statev poured the brandy and raised his glass with the toast: "Congratulations to Konstantínos Kapidaghlís and Sofía Zissis. And…" He paused for a moment, and then continued through a mischievous grin, "To all young people contemplating marriage."

Eléni and Andrei glanced at each other briefly and then turned away to conceal their embarrassment. Marieka shook her head ever so slightly, looking at her husband with disapproval.

When the afternoon slipped into early evening, Andrei rose from his chair, thanked his hostess and the young women for their hospitality and followed Mr. Statev to the door. "Thank you for having me to your home and for a memorable Palm Sunday, sir. May I visit you tomorrow during my lunch hour? Perhaps you will write the letter we discussed."

"Yes, tomorrow at noon. I do not promise you the letter, you understand. First I must talk to Eléni."

"Yes, yes — of course. But I think…good night."

Mr. Statev closed the door behind Andrei and returned to the parlor. "Marieka, Maria, would you please allow me a few moments with Eléni?"

Mother and daughter left the room, exchanging knowing glances with Eléni, who stood facing Statev. They had barely left the room when Eléni asked, "Did Andrei…Mr. Atanasov say anything?"

"What did you want him to say, Eléni?"

"Please don't tease me, Théo."

"I'm sorry. I shouldn't tease. Yes, he asked to see me tomorrow about a letter to your father."

"What did you tell him?"

"That he could come to my office at noon for an answer, and that I had to ask you first."

"Yes, yes, please write the letter, Théo."

"I'd be happy to. It seems that your father and mother will have more good news this Páscha."

74

SOZÓPOLIS, BULGARIA

"Eléni, Eléni, wake up."

Eléni strained to open her eyes. Sofía pulled at Eléni's blankets in a frenzy of excitement. "Get up, Eléni. Help me get ready."

Eléni heard the calls of seagulls as they flew over the house. She turned over. "It's early, Sofía. Let me sleep a little more."

"No. It's time to get up, Eléni."

"Just a few more minutes," she pleaded.

In a huff, Sofía left the room and ran down the short hallway toward her parents' room.

Eléni lay back on her pillows. Her window was open to the fresh air of the spring morning. It was the sixth of April. Winter had lingered into late March and now finally given way to the earth reborn. On every tree, hundreds of tender leaves screened the view of the sky, and tens of thousands of birds cast shadows as they flew north on their annual migration along the coast of the Black Sea. Their beating wings affirmed the season.

Sleep gave way to Eléni's remembrance of the events of the past week. Andrei had visited Mr. Statev the day after Palm Sunday to obtain a letter of introduction to her father. Eléni's mind raced, wondering when Andrei would come to Sozópolis.

"Eléni, get up before Sofía drives us crazy," Eléni's mother complained as she came down the hall and entered the room. "She is so excited. Come. Help me to get her ready. Your *babás* couldn't stand it. He's already dressed and getting ready to leave the house to have his morning *kafé* with *pappoú*."

"What time do we have to be at church, *mána*?"

"Pater Elefthérios expects us mid-morning. What a week this has been. Late nights at church, *Páscha* yesterday. We'd all rather sleep, but Konstantínos must return to Pyrgos today."

Eléni stretched one last time and forced herself out of bed. "Did they decide the date that they'll be crowned?"

"The last Sunday in May. That will give Konstantínos time to find a place for Sofía and his children. Sofía will have her hands full. Zenóvios is nearly her age. How can he call her *mána*?"

Eléni heard the worries pouring out of her mother's mouth but had no concern. Konstantínos would make everything work. She knew he would.

A few minutes before eleven o'clock, Hristodoúlos returned home and called from the parlor. "Is everyone ready? Aleksiev and Sultána will take my mother to the church. Konstantínos's family is gathering at Décimos's house. Are you ready?"

"Yes, quiet. We're coming," said Vasilikí. "Wait until you see Sofía – she is so beautiful."

Sofía was beautiful. Eléni, Smarágda, and their mother had lavished their attention on the fifteen-year-old. Dark curls circled her brown-eyed, olive-skinned face, and a soft smile played on her deeply colored lips. She wore the white lace veil Eléni had sent to her from Pyrgos. It would cover her head and hide her face until the moment she received the ring signifying her betrothal.

The family hurried out of the house to walk to the church. Neighbors greeted them with *"Hristós Anésti"* in passing and congratulated Sofía on her betrothal. Her sister, Sultána, and her husband, Ioánnis, and more family and friends joined the procession along the way. As Sofía and her family approached the church, Konstantínos's brother, Ménas came forward to greet them. Pater Elefthérios and Konstantínos were waiting inside, in front of the *ikonostásion*.

Sofía and Konstantínos stole glances at each other as Pater Elefthérios blessed the rings they would wear. He held them over first one and then the other of their heads and chanted the ancient words: "The servant of God, Konstantínos, is betrothed to the servant of God, Sofía, in the name of the Father, and the Son, and the Holy Spirit." After he placed the rings on the couple's fingers, he congratulated them.

Sofía moved her veil away from her face to allow Konstantínos to see her adoring smile. She clung to her betrothed's arm, and together they led the procession to the Zissis home.

By mid-afternoon, Konstantínos had left to return to Pyrgos. When his mother, Theófano, gathered his three children to take them to her home with her, Sofía hugged and kissed them, and her new mother-in-law. Zenóvios, who was less than one year younger than she, groped for words. "Goodbye, Sof...what should I call you?"

"Sofía, Zenóvios." She assured him with a smile. "Just Sofía."

After the house emptied, Sofía babbled to her sisters and mother about all the preparations she had to complete before May the thirty-first, just eight weeks away. "You will help me, won't you, Eléni? Will you make my wedding dress? It will be wonderful to live in Pyrgos."

Eléni thought about Sofía's words, and looked at her. She was still half a child, and in Pyrgos, she would not have the direction and stability that her mother and father provided. Eléni wondered how much she would have to substitute for her parents. What would Sofía expect of her?

The answer came immediately from Sofía's lips. "I'm lucky that you'll be there to help me, Eléni. You'll tell me what to do to make Konstantínos happy and you can help me with his boys. Haríklea is only three, so she won't be a problem."

Eléni started to worry that her role would be both sister and mother to Sofía, but decided that there was no sense thinking about it now. Elenko would be there too, and Konstantínos would be more likely rely on his sister to guide and help Sofía. By then, she hoped, perhaps her own situation might change. *Perhaps Andrei?* she thought.

Hristodoúlos, Aleksiev, and Konstantínos's father, Stéfanos, left the women as soon as they could and strolled across the city to their retreat, the *kafeneío*. Hristodoúlos worried about Aleksiev, who sipped increasingly at the little bottle that he carried in his coat pocket. And he was saddened to see how stooped Stéfanos had become.

They relaxed at Aleksiev's corner in the *kafeneío,* away from the turmoil that had filled the home of the newly betrothed. Stéfanos was no longer just a friend. Now he was *symbétheros,* an in-law to both Hristodoúlos and Aleksiev. They decided to commemorate their new relationship with *rakí.* A few minutes after they were served, three fishermen came through the door. A well-dressed young man followed them.

"Did you have a good trip, Petros?" Thanási asked.

"Excellent," said one of the fishermen. "We filled the bottom of our boat and sold the catch at Pyrgos last Thursday. I decided to stay there with my sister for *Páscha.*" He waved his hand toward the stranger. "We picked up this fellow on the way back," he said, and then to Thanási, "Give us *rakí.*"

Thanási turned to the young man, "And you? Would you like *rakí? Kafé?*"

"No, thank you," he said. "Nothing." Andrei spoke Greek with an insignificant accent. "My name is Andrei Atanasov," he went on. "Can you help me find the home of Hristodoúlos Zissis?"

"I could have given you directions," intruded Petros.

Thanási winked at Petros. "I can tell you how to find his home. Do you want to see his home, or him?"

"Him, of course."

"Well there he is, the youngest of the three old men sitting at the corner table." Thanási called out, "Hrístos, there's someone to see you."

Andrei saw a man turn his head to look toward him. "Petros? *Hristós Anésti.* What can I do for you?"

"*Alithós,* Hrístos. Not me." Petros nodded his head toward Andrei. "This young dandy here."

Andrei stepped forward. "Kyrie Zissis?" he asked.

Hristodoúlos rose from his chair and waited, while Aleksiev and Stéfanos looked at the young man with curiosity.

"*Hristós Anésti*, Kyrie Zissis."

"*Alithós*," Hristodoúlos responded. "How can I help you?"

"It's personal, Kyrie. I have a letter for you from Kyrie Statev."

"Georgi Statev?"

"Yes."

"What about?"

"About me...and it's about..." He gave up, took a deep breath, and said, "It would be better if first you read it and then we talked. Kyrie Statev wrote it in Greek for you."

Hristodoúlos gave him a concerned look and held out his hand. "Give it to me."

Andrei reached into his breast pocket and took out a letter that was sealed with red wax and addressed to "Kyrie Hristodoúlos Zissis."

"Sit while I read this," Hristodoúlos ordered.

Aleksiev and Stéfanos watched intently. Hristodoúlos carefully broke the seal and opened the letter.

"What does it say?" asked Aleksiev.

Hristodoúlos scanned the letter for a moment and then said, "Kyrie Statev writes about Eléni. Since you are her grandfather I might as well read this aloud."

"Quietly, please, Kyrie Zissis," Andrei begged.

The three men moved their chairs closer together. Hristodoúlos read aloud in a hushed voice, but he had difficulty, for both his eyesight and his ability to read were limited. He turned to Andrei. "I can't see well in this light. Perhaps you can read this to us, Kyrie Atanasov."

Andrei took the letter and read in a whisper.

Dear Kyrie Zissis,

    Your daughter, Eléni...

"Speak up, young man," Aleksiev commanded. He wheezed, reached into his pocket for the little bottle he depended on and took a sip.

Andrei cleared his throat and started over:

> Your daughter, Eléni, has lived with my family this past year. She is a fine young woman, works hard, respects her elders, and attends church regularly. Eléni is like a sister to our daughter, Maria, and a second daughter to us.
>
> This letter is to introduce Kyrie Andrei Atanasov to you. We met Kyrie Atanasov at church, and at his request, and after making inquiries about him, we invited him to our home for dinner on Palm Sunday to meet your daughter. I did not think that I should write to you about this until after his visit to our home, since I was not sure that it would be necessary.
>
> Kyrie Atanasov expresses a serious interest in Eléni, and Eléni assured me that she feels the same way about him. I asked his employer, Kyrie Zurkov, about his character and prospects.

Andrei hesitated for a moment and looked at the men. Their eyes were focused on the paper in his hands as if the ink on the page was speaking directly to them. Andrei continued.

> Kyrie Zurkov, as you probably know, is the highly respected owner of one of the largest apothecaries in Burgas. He owns an apothecary in Sozópolis as well. Kyrie Atanasov is an apprentice to Kyrie Zurkov, who regards him as an excellent employee — hard working, honest, and a gentleman. Kyrie Zurkov told me that Kyrie

Atanasov is a member of a good Bulgarian Orthodox farming family from Kayali.

It was a pleasure to have Kyrie Atanasov as a guest in our home.

The rest, I leave to him.

With my best regards,

Georgi Statev

The men turned to Andrei. "Well?" asked Aleksiev.

Hristodoúlos nodded at Andrei encouragingly. "Go ahead, Mr. Atanasov. Aleksiev Vserkosov is Eléni's grandfather and Stéfanos Kapidaghlís is one of my closest friends. In fact his son was just betrothed to my youngest daughter."

"Yes, Konstantínos. I know of him," said Andrei. He sat forward in his chair, and said, "Kyrie Zissis, I want permission to ask Eléni to marry me."

The words stunned Hristodoúlos. He had just seen Sofía betrothed, and now this young man was asking for Eléni. "Well," he said softly. "Well," he repeated, with greater authority, "since Kyrie Statev vouches for your character, I ..."

"Praise God, Hrístos." Aleksiev interrupted. "Twice-blessed in one day," he exclaimed, unable to contain himself.

Hristodoúlos continued. "When would you marry? If she accepts you that is."

"I won't be able to marry for two years. It will be a long betrothal." Andrei looked for a sign of rejection.

Hristodoúlos regained his composure. "Why?"

"I won't complete my apprenticeship for two years. Then I'll have a good profession and a future to offer Eléni, if she is willing to wait."

Aleksiev asked directly, "What do you expect Eléni to bring to the marriage?"

"Only herself. I have little now, but my profession will provide a good life for us."

"Good," Aleksiev responded. "We, too, have little. Give the young man permission to see Eléni, Hrístos."

"Yes," he said. "Yes, of course," and he reached out to shake Andrei's hand.

"Where will you stay tonight, Mr. Atanasov?" Aleksiev asked. "We have room for you."

"Yes, go with my *symbétheros*," Hristodoúlos told Andrei. "Tomorrow morning he'll bring you to my home and you can speak to Eléni."

By noon on the next day, Andrei, buoyant, was on his way back to Burgas. Earlier that morning Eléni had promised to marry him; their betrothal would be in June. At lunch, Eléni, Vasilikí, and Sofía hardly touched their food. There was too much to talk about. Smarágda was the only quiet one. Eléni noticed, and after lunch, she asked her sister to take a walk with her. They followed the shore path on the south side of the town to the beach and sat on an outcropping of rock to watch the gulls sweep over the waves.

Smarágda rested her head on Eléni shoulder and closed her eyes.

"Have you heard from Dimitrios?" Eléni asked.

"Not for months. He promised to write, and to return by Páscha. I asked his mother about him just yesterday. She hasn't heard anything from him either."

"Dimitrios is different. His ideas about life aren't the same as the men talk about here."

"But he promised to return," Smarágda sighed. Tears welled in her eyes.

"And he will," Eléni said with more certainty than she felt. "Would you leave Sozópolis to be with him?"

Smarágda's answer was ready. "Yes."

"Then be patient. He is bound to return to visit his family. Konstantínos saw him in Athens."

"Why didn't you tell me? Was he well? Did he ask for me?"

Eléni avoided the questions. "Listen," she said. "At sixteen, Dimitrios left Sozópolis to work in Anchíalos. Then he worked at the docks in Pyrgos. I heard *babás* and *pappoú* talk about him with his father. He said Dimitrios thinks only about how bad kings are, and how greedy business owners are, and that everyone should have an equal share of everything. He said that Dimitrios wants things to change. A simple life in Sozópolis and Pyrgos isn't enough for him."

Smarágda took up a handful of sand and sifted it through her fingers. "Dimitrios's father is right. Dimitrios worries about people, and about what he thinks is unfair and wrong. When he told me about the men he talked to in Odessa and Varna, his words worried me. But he is exciting to listen to, even though I don't understand everything he says."

Eléni sighed. "Isn't there anyone else for you?"

"No." Smarágda raised her eyes to her sister, and in them Eléni saw a determination that surprised her. "He's the one I want. Oh, Eléni, he has to come back." Dimitrios returned to Sozópolis during the last week of August. Within an hour of his arrival he knocked at the door of the Zissis home. With a wiry body, long, straight, black hair, and pale, chiseled face — accentuated by the dark shadow of two days growth of beard — he appeared threatening.

Vasilikí opened the door. "Dimitrios? You're back?"

"In time for the grape harvest, and ..."

"Who is it, *mána*?" Smarágda called, while walking into the room.

"It's me," Dimitrios answered.

She ran to the door, but was blocked by her mother.

"Come in," Vasilikí said. "Smarágda can visit with you here." She motioned him to a chair and pointed to another across the room for her daughter.

Alert to the possibility of intimacy, Vasilikí stationed herself in the kitchen, just out of earshot, but in a position to glance down the hallway from time to time to satisfy herself that Dimitrios was visible. Smarágda sat safely across the room from Dimitrios, out of her mother's sight.

"Why didn't you write to me?" Smarágda whispered. "You saw Konstantínos in Athens. Why didn't you send me news?"

"I'm here now."

"Why? Why do you come here if you didn't even think of me when you were away?"

"But...but I did think of you. It's just that I didn't know what to write or what message to send."

"Why are you here now?"

"You know."

"No, I don't know. Tell me the reason."

"I must speak to your father first."

"About what?"

"About us."

"What about us? You'd better talk to me before my father."

Dimitrios stood up and stepped toward Smarágda, his open arms inviting her. Just then, Vasilikí peaked down the hallway. "Do you need something, Dimitrios? Some water?"

"No. No, thank you, Kyria Zissis. I just wanted to stretch my legs." He sat down again, and looked into Smarágda's eyes. "You're right. I should talk to you first. You know that I want you to marry me — I asked you to wait before I left for Athens. I want to marry you, and I want you to come to Athens with me. I must talk to your father."

"You'd better ask me first whether I want to marry you. Athens is far away from my family and the life I know. What would we do there?"

"I know it's far away. But in Athens we'll be among Greeks. Here we are few, overwhelmed by Bulgarians. There I can be Romiós and Greek. I'll never be able to do what I want here."

"What do you want to do?"

"I want to marry, work, and raise a family," he replied, looking at her pleadingly. Then he frowned. "But I also want to be part of something bigger, a movement to change the world. I can do that in Athens, but not here."

Smarágda fell silent for a moment, and then asked, "Would we marry soon?"

"When the fishing season is over in October I'll have enough money to take us to Athens. My friends promised me work at the docks in Piraeus. Will you come with me?"

"Talk to my father and ask his permission."

Dimitrios called down the hallway. "Kyria Zissis."

"Yes? What do you want, Dimitrios?" Vasilikí asked, hurrying toward the parlor.

"When will Kyrie Zissis be home?"

"Later in the afternoon when the fishing fleet returns," she said. She came into the room and saw Smarágda's glowing face.

"May I come to see him this evening?"

"Yes, yes, this evening," she told Dimitrios, and whispered to herself, "Finally."

The next morning Hristodoúlos hurried to Aleksiev's home. "How is he, Sultána?" he asked.

Kyria Sultána showed him to the bedroom. At the door, she crossed herself and whispered, "I hope, soon. He suffers so."

Hristodoúlos stepped to Aleksiev's bed. His face twisted in grief at what he saw. Aleksiev had lost half his weight, his eyes were sunken and dark, and his open mouth issued a rattle as he gasped to fill his lungs. "Aleksiev, can you hear me?"

Aleksiev answered in a halting voice. "Yes, fool. Not dead. Yet. Soon. Remind Pater Elefthérios."

"Aleksiev, good news. Smarágda will marry Dimitrios Parousis."

Kyria Sultána crossed herself again, whispering, "May God protect them."

Aleksiev heard her, and chuckled. "Dimitrios. Good boy. Head in clouds. Work hard. All right."

"They'll leave for Athens after they marry," Hristodoúlos went on.

"Only Sultána will be left in Sozópolis," sighed Kyria Sultána.

Aleksiev drifted away. "I'm tired," he said faintly. "Tired."

Aleksiev did not hear Pater Elefthérios fulfill his promise. The priest forgave all the real and imagined petty slights he'd suffered under Aleksiev's scorn of the clergy, especially those who were Romiói, for the abuses were insignificant when measured against the appeal the dying man had made to him weeks before. Pater Elefthérios conducted the funeral service with prayers and chants that seemed to emanate from his soul.

All four of Aleksiev's granddaughters were there. Eléni accompanied newly wedded Sofía and Konstantínos on the trip from Burgas. Sultána held her baby, Thomás, in her arms. Her proud husband, Ioánnis, stood next to her. Dimitrios and Smarágda, not yet betrothed, positioned themselves discretely on either side of his parents.

Surrounded by her daughters, Vasilikí wept at the loss of her once powerful father. They supported Kyria Sultána, who both mourned her husband and gave thanks that his suffering was over.

At the *makaría*, Hristodoúlos turned to Stéfanos. "Praise God, Aleksiev lived long enough to see Sultána and Sofía married, hold his first great-grandson, and know that his other granddaughters were betrothed."

"He died blessed," said Stéfanos. "You and I are left now, with the women. Our children are leaving."

"One by one," Hristodoúlos mourned.

CHAPTER SIX
1905
MÁVROVO, KASTORIA
VILÂYET OF MONASTIR, IN THE OTTOMAN EMPIRE

Dimitráki dropped to the ground from the top of the wall and crouched. Hidden from view, he lingered for a moment, hiding at the side of an outdoor wood-fired oven. It was where his mother baked bread each week, slow-cooked lentils and beans in clay pots, and on feast days roasted or braised meat. Satisfied that he had not been noticed, he crept quietly into the house and slipped into the room he shared with his brothers.

Kóstas' hands grab him. "Where have you been? *Babás* will call us at any minute."

Dimitráki shook himself loose from his older brother and concealed a slingshot under his straw-filled mattress. "I got a blackbird. Too small to pluck or roast," he complained.

"*Babás* will skin you alive if he finds out that you made another sling shot. Killing *Pasás* with your first one was a big mistake. He was *babás'* favorite rooster."

"I didn't mean to kill him. I was only practicing."

At the eastern shore of a mountain lake, the boys' village, Mávrovo, was in the western region of Macedonia that had witnessed the triumphs of King Philip of Macedon, Alexander the Great, and Octavian and Anthony, who crossed the mountains to bring vengeance to Caesar's assassin, Brutus, at Phillipi. It was here that Alexius I, Emperor of the Byzantine Empire fought the Norman, Robert Guiscard, and defeated his army at Kastoria in the eleventh century. A few years later, Bohemund, Guiscard's first son led his knights through the city on his way to Constantinople on the First Crusade. After a period of absorption by the Serbian Empire, Ottoman forces surged through the Balkans in the fourteenth century, and brought Kastoria and its people under the rule of the Sultan. For the next five hundred years, they were members of the Sultan's Orthodox Christian flock, fleeced regularly by him and his subordinate governors.

Appointed by a Bey, who governed an administrative division called a Vilâyet for the Sultan in Constantinople, a Kaimakan ruled the Sanjak of Kastoria, one of several smaller units within the Vilâyet that were within the Bey's purview. The Sanjak contained the city of Kastoria, and many ethnically disparate villages within its border — Albanian, Bulgarian, Greek, Serbian, Turkish, and Vlach. A Jewish community lived with the city, and Gypsies and their camps came and went with the seasons.

The seven-foot-high mud-brick wall that Dimitráki had climbed secured a barn that housed the family's animals and farming implements, their outdoor oven, and their home. It protected them from Gypsies, thieves, and marauding Bulgarian *comitadjis*, the irregulars who sallied from hiding places in the defiles of the Grámmos and Vítsi mountains to terrorize villagers and make off with their livestock. Their purpose was to make Macedonia Bulgarian.

A late September wind blew down from Mount Vítsi and chilled the valley with a first hint of autumn. Whitecaps on the lake mimicked the snowdrifts that would form on top of winter's ice in

December. Apple and pear orchards were bare of fruit. It had been harvested and stored, or shipped on the backs of caravan mules to the markets of Monastir and Salonika.

Preparing to leave his home, Kóstas and Dimitráki's father, Athanásios Mavrovitis, stood before a mirror in his bedroom to adjust his *fez* and groom his mustache. Once outside, he opened a gate in the wall and then turned toward the house, calling, "Kóstas. Dimitráki. *Haíde*, we are late for church. The bishop honors us this morning."

The boys hurried after their father. They wore dark, mended trousers, short jackets, and frayed but clean and ironed shirts, buttoned to the neck. Their shoes were roughly used, and ill fitting. Their pale white scalps showed through closely cropped hair.

In the village church, Dimitráki stood in awe before the tall, black-bearded Metropolitan Bishop of Kastoria, Germanos Karavangélis. Resplendent in his brightly colored, embroidered vestments and wearing a regal crown, he conducted the liturgy with the assistance of the village priest. The setting was unusual. There was a pistol on the sacred altar and a black-robed assistant crouched before the Panaghía in front of the *ikonostásion*, with a Mannlicher rifle at the ready.

Had he been older, Dimitráki's father would have explained to him that the bishop needed protection when he visited his Greek-speaking parishes. Karavangélis was answerable to the Patriarch in Constantinople, and the Patriarch was, in turn, accountable to the Sultan for civil administration and peace among the Orthodox Christians of the Sankjak. Karavangélis was therefore a target for the rifles of the Bulgarian *comitadjis*. Few knew that Karavangélis was the secret leader of the *andártes*, the Greek irregulars who brought death and devastation to Bulgarian villages in the mountains that surrounded the lake. He furthered the Patriarch's goal by preventing the expansion of the Bulgarian church, the Exarchate. Some thought that he worked to make it possible for the government of Greece to annex Macedonian territory.

When the liturgy ended, Dimitráki followed his father to the front of the church to receive *antídoron* from the bishop. Explosions of rifle shots froze time at the instant that the boy touched his lips to the powerful hand that dropped a small piece of blessed bread into his palm. The bishop turned, snatched his pistol from the altar with one hand, and with the other lifted his *ráso* away from his ankles. He and his assistant broke into a run, escaped out the side door of the church, mounted their horses and galloped toward Kastoria on the wagon road that circled the lake.

Screams came from beyond the wall of the churchyard cemetery. Athanásios and his sons followed the other worshippers out of the church and rushed toward the commotion. Dimitráki and his brother edged through a small crowd that circled the bodies of two men who lay motionless in the dust, their blood seeping into wagon tracks. They had been serving as guards for Karavangélis. Women fell to their knees and wailed laments beside them. Dimitráki squatted and stared at the bloody pulp that had been a man's face. Flies had already gathered.

"Are they dead, *babás*?"

"Yes. They feel no pain."

"Why?"

"The Bulgarians," Athanásios spat as he took Dimitráki by the arm and pulled him to his feet. "That's what they'll do to you, and to you too, Kóstas, if you aren't careful. Stay close to home. Protect your mother and sister."

Athanásios hurried his sons along as a group of men ran toward the church from the lake's edge. They were part of a band of volunteer guerilla fighters from Crete. They stopped for a moment to see what had happened, then spread out, moving away from the lake to hunt the *comitadjis*, spill blood, and add to their collection of Bulgarian ears.

Later, in the afternoon, a group of the village elders gathered in Athanásios's home. "The bishop plays a dangerous double game,"

Athanásios told them. "What do you think, brother?" he asked, turning toward Michaelis.

Michaelis, whose thick, black hair fell to his shoulders, leaned forward on the divan and set his glass on the low table before him. He tapped on its surface with his index finger, shifted his position, stroked his thick beard and pulled his lambskin cape up to cover his shoulders. The elders waited for him to speak. When he did, his deep-throated, deliberate speech gave weight to his words. "Brother, the game Karavangélis is playing will get us and our families killed. What is going to happen if the Kaimakan finds out that the Cretans are camped close to Mávrovo? Do you think Karavangélis will be able to talk us out of trouble?"

"He's right," Petros said, looking around the table at his neighbors' faces. "Karavangélis can make the Kaimakan do whatever he wants — even attack Bulgarian strongholds with Turkish troops. But if that infidel finds out that Karavangélis is telling our *andártes* when to attack his Turkish soldiers, I'm afraid to think of what will happen."

"I'll talk to the leader of the Cretans and ask him to keep away from Mávrovo," Athanásios assured him. "Kallíope lets them bake bread in her oven. I'll have Kóstas and Dimitráki run the kneaded loaves and baked bread back and forth at night. That will keep the Cretans away. Agreed?"

Michaelis, Petros, and the others nodded their approval.

Athanásios lifted the bottle. "One more *rakí* before you leave. Drink to the boys that died today." He poured liquor into each of the men's glasses and then raised his, saying, "May their memory be eternal."

The village men quietly murmured, "*Amin*," and drank.

MONTELEONE DI CALABRIA, ITALY

Leonardo sat on a pile of rubble that had been his home. Days before, the earth's crust had heaved, making it impossible for him to stand. He had dropped to his knees, shut his eyes, and prayed frantically. He had felt the sudden jolts of sun-baked rocks rupturing in the Calabrian landscape before. They were reminders of the periodic eruptions promised by Mounts Aetna in Sicily, and Vesuvius in Naples. Now, Leonardo understood the stories of the destruction his village had experienced more than one hundred years before.

His mother, Assunta, had sent him to see whether anything remained of their home. She and his sister and brother were fifteen hundred feet below the eminence on which their town stood, or had stood, safe at a temporary camp on the coast of the Gulf of Sant'Eufemia. The news they heard about the thousands killed, and the devastation of villages throughout the region, made them count their blessings.

Leonardo watched others sort through the rubble of their homes looking to salvage what they could. Someone had already taken everything of value or utility from what was left of his home. He got up and moved listlessly toward the Bay, passing ancient columns that lay on the ground, finally having succumbed to nature's violence. They had stood for more than two thousand years, artifacts that had witnessed the time of Magna Graecia, when ancient Greek colonies prospered in Panticapaeum and Phasis on the shores of the Black Sea, along the Bosphorus, and on the reaches of the Aegean and the Mediterranean seas, westward to the Pillars of Hercules.

Leonardo felt helpless. Everything was gone.

More than three years before, Leonardo's father, Vincenzo Perna, had abandoned his family for a life of banditry. Landless and without hope of employment, he had been desperate. The path he chose seemed almost inevitable. He appeared infrequently, always in the middle of the night, to give his wife a few coins, see his children, and assert his conjugal rights. He always left before dawn, disappearing into Calabria's wilderness. Leonardo came to think of his father as dead, and at fifteen had assumed responsibility for his family.

Leonardo had recently returned to his family from Avellino where he had completed his apprenticeship as a tailor. He had sent small amounts of money to his mother from what he earned working late into the night. Short, slender, and shy, he made up for an unassuming appearance and inexperience with hard work, persistent good humor, and an engaging smile.

Walking with his head down, he thought about his future, worrying whether now, after the destruction, there would be anyone able to pay for the services of a tailor. "Who would pay for new clothing now?" he asked himself. "No one," he answered his own question. Food to ease hunger, and shelter from the elements — these would be the priorities for a long time.

Rather than give in to the fears of the moment, Leonardo raised his head and walked purposefully down the hill toward the Gulf and his family. In the distance, he saw a ship steaming west. It followed the late afternoon sun away from the misery in Calabria and toward a far off opportunity that everyone talked about. At that moment, Leonardo made his decision. He had discussed the possibility with his friends in Avellino and been uncertain, afraid. All he had ever wanted was to work here, in Calabria, close to his mother and siblings. But when he looked back toward the town that had been his home, all he saw was ruins. "There is nothing here. I have to go," he said to himself quietly. Then, inside his head he shouted: "I am going. To America."

SOZÓPOLIS, BULGARIA

Hristodoúlos sat alone at the table in the corner of the *kafeneío*. He stared blankly at the empty chair Aleksiev had claimed as his own for more than fifty years. The chairs to his left and right were empty too. Zísos had left first, and then Aleksiev, and finally Stéfanos had perished at sea in a sudden, violent storm. He had been too old to fish, but one day while walking on the quay, he decided to avoid the boredom of home and seek the company of younger men. He begged a place on a boat from its captain, a friend who was preparing to sail to the village of Vasiliko for a cargo of charcoal. A few hours later, the Black Sea claimed Stéfanos and the entire crew. Their bodies washed ashore on the coast south of Sozópolis, close to the remains of the boat.

Through the years, Hristodoúlos had helped to remove his friends' bones from their graves, gently cleaned them with wine, and then placed them ceremoniously into their boxes. Tearfully, relatives would write the name on a box and set it on a shelf in the graveyard ossuary. When he took Stéfanos's white skull from his widow's hands and placed it in its box, Hristodoúlos had said, "You've made room for me, friend. Soon I will lie here in my grave until my bones are clean. Then I will join you."

At sixty-seven, Hristodoúlos worked the fields and served as a crewmember with one or another *kapetános* who knew the ways of the sea and its fish. However, when he returned home to Vasilikí from field or sea his fatigue was greater than he had ever known.

On days that he did not work, he wandered about town, talked to friends, and gathered news. Vasilikí visited with neighbors, lit candles, and prayed at the church, or at the *ikonostási* in the corner of their bedroom. They lived alone in their empty house.

Their daughter, Sultána, had given her husband, Ioánnis, a son, Thomás. He was Hristodoúlos's first grandchild — a grandson — a male descendant. Happily, for the aging grandfather, the boy lived in Sozópolis. Whenever Vasilikí and Sultána permitted, Thomás accompanied his *pappoú* on walks about town, to the beach, and to the quay at the small harbor where he would sit in a bobbing boat and listen to his grandfather's stories.

Dimitrios Parousis had surprised everyone after his marriage to Smarágda by settling down in Sozópolis. Two children, Gíorgos and Vasílis, arrived within one year of each other.

Hristodoúlos and Vasilikí missed Sofía, who had left for Athens with Konstantínos and their grandchildren two years before. Every few weeks, an envelope arrived with a long letter from Athens. They waited for news about the birth of Sofía's third child, who would join the three she cared for in Athens — Haríklea, from Konstantínos's first marriage and two of her own: Hrístos and Theanó. Konstantínos's sons Stávros and Zenóvios were in Paris, working in its fashion industry.

The grandchildren who were near to him were too young to fill Hristodoúlos's days, but of the right age to keep Vasilikí busy from dawn to dusk. He had days with little to do. Often, he would walk across Sozópolis to the *kafeneío* to take his old place in the corner, drink a glass of wine, and enter into silent communion with the ghosts of his old friends. If when he arrived he found new customers sitting at his friends' table, taking pleasure in its comfort and vantage point, Hristodoúlos would turn from the door and retrace his steps home, saddened that he could not visit his memories of Aleksiev, Stéfanos, and Zísos.

Now it was mid-October. The end-of-the-season tuna catch was good. Hristodoúlos had spent the past few days with the men, cleaning tuna, cutting them into inch-thick steaks and placing slices of fish between layers of salt in wood casks and earthenware crocks. In the cool recesses of Sozópolis's first-floor storerooms the salt from Anchíalos's saltpans on the north of Burgas's great bay cured the tuna to produce *lakérda*, a staple winter food.

Stored close to the *lakérda* were crates of prized *tsíri*, the dried, brown-black, stick-like mackerel that had been harvested from the sea in early spring, then salted and air dried and hidden in boxes of wood ash to protect them from hungry mice. From time to time, Vasilikí would descend to the storeroom, sift ashes through her fingers to find a few dried fish and then roast them over an open fire until the fat they released flared and sputtered in the flame and their flesh became soft and pliable, easily separated from the bone.

She placed strips of the fish into glass jars to marinate in vinegar, minced dill, and a little olive oil while singing:

> Tsi-, tsi-, tsi-,
> Young maidens at the sea,
> Preparing little *tsíri*,
> They pour *krasí* so freely,
> They clean the fish all day,
> The bones they throw away,
> They serve *mezés* to sweethearts,
> And dance along the bay.

The cycle of life went on. Soon it would be winter, and as in all winters past, the people would stay sheltered in their homes waiting for spring, the reappearance of the annual run of mackerel from the southern shores of the Black Sea, and earth's rebirth at the time of the *Anástasi*.

BURGAS, BULGARIA

Eléni handed her baby to Maria and turned to stir a pot of lentil soup that bubbled on the stovetop. Sitting on a chair in the corner of the small kitchen, Maria balanced little Evangelía on top of her swollen belly. "I'm so uncomfortable," she said. "Thank God the baby is due in the next week or two."

"I wish I didn't have to cook and keep house," Eléni complained. "I'd love to work with Kyria Anthoula and hire help."

"Listen, Eléni, do you want to shame Andrei? He works hard. Be satisfied that you have a such a good husband."

"I am. But I'm bored."

Evangelía started to fuss and nuzzled at Maria's breast. "She wants to nurse, Eléni. Here, take her, and I'll stir the soup."

A moment later Evangelía found Eléni's breast and quieted, focusing all of her energy on sucking.

96

"Are you happy at home, Maria? I know you love Vasílis, but are you happy just being at home? Don't you miss Kyria Anthoula?"

"Of course I'm happy. I have a husband, a home, and I am going to have a baby. You know that I never liked working as much as you." Maria stirred the lentils for a moment and changed the subject. "How are Konstantínos and Sofía?"

"Sofía will have her baby soon."

"And Konstantínos? Is he happier in Athens than he was here?"

"I think so. He worries a lot about the Greeks and Bulgarians fighting in Macedonia."

"Why are they fighting?"

Eléni's interests ranged further than Maria's, and she took the question seriously. "Konstantínos writes that Greece wants to expand its territory. Andrei heard angry talk in Pyrgos and Varna about what the Greeks are doing to Bulgarian villages." Eléni shifted Evangelía to her other breast.

"Vasílis told me the same thing," Maria said. "He heard Bulgarians arguing with Greeks in the city."

"Andrei says that his Greek customers up and down the coast are worried."

Maria gave the soup one last stirring and then turned impatiently. "Enough, Eléni," she said, sitting down again. "Let the men worry about politics. What other news do you have?"

"Smarágda visited me last week. Can you keep a secret?"

"What?"

"She and Dimitrios are taking their children to Athens soon. They haven't told my mother and father yet."

"Why are they going?"

"Dimitrios always wanted to leave. Now I think he has to. He's is in trouble."

"What kind of trouble?"

"He has been complaining in public meetings about Prince Ferdinand and the government in Sofía. Smarágda told me that he was in front of the student demonstrations here in Burgas. Andrei thinks they are revolutionaries, like the ones in Russia. Smarágda is afraid he'll be arrested."

"Vasílis says those students should be shot," Maria said dismissively. She got up from her chair. "It's getting late, and I have to finish preparing dinner. Vasílis hurries home from work excited to see how much my belly has grown. He won't go on any more trips to Varna or Constantinople until after the baby is born."

Eléni took her contented baby from her breast and buttoned the front of her dress. "I wish Mr. Zurkov wouldn't send Andrei to deliver medications to the small cities on the coast. Sometimes he is away for two days waiting for a boat, or for good weather. Zurkov is thinking of putting Andrei in charge of his apothecary in Sozópolis."

"That would be wonderful." Maria started toward the door.

"No, it wouldn't. I don't want to live in Sozópolis. It's too small."

Maria hugged Eléni, kissed Evangelía on her cheek and left. When Eléni closed the door, she wondered how Maria could be indifferent to events and completely content with her life. "I need more," she said to herself.

KALITHÉA, ATHENS, GREECE

The cold, damp December evening made Konstantínos thankful for the warmth of the kitchen and the hearty fish stew Sofía had prepared for his dinner. He sat at the kitchen table, now cleared of dishes, and opened an envelope while listening to Sofía and ten-year-old Haríklea put Hrístos and Theanó to bed. Sofía, heavy with the baby in her womb, was grateful for Haríklea's willing help.

Two letters had arrived during the day. One was from Konstantínos' son Zenóvios in Paris, and the other from Dimitrios Parousis. Konstantínos knew that Sofía would be excited to hear news from Sozópolis.

Konstantínos took his new reading glasses from their case and seated them on the bridge of his nose. He was not yet used to wearing them and had admitted to their necessity only as it became more difficult for him to thread a needle. He took a minute to roll and light a cigarette and then began to read. Sofía came into the kitchen and placed a long-handled, brass-coated *ibríki* on top of the hot coals in the brazier. They radiated enough heat to warm the room against the chill of a misty evening that promised rain.

Sofía added sugar and pulverized coffee to the pot, stirred the mixture and let it simmer until creamy foam formed a layer on top of the dense coffee. She filled a demitasse and served it to Konstantínos, who was too absorbed in his reading to acknowledge her. Sofía sat and waited patiently, watching Konstantínos's facial expressions and listening to his soft sucking at the lip of the coffee cup. Aromatic tobacco smoke filled the room. When he finished reading, he set the letters before him, took off his glasses and rubbed his eyes. He dabbed at his mouth with a napkin, and shaped his mustache with his fingers.

Sofía could wait no longer. "Tell me, Konstantínos, what do the letters say?"

"Zenóvios writes that he and his brother are well and working hard. Stávros loves Paris. Zenóvios says that the boy struts about Parisian streets showing off his clothes and manners."

"Stávros is fourteen," Sofía said with disapproval. "I hope Zenóvios is watching him."

Konstantínos smiled. "Sofía, my sons are well-raised. They are men now. They work hard, and they won't shame themselves or us."

"But, Paris — and they're so young. Everyone knows about Paris."

"They'll be fine. Zenóvios writes that business is good, and that Kyrie Pappanikoláos is happy with them." He stopped for a moment and said with pride, "Of course he's happy with them. I taught them."

He went on. "Zenóvios asks whether I'd like to work in Paris for a few months each year. He writes that I can make good money there."

"No. Would you go?"

"Well ..."

"How long would you be gone? What would I do without you? I'd be alone, and I'd miss you."

"You have Haríklea to help you, and by the middle of December you'll have company."

"Who?" she asked. "Is it in the letter? What does it say?"

"Dimitrios and Smarágda and their two children will be here in a few days."

"That's wonderful."

"He asks if they can stay with us until he starts work and finds a place to live. You'll have company and help."

Sofía was on her feet, her face alive with excitement. "I haven't seen them for two years. Smarágda will have all the news. She will help with the baby, and we'll shop together. If you go to Paris, I won't be alone."

"Don't rush me out the door, Sofía."

"Does he say anything about my family? Your brothers?"

"No. Dimitrios isn't a letter writer. He just talks a lot. They're well, they're coming, and he has work promised to him at Piraeus."

Sofía cleared the table and went to look after the children. Konstantínos stared first at the letter before him, and then, shaking his head slowly with concern, at the newspaper headlines.

Earlier in the day, he had fitted two members of parliament for suits and listened to them discuss events. While Konstantínos had marked a correction on a jacket, a short, corpulent parliamentarian had growled, "British ships blockaded Mytilíni and Lémnos."

Konstantínos wrote a note on the order slip, removed the man's jacket and chalk-marked the rear seam of his trousers while his client continued. "London wants reform in Macedonia — for the

Sultan to return to the *status quo* before the Greek and Bulgarian uprisings."

His comments were directed to the second politician in the room, a tall, distinguished man who sat admiring himself in a mirror. Smoothing his silver hair he responded, "The Sultan will feel more pressure to make changes in Macedonia and keep things stable in his Empire."

The chubby man turned abruptly to his silver-haired friend. "The British cannot stop us from saving the Greeks in Macedonia," he said, twitching in annoyance at Konstantínos, who tugged at the trousers and re-marked the seam. "Or from Macedonia joining Greece. Pavlos Melas left the regular officer corps and died a national hero fighting the Turks in Statista. Church bells rang for him. The people are behind a greater Greece. Our *andártes* are doing even more damage to the Bulgarians with help from Cretan volunteers. It's only a matter of time." He broke off, frowning. "Hurry, will you, Konstantínos?"

"Yes, yes, Kyrie. I am almost finished." Konstantínos near choked in frustration. *You arrogant, pompous politician,* he thought. *When have you fought, or made any sacrifice for Greece?*

The tall man rose from his chair and removed his jacket in preparation for his fitting. "The Turks have their hands full trying to maintain control over Macedonia," he said. "There are thousands of Turkish soldiers helping our *andártes* destroy Bulgarian and Serb villages, thinking that they are protecting the Sultan's lands."

"There, Kyrie, I have finished marking your trousers," Konstantínos told his corpulent customer, who stepped behind a curtain to change.

The tall, patrician handed his coat to Konstantínos, and stepping before the mirror continued, "Eventually Macedonia will be part of Greece, but first we, the Bulgarians, and the Serbs must rid ourselves of the Turks. Then we can decide who gets Macedonia."

Konstantínos helped his client into his new coat. He smoothed the material over the man's shoulders and checked the length of the sleeves. Tugging at the coat's skirt, and then buttoning it in front, Konstantínos commented, "Excellent fit, sir. Your coat needs no adjustments."

The politician paid little attention to his tailor. He continued talking to his friend, who came out from behind the curtain holding his newly chalk-marked coat and trousers in his hands. "Sometimes I wonder about the way Karavangélis and the other bishops use the Turks. They seem to be working for Greece's benefit, but may have it in mind to keep Macedonia under the Sultan, and therefore under the control of the Patriarch. The church has its own ends."

"You know how it will be decided, my friend," the fat man said.

Konstantínos could contain himself no longer. "With guns," he interjected. "And with young men's blood."

CHAPTER SEVEN
1906
CHICAGO, ILLINOIS

Leonardo's familiar way of life ended in a cataclysm that had devastated Calabria. His new life thrust him into a sense-exploding world of a ship's thunderous engine, the pounding of the sea against a creaking steel hull and the roar of a train hurtling west.

On the first evening of the voyage from Naples to New York Leonardo stood on the deck of his ship and gazed eastward toward Italy. A tall and slender young man watched Leonardo for a time, and sympathizing with the signs of homesickness and despair that he saw, stepped up and said, "Beautiful evening, no? I am Enzio De Lucca. Is this your first trip to America?"

Leonardo looked at the fashionably dressed stranger who wore a bowler hat. "Yes. First trip. My name is Leonardo — Leonardo Perna."

It was Enzio's second round trip from Chicago to Calabria, and while not yet twenty, he had the air of an experienced traveler. He took off his hat, revealing a prematurely receding hairline, ran his fingers through his hair and put his hat back on, saying, "Let's have dinner together."

Leonardo was happy for the company. Within a few hours, they had finished dinner, exchanged life stories, and developed a basis for a friendship.

"Do you know anyone in New York?" Enzio asked.

"Only the cousin I am supposed to go to. I really don't know him. I am using his name and address on my papers."

Enzio's eyes widened with an idea. "Why not come with me to Chicago?"

"Where is that?"

"Chicago is in the middle of America, close to a lake that is like a sea. It is full of Italians. Come with me, Leonardo. My uncle will help you, I know he will."

Three weeks later, the young men stepped off their train in Chicago and made their way to a shop front close to Halsted Street. The sign above the door announced:

LAUNDRY – FRENCH CLEANING – CARPETS

Enzio nudged Leonardo toward the doorway. "Go in, go in," Enzio urged. He eased himself in front of Leonardo, and then took his friend by the arm and pulled him through the door. "Uncle Giovanni," he called. "Uncle Giovanni, I'm back."

Leonardo saw hands open a way through a wall of hanging garments; a gray-haired, heavyset man wearing thick-rimmed spectacles followed. He surrounded Enzio with his arms. "Enzio. How is your mama? Is she well? And your papa — he was lucky to marry my sister. And his family?"

"Everyone is fine, Uncle. They send you thanks and kisses." Enzio had carried an envelope filled with American dollars to his mother — a gift from his uncle to the sister who cared for their parents.

"Bravo, bravo!" Giovanni exploded, clapping his nephew on his back. "You look good, my boy. Calabrian food and air. That will do it."

Pulling himself away from his uncle, Enzio motioned toward Leonardo. "Uncle, this is my friend, Leonardo — Leonardo Perna." Then he turned to Leonardo to complete the introduction. "Leonardo, this is my uncle, Signore Giovanni Arcudi."

"Are you from Calabria?" Arcudi asked.

"Yes, signore, from Monteleone."

"Beautiful town."

"No more, signore."

"Ah, yes. *Tragedia. Sfortuna*," he said, shaking his head. "A terrible thing."

Leonardo's lips trembled.

Enzio saw Leonardo's pain and asked briskly, "Uncle, do you have work for Leonardo? He's a fine tailor."

Arcudi looked at Leonardo critically. "Did you apprentice?"

"Yes, signore, in Avellino," Leonardo answered, regaining his composure. His facial expression revealed both concern and hope.

"Good." Arcudi thought for a moment and asked, "Where do you ..." He stopped himself. "Business can wait," he said, winking at Leonardo. "Come, we'll eat, drink a little wine and talk about the future. There are possibilities, Leonardo. Don't worry."

Enzio grinned at Leonardo, whispering, "He likes you."

Leonardo sighed, and then picked up his worn suitcase and followed Enzio and his uncle out the door.

VARNA, BULGARIA

The small coastal ship that carried Andrei slipped into its berth at Varna's port just as a second ship approached its mooring on the opposite side of the wharf. The city and the homes that lined the hills high above the bay were clearly visible in the bright light of the June morning. The fresh air and smell of the sea had invigorated Andrei, and piqued his excitement about what lay ahead of him.

While he waited on deck for the ship's crew to make final preparations for passengers to disembark, he studied a bearded man who stood at the rail of the ship that had just arrived on the opposite side of the wharf. The black *ráso* and veil-covered *kalimáfi* identified him as a celibate priest. Andrei heard shouts above the noise of the engines and the commands of the officer directing the crew, and then he saw a large crowd marching on to the wharf. The people focused their eyes on the cleric and shook their fists, screaming at him.

"Go home, Phanariote."

"Exarchist bishops for Bulgarians."

"No Greeks."

"No Neofoti."

Andrei hurried down the gangway and edged past the angry demonstrators. He made his way clear of the harbor area and then found his way to the hotel where he would meet his business contact, Kiril Vasilov. A message was waiting for him when he registered.

Mr. Atanasov,
Please meet me in the lobby this afternoon at three o'clock.
Kiril Vasilov

With almost two free hours, Andrei left his suitcase and portfolio in his room and hurried out of the hotel into the streets of Varna to explore what he could of the city before his appointment.

He found Varna's buildings more elegant in their style than any in Burgas. Making his way up the hill behind the bay, he walked along tree-lined streets that offered eastward vistas of the sea from a point higher than he had ever been. On the way back to the hotel, he came across a massive cathedral with cross-studded domes. He asked a passing military officer its name. "You don't know?" the young officer asked in amazement. "That's the Cathedral of the Assumption. Prince Alexander built it when Bulgaria became a Kingdom, when we won our freedom from the Ottoman Empire and the Greek Patriarch." He marched off down the street, stopped for an instant and called over his shoulder, "That's what it stands for."

That night, Andrei sat opposite Mr. Vasilov at a table in the hotel's restaurant. They had concluded most of their business early in the evening, and having agreed to finish their work the next morning, enjoyed a relaxed dinner.

Vasilov, twenty years Andrei's senior, was a native of Sofia. His manner and dress were urbane, even more elegant than the affluent Bulgarians in Burgas. A thin mustache complemented his long, slender face. Clothing of finely woven material fitted his athletic body perfectly. Andrei listened to Vasilov speak casually to other businessmen in the lobby and at adjoining tables in Bulgarian, French, German, or Greek. He moved easily from language to language.

When their table had been cleared, Vasilov sat back comfortably in his chair and asked, "What do you think of Varna?" He knew it was Andrei's first visit to the city.

"I like it very much. I did not know it was so big."

"Yes, it's big. And growing. It will change more, just as Bulgaria is changing. You haven't been to Sofia, have you?"

"No."

"Sofia is transformed. Twenty years ago, it was nothing more than a large, dirty village with cows roaming in from the surrounding fields. Wild dogs ran in packs cleaning the streets of dead animals, even horses. Now it's a European capital with more people and many more problems."

Vasilov stopped talking, seeming to gather his thoughts. The fingers of his right hand held the stem of his glass. He turned it slowly, causing the candlelight that passed through crystal and red wine to cast kaleidoscope-like patterns on the tablecloth. In silence,

Vasilov gazed at the patterns while his left hand toyed with a gold watch chain that flowed into his waistcoat pocket.

He looked up. "Did you see what happened at the wharfs today, Andrei?"

"You mean the mob?"

"Yes."

"I didn't stay long. They seemed to be angry at the priest on the ship across from the one I was on."

"Not just a priest," Vasilov said. "That was Neofoti, the new Metropolitan Bishop of Varna. He was appointed by the Patriarch of Constantinople."

"Why was the mob angry?"

"I'll tell you. But first, let me ask you — what do you think about the relationship between Greeks and Bulgarians in Burgas?"

"Well," Andrei answered. "I'm married to a Romiá from Sozópolis. She had a Bulgarian grandfather on her mother's side. Our families get along well. Many Bulgarian men take Romiá as brides. I speak Greek at home with my family."

Vasilov leaned forward impatiently and pressed. "No, not your family. What are the people's feelings about what is happening in Macedonia? How are the Greeks and Bulgarians getting along?"

"Oh, I see. I have heard angry words in the streets of Burgas. Bulgarian thugs talk about throwing out the Romiói and sending them to Greece. But that would mean family members fighting each other. I don't think that will ever happen. What was the mob about today?"

"Today was a prelude — a beginning — of what's about to happen in Bulgaria. I want you to repeat everything I tell you to Mr. Zurkov."

Vasilov refilled his wine glass, sat back in his chair and began to talk. Andrei listened attentively. From time to time, Vasilov glanced about the room, pausing as if to determine whether others at nearby tables might be listening to him.

"Since this is your first trip to Varna, you don't see the changes that have taken place. A few years ago, the people in Varna were almost all Turks and Greeks. Now the Bulgarian population has grown, as it has in Burgas. Why?"

Andrei looked at him blankly.

Vasilov did not wait for him to formulate an answer. He struck the side of his wineglass with his fountain pen as he announced each reason.

Ting — "Hungry peasants are moving to larger towns to work in factories, and they're jealous of the wealthy Greeks they find there — the middlemen merchants who buy peasant products cheaply and make fortunes in trade. The socialists are making the most of it."

Ting — "Politicians want Macedonia to become part of Bulgaria just as Eastern Romylia did. They're behind the *comitadjis* fighting in Macedonia."

Ting — "Bulgarians want their own language, schools, and churches. We don't trust the Orthodox Patriarch of Constantinople — a Greek picked by the Sultan."

Vasilov paused, but he wasn't finished. His litany went on as if rehearsed.

Ting — "Things are going badly for the Bulgarians in Macedonia. The Bulgarians want revenge."

Ting, Ting — "The pot is boiling. The Bulgarian Patriots, Dragulev's organization, is militant and includes Bulgarian veterans from Macedonia. They led the mob you saw today. And they're the ones who'll cause trouble for the Greeks in the cities and towns up and down the coast of the Black Sea."

Andrei sat wide-eyed. "What...what happened to the Metropolitan?" he asked.

"He never got off the ship. It left for Constantinople with him on board. They say that he plans to return. I hope not, for his sake, and for the sake of all the Greeks in Varna. He is a symbol. He would only create more antagonism and hostility."

Andrei leaned forward toward Vasilov, putting his forearms on the table. "What do you think will happen in Burgas, Mr. Vasilov?"

"I'm not sure. Perhaps a catastrophe. My advice to Zurkov, and to you, is to stay clear of Greek communities. Reduce inventories in Zurkov's apothecaries in Sozópolis, Burgas, and Anchíalos. And when it arrives, keep most of the stock you ordered today in a safe, out-of-the-way warehouse in Burgas."

Andrei slept little that night. In the morning, he finished his business with Mr. Vasilov over breakfast. Vasilov's parting words were, "Get home safely, Andrei, and tell Zurkov everything I've told you."

PIRAEUS, ATHENS, GREECE

Dimitrios Parousis strained his muscles and lifted a heavy sack. It was noon. An unrelenting Athenian summer sun made the ship's steel hull impossible to touch and its hold an oven. His torso was covered in bizarre patterns, etched by streams of sweat that ran through a layer of salt that clung to his body. Labels with the name of the saltpan he had worked at in Anchíalos identified each sack of this shipment. There, he had sweated loading ships bound for ports on the Black Sea, and Constantinople and Piraeus.

Dimitrios' work on the docks brought him into contact with young socialists in Athens, and their political organizations at Piraeus's waterfront. He did not have the intellectual tools to make sense of the ideas he heard, but was nonetheless convinced that when their goals were achieved, landholders, factory owners, and bankers in Bulgaria, Greece, and Crete would use independence from the Turk selfishly. Sometimes, he woke in the middle of the night with his mind racing among disjointed ideas about how to change the world.

Exhausted, Dimitrios hurried home at the end of this July day looking forward to his dinner, rest, and the cool of the evening. Smarágda greeted him with a kiss and an order, "Wash up and change. Konstantínos arrived home from Paris this afternoon. Sofía asked us to dinner."

Smarágda finished nursing her son, Vasílis, while Dimitrios went out to the pump to fill a bucket with water. In a few minutes, they were both changing their clothing in their small bedroom. "How does Konstantínos look?" Dimitrios asked. "Is he well?"

"Yes, he's fine. I was worried about him when he left for Paris so soon after Sofía's baby died. But I was even more worried about Sofía. The baby was just a few weeks old, and she was devastated."

Dimitrios buttoned his clean shirt. "I'm glad we got here in time for you to help her. She'll be fine now that Konstantínos is back."

Smarágda looked at herself in the mirror and pinned up her hair. "Sofía was so strong after she buried little Vasilikí. I suppose that she had be, for Konstantínos's sake and her own. She never told me how she felt about Konstantínos being so far away, but I know she missed him. She wants to have another baby as soon as she can."

When they arrived at Konstantínos and Sofía's house, they found the family seated in the courtyard. Sofía had set a table for their dinner of fresh salads and fish soup under a great mulberry tree. After they finished their meal, Haríklea and Theanó took charge of putting their little cousin, Vasílis, to bed. In the soft twilight, Konstantínos satisfied his family's curiosity about Paris. "You should see the Eiffel Tower," he exclaimed, raising a hand high over his head. "It's as high as the Acropolis. No. Higher. And Notre Dame, the great cathedral — it is larger than any church in Athens, and different. The Francs all follow the Pope and Rome."

"Tell us about the women and their clothing." Smarágda waited, watching him wide-eyed while he sipped at his demitasse and drank a little water.

"Ah," he began, "you should see the women in their carriages entering the Tuilieres Gardens." He went on, describing wide boulevards and fashionable people who drove past, or walked along in pairs and in groups. "They enjoy displaying themselves," he explained, "and observe and comment on others they pass, laughing at clever remarks." Konstantínos's arms and hands flowed about his body as he tried to create visual impressions of hats and dresses, capes and coats. "You've never seen so many beautiful women in beautiful clothing." He went on answering questions until twilight faded into darkness.

Stellar constellations appeared that had existed in the sky above Athens since it was founded — Draco, the Little Bear and Great Bear, Cassiopeia, and their myriad companions sparkled in their permanence. Dimitrios and Smarágda left the garden for their home with little Vasílis asleep in her arms, and Konstantínos and Sofía sent their children to bed. Finally, in the privacy of their room, they expressed verbally and physically months of pent-up passion.

Weeks passed, and from time to time, while the women shopped or chatted in the kitchen, Dimitrios sat in the garden with Konstantínos to drink coffee and smoke, and talk about politics and current events. One afternoon, Konstantínos described the socialist movement in Paris to Dimitrios.

"See?" Dimitrios said. "People can stand up to the bankers and industrialists. We can do it here, too."

"Patience," Konstantínos advised. "Change does not happen overnight." He knew that Dimitrios would ignore his advice, and that his brother-in-law's feelings about society's wrongs were too passionate for patience. His frustration with the world could be relieved only through action.

Dimitrios became a willing, regular member of a group that struck out at authority and the government at every opportunity. More than once, Smarágda went crying to Sofía when Dimitrios staggered home bruised and bleeding from a confrontation in the streets. Konstantínos cautioned Sofía that the problems would likely become more serious for her sister and Dimitrios. "Sooner or later," he warned, "Dimitrios will get involved in something that will seriously hurt him and his family. He can't help himself."

SOZÓPOLIS, BULGARIA

Hristodoúlos and Vasilikí took turns cuddling their granddaughter, Evangelía, while Andrei and Eléni went for a walk along Sozópolis's sandy south beach. Andrei had finished stocking Zurkov's pharmacy in the morning, and they had taken advantage of the warm July afternoon to be together.

Andrei stopped and looked out over the sea. "It's so peaceful in Sozópolis. Are you sure that you don't want me to take over Zurkov's pharmacy here?"

"I'm sure." Eléni motioned toward the town. "Sozópolis is too small. What would I do here when Evangelía grows up? In Pyrgos I can go back to Kyria Anthoula's, or even open my own dress shop."

"You don't have to be a dressmaker. I earn enough to support my family. And we may have more children to keep you busy."

"Of course you earn enough for us. And I would be happy to have another baby. But I enjoy dressmaking, and the people I meet, and the excitement of the business."

"What you enjoy isn't as important as your safety, and Evangelía's. I told you about Mr. Vasilov's warnings."

"Oh, nothing is going to happen in Pyrgos. Who would want to hurt us?"

Andrei turned to face her. "Eléni, last night at the *kafeneío* a *kapetánios* told us that the day he left Varna there was a riot at the Greek hospital. Last week a Bulgarian mob surrounded Ághios Nikoláos, threatened the priest and terrified the Romiói in the church. If it is happening in Varna, God knows what will happen in Burgas."

Eléni put her arms around her husband and pressed her face against his chest. "I can't come back here," she said. "I can't live the way women do here."

They held each other for a moment. Eléni stepped back and clasped her hands together. "Should we go to Athens, with Konstantínos and Sofía, and Dimitrios and Smarágda? We'd be safe there."

Andrei shook his head. "This is my country. The trouble will pass. You would be safe in Sozópolis until it does. Then we could take up our lives again in Burgas — perhaps even with you having your own shop. Think about it and we can talk more."

Eléni sighed and put her arms around him again. "All right, Andrei. Next week."

BURGAS, BULGARIA

The next day Eléni and Andrei left Sozópolis and returned to Burgas with their baby. The city's streets were empty except for men who clustered together on corners or roved in bands. Andrei held little Evangelía in his arms, leading Eléni and the porter who carried their luggage. He kept them close to buildings and backed them into doorways to avoid passing groups of men.

They heard urgent voices. "Andrei. Eléni."

Georgi and Todor Statev hurried toward them.

"Théo Georgi." Eléni hugged and kissed both men. Georgi grasped Andrei's arm and peeked at Evangelía, who gave a little cry, opened her eyes, closed them again, and fell back to sleep in her father's arms. "Go home," He directed. "And stay indoors."

Todor looked over his shoulder and then down the street. His voice was anxious. "We'll walk with you. It's Dragulev and his troublemakers. He's holding rallies in support of the *comitadjis* in Macedonia. He says that Greeks here in Bulgaria send money to Greeks in Macedonia — I'm sorry, Eléni — that Greeks here are helping to destroy Bulgarian villages and kill Bulgarian peasants."

"And worse," Georgi went on. "Dragulev is telling Bulgarians to wipe out Greeks in Bulgaria, just as Greeks are annihilating Bulgarians in Macedonia."

They came to a corner. Todor took his brother by the sleeve and pulled him. "Come Georgi. This way." Georgi started down the street with his brother, but he turned for an instant and called to Andrei: "Hurry. Hurry home. And be careful."

Within a few minutes Andrei, Eléni, and Evangelía had reached the safety of their apartment. Andrei found a note from Mr. Zurkov. It asked him to come to the shop as soon as possible. "Feed Evangelía and put her to bed," he said, kissing Eléni at the door. "I'll go to see Mr. Zurkov for a few minutes and be back in time for us to have dinner."

Eléni frowned. "Do you have to go into the streets? I'm afraid."

"You're safe here. And no one will bother me."

She gripped his sleeve. "Hurry back, Andrei."

The apothecary was dark when Andrei arrived at its door. He looked up and down the street. There was no one there to see him. He knocked on the door. "Mr. Zurkov, Mr. Zurkov," he called in a low voice. The front door opened a crack. "It's me, Andrei," he said. The door opened wider.

Zurkov grasped both of Andrei's arms. "Andrei. Come in." Zurkov quickly locked the door behind the younger man and pulled him further into the darkness. He asked frantically, "Are you all right? Are they rioting in Sozópolis?"

"No. Sozópolis is quiet."

"Good. Thank God, I listened to Vasilov and didn't restock this place or the store in Anchíalos. I was worried about Sozópolis."

"Do you think the shops are in danger?"

"You saw the mobs in the streets. Dragulev and his rabble destroyed a Greek church and school today. Worse, there are rumors about what is going to happen in Anchíalos."

"When? What are they going to do?"

"Tonight. Tomorrow. Soon. I don't know what. Only that it will be bad."

"What about the store in Anchíalos?"

"There's nothing I can do about Anchíalos. For now, I want you to take all the morphine and whatever other drugs you can carry out of this store. I'll do the same. I'll light the lamp for a few minutes."

When they finished packing, Zurkov led Andrei to the door. Before opening it he ordered, "Stay home tomorrow. I am going to lock up tonight and not open again until things quiet down. I will send for you when it is safe."

Burdened by two sacks full of Zurkov's stock, Andrei left the apothecary and hurried home, avoiding the main streets and their milling crowds of men.

MÁVROVO, KASTORIA
VILÂYET OF MONASTIR, IN THE OTTOMAN EMPIRE

The Kaimakan glowered scornfully at two Cretan *andártes* who were bound and lying in the dust, their feet tied by long ropes to saddles of his cavalry escort.

"Kyrie Athanásios, what are these men doing in Mávrovo?" the Kaimakan demanded.

Dimitráki and his brother, Kóstas, peeked through a crack at the side of the gate, watching their father stand humbly, head bowed before the Turkish overlord. "I'd like to kill that Turkish dog," Dimitráki snarled. He was embarrassed to see his father cowering before the Turk — head lowered, body stooped, and arms spread, palms upward, in the manner learned from his father, and that had been passed down from his father's father, and before, through generations.

Athanásios answered the Kaimakan. "I don't know why they are here, *Aféndis*. I haven't seen them in our village until now, when your men brought them here."

The Kaimakan ordered his escort, "Take these infidels out of the village on to the road to Kastoria, and tie them to a tree. Wait for me." The governor motioned to his mounted soldiers and they dragged their captives along the wagon-wheel-tracked road as if they were logs. Controlling their emotions, Athanásios and several other village elders watched the young men's bodies bounce off rocks and clods of earth, leaving trails of blood behind.

"*Aféndis*, honor me and allow my wife to serve you *kafé* and a sweet." Athanásios led the Kaimakan into his home, calling, "Kallíope, we have a guest."

Kallíope looked into the parlor and saw the two men taking their places on a divan. She hurried.

The Kaimakan casually opened one of three books that rested next to him. "More books, Kyrie Athanásios?" He glanced at a page and closed it dismissively. "You are an elder. You should spend more time controlling events in your village, not reading books."

"I tend the fields and orchards in the growing season, *Aféndis*, and consult with my neighbors when they ask my opinion. In winter, books are a comfort. They fill my time and my mind."

For several minutes, they talked of the weather, of crops, and of fishing in the lake, deferring the issue that concerned them both. Almost silently, her head covered with a shawl, Kallíope entered the room carrying a tray. On it were two of her best porcelain demitasse cups, brimming with frothy coffee, two small plates, each just large enough to hold a teaspoon that cradled deep black-red candied cherries and two glasses of cold water. She set these on the low table in front of the divan and left the room without saying a word. The men ate their sweet, drank their cold water and began to sip their coffee.

When he spoke again, the Kaimakan's face was threatening and his voice harsh. "Kyrie Athanásios, there are bands of rebel fighters hiding in the mountains and along the east coast of the lake near your village. You and I have known each other for a long time, but

I warn you, whoever helps them will suffer the same fate as the two that we caught today."

The Kaimakan set down his cup and rose to leave. Athanásios jumped to his feet, and taking a small leather bag from his pocket said, "*Aféndis*, please take this small gift in gratitude for your protection of this village. And we'll have a fine apple crop to share with you this fall."

The Kaimakan weighed the gift in his hand. He knew it was more gold than Athanásios could afford. He also knew that likely as not, this clever old man would recover part of the gift from other elders. He had learned the ways of *bakeesh*.

"Send your young men out later to see what happens to *andártes*, Kyrie Athanásios. This time ..." He paused and pocketed the bag. "This time," he emphasized, "I'll overlook the fact that we caught them near your village."

One hour later, Dimitráki accompanied his father, brother, and other villagers along the road to the outskirts of Mávrovo. There, they found the broken bodies of the two young Cretans lying face down in dirt stained by the blood that had poured from their gaping throats. The villagers carried the bodies to the church, where women prepared them for burial. The priest hurried a funeral service for the unnamed. The last shovelful of earth covered the bodies before nightfall.

Late in the night, Dimitráki sat up, startled awake by his own scream. His dream was so real that he looked for the Kaimakan's blood on his hands and body.

Awakened by Dimitráki's shriek, Kóstas asked, "What's wrong? A nightmare?"

"Yes. But someday it will be true."

"What?"

"Someday I will kill him."

"Who?"

"The Kaimakan," Dimitráki answered. He pulled a blanket to his neck and fell asleep smiling.

SOZÓPOLIS, BULGARIA

"Hrístos. Hrístos, wake up," Vasilikí shouted. She shook her husband. "The church bell is ringing. Something has happened."

Hristodoúlos forced himself out of a deep sleep and sat up. The evening had been warm. The windows and shutters were open, inviting in the sea breeze. The sounds of the church bell and the commotion in the street outside their home finally cleared his mind. "What? What's wrong?" He went to the window and saw a red glow in the sky to the north.

"Fire," he murmured. "There's a fire."

Hristodoúlos pulled on his clothes. "I'm going to the harbor. Go and tell Ioánnis to meet me there." He paused, assessing the situation for a moment. "After you send Ioánnis, stay with Sultána."

When he reached the quay, Hristodoúlos found a crowd of men gaping at a flickering red sky to the north. Pater Eleuthérios, gray-bearded and rotund, held a cross in his hands and, half asleep, mumbled prayers. Hristodoúlos caught sight of Décimos Kapidaghlís in the dim light and rushed toward him.

"What's happening?"

"It's Anchíalos," Décimos gasped. "Anchíalos is burning. The sky is red over Pyrgos too."

"Why?"

"A boat arrived from Pyrgos just before dark. The *kapetános* told us that there was fighting in Anchíalos — that a mob and some militia attacked Romiói. They hid in *Ághios Giorgios*. And there are riots in Pyrgos."

Hristodoúlos moaned. "Aleksiev told us this would come." He asked, "Has anything happened here? Has anyone been hurt?"

"Some stores were looted. And Pater says the church was broken into. He doesn't know if anything is missing yet. Whoever did it is gone."

"My God, what's happening to Eléni and Evangelía?" Hristodoúlos crossed himself and prayed aloud, "Panaghía, protect them."

BURGAS, BULGARIA

Eléni heard gunshots. She peeked into the street from the slit at the side of a curtained window. Men ran past under her darkened room shouting slogans and obscene curses. Evangelía slept fitfully in her crib, her eyelids quivered at each loud noise.

"Andrei, where are you?" Eléni thought. "Hurry home. I'm frightened."

Finally, she heard Andrei's feet pounding up the steps that led to their apartment. She rushed to the door, opening it just as he reached to unlock it.

"Andrei, what's happening? I heard shots. There are men yelling in the streets."

"Hurry, there's no time to explain. Dress Evangelía and pack enough clothes to go to Sozópolis for a few days."

"Why? How will we get there at night?"

"No questions now. It's dangerous here, and I want you and Evangelía out of Burgas now, tonight."

Andrei took Eléni by the arm and led her into their bedroom. The bags that she had unpacked the day before were in the corner of the room. He placed them on the bed.

"Pack," he directed. Eléni started throwing in clothes almost at random. "Hurry," Andrei kept saying. "Hurry, Eléni."

"Just tell me what's going on, Andrei. I want to know."

Andrei spoke quickly. "Mr. Zurkov told me that the Greek Church was on fire ... all of Anchíalos is burning. Bulgarian militia and mobs attacked the city. Some of them returned to Burgas and joined up with the local thugs. They're breaking the windows of the businesses owned by Greeks. They're setting fires." He hesitated. "Kyria Anthoula's shop is in flames."

Eléni flinched at the news. "Where is she? Is she all right?" She picked Evangelía up from her crib and dressed her. Half asleep, the baby fussed and cried.

"Yes, she's all right, but frightened. I met her close to her shop. She was talking to two men, a *kapetános*, an old friend of her husband, and his first officer. She told me that she was afraid for her life and was leaving on his ship tonight. I asked him if you and Evangelía could go with her."

Eléni turned to him. "You are coming too, aren't you?"

"No." Seeing the look on her face, he went on, "Eléni, I've nothing to fear, I'm Bulgarian. Mr. Zurkov will need me when things quiet down."

"I won't leave without you." Eléni lifted Evangelía. "You're coming with us, or we're all staying here."

He shook his head. "No. You are leaving with Evangelía tonight. The *kapetános* will drop you off in Sozópolis. I will join you there in a few days and bring you back when things are safe. No arguments. He told me to have you on his ship within the hour or he'll leave without you."

Eléni looked at her daughter and realized this was no time to quarrel.

Andrei led Eléni through the streets. She held Evangelía close, muffling her baby's cries. They joined a growing throng of men, women, and children who surged toward the bay. Behind them, shouting mobs, the sounds of glass breaking, and the bark of guns turned people's fear into panic. Those who could ran.

Andrei grabbed Eléni's skirt with his left hand. He held it curled about the handle of the suitcase and pulled her along. He used the bag in his right hand as a battering ram to push through the jam of terrified families. When they reached the wharf, Andrei's eyes searched the deck of a ship for the captain who had promised Eléni transport. Eléni spotted Kyria Anthoula waving her arm as if she were leaving on a voyage, stylish even now, her pretty handkerchief acting as a signal flag.

"There — there, Andrei. Kyria Anthoula," Eléni cried.

Andrei wedged himself through the crowd toward the gangway of the ship. There was a momentary opening, and he pushed Eléni and Evangelía forward, handing the suitcases to a crewmember.

"Run — go to Kyria Anthoula. Find the *kapetánios*. I'll keep back the crowd. Hurry."

Eléni cocooned Evangelía in her blanket and clutched her close to her chest. She climbed the gangplank and rushed into Kyria Anthoula's arms just as the captain ordered his crew to raise the gangway.

Eléni turned back, searching the crowd for her husband. "Andrei. Where's Andrei?" Her eyes spied him the instant he went down under the feet of desperate people who were trying to reach the gangplank. "Andrei!" she screamed. "I can't see him. Andrei!" She pushed her way along the ship's railing. "Please – please – let me off the ship."

It was too late. The kapetánios shouted orders from the bridge and his crew cut the ship's hawsers with axes. The engines roared and powered the ship into the bay, away from the hopelessness of those left behind.

Stunned, Eléni stared back toward the pier. Quietly, Kyria Anthoula put a blanket around Eléni's shoulders, tenderly smoothed her hair, and took Evangelía from her arms. "Sit, Eléni. Here, next to me. Sit down." Anthoula led her to a deck hatch, where Eléni sat in shocked semi-consciousness. Unaware that the ship headed east out into the Black Sea, and then changed its course to the south, toward the Bosphorus, she moaned softly and rocked her body with her arms across her chest.

At dawn, Eléni suddenly jumped to her feet and looked over the ship's rail to the west. She did not recognize the long, low-lying coastline, cloaked in a gray mist. The ship had reached that part of Thrace's coast known to the ancients as Salmydessos — a place of shipwrecks. Evangelía's cry startled her.

Kyria Anthoula, who was only half-awake, held Evangelía close. Eléni nudged Kyria Anthoula and took her baby in her arms. "Where are we? What happened to Andrei?"

The haggard seamstress, whose fatigue and disheveled hair aged her ten years, rose to her feet and wrapped a blanket about Eléni and Evangelía. "Quiet, child. Be calm. The *kapetános* said it was too dangerous to anchor at Sozópolis last night."

Eléni looked around frantically. "Where are we going? What happened to Andrei?"

"I don't know." Anthoula's voice was soothing. "He stumbled, or was pushed down, but we were gone before I could see anything more. He is all right. Don't worry."

The captain left the ship's bridge to assess the condition of his refugee passengers and exchange a few words with them. He approached Eléni and Kyria Anthoula, and asked, "Ladies, are you all right?" He saw the baby in Eléni's arms. "Is there anything I can do for you? For your baby?" He hesitated for a moment. "Please, use my cabin," He carried their suitcases and led them. "I'll have food brought to you. Tell me if there is anything you need."

"Where are we going?" asked Eléni.

"To Volos," he replied.

"Where is Volos?"

"In Greece."

"But my husband — my mother and father — how will they find me? I want to go home."

The captain's voice was gentle. "Kyria, there is no going back. My ship must be in Volos on schedule, and, no matter what, I won't return to a Bulgarian port until I know that it's safe."

Kyria Anthoula put her arm around Eléni. "Come, Eléni. Come to the cabin and rest. Everything will be all right. I'll send word to Burgas and Sozópolis about where you and the baby are and soon you'll be with your family."

In a daze, Eléni followed the captain to his cabin, washed Evangelía, and fed her from the food the ship's cook brought to them. She did not see the entrance to the Bosphorus, or Constantinople, or the straits of the Hellespont. She sat quietly, trying to order her mind. Her hand touched the chain at her neck and her fingers grasped the little bag that contained the amulet her mother had given to her and *pappoú* Zísos' ancient silver drachma.

VOLOS, GREECE

Immediately after they stepped on the wharf at Volos, Kyria Anthoula, who had hidden gold liras in her clothing, told Eléni that she was going to bribe the officials and buy passage to Piraeus.

"Don't leave me, Kyria Anthoula. What will I do?"

"Take care of yourself and Evangelía. I have only enough money to get to Athens and live there until I decide what to do."

"But what will I do alone with my baby?"

"You'll survive until I find Konstantínos and Sofía and send help to you."

Eléni shuddered. Soldiers were herding refugees away from the port — others that had been on her ship, and from ships from Varna and Mesémbria. Evangelía started to cry.

"Take care of the little one, Eléni," ordered Kyria Anthoula. "Go wherever the soldiers take you. I'll learn where you are, and we'll come for you."

"Please, find out what happened to Andrei. Write to my parents. Tell them where we are. Find Andrei. Please."

A soldier took Eléni by the arm. "Come with me."

Eléni reached out toward Kyria Anthoula, then resigned herself and followed the soldier.

EFXINOÚPOLIS, MAGNESIA, GREECE

Two days after they left the ship, Eléni and Evangelía arrived at Efxinoúpolis, a camp for refugees in a region south of Volos. In the morning light, Eléni surveyed row on row of dismal wooden huts. *These are shacks*, she thought as a non-commissioned officer led her to one of them. Eléni stepped inside holding Evangelía over her shoulder. "This bed is for you and your baby," he announced. "The other beds are for other refugees. You'll share."

Eléni sat on the edge of the bed, held her baby, and cried. "Soon, darling. Soon they will come to get us and we will go home. Soon, please God."

At first, she was sure that her rescue was only a day or two away, Eléni spent hours watching the road that approached the encampment for signs of Andrei, or of Konstantínos, praying that one of them would come to take her and Evangelía to a place of safety. Soon, circumstances forced her to concentrate her energy on sustaining their lives.

Winter came. Cold winds swept down from the northern Aegean Sea, bringing first rain, and then ice, snow, and biting cold. Neither she nor her child had sufficient clothing or blankets, and food became scarce. Dysentery, pneumonia, smallpox, and childhood diseases provided both the angel of death and the priests who were available with continual work. Eléni saw soldiers pull a wagon stacked with bodies past her shelter on the way to cremation fires that were hidden beyond view. Horrified, she watched a woman who had shared her hut carried to a waiting cart. Sickness and death were constant companions.

One morning, after a light snow had covered the ugliness of the camp, Eléni took her place in a long line of shivering women and waited to receive a share of crude gruel. When a rumor spread along the line that there was not enough food for everyone, the women rushed forward, shoving each other to gain advantage. One pushed Eléni out of the way, almost dislodging Evangelía from her arms. A rage shocked Eléni out of the torpor that had gripped her for days. She looked around until she saw a familiar face. "Here, Alíki, hold Evangelía for me." The woman took Evangelía in her arms, and Eléni lunged forward, reached the serving table and pushed two soldiers aside. She raised her arms and cried, "Stop. All of you. Stop. Control yourselves."

The women froze for an instant, but then struggled forward again. When one pushed to the table, Eléni pulled her to the ground by her hair, and stood over her with a threatening raised arm. The others hesitated.

"Stand where you are. We'll share what there is."

Surprising even herself, Eléni took control. She elbowed a guard out of the way and motioned a woman forward. One by one, they passed her, their pots and cups outstretched to receive the gruel she ladled. Serving Alíki's portion and her own last, she took Evangelía back into her arms and walked away grimly. The women stared after her.

In the days that followed, the refugees began to look to Eléni for advice and leadership. She bartered her sewing skills for cloth and other necessities that survivors stripped from the bodies of the dead and made warm clothing for them, and for Evangelía and herself. She badgered the military into providing rudimentary huts with tubs for bathing and washing and had the men dig outhouses. But gradually, the grip of winter squeezed out of her the satisfaction she had gained from her effort.

In late January of the new year, Eléni lay huddled under a blanket, holding Evangelía close to keep her warm. A cutting wind blew snow through cracks in the wall of the hastily built shack that served as their shelter. Three other women claimed corners of the windowless room. There was no privacy. Eléni heard a knock at the door. A voice called, "Eléni Athanasíou. There's someone to see you." She resisted waking, wanting to remain adrift in dreams of happy winter days at home with her sisters and parents. Only in her dreams could she escape the nightmare of the refugee camp.

The knocking persisted. "Eléni, Eléni Athanasíou?" She responded to the Greek version of her husband's surname and opened the door a crack. There was a soldier there. "The man who brought this is waiting for you with the colonel," he said, handing an envelope to her.

Eléni recognized the seal on the back of the envelope. *Konstantínos!* She stepped outside and looked frantically to the left and right of the hut before turning to the soldier, "Where is he? Where?"

"At the commander's house."

She crushed the envelope in her hand, turned back into her hut, wrapped Evangelía in a blanket, and clutching her child close to her hurried out the door and toward the colonel's home. As she approached it, she saw a slender, bearded man stepping out into the light. He carried a large bundle.

"Eléni?" he called.

She recognized his voice. "Dimitrios? Is it you?".

"Yes." For a minute, Dimitrios Parousis encased Eléni and Evangelía in his arms. Then they walked to a fallen tree at the edge of the camp and sat close together. Dimitrios set his bundle on the ground and held Evangelía while Eléni smoothed out the creases of the crushed letter. She looked at the neat handwriting, hopeful that the words would bring good news.

Embarrassed, she said, "Read this to me, Dimitrios."

He took the letter, paused for a moment, and read:

My Dear Eléni,

Dimitrios found you. Thank God.

Kyria Anthoula came to us a few days ago and brought news that you were somewhere near Volos. Dimitrios left Athens to search for you. He will give you some money to help until we can bring you to us.

Dimitrios will tell you about your mother and father, and about Andrei.

Kisses from Sofía, Smarágda, the children, and me.

Konstantínos

"What about Andrei?" Eléni grasped the front of Dimitrios's jacket. "What news is there? Is he well? Is he coming for us?"

Evangelía started to cry, frightened by the tone of her mother's voice. Dimitrios looked into Eléni's anxious face, and then down at Evangelía. He cradled her close in his arms and rocked her gently.

"Dimitrios, say something. Talk to me. What has happened?"

"Konstantínos, Sofía, Smarágda, and the children are well," he said. "Kyria Anthoula is working with Konstantínos and will soon open her own shop. I work at the docks, and ..."

Eléni interrupted. "Where is Andrei?"

He took a deep breath. "Prepare yourself, Eléni. The news is not good."

"Just tell me."

"Your father is very ill. Cancer. He may not live until *Páscha*."

"Oh, no...what will *mána* do?" Tears filled her eyes. "Thank God Sultána is there to help her." Then she took hold of his jacket again. "But tell me about Andrei."

"Andrei..." Dimitrios hesitated, and then blurted out, "He is gone."

"Gone? Gone where? What do you mean?"

"He is dead."

"No, no!" Eléni's eyes showed fear. "How?"

"Andrei fell when you ran up the ship's ramp. The panicked crowd trampled him. It was an accident."

"What will I do? What will Evangelía and I do?" She took Evangelía back into her arms and rocked her back and forth. Eléni felt lost — abandoned. Her grief was secondary to her terror. She was alone in this miserable camp, barely able to survive — without a husband. "What will we do? What will I do?"

"You'll be strong and wait here," Dimitrios said. "The colonel won't let anyone leave. Athens wants to make Efxinoúpolis and Nea Anchíalos permanent towns for the refugees from Bulgaria."

"Take me with you now."

"I can't, Eléni. They won't let me." Dimitrios moved the bundle to Eléni's feet. "Take this. There's food in it. Sofía and Smarágda sent warm clothing. And you'll find Konstantínos's address on a sheet of paper." He lowered his voice. "Konstantínos hid a bag of small gold coins in a shawl. Use them to bribe the soldiers when you must."

"Take us to Athens, Dimitrios," Eléni implored. "Take us to Sofía and Smarágda."

Just then, a soldier passed, his attention riveted on the bundle that Eléni held. Fearful, she kissed Dimitrios on the cheek and whispered, "Soon, please, soon, Dimitrios."

She slung the bundle over one shoulder, picked up Evangelía, turned, and walked away. Evangelía looked quizzically at her uncle over Eléni's shoulder as he faded into the distance.

Weeks later, as Eléni approached her hut with an armful of wet laundry she heard her name called. "Eléni. Eléni." A small group of women hurried toward her. At each step, their labored breaths turned into puffs of smoke-like mist. "Eléni. Our food. They've taken our food."

"What? Wait. Let me put my laundry away."

Eléni hurried inside, put her laundry on a rough table, and commanded the woman who was sitting on a bed and holding Evangelía on her lap. "Aspasia, take care of Evangelía for a few minutes."

Evangelía reached for her mother and started to cry. "Shh, darling. I'll be right back. Théa Aspasia will be here with you." With that, Eléni covered her head and shoulders with the shawl that her sisters had sent to her and went out to the women.

One of them stepped in front of the small crowd of anguished faces and grasped Eléni's shoulders. Her high-pitched voice was shrill with anger. "Eléni, when our food carts arrived from Volos this morning, the soldiers took them away. We have no food. Why do they do this to us? We are Greeks, like them."

"Turk — Bulgarian — Greek. What does it matter? Pigs don't have nationalities."

Another spoke up: "They pushed us away. One officer took out his pistol and pointed it at us."

"Was the colonel there?" asked Eléni.

Three or four voices answered, "No."

Eléni looked toward the snug home at the edge the encampment, the place where the colonel lived comfortably. The sight of smoke rising from its chimney infuriated her. She imagined the warmth of his fireside and his amply filled pantry.

Eléni called back to the woman inside the hut. "Aspasia, stay here and take care of Evangelía. I'll be back as soon as I can." Turning to the growing group of women Eléni commanded, "You. All of you. Come with me."

Eléni forced herself to ignore Evangelía's cries and marched in long, strong strides, her eyes set on the colonel's retreat. As she progressed, she called to other women, "Come. Come and get your food. Come with us."

One by one, overcoming their fear, the women of the camp joined her, swelling the number of her followers. Their men gaped at the women.

Eléni cried out "Bread. Bread. Give us our bread." The women took up the chorus and moved close to the soldiers who protected the colonel's home. They readied their rifles.

Eléni strode up to the first soldier. She brought her face to within inches of his, slapped him, and took his rifle. In moments, her followers had disarmed the other two guards and had them lying helpless on the ground.

The colonel, wearing a dress uniform, opened his door with an air of authority and disdain. "What...what is this? How dare you. Leave. Leave at once," he ordered, waving his arm toward the shelters. "Get back to your quarters!"

He was a small, emaciated man whose face twitched nervously. As he spoke, the movement of his mustache, twisted to sharp points on either side of his thin-lipped mouth, punctuated his speech. Even his arms and hands moved spastically to the rhythm of his words.

"Where is our food?" Eléni demanded.

"I don't know what you are talking about," he answered.

Eléni stepped forward, and grabbed the colonel by his tunic, pulling him from the door and throwing him to the ground. She sat on his chest, pinning him, and slapped his face in a fury, first with one hand and then the other.

"We're starving," she cried, her hands pummeling his head. "Give us our food."

"Stop, stop!" His voice rose to a scream.

Eléni stared at him. The man's face was beet red and his nose was bleeding. She spoke through gritted teeth: "Give us our food today, and every day, or I swear to the Panaghía, the next time this happens, the whole camp will come after you. We'll kill you. Now, tell your men to take us to the food."

"Get off me."

Eléni stood up, allowing the colonel to stagger to his feet. He reached into his pocket for a handkerchief, which he held to his nose to stem the flow of blood. He did not meet Eléni's eyes but turned to order the astonished guards, "Take these women to the food carts."

The soldiers drew near. "Keep their rifles until we have the carts safe," Eléni ordered the women. After watching the women follow the soldiers back down the hill, the humiliated colonel stumbled back into his house.

CHAPTER EIGHT
1910
CHICAGO, ILLINOIS

The small fitting and sewing room at the back of Signore Arcudi's establishment was Leonardo's realm, and Arcudi recognized Leonardo's contribution to his business on the new sign in front of the shop.

LAUNDRY – FRENCH CLEANING – CARPETS – TAILOR

There was not enough business for Leonardo to devote all his effort to his trade. He spent many hours away from sewing to tend the counter and sort laundry, and he beat-clean carpets that hung on lines behind the shop. In the summer, the work brought him near to collapse — the heat and high humidity were unbearable. In winter, he welcomed the work as a means to get warm, at least until the cold made his eyeballs hurt.

Leonardo sent money to his mother every month and saved toward the day that he would bring his family to join him. He heard little of his father, except that he occasionally appeared in the middle of the night, washed, spent a day eating and resting and then snuck out at dark to join his bandit group carrying a package of food and a bottle of wine.

One bare bulb supplemented the light that came through the single high window in Leonardo's workroom. Arcudi had been one of the first in the neighborhood to contract for electricity. The room's contents — a table, foot-treadle sewing machine, mannequin, pinking shears, needles and thread, and other tools of Leonardo's trade — revealed its function. He loved this space and was never happier than when he wore a thimble and held a sewing needle in his fingers.

Until he moved into his own small apartment, Leonardo had lived in a boarding house on the West Side of the city, close to Halsted Street. Italian, Greek, and Bulgarian bachelors filled its rooms, conflating their languages and their music. They learned to speak English from their bosses, whether at the stockyards, slaughterhouses, or on railroad gangs, and from the many Irishmen who worked by their sides. Leonardo used a mixture of Italian, Greek, and English in conversations with friends, or in serving customers at the counter of Signore Arcudi's shop.

Petros Angelopoulos admired himself in a three-way mirror. He twisted his body to the left and then to the right to see how he looked in his new suit.

"No move, Petros." The irritation in Leonardo's voice was clear. He pinned corrections to the suit's coat while Petros squirmed. Leonardo raised his voice. "No move or I don't finish." He marked a seam with tailor's chalk.

Enzio had introduced Leonardo to his Greek friend. The three young bachelors had bonded, and shared adventures on their days off from work.

"Leonardo, can look thin?" Petros said in English.

Leonardo smiled. "*Assolutamente. Sì.* Ladies love you."

Petros Angelopoulos was impatient. His round, smooth face was topped with black, slicked-back hair that looked like a woman's cloche hat. His belly swelled under the vest Leonardo had sewn for him.

A voice called from the front of the shop, "Leonardo, are you back there?"

"Enzio? Come back here," answered Leonardo.

Shaking snow from his coat, Enzio entered the little room. He filled it with his energy.

Leonardo looked up. "I'm making Petros more handsome than he deserves. A peacock."

"Petros, you stuffed. You can move in jacket?" Enzio asked. And then, in Italian to Leonardo, "What have you done to him?"

"No move," Leonardo ordered. Petros froze in place.

Enzio stood in front of Petros, almost close enough for their noses to touch. "It true, Petros? You take Leonardo, me to church dance to meet Greek girls?"

Enzio had hounded Petros to take him and Leonardo to the pre-Lenten carnival dance from the time he met Petros' sister, Marina. She had picked up a carpet at the counter of Arcudi's shop while Enzio was visiting. The young men liked Marina and her dark-haired, olive-skinned girlfriend. They looked so Italian.

"Enzio, Leonardo — yes, I take. But do favor. Greeks not like stranger near daughter. No make trouble."

While Petros changed into his street clothing, Leonardo sorted laundry and Enzio groomed himself in the mirror. He combed his hair. "Beautiful hair, no, Leonardo?"

Leonardo finished sorting the laundry, put on his suit coat and closed the shop, ushering his friends out and locking the door behind him.

ATHENS, GREECE

Eléni left the palace and skirted Syntagma Square and the *kafeneía* that surrounded it to avoid boorish comments from the men seated there at outdoor tables. She hurried toward the railroad station, eager to share her experiences with her family. Her thoughts made her smile. *Now that I go to the palace and sew for the princess, life in Efxinoúpolis is only a bad dream.*

A man had been hiding from view at the side of the road when Eléni battered the colonel at Efxinoúpolis. With his heavy growth of beard and furtive movements, the stranger might have been a *kléfti*, one of the Robin Hood-like bandits romanticized in Greek poetry and song. But he was only a refugee who had walked the long distance from Nea Anchíalos to Efxinoúpolis in search of missing relatives from Bulgaria.

The man saw the colonel reappear at the door of his house as soon as Eléni and her followers were out of sight. The twitching officer called guards near to him and gave them orders, pointing in the direction Eléni had taken. The cautious man was experienced enough to know what the officer's orders might be. He hurried after Eléni and followed her to her hut.

Eléni had barely sat on the edge of her bed and taken Evangelía into her arms when she heard a knock at the door. She covered her shoulders and Evangelía with a shawl, and holding her baby, opened the door a crack to see who it was. "What do you want? Who are you?" she asked the tall, wiry man at the door. He frightened her. His clothing was dirty and worn, his hands rough, and he cowered like a trapped animal.

"Kyria, I am Spíros Stamatiou. From Anchíalos in Eastern Romylia. I live in Nea Anchíalos. I saw what you did to the colonel. They're going to come after you." His voice was sincere and concerned. It overcame her fear.

"Who's coming for me?"

"The soldiers. You must go away. The colonel won't leave you alone after what you did to him."

"How do you know what I did?"

"I watched from the road. You were amazing. The colonel will never forget. He'll get even."

"He wouldn't dare hurt me," she answered. But her face showed fear.

Evangelía's arms reached around Eléni's neck, arousing her maternal protective instinct. "Where would I go?" she whispered, her courage failing.

"Where's your husband?" the man asked.

"Dead."

"Come with me to Nea Anchíalos. My family will protect you and your baby." He nodded his head and pointed his finger toward the road. "*Haíde.* The soldiers must be on their way already."

Eléni was frantic. She knew in her heart that the man was right — the colonel would want vengeance. She had humiliated him, and he would be afraid that she would report his corruption. She looked into Spíros' eyes and decided. "Wait until I gather some things."

Eléni put Evangelía on the bed. "Watch *mána* for a minute," she said, trying to keep her voice light. "Then I'll pick you up and we'll go for a walk."

The other occupants of the hut lay mute, staring as Eléni gathered her few possessions. She hid the gold pieces Dimitrios had brought to her in her bodice.

Ready, Eléni picked up Evangelía, made the sign of the cross with her free hand, took her bundle and opened the door.

Spíros was waiting.

Eléni nodded grimly. "Let's go. God be with us."

Eléni and Evangelía found shelter in Nea Anchíalos with Spíros, his mother, a sour, black-enshrouded widow who resented every moment of Eléni's existence, and Spíros's barely pubescent sister, who seemed always to be clinging to her mother. "What did you bring home?" his mother snarled at Spíros. She answered her own question with a face twisted in derision. "A widow. Not a young bride. Not someone to take care of me when I grow old."

Eléni was grateful that she had been saved from the colonel, and for the protection provided by Spíros. But being a widow in a bachelor's home, and being asked contemptuous questions by his mother and observed by prying eyes, shamed her. She bought some relief from the venom directed at her by pretending a messenger had brought her a gold coin from her relatives in Athens. The crone snatched the coin. "Well, this is something to pay us for our trouble," she grumbled as she hid it in her purse. "When will you get more?"

Spíros paid constant attention to Eléni. His eyes followed her when she went behind the curtain screen that provided privacy for washing and changing, and he seemed always to find a reason to touch her or press against her. His mother noticed. "Good, Spíros. Make use of her now. Later you can find a virgin bride to bring home to me."

A month passed. One morning in March, Eléni awoke sensing that the air had softened, and the light had changed. She rushed out to wonder at the early morning, leaving Evangelía sleeping on her bed. She remembered looking out the window of her home in Sozópolis an eternity ago when the first signs of spring had lifted her spirits.

Spíros stepped up behind her and put his arms around her waist. One of his hands crept cautiously up to cup her breast. Eléni lunged forward, breaking his hold. She turned with a wide-legged stance, as if ready to defend her life. "No, Spíros."

"It's me, Eléni. Calm yourself."

"How dare you?" She spat the words at him indignantly. "How dare you touch me that way?"

"I only... I wanted ..."

"I know what you wanted. No."

"But I love you, Eléni.

"No."

"I do. And I love Evangelía."

Eléni's mind raced. She was indebted to Spíros, but she found him repulsive. The thought of submitting to him turned her stomach. She had to think only of Evangelía and herself. She had to get to Athens. Suddenly, her voice softened, and without realizing her intent, she uttered manipulative words for the first time in her life. "It would never work. Especially not here," she said gently.

"What do you mean?"

"I can't be in your mother's home. I have to find my family. I have my own mother to take care of."

"Then where?" Spíros asked eagerly. "Where?"

She looked into his eyes. "Athens."

Several weeks later, Spíros arranged their escape to Volos by horse cart. Once there, they bought passage on a boat to Piraeus with Eléni's remaining gold coins. A few hours after their arrival in Piraeus, Eléni located Konstantínos and Sofía in Kalithéa. They welcomed her and Evangelía into their home with relief and joy. "We didn't know where you were, Eléni," Sofía sobbed, hugging her sister. "Dimitrios went to Efxinoúpolis to bring you here, and you were gone. We didn't know where to look for you."

A comfortable room, with a bed for her and another smaller one set next to hers had been waiting for Eléni and Evangelía for months. Spíros made do with a makeshift cot in the storeroom.

In the days before they arrived in Athens, Spíros pressed Eléni to marry him. She fended him off with vague promises and reminders of the obligation that he had to his mother and sister. To her relief, shortly after she moved in with Konstantínos and Sofía, Spíros was on his way back to Nea Anchíalos, giving Eléni disturbing assurances that he would return.

Eléni found Kyria Anthoula, who embraced her with tears and apologies for having left her behind at Volos. She went to work in her teacher's small shop. Clients grew loyal to Eléni, and referred friends directly to her. Kyria Anthoula gracefully accepted Eléni's success.

Spíros returned to work at Piraeus's docks with Dimitrios Parousis twice in the first year that Eléni was in Kalithéa. Strenuous days exhausted him, and he had few opportunities to press Eléni about their relationship. She worked long hours at her shop, often on Sundays, and was surrounded by family at home. On each stay, Spíros was in Athens just long enough to save a little money to take back to his mother and sister.

In the second year, Spíros moved to Kalithéa to live near Eléni and work with Dimitrios. He contrived to visit at times that courtesy required Konstantínos and Sofía to invite him to stay to dinner. His intrusiveness and attempt at familiarity made Eléni and her family uncomfortable.

Once, alone with Sofía, Eléni confided, "Sofía, Spíros worries me. I feel guilty that I used him to escape Efxinoúpolis, and you have been good to him because he saved me. But he frightens me."

Excited by her success at the palace, Eléni boarded the new train that ran from Athens through Kalithéa to Piraeus. She could afford the luxury of sitting in a modern train and not in a carriage behind a braying, smelly donkey, or worse yet, walking for hours on a scorched and dusty road. August was an impossibly hot month in Athens. Nevertheless, people filled the streets that buzzed with the name 'Venizelos'. The Cretan political giant, recently elected to the new assembly, was about to return to Athens from Switzerland. Rumor had it that he was going to form a government.

Eléni was ignorant of all this.

Eight months before, in January, a fire at the palace had brought Eléni good fortune. The flames spared King George, his family, and their living quarters, but smoke filled the private rooms, and its acrid smell clung to every garment in the closets.

While being fitted for a uniform, the commander of the palace guard talked to Konstantínos about Princess Sophie's need of fresh clothing. Konstantínos recommended an excellent Greek seamstress. "Kyria Eléni designed and made fashionable clothing for wealthy women in Bulgaria," he said. "I'm sure that the princess would be happy with her work."

The next day an officer appeared at the door of Konstantínos' home and in the name of Crown Prince Constantine commanded Eléni to present herself at the servant's entrance to the palace on the following morning at nine. "Bring samples of your work for Princess Sophie to inspect," were the officer's final orders.

Within hours of Eléni's interview with the young princess, she and Kyria Anthoula were busy cutting and sewing the first of many dresses that the princess ordered for her daughters and herself. Eléni was once again with Kyria Anthoula, this time not as an apprentice, but as a partner.

When she arrived home from the palace, Eléni found six-year-old Evangelía playing with her five cousins. Eléni's sisters, Sofía and Smarágda, were sitting under the shade-giving mulberry tree, cleaning vegetables, and chatting while they watched their children.

"*Mána*," Evangelía called, running to her mother.

"Come, my treasure, let me hug you." Eléni lifted her daughter and covered her face with kisses.

"Sit down, Eléni," ordered Sofía. "Drink some cold water. You must be parched. Tell us about the palace and your princess."

Eléni sat with her sisters, accepted a glass of water from Sofía and drank deeply. Evangelía snuggled in her mother's lap.

"Princess Sophie loved the dress I made for her. She asked about our family, and about how we are managing in Athens. She is so kind."

"Does she really speak Greek?" Smarágda asked. "I thought she was German."

"Perfectly, even though she was born in a place called Prussia."

"Where is Prussia?" asked Sofía.

"I don't know," Eléni admitted. "Let's ask Konstantínos later. He'll know."

"Are you going back to the palace?" Smarágda asked.

"Yes. Soon. The princess ordered four summer dresses, two for each of her daughters. Helen and Irene are perfect little princesses. They love trying on dresses and posing for their mother."

"It must be wonderful to be a princess," Smarágda said pensively. "No worries about money. Everything done for you."

"Every woman suffers, Smarágda," Sofía said. "There's no birth without pain. Women serve their families, even princesses."

"But to be a princess ..."

"Enough dreaming," Eléni interjected. "Vasílis is climbing the wall again. You'd better get him down before he breaks his neck."

"Vasílis, I'm going to kill you. Get down. Down from that wall. You and your father — always looking for trouble."

"What's happening with Dimitrios?" Eléni whispered to Sofía.

"I heard you, Eléni," Smarágda said wearily. "It's the same as always. Dimitrios gets involved in every political happening. Last year he supported the military uprising, yelling '*Enosis* for Crete, or war!' He could have been killed. Now he joins the mobs at night. They scream for Venizelos to head the government. I don't know where he gets the strength after a day at the docks. He's never too tired to leave me alone at night."

Sofía sighed. "What have you decided about Spíros, Eléni? You should get married again."

"Please, Spíros is not ..."

"He is not Andrei," Sofía finished.

"No, he's not Andrei. I know what I owe Spíros. If he hadn't helped me escape, Evangelía and I might not be here."

"Dimitrios says that Spíros works hard," Smarágda said. "And he supports his mother and sister."

"Enough about Spíros. I need to lie down for a little." Eléni lifted Evangelía from her lap.

Sofía called to her daughter. "Theanó, play with Evangelía while Théa takes a nap."

In the coolness of her room, Eléni drifted into a half-sleep. Her mind went back to Efxinoúpolis and the feeling of power — of triumph — that she'd had as she led the women away from the house of the crestfallen colonel. She thought about how she had met Spíros and the dilemma their uncomfortable relationship had created.

Eléni rose from her daydream and sat on the side of the bed, her hands folded in her lap. *What shall I do with him?* She closed her eyes and breathed slowly and evenly for a time. When her eyes opened, she whispered, "Konstantínos. I will ask Konstantínos."

A few days later, on a Sunday morning, Eléni contrived to be alone with Konstantínos. Knowing that he preferred to sit in the garden under the mulberry tree on Sunday mornings with his coffee, cigarettes and newspapers at hand, she feigned not feeling well and stayed behind when the others went to church. A dignified, fifty-one-year-old gentleman, he looked more a professor than a tailor. He kept his graying mustache meticulously groomed, waxed to sharp points at the tips. Like most literate Greek men of his time, he was an avid reader, especially of the myriad Athenian newspapers.

Eléni brought a glass of cold water to him in the garden and set it next to his coffee. "Would you like me to make another cup for you, Konstantínos?"

"No, thank you. Water is fine." He drank and wiped his mustache dry with an embroidered napkin. "It's so good to be here in the garden. Look how clear the day is. The sky is miraculously blue. It is the temple God created for us to worship him in — better than the cathedral." He looked at his newspaper for a moment, and then spoke again. "Next month, I'll be off to Paris. Stávros and Zenóvios have learned so much about the business that they teach me now."

"How long will you be gone this time?"

"About four months. Sofía is pregnant — I'll return in time for the birth."

"She didn't tell me." Eléni crossed herself. "May her delivery be easy." Eléni was reminded of the baby Sofía had lost — the one she had named after her mother. "I am happy that you will have a baby to take the place of little Vasilikí."

They sat quietly for a moment. Konstantínos smiled and looked up. "Now sit down and tell me what is on your mind."

"Oh, nothing."

"Come now. You didn't stay home for nothing. We have shared secrets. I watched you grow up, and I asked you to give me advice when you were much younger. You've been hovering about for a reason. Tell me."

Eléni pulled up a chair sat down facing him. "What do I do about Spíros?"

"What do you want to do?"

"Oh — I don't know. He never leaves me alone. He wants me to marry him, and he helped me get to Athens with the idea that I would."

"How did he get that idea?"

She blushed. "I know I led him on. I'm guilty."

Konstantínos reached out and took Eléni's hand. "Listen. I can't say that what you did was good. But you were alone, and responsible for Evangelía."

"I misled him. I had to. I had to get to Athens."

"Men — and women — do what they think they must to survive. I'm ashamed of some things that I did on the battlefield, but I had no choice, at least I thought so at the time."

She stood up and paced back and forth. "The thing is I didn't love Spíros then, and don't now. I don't even like him. And now I

144

don't even need him. I can provide for myself and for Evangelía. There is no reason to marry Spíros except to reward him for helping me. That's not good enough."

Konstantínos busied himself. He rolled a cigarette and lit it, took a puff, expelled the sweet-smelling smoke and looked at Eléni. "Well, let me suggest something that may shock you. But give it some thought."

She sat down again, and looked at him intently. "Tell me."

He spoke slowly. "Our future isn't here, Eléni. Not in Athens. Not in Greece. Bulgaria, Serbia, and Turkey are building their armies. Venizelos is a strong leader with great ambitions. He wants Greece to be the master of her own destiny. The Macedonian question is unresolved — Greece wants to expand its territories. War will come."

"When? When do you think Greece will be at war?"

"Next year. The year after. Not much later." Konstantínos took another puff on his cigarette. "Let's talk about our family. You want the best for Evangelía?"

"Of course."

"You want to bring your mother from Sozópolis?"

"Yes."

"And Sultána and her husband?"

"Yes, them too."

"As for me, two of my sons are in Paris. Paris is not the answer. There's too much trouble in Europe. Haríklea and the children are here, with one on the way."

"God help us."

"We can pray for help, Eléni." Konstantínos looked at her, his cynicism revealed in a slight smile. "However, in most things we have to help ourselves."

Eléni was puzzled. "What does this have to do with Spíros and me?"

"Remember when I asked you about my marrying Sofía? It was after I came back from the war in Greece — at my welcome home party — at the Stoyanni's home in Pyrgos."

She smiled. "What a wonderful party that was. We were all so happy."

"I told you then that Athens and Greece were not the long-term answer for me."

"I remember. I didn't understand then and I don't now."

"Where are the Greeks who are leaving Turkey, Bulgaria, and Greece going? Where are the ships that leave Piraeus every week taking them?"

Eléni hesitated before she answered. "America?"

He nodded. "Yes, to America. America must be our dream. A place away from war and suffering. A place that is safe — with opportunity."

"But how?"

"Spíros is the answer. You must convince him to go to America. Marry him before he leaves and follow him there with Evangelía. We'll join you there, one by one."

"You want me to marry Spíros?" Eléni cringed, crossed her arms across her chest, and hugged herself.

"Eléni – think about your future, and Evangelía's. I fear for us here. I make uniforms for military officers who talk about nothing but conquering Turkey and taking Constantinople. War will consume Greece and its people." He got up and paced toward the tree and back, stopping in front of Eléni. "The time of kings and queens is passing. In a few years, your princess may not be here to order dresses. But in America — everything is possible."

"Is it fair to Spíros?" she asked. "And…and how can I submit to him?"

Konstantínos' voice was gentle. "Marriages for convenience aren't new to us. Think about saving Evangelía and your mother. This may be your chance. Think about it. If you want, we'll talk again."

Eléni got up and walked across the garden and into the house with her head down. She stepped into her quiet room. *America?* she thought. She sat at the foot of her bed. *If I stay here, we may be caught up in a horrible war. America is a strange place. I know no one there."* She paced the room for a few minutes and sat down again. *Either way, I don't know what the future will be. In America, there are no wars. Evangelía would be safe. Spíros? Well, I can manage him.* She lay back on the bed and closed her eyes. *Andrei, what should I do?*

Eléni came out of her trance when she heard her sisters and the children entering the garden. *"Mána, mána,"* called Evangelía. "Yes, darling. I'm here," she answered. Then, in a whisper, she said, "We're going to America, my darling."

CHAPTER NINE
1912
KASTORIA
VILÂYET OF MONASTIR, IN THE OTTOMAN EMPIRE

Dimitráki held a pistol close to his chest, crouched low in the fading light, and inched sideways with his back pressed against a mud-brick wall. Muck from the road that ran between the walled row of home gardens and the lakeshore covered his worn shoes. Three boys, members of his band of young *andártes*, crept alongside him.

Dimitráki's heart pounded in his chest. He thought he could hear it.

Winter snow covered Mount Vítsi. It chilled the March air that flowed down its slopes into the valley and over the lake. Dimitráki trembled with cold, and fear. But there was no turning back. The eleven-year-old boy was determined to kill the Kaimakan, the Turk who he had seen humiliate his father.

Dimitráki raised his head slowly and spied over the tile-topped wall of the Kaimakan's garden. In the twilight, he saw the small bedroom balcony that overlooked the lake. Ducking down he motioned to his accomplices to hug the wall. In a few moments, a squeaking hinge alerted him. Peering over the wall again, he watched the Turkish governor step onto the balcony for an evening gaze at the lake. *There he is*, he thought. His fingers adjusted the flint and flash pan of his prized muzzle-loading pistol a final time. He cocked the trigger, set the pistol on top of the wall, aimed and fired.

The flash singed Dimitráki's eyebrows and lashes. Flame shot out from the muzzle of the overcharged weapon and chased the lethal ball like a lightening bolt. Its thunder echoed across the lake.

When he turned to run, Dimitráki's comrades were nowhere in sight. They had already escaped into the city. Dimitráki darted along the lakefront toward the narrow neck of land that led to the road to Mávrovo. But his pistol's roar had alerted the guards at the entry to Kastoria, and he ran right into the arms of the Turkish soldiers who were rushing toward the Kaimakan's house. They threw him to the ground and pinned his arms. Dimitráki's head rang from the soldiers' slaps and punches. When the Kaimakan appeared, he hovered over the captive with his fists clenched and shouted with rage, "You unbeliever. Christian assassin. Enemy of the Prophet. You'll die for this." Dimitráki's ball had missed, splintering the doorframe a few inches from the Kaimakan's head. In his fury, the Kaimakan kicked the boy in the stomach and marched off yelling, "Throw him in prison."

In the early morning hours, the boy lay curled up on the floor of a cell, hugging his knees, shivering, and sick with fear. A guard sitting on a stool watched him and sneered, "Unbelieving pup, this is what we are going to do to you tomorrow." He put his hand above and behind his head as if holding a rope, twisted his face and stuck out his tongue. "That's how you'll look in a little while, when you hang."

Dimitráki choked back tears.

Late the night before in Mávrovo, Dimitráki's father heard what had happened to his son from his frightened cohorts and their parents. Athanásios mounted his horse and arrived at the

Kaimakan's house before dawn, escorted by Turkish sentries who had recognized him at the city's gate as one of the respected elders of his village. The Kaimakan received his old acquaintance sternly, offering him neither a seat, nor any other hospitality.

"You know why I'm here, *Aféndis*. My son is in your jail. What will you do to him?"

"What happens to all assassins? He'll hang."

Athanásios's body slumped. "He is just a boy. He didn't know what he was doing."

"He knew what he wanted to do. He didn't think about the consequences if he was caught. I've no alternative — he'll hang."

"*Aféndis*, I'll punish the boy. I promise that he'll never enter Kastoria again."

The Kaimakan was silent.

Athanásios raised himself to full height. "Perhaps you can punish the boy some other way, and then allow me to take him home. That would show the young men of Kastoria what happens to boys with foolish ideas. And he'll be an example to others in Mávrovo when they see what happened to him."

"What of the damage, of the injury to my pride and person, of the fear in my home — who will remedy these affronts?"

"Of course you must be compensated, *Aféndis*." Athanásios reached into his pocket and took out a leather purse. "What will you do to the boy?"

The Kaimakan studied the purse in Athanásios's hand, and said, "Perhaps a good beating to the soles of his feet will teach the lesson. What do you think, Kyrie?"

"Yes. Yes, of course. But not so much that he won't be able to walk again." Athanásios held out the purse.

The Kaimakan hesitated, but then extended his open hand. "Of course."

Athanásios dropped the purse into the Kaimakan's palm. "Please, take this to compensate you for your injuries."

The Kaimakan weighed the heavy purse of gold coins in his hand.

"Praise Allah the Merciful, Kyrie. He has softened my heart. Your son will have his punishment this morning. You can take him home on your horse, which, I remind you, I allow you to ride as an exception to the rule for everyone else. But be warned. If your son ever steps into Kastoria again, or causes any trouble, he'll lose his head." Athanásios bowed low, voicing his gratitude to the Kaimakan for his great generosity and suffering in silence the knowledge that he would never be able to fill his purse with gold again.

Later that morning, Athanásios watched the soles of his son's feet beaten until they bled. They swelled to the size of melons. The boy lost consciousness after the first few blows, but not until he screamed obscenities at his tormentors. Through it, Athanásios managed to maintain his dignity.

SOZÓPOLIS, BULGARIA

Vasilikí sat on a comfortable chair by a window in the place that had once held an Ottoman divan. An icon of a seventy-year-old widow of the Balkans, she wore a black dress that fell to her ankles, and a black shawl that covered her head and shoulders against the chill of the March morning. While she embroidered, she thought about her daughters and grandchildren.

It was the day after Evangelismós, her granddaughter Evangelía's name day, and this year, the day after Páscha. In a rare coincidence, religious commemorations of the Annunciation and the Resurrection fell on the same day, the twenty-fifth of March.

Vasilikí's fingers stopped their work when she heard footsteps on the stairs that led to her front door. She put aside needle, thread, and the bed sheet whose borders she was embroidering and looked up to see her daughter. Sultána put an envelope down on the doily that had covered the round table in the center of the room for more than forty years and kissed her mother. "*Mána,* there's a letter from Eléni."

"Is it from Konstantínos?" she asked. Vasilikí's animated bright-blue eyes belied her age.

"Yes, he wrote for Eléni. She sends you love and kisses, and great news." Sultána brought a chair from the center of the room and sat next to her mother.

"What? Read it to me."

As he had no son, Aleksiev Vserkozov had insisted that Vasilikí learn to read and write. He paid the priest that preceded Pater Elefthérios to teach her. But Vasilikí's daughters were not given the opportunity — Hristodoúlos thought it unnecessary. Soon after he died, Sultána came to her mother and asked, "Teach me to read, *mána.*" She was the only one of Vasilikí's four daughters who learned to read and write.

"*Mána,* Eléni is married again."

"To that man from Anchíalos? The one that Konstantínos wrote to us about — the farmer?"

"Yes, they were married in January. He's leaving for America." Sultána fell to her knees before her mother. Her eyes glistened and she went on excitedly. "*Mána,* Eléni is going to follow Spíros to America with Evangelía. Konstantínos writes that when Spíros and Eléni are settled, he, Sofía and the children will follow, and then — it will be our turn."

Vasilikí's face darkened. "I can't. I can't leave Hrístos. Who'll go to the cemetery?"

"We have to leave. Ioánnis says that war is coming, and he will be forced to fight for Bulgaria. What would happen to the children and me? You can't stay here alone."

"Go. Leave soon. Don't worry about me. Décimos and Olga will watch over me. So will Chrysóula. She's like one of you to me. I won't be alone."

Sultána put her arms around her mother and kissed her. "How can we leave you behind?"

"I know. I know, my darling. But you must make your own lives."

Sultána kissed her mother again and held her hand.

Vasilikí looked out the window at a darkening sky. The wind gusted and a light rain began to fall. The shore of the Black Sea faded from view.

PIRAEUS, GREECE

In the January following her talk with Konstantínos, Eléni carried out her decision to cross the ocean to America and safety. She married Spíros in Kalithéa on a cold winter afternoon. Konstantínos rewarded the priest who joined the couple generously, for it was the second marriage for Eléni — one barely tolerated by the Church – and the black-robed cleric conducted the ceremony with studied condescension.

The morning of the wedding, Eléni had dressed Evangelía in white and placed a crown-like wreath on her that was similar to the *stéfana* that would grace the couple's heads during the wedding ceremony. "There, my darling. Aren't you beautiful? You'll look just like *mána* today."

"Is Spíros going to live with us?" Evangelía asked.

"Yes, my treasure. And now you will have your own bed and your own room."

"But I want to sleep with you."

"You can't anymore. You are a big girl. And I will be close to you, right in the next room."

Evangelía put her arms around her mother's neck and cried, "No. No, *mána*. I am afraid. I want to sleep with you."

"Shh, darling. Everything will be fine. You'll see."

Eléni tried her best to be celebratory. She smiled, held Spíros's arm and pretended affection for him. Spíros, elated to have finally won Eléni, was oblivious to the feelings of his bride. He drank deeply of the *rakí* and *retsína* that Eléni's brothers-in-law provided for the wedding feast, so that he was drunk and incoherent when he fell asleep on top of Eléni after consummating the marriage. She pushed him off her body. Turning, she curled up with her knees to her chest and buried her face in her pillow. Eléni remembered her loving wedding night with Andrei. Tears streamed down her cheeks. "Forgive me, Andrei," she whispered. "I did this for Evangelía. Forgive me." In the next room, Evangelía cried herself to sleep.

In the days that followed, Spíros held Evangelía and kissed her, and told her how pretty she was and what a lovely bride she would be. None of what he did or said changed her opinion of him. She disliked Spíros even more now that he had become her stepfather. She was happy on the April day that Spíros boarded the *Macedonia,* the ship that would take him far away. That night she was in her mother's arms again.

A letter arrived from Spíros in June. An educated hand had written it and addressed the envelope to Konstantínos. Spíros reported that he had joined his friend in a region called Minnesota. He asked Konstantínos to advance passage money for Eléni and Evangelía and promised that he would repay Konstantínos as soon as she arrived and went to work with him.

"Give Eléni this address," the letter directed: "211 East 7th Street, St. Paul, Minnesota. The officials at Ellis Island will help her send a message to me when she arrives in America."

Eléni and Evangelía shuffled in a line that moved toward the double-doors of the embarkation building. With each of their steps, émigrés raised wisps of dry dust from the sun-baked street. In the heat of the July morning, Eléni's clothing stuck to her back. She was excited and fearful. Evangelía held her mother's skirt with both her hands.

Konstantínos and Sofía, Smarágda and Dimitrios, the children, and Kyria Anthoula were there. They stood behind a barrier with their eyes fixed on Eléni. She looked back as she stepped into the shade of the building to see Kyria Anthoula dabbing at her eyes with her lacy white handkerchief. Evangelía saw her aunt, her Théa Sofía, move her baby Calypsó's little hand up and down; her cousins were waving goodbye.

In the processing room, Eléni and Evangelía were subjected to a rudimentary physical examination. Embarrassed by how the doctor probed the women in the line in front of her, Eléni balked when her turn came. A nurse chided her. "Now, now, Kyria. Cooperate with the doctor. We have no time for modesty. If you aren't healthy when you get to America they'll send you back."

Eléni and Evangelía passed the medical examination and took their places in another long queue, one of women and children. They were herded onto the ship and crewmen led them down multiple gangways until somewhere below the waterline they entered a cavernous space filled with stretched canvas bunks stacked three and four high. On each was a single blanket.

Eléni selected two bunks, cramming what few possessions she had on to one of them and cuddling Evangelía in her arms on the other. The ship left its mooring and entered the Bay of Salamis. Within minutes, its rocking motion and stale air made passengers queasy. Conditions grew worse when the ship passed the Straits of Gibraltar and entered the Atlantic Ocean. The ship's keel, twisting in mounting swells, groaned. That frightening sound, and the noise of pounding engines and howling propeller screws made sleep almost impossible. Dank, cold moisture condensed on the bare metal of the ship's hull.

There was one communal toilet, but no bathing facility. The passengers made the most of cold water and a sink. The smell of unwashed bodies, slop buckets, and vomit was unbearable. On days that weather permitted, Eléni and Evangelía huddled close together on the third-class deck and breathed fresh, cold sea air.

Being seasick, they ate sparingly of meals that consisted mainly of stews of the least expensive ingredients, self-served from huge tureens.

Some passengers played cards or sang songs to pass the time. Others stared blankly into space. Eléni held Evangelía close to her in their bunk, often singing to her. She encouraged her daughter despite her own depression and anxiety. "It will be wonderful when we get there, *hrisó mou*. Soon this will be over and we'll be in America." She washed Evangelía's face and hands every day, and brushed her hair. "We'll buy pretty ribbons for your hair when we are in America, my love," she promised her child.

After seventeen horrendous days and nights, they disembarked at Ellis Island. Officials directed them through one processing station after another. Eléni's confidence grew once they were on solid ground and in a clean dormitory with a place to wash. They both developed appetites. "Eat, my darling," she told her daughter. It's good food. Not tasty, the way we cook, but it will make you strong." Eléni was grateful that in a matter of two days Evangelía had regained her color and energy.

Eléni did not have enough money to buy rail tickets to St. Paul. Social workers helped her send a telegram to Spíros. When she received the funds that he wired to her, she purchased tickets and boarded a train with Evangelía. She had no knowledge of the language, or of how to purchase food, or where she and Evangelía were going. Eléni held her daughter, encouraged her and prayed to the Panaghía.

The train rumbled through vast forested mountains and endless farmland. The country seemed as large as the ocean they had crossed. In Chicago, railroad yard gangs disconnected the car they were in from its place in the train and connected it to another for the trip further west. The jolts, and the noise of the railroad yard upset them.

Hours after the train left Chicago, a conductor motioned to Eléni to get off the train. They had arrived in St. Paul, and Spíros was waiting for them on the station platform. They greeted each other tentatively. "We're here," Eléni said. Evangelía cringed at the sight of her stepfather.

"Yes. Good. It's good to see you." Spíros's every word and movement was hesitant. He picked up their bags. "Come. We'll go to our house."

The house was little more than a log cabin with a fireplace and a wood stove. Spíros celebrated his wife's arrival with a bottle of wine. Later, not wanting to rouse Evangelía out of a deep sleep, she gave in to Spíros's sexual demands.

On her third morning in St. Paul, Eléni knelt and hugged her daughter at the door of their cabin. Sobbing, Evangelía listened to her mother. "I will be home tonight, Evangelía. You are a big girl now. Be brave. You can take care of yourself. Play outside, but stay close to the house. Eat when you are hungry. Be careful."

With a kiss, Eléni turned from her daughter. In turmoil, she followed Spíros and several other men and women for over a mile to a meatpacking plant in South St. Paul, feeling constant anxiety for Evangelía. Spíros exchanged a few cursory words with a gruff, bearded fellow who peered at Eléni through squinted eyes that were barley visible under his shaggy eyebrows. He outfitted her with gloves, apron, and boots, and motioned to her to follow Spíros and the rest of the shift's workers. They led her to the plant's killing floor, where she learned new skills — how to thrust a knife into the throat of a squealing pig that had been stunned by a sledgehammer blow to its head — how to disembowel it and sort its offal while maintaining her balance on a slippery, blood-covered floor.

She retched for the first few hot, humid, late summer days, more sickened than she had been in the stench of a third-class hold in heavy seas. When a whistle blew ending a shift, Eléni would rise from a crouch and groan, her hands, arms, apron, and boots covered with the gore that was everywhere on the floor of the slaughterhouse. She adapted to the horror and found that she could tolerate it. Eventually, the heat of late August and September was defeated by chill autumn winds, and finally she numbed to the routine. The reek of blood and intestines rose on the steamy condensation of moisture in the cold, concrete room. *I'm in hell*, she thought. *Hell isn't hot. It's cold, and it stinks.*

Eléni spent Sundays close to her daughter — washing, cooking, and telling her stories about Sozópolis and her family. When she was not too exhausted, she took Evangelía to church, with Spíros trailing along. Otherwise, he spent his free time with his friends, drinking and smoking, and arriving home in time for dinner and more wine.

Evangelía became listless. Alone in the rudimentary one-room cabin, she did little all day but huddle by the fire to keep warm. "*Mána*, why can't we go back to Théa Sofía's house?" she asked. "It is warm there, and I could play with my cousins."

Evangelía ran to her mother's arms when she came through the door after a long day at work. Eléni kept her at arm's length until she removed her soiled work clothes, washed, and changed. Finally hugged and kissed, fed and nurtured, Evangelía slept with her mother.

Exiled, Spíros slept alone.

One day they heard alarming news from their Greek fellow-workers. Greece, Bulgaria, and Serbia had attacked Turkey. The following Sunday they went to the Greek Orthodox Church of the Theotókos in Minneapolis to pray for their families in Bulgaria and Greece, and to learn as much as they could about the conflict. They waited for letters from Sozópolis and Kalithéa.

On a mid-December night, Eléni left the slaughterhouse to find Spíros waiting for her in the street. She stopped for a moment to look up into the dark sky and took a deep breath to cleanse the smells of her long, backbreaking day from her lungs. Falling little white flakes melted on her face, refreshing her. The cold made her shiver.

"Come. Come, Eléni, let's go home," Spíros urged. "It's freezing. Evangelía is waiting."

Eléni looked at her husband with disgust. He was even less the *palikári* than he had been in Greece. He showed little of that bravado and manly strut, the air that young Greek men flaunted to affirm their masculinity. She squared her shoulders and set out for her home. Walking through the light snowfall, Spíros followed a few steps behind his wife. His head was down. The more dejected and submissive Spíros became, the more Eléni despised him.

Spíros heard his wife scream. "Evangelía. Evangelía." Eléni ran forward toward a crowd in front of their home. The door was open and men were rushing in and out with buckets in their hands. Smoke filled the air.

"Evangelía." Eléni shoved her way through the bystanders who were watching the fire brigade. By the time Spíros got to her, Eléni was on her knees holding Evangelía tightly. They were both crying. When he bent to comfort them, Eléni turned aside and lifted Evangelía in her arms.

"I'm sorry, *mána*," the child sobbed. "I'm sorry. The fire came out of the fireplace when I put wood in it."

"Shh, Shh, Evangelía. It's all right. It wasn't your fault."

That night the bitter smell of charred wood and smoke filled the cabin. Spíros snored loudly. Eléni could not sleep. She held Evangelía close and tried to shut out her husband's irritating noises. Her mind raced, thinking about what to do.

She was angry with herself. She remembered how she had survived Pyrgos, and the voyage to Volos, and escaped Efxinoúpolis. She had succeeded in Athens and made dresses for royalty. Now, here, in what was the land of opportunity, she wallowed in animal filth, leaving Evangelía alone all day.

I never should have married Spíros, she thought. *What for? To have Evangelía end up in this miserable place? To work like a mule for pennies?* A few moments passed. "It's over," she said quietly. Her resolve brought her relief. She turned to Evangelía, kissed her, and fell soundly to sleep.

In the morning, Eléni told her husband, "I am not going to work today. I'll stay home, clean this place up and take care of

Evangelía. I decided that we are going to leave here. We are going to Chicago. They say it's a big city and has many Greeks. Maybe I'll find work there with the needle again."

"You've decided?" asked Spíros. He pulled himself up to full height. "You're my wife." He spoke loudly. "I'll decide."

She shook her head. "No. I'm leaving. That's what I am going to do – with you or without you. You can come along or not. I don't care."

"You can't just leave me, Eléni."

"Don't try to stop me." Her voice became menacing. "Don't try."

Spíros put on his coat, and left for work without looking at her or saying another word.

MÁVROVO, KASTORIA
VILÂYET OF MONASTIR, IN THE OTTOMAN EMPIRE

Athanásios was reading when he heard Dimitráki tap on the window.

"*Babás*, someone is knocking on the gate and calling for you."

"Go, open the gate. See who it is."

Dimitráki rushed to the gate, for he was again able to walk and run. When his father brought him home incoherent with pain the night that he had been bastinadoed, his mother immediately set about retrieving moldy bread from the box she kept to produce and store it. Its curative power over infection and possible gangrene was knowledge passed down from generation to generation. With the moldy bread and water, she made a paste that she applied to Dimitráki's feet. She kept them lightly swathed in bandages, and each day cleansed them and re-applied fresh poultice. Neighbors provided her with more of the preparation when she had none left. Gradually, Dimitráki's feet had healed.

Mávrovo's schoolmaster, Kyrie Mantópoulos, and several village elders waited outside of the gate. "We must see your father," Mantópoulos said as they walked past the boy and toward the house. Athanásios watched them, calling to Kallíope, "We have guests, Kallíope. Open the front door and bring them to me."

"What is it? What's going on?" Athanásios asked as they filed in. He motioned to them to sit down.

Mantópoulos untied a canvass wrapped package, took out a flag with a white cross against a blue field, and proudly held it up, saying, "Look. The flag of Greece. I am going to raise it today, Kyrie Athanásios, either at the school or at the top of the *tzamí*." The schoolmaster's eyes were shining. "The army of Greece is already near. Our saviors have come."

The rest of the group looked at Athanásios for his reaction.

"What do you think?" asked one of the elders.

"Caution," Athanásios said. "That's what I think. The Turks are still here. There are Turkish battalions in and around Kastoria. Be careful. Wait."

One of the men spoke up. "My cousin came across the lake in a boat last night from Aposképos. He says that before he left he saw a group of Greek cavalry approaching his village from the north."

Athanásios shook his head. "There are Turkish soldiers between them and us. We have waited over five hundred years to be free. We can wait one or two more days."

Mantópoulos's face showed his disappointment. He rolled up the flag, put it under his arm, and silently left.

Mid-morning on the next day, screaming and the sound of galloping horses startled Athanásios who sat reading in his parlor. He ran out of the house, and looked into the street through an opening in the gate. Seeing Turkish cavalry, he called to his wife. "Kallíope, find the children. Take them to the orchard and hide."

He followed the cavalry toward the center of his village, where the blue-and-white flag of Greece, rippled at the top of the *tzamí's* minaret. *That fool*, he thought. *That romantic, patriotic, teacher-fool.*

Kóstas and Dimitráki rushed to their father's side. "Where is your mother?" he asked them.

"She took the girls and our brothers to the orchard. We came to help you," Kóstas responded.

"Run to every house and tell the people I said for them to go to the fields and hide. Be careful. Don't be seen."

Athanásios edged along the walls that bordered the street toward the *tzamí*. He saw that the Turkish cavalry had already torn the flag down, captured Mantópoulos, and arrested a group of men. The prisoners were sitting on the ground, hunched down in terror of the mounted soldiers that surrounded them. Athanásios turned into a garden to hide himself, and spied through the branches of a tree that stood next to the garden wall. He watched as a soldier forced one of the prisoners to his knees. An officer raised a saber and in an instant struck off the man's head. The other prisoners were dazed, stunned by the sight of a headless body pouring its blood into the dirt. They were immobilized by fear.

Athanásios heard a familiar voice whisper, "Kyrie Athanásios, stay where you are. Don't move." The Kaimakan stepped behind Athanásios. "Don't talk. My men caught your sons. I ordered them to take the boys behind the church, away from the prisoners. Go. Take them and leave the village."

"What is going to happen to my people?"

"The cavalry commander will execute every man over fifteen that he can find, and then he'll burn the village." The Kaimakan stepped in front of Athanásios and stared into his eyes. "Kastoria will be burned tomorrow or the next day."

Athanásios said nothing. He walked away quickly, skirting the village to reach the church, where he found his sons guarded by two of the Kaimakan's soldiers. They released the boys. Crouching, they followed their father into the fields and buried themselves in the high grass. Terrified, they listened to the screams of men being mutilated and killed.

The Turks butchered Mantópoulos and dragged his body through the streets of Mávrovo as an example. They had set a few homes on fire when, without warning, they mounted their horses and took flight. Athanásios saw them galloping toward Kastoria. "They may have received a message that the Greek army is near," he told his sons.

Within hours, a fishing boat came to Mávrovo with information that the Turks were leaving. Although Athanásios and his family's lives were spared, and their home undamaged, the joy that should have accompanied the news that the Turkish yoke was about to be lifted from them was lost in the trauma of the executions of friends and neighbors, and the destruction of many homes. That night, the people were terrified at a report that hundreds of Turkish soldiers were on the move toward the south of the lake. At dawn, they realized that the troops had been marching not toward Mávrovo, but eastward, in retreat.

Athanásios and his family, others from Mávrovo, and villagers from around the lake flooded Kastoria to welcome the army of Greece when its soldiers entered the city. In the rush to save himself and his troops, the Turkish army commander abandoned the Kaimakan and his family. They, fearing for their lives, hid in their shuttered house by the lake until Greek soldiers dragged the once powerful governor to the cathedral in manacles. He and his family sat on its steps before angry, vengeful men and women.

Dimitráki, his jaw set, left his father's side, pushed himself to the front of the crowd and slipped past a soldier.

"See? My feet have healed," he screamed, kicking the Kaimakan in the stomach. "Die, you dog."

Athanásios seized his son by the arm and pulled him away.

"Kyrie Athanásios, my old friend," the Kaimakan moaned. "Help me. Tell them I was just."

Athanásios looked at the humbled Kaimakan. "I acknowledge the debt I owe you for my life, and the lives of my sons. I am grateful to you, and I apologize for my son. But we were never friends. May Allah bring you mercy."

Athanásios turned away, and holding his son by the neck, pushed him ahead toward the road that led to Mávrovo. "Dimitráki," he said quietly. "Dimitráki — after the feast day of Ághios Nikoláos I am going to take you to the monastery, to Mavriótissa. You'll stay with the monks for as long as it takes you to learn to control your anger and to trust in God."

CHAPTER TEN
1913
CHICAGO, ILLINOIS

On his way out on the morning after Eléni told him of her decision to move to Chicago, Spíros announced, "Tonight we'll make plans to move to Chicago." Eléni smiled at him and shook her head. "Good. That's settled. But remember — there will be nothing between us in Chicago. Nothing. You will live with us. That's all. Close the door behind you."

Before they left St. Paul, the priest's wife took Eléni aside after a Sunday service and instructed her, "When you get to Chicago, go to Hull House. Here is the address." She handed Eléni a piece of paper. "It's an old mansion," the *presvytéra* explained. "We know that Greeks go there to find jobs and places to live."

The *presvytéra* was right. Hull House's American social workers helped Eléni and her family find furnished rooms on the day they arrived. The next day, Hull House sent Spíros to a job in a Southside slaughterhouse. Encouraged, Eléni went to Hull House to meet with a social worker in hopes of finding work. A dark-haired, olive-skinned young interpreter named Katina translated for her.

"You were a seamstress in Greece?" Katina asked.

"Yes," Eléni answered, adding timidly, "I sewed some dresses for Princess Sophie and her daughters."

Katina was wide-eyed at the response. Excited, she told the social worker about Eléni and went to fetch her brother from a nearby room.

"Kyria Stamatiou, this is my brother, Petros Angelopoulos. I told him that you sewed dresses for the Princess of Greece."

"*Háiretai*, Kyria. Did you go to the palace?" Petros asked. "Is it wonderful?"

"Yes, I went to the palace. It is beautiful, and the princess is kind. But that was long ago. I want to sew again. Here."

"Ah, you want work?"

"Yes. As a seamstress."

He thought for a moment. "Can you meet me here tomorrow? I'll take you to a man who might help you."

The next morning Leonardo was tending the counter at Arcudi's shop when his friend Petros walked in with Eléni.

"*Buon giorno*, Leonardo."

From behind the counter, Leonardo smiled, "*Kali méra*, Petros."

"Leonardo, this Kyria Eléni Stamatiou. She come Chicago *con sposo, apo* Saint Paul," Petros said, mixing Italian, Greek, and English. "I meet Hull House. Kyria Stamatiou seamstress Need work. You use help? Business good."

"*Háiretai*, Kyria," Leonardo said to Eléni. Their eyes made fleeting contact.

Eléni smiled. *I wonder how old he is*, she thought.

His face reddened. Eléni was two inches taller than he. He stammered. "I don't know, Petros."

"Don't know what?" interjected Signore Arcudi. He appeared from behind a rack of clothing.

Leonardo introduced Eléni and explained her circumstances.

"Leonardo, what do you think?" Arcudi asked. "Business is good. Do you need help?"

Eléni listened to them speak in Italian, not understanding what they were saying.

"Leonardo," Arcudi repeated. "What do you think?"

Eléni looked directly at Leonardo again with her soft, brown eyes, and realized that she distracted him. He looked down. She smiled, thinking, *Nice man. Shy.*

Finally, Leonardo responded. "Maybe we try for a week or two."

"*Buono*," confirmed Signore Arcudi.

"We try, Kyria Stamatiou." Leonardo's Greek was good enough for her to understand.

Eléni and Leonardo worked together for one week, and then two. Weeks and months passed. They beat carpets in the lot behind the store, sorted laundry and dry cleaning, served customers at the counter and sewed alterations and repairs. Leonardo admired her skill as a seamstress. They attracted more business in alterations and were sewing dresses and suits to order. Signore Arcudi was ecstatic.

With guidance from Hull House, Eléni found the Greek Orthodox Church and a school that taught Evangelía both English and Greek. The children's lessons stressed the glory of Greece, and the duty of every Greek boy to rescue Macedonia from the Turks and Bulgarians.

Except for the time she attended school just a few blocks away from Arcudi's shop, Evangelía was constantly with Leonardo and Eléni. They taught her the skills of the needle and the magic of turning bolts of material and yards of thread into stylish garments.

Eléni grew comfortable with her life in Chicago. Its large population of Greeks gave her a sense of security, and she enjoyed working at Signore Arcudi's shop. The limits she imposed on her relationship with Spíros had made her life with him tolerable. But one night, soon after their arrival, Spíros arrived home late, drunk, and hotheaded.

"Eléni," he yelled while climbing the stairs. "Eléni," he called again, stumbling into the apartment and waking her. "Where are you?" He staggered into her bedroom and pulled off her bedcovers.

Evangelía, nestled in her mother's arms screamed, "*Mána!*"

She jumped out of her mother's bed as Spíros tumbled in, groping for his wife and shouting, "I am your husband."

Eléni rolled out of the bed, turned, and threw the sheets and blankets over Spíros' head and arms. "Stop, you worthless *bekrís* or I'll kill you."

Spíros whimpered from under the covers, "Eléni. You're my wife. You ..."

"I nothing. You can work, drink with your friends until you can't walk, and visit *pórni* for all I care. But never touch me."

Spíros did not hear her last words. He was snoring.

"Help me, Evangelía," Eléni said to her frightened daughter. "Come, help me. It's all right." They pulled Spíros off the bed and dragged him by his feet into the next room, where they threw a blanket over him and left him on the floor. Once they were back in bed, Eléni held Evangelía close to her. "Sleep now *hrisó mou*. Everything is fine. He won't bother us anymore."

Eléni was right. Spíros left for work the next morning before she could look him in the face. He occasionally accompanied Evangelía and Eléni to *Ághia Triáda*, the Greek Orthodox Church at Halsted and Harrison Streets, but rarely went to her place of work, where he knew he was unwelcome. The easy relationship Eléni had developed with the little Italian shamed him. He turned to *rakí* and the companionship he found in the *tavérnas* of Greek Town for solace, and one night boasted that he was returning to Greece to fight in the First Balkan War. His courage left him with the sobriety that accompanied the morning sun.

Eléni felt unburdened. It was as if Spíros no longer existed. Evangelía ignored the man completely.

The Greek community welcomed the end of the Balkan Wars — except for the fact that Turkey held Constantinople. Salonika, the second city and a prized commercial center of the Ottoman Empire was in Greek hands, and was again called Thessaloniki. Greece, Bulgaria, and Serbia partitioned Macedonia among themselves.

Eléni worried constantly about her family in Greece and Bulgaria. In late August, a letter arrived. There was a seal on the back of the envelope: K.TSV.KAPIDAGHLIS. Anxious and excited, Eléni took the letter to Hull House and found a Greek woman to read it to her.

My Dearest Eléni, We kiss you.
>   Kisses from Sofía, Smarágda and Dimitrios, and Sultána.
>   Sultána is in Piraeus with us. She escaped from Bulgaria with her children just after the war ended. They are well.
>   We heard from Décimos and Chrysóula that they and your mother are fine. They look after her. Chrysóula is like her daughter.

The social worker hesitated. Eléni took the small bag that hung from her neck between her thumb and forefinger and pressed the little coin Chrysóula had given to her.

"What else does he say?"

The social worker began to read again, but in a low voice.

I have bad news.

Eléni crossed herself and closed her eyes for a moment.

Sultána is alone. Her beloved husband Ioánnis was killed in the war somewhere in Serbia, on a mountain named Kitka. Your cousin Orthodoxos Zissis died on the same day. They were conscripted because Greeks in Romylia are Bulgarians now.

Smarágda and Dimitrios decided to stay in Greece. Dimitrios is political, and joined secret societies. He will not leave.

Sultána and her children are with us in Kalithéa. She is not ready to make any decisions.

I will join Stávros and Zenóvios in Paris soon. With the war over, I can travel without worrying about my family. I will go for several months to put more money aside for us to come to America.

Our kisses to you and Evangelía,

Konstantínos

Eléni left Hull House and walked directly to Holy Trinity, where she lit candles for Ioánnis and Orthodoxos. In the serenity of the church, and the glow of its oil-lit lamps, she thought only of bringing her family to America.

On her first Christmas Eve in Chicago, Arcudi handed Eléni an envelope. "This is present — *Il Natale* — Christmas — for you, Evangelía. For good work."

She opened the envelope and in it found a ten-dollar bill. "Ah, Signore, *mille grazie*." She wanted to tell him more, but she did not know the words in Italian or English.

CHAPTER ELEVEN
1914
CHICAGO, ILLINOIS

Eléni and Leonardo were enjoying lunch at a table under the trees in the lot behind Arcudi's shop when Leonardo asked, "Do you remember what you said about New York?" His growing ability to speak Greek, and hers to speak Italian made communication between them comfortable.

"Yes. Try *dolmádes*, Leonardo." She put three of them on Leonardo's plate. "Just rice, no meat."

Leonardo tried one of the little rice filled grapevine leaves. "Good. They have mint and parsley. No?"

"Yes. Mint, parsley, pignoli, currants, olive oil. What about New York?"

"I met a man yesterday at the Italian Club — a dressmaker. He says lots of work and good money in New York."

"How much money I need to move New York?" she asked. "You think I find work fast?"

In the days that followed, they often talked about the possibilities in New York, as if their futures intertwined.

173

In June, world events made it impossible for Eléni's family in Greece and Bulgaria to come to America. Within a month from the day that newspaper headlines screamed about the assassination of Austria's Archduke Ferdinand in Sarajevo, war engulfed the Balkans and the rest of Europe. And once again, Russian warships steamed past Sozópolis on a course set for the Straits of the Bosphorus.

Eléni focused on how she could get to New York. Spíros was a problem — a problem that she would solve when her plan was in place. Her relationship with Leonardo was another question. She liked him the day she met him and immediately felt at ease around him. Little by little, through the year that they had worked together, Leonardo and Eléni had developed a familiarity. Their rapport grew with small kindnesses. Leonardo might present Eléni with a cup of coffee or a treat at lunch, and Eléni would reciprocate with a piece of *baklavá*, or a bowl of rice pudding from her kitchen. He had been caring for Evangelía, and had shown great patience with her as he helped to teach her to sew.

Eléni talked about Sozópolis and her life there, about Andrei, Pyrgos, and her struggle in Greece. Leonardo shared his memories of Monteleone, of the earthquake, and of his family, whom he desperately wanted to bring to America.

Leonardo found that he felt breathless when he leaned over Eléni's shoulder to help her with a problem at the sewing machine and her hair brushed his face. Eléni's throat tensed and she would stop breathing for a moment if her hand touched Leonardo's as they draped material over a mannequin. Their emotions wound more tightly each day — springs without release.

On a crisp, clear fall morning that ended a hot, humid Chicago summer, Eléni found herself alone in the shop. Petros appeared at the door, and removing his hat announced, "Kyria Eléni, Leonardo won't be in today. He isn't feeling well. It's his stomach."

174

Eléni worried about Leonardo all morning. In the mid-afternoon, she told Signore Arcudi that she had to attend to personal business and left the shop.

Eléni knew that Evangelía was already at their flat. She hurried there and told Evangelía, "I'll be home later, after work. You can make *keftédes* for me. We will have greens and rice with them. Everything is in the icebox." Evangelía loved to cook and welcomed the opportunity to prepare dinner.

Eléni took a bowl of lentil soup from the icebox and made a small package of it with some cheese and bread. On her way out, she stopped at the wall mirror in the entry and brushed her hair. She knew where Leonardo lived. She and Evangelía had delivered a note from Signore Arcudi to his mailbox several weeks before. When she arrived, she climbed the stairs to the third floor of the four-story building, grateful she had not seen anyone she knew. She knocked on the door of Leonardo's room.

"*Si? Chi è la?*"

"Leonardo, *sono io*, Eléni."

"Eléni? Wait minute." Seconds passed. "Come in."

Eléni hesitated for a moment and then entered the room. Leonardo was in bed, wearing a robe and, despite the heat, was hidden under sheets.

"Leonardo, are you all right? I brought you something to eat." She left the door half open behind her.

"I'm better. But I am not dressed." He pulled the covers up, close to his neck. Looking to the door he said, "Maybe you should leave. Thank you for the food. Just leave it on the table."

Eléni approached Leonardo's bed. "I've been worried about you. Do you have a fever? Let me touch your forehead."

She stepped forward and put the back of her hand on Leonardo's brow. His breath caught in his throat. With no consciousness of what she was doing, she bent over and kissed Leonardo on his forehead. She moved her head away, but then returned to kiss his lips. Leonardo lips responded. He sighed and touched her face.

175

Eléni ignored the difference in their ages, her marriage, and the insanity of her feelings. She went to the door, and closed and locked it before testing its security. "Turn your head Leonardo." Moving to his bed, she undressed and slipped under the sheets. Her emotions overwhelmed her, and she opened herself to Leonardo with tears streaming down her cheeks.

The weeks that followed were difficult for them. They did their best to keep their affair a secret. At work, they touched or held each other's hands when they could, and using the ruse of a backlog of orders, came to the shop early, or stayed late, to make love hastily on the floor of their sanctuary. When she found an excuse to be out alone, she stole up the stairs to his apartment for an hour of passion.

Signore and Signora Arcudi noticed the change in Leonardo and Eléni's relationship, chose to ignore how far it had progressed and closed their eyes to obvious signs of intimacy through the winter months and into the New Year.

A Greek couple, Leonídas and Evanthía, who had emigrated from the Peloponnesos, lived next door to Spíros and Eléni. The young women sought emotional support from each other and became friends. Spíros's drinking and sulkiness prevented his developing a friendship with Leonídas.

After church one Sunday in March, Evanthía walked home with Eléni, keeping a few steps behind Leonídas and Spíros. Evangelía had gone to spend the afternoon at a friend's house.

"Eléni, I want to ask you something?"

"Yes, ask."

"You are happier. Why? What has changed?"

Eléni blushed. "I don't know what you're talking about, Evanthía. Work is going well. I am saving money, and we will move to New York next year. That makes me happy."

"No, Eléni. There is something else. Or someone else?"

"Enough, Evanthía."

"All right. I'm glad for you, whatever the reason. I'll miss you when leave."

Eléni looked down. *I don't know anyone in New York,* she thought. *If Leonardo were there... What will I do about Spíros?*

CHAPTER TWELVE
1915
CHICAGO, ILLINOIS

"We baste the hem so it will be easy to sew straight on the machine," Eléni explained. Evangelía sat opposite from her mother watching and listening. "Look. Baste with one long stitch, and then two or three short ones. See? When we finish basting, we'll put the dress on the mannequin to be sure that the hem is even. Keep the material smooth, and ..."

"Eléni," Leonardo called from the front counter. "A man wants to see you."

"Coming," she answered. "Here, *hrisó mou*. Try a few stitches. I'll be right back."

Evangelía took the dress, needle, and thread in her hands and focused on her task. Now eleven, she was slender, had long dark hair and intelligent brown eyes. She stitched the hem with confidence.

Eléni walked the few short steps from the workroom she shared with Leonardo. A sweating, disheveled man waited at the counter.

His trousers and shoes showed signs of the Southside stockyards. His smell confirmed where he worked.

"Kyria Eléni?" he asked in Greek.

"Yes. What do you want?"

"I bring bad news. Spíros ..."

"What?" she interrupted.

"Dead."

"Dead?"

Eléni's mind raced. *He's dead*? she thought. *Oh, God. I'm free.* She crossed herself, praying silently, *God, forgive me. I didn't wish him dead.*

Leonardo put his arm around Eléni's shoulder and spoke quietly to her. "Stay here, Eléni. I'll find out what happened." He followed the messenger out the door.

Moments later, Signore Arcudi stepped into his shop, mopping his brow with an expensive linen handkerchief. He took off his suit coat and cried, "*Madonna*, the heat will kill me. Eléni, where was Leonardo going?"

Eléni stared at him. She showed no effect.

"Eléni, what's wrong? It's me. Giovanni. Giovanni Arcudi. Eléni."

"Signore ... *scusa* ... *ma* ... *sposa* ... *morte*."

"Dead? Spíros is dead?"

"*Si*. Leonardo go."

Arcudi saw that it was useless to try to talk to Eléni. He locked the front door to the shop, put up the 'CLOSED' sign and lowered the blinds. Taking Eléni by her arm, he led her to Leonardo's sewing room. Evangelía, who had been diligently basting, looked up from her work.

"Evangelía, sit with your mama. Wait for Leonardo. *Brutta notizia, solo molto dolente* ... you papa dead."

"Spíros?"

"*Si*. Yes."

Eléni's arms embraced Evangelía. They held each other tightly. Neither of them cried.

"I close shop. Wait for Leonardo. Go home. What you want. Leonardo tell what happen. He help."

When Leonardo returned two hours later, his shirt was soaked in perspiration. "Spíros fell. Maybe the heat. A machine crushed him."

Three days later, Eléni stood at Spíros' graveside oblivious to the prayers being chanted by the priest. She prayed silently for Spíros. But most of her prayers were for herself. *Help me Panaghía. Forgive me God. I didn't want to hurt Spíros. I am sorry I …*

"*Mána*, come. Théa Evanthía says we can go now." Evangelía tugged at her mother's dress.

Evanthía took charge at the *makaría*, with Leonardo's help, and watched how attentive he was to Eléni's needs. The two responded to each other like husband and wife.

In August, Eléni visited Hull House and dictated a letter to her sister and Konstantínos.

10 August 1915

My dear Sofía and Konstantínos, I embrace you and kiss you.

I have terrible news. Spíros is dead. He collapsed at work, and a machine crushed him.

My employer, Signore Arcudi, and his wife, are helping me. A friend, Evanthía, and a young Italian man who works with me, Leonardo Perna, were with me through the funeral. Leonardo and I are good friends. He is an excellent tailor and helps me to teach Evangelía our work.

I will stay in Chicago until I have saved enough to move to New York City. Leonardo learned that there is a lot of work there, and good money. He will probably go there with Evangelía and me.

Evangelía is growing up. She attends a school where she learns Greek and American. She spends most of the day close to me.

Are your sons safe in France? What is happening in Sozópolis? Do you have news about my mother?

I pray that we will all be together again.

Embrace and kiss Smarágda, Dimitrios, Sultána, and their children for me.

With many kisses,

Eléni

MAVRIÓTISSA, KASTORIA
THE KINGDOM OF GREECE

The priest chanted, "*Eiríni pási*," and Dimitráki returned the priest's prayer for peace to all with the response, "*Kai to pnévma sou*," — the prayer that the priest's spirit would also find peace.

Brother Dimitrios stood next to his student at the liturgy and led him in the text, rhythm, and melodic direction of the chant by pointing to passages in the book that lay on the lectern and waving his finger descriptively in the air. The monk had tested the boy's voice and found that he had the talent to become a cantor. Much to the bearded, black-covered Brother Dimitrios's relief, the cracking alto that had tortured him for months, changed late in the summer. Dimitráki now had a clear, expressive tenor voice.

More than three years had passed since Dimitráki's father had hired a boatman to transport the boy across the lake to the monastery on the far side of the promontory that held Kastoria. Kyrie Athanásios consigned his son to be civilized by the monks there.

The monastery, named 'Mavriótissa' was a thousand-year-old remnant of the Byzantine Empire and its religious tradition. Hidden in a cove, it rested at the place a contingent of Emperor

182

Alexius I forces landed in 1083 to attack Norman invaders that held Kastoria. Alexius was victorious, and as a result, the Normans were expelled from Macedonia. He ordered construction of the monastery in thanksgiving for the victory.

Sited on a narrow, half-moon shaped shelf of land, Mavriótissa stood between the lakeshore and the foot of a small mountain, whose steep slopes fell sharply to the lake and provided the isolation the monks required for their religious life. For generations, it relied on the faithful across the lake, the people of the villages of Mávrovo and nearby Krepení, and the monastery's land holdings around those villages for sustenance.

Ancient Byzantine frescoes covered the interior walls of Dimitráki's place of learning, a church dedicated to the Virgin Mary Mavriótissa. But early in their five-hundred-year occupation of Macedonia, the Turks had imposed on their Christian subjects the Islamic prohibition on depictions of the human form. So, in acts of desecration, they scratched out the eyes of the Virgin, Christ, and the Saints in the frescoes. And they covered with plaster the sacred images on the exterior walls of both the main church and the small chapel of St. John the Theologian that adjoined it.

Dimitráki's adjustment to the monks and their way of life had been difficult. On his first day, the abbot introduced the boy to the monastic who would be his spiritual father and mentor. "Dimitráki, this is Brother Dimitrios. He will teach you and guide you." The boy kissed the young monk's hand and followed him outside to a place under a plane tree by the lake.

"Do you know why your father brought you to us, Dimitráki?"

"Yes. I think so."

"Whatever you think the reason, the most important is that your father loves you."

"How long will I be here?"

"Let God decide, my son."

"What will I do?"

"Do? You will pray for mercy and guidance, we will study and talk together, and God will lead you."

"When will I start, Pater?"

"Now. Let's go into the chapel and pray for guidance."

The monastery's living facilities were limited to a one-room house for the abbot and, in a separate structure, several small cells for its monks. The abbot assigned an uncomfortable, unfurnished cell to Dimitráki for his stay at Mavriótissa. It was pleasant in the summer when the water of the nearby lake tempered the air and kept him cool through the night. In winter, the boy shivered, huddling on a bed of straw under a coarse blanket. In addition to the food that Dimitráki carried to Mavriótissa for his own consumption, he frequently brought gifts of beans, fresh fruit or vegetables, cheese, or olives sent by his father in gratitude to the monks.

Every night, whether hot, temperate, or freezing, Brother Dimitrios roused Dimitráki from his sleep to assist in one or more of the myriad calls to prayer that punctuated the monks' life. In the dark hours of the night Dimitráki intoned ancient chants while the monastics prayed before icons that shimmered alive in the red glow of oil-lamps.

Although Dimitráki's feet had healed from the beating they received at the hands of the Kaimakan, they ached when he stood or walked for any length of time. In the beginning, they ached constantly as he stood during his long lessons in modal singing. He learned the cantor's role in the ancient church's liturgy, and in weddings, baptisms, and funerals.

For three years, Dimitráki lived at the monastery all year round, except for times of planting or harvest when he would shuttle back and forth across the lake to work in the fields on his father's farm.

After the first few months, Kallíope, commented to her husband, "Dimitráki hasn't made trouble for his brothers for days now, and I haven't seen his *andártes* anywhere."

In his third year, Dimitráki was at Mavriótissa for all of the forty days of the Great Lent that preceded Páscha. The Resurrection service was newly brilliant and transcendent for him, perhaps because he participated with the monastics in their rigorous preparation and fasting. Mental and physical discipline had prepared him for the spiritual experience.

Brother Dimitrios effected the change in Dimitráki through the hours he spent in conversation with him in the chapel, or under the shade of the cyclopean plane trees that bordered the lake. For his lessons, the good monk mixed principles of Christian theology, moral philosophy, and ethics, with stoic philosophy and traditional proverbs. Dimitráki responded. Talking with his mentor was not like his experience at school. He matured, and learned that he enjoyed using his mind.

At the conclusion of the liturgy on the first Sunday of December, Dimitráki stood with his mentor before the Royal Doors that concealed the sanctuary of the main church. A little earlier, he had received Holy Communion. Brother Dimitrios asked him to stay in the church until it was empty, and now stood facing him. "You are ready to leave us, Dimitráki," he said.

"Leave?"

"Yes. I spoke to your father yesterday and told him that you have done well, very well. I told him there would be no reason for you to stay with us any longer unless you decided to become a monk or a priest. I know that that is not your wish."

The boy had become a young man, and the young man had lost the brashness of the boy. He did not know how to respond to his teacher and friend.

Brother Dimitrios understood Dimitráki's silence.

"Say nothing. You have done well and God is pleased with you. Go with my blessing and be a good man, always."

Not daring to look into the monk's eyes for fear of crying, Dimitráki bowed, took his teacher's hand and kissed it. He hurried to his cell and gathered his things. Knowing that his days of study at the monastery had ended, Dimitráki stepped purposefully on to the ice in the silver twilight and walked across the lake toward the lamp-lit windows of Mávrovo. Brother Dimitrios's blessing gave him a great sense of peace and fulfillment. He wanted to honor his mentor. "I will be a good man," he said loudly enough to be heard, had there been anyone to hear him. "I promise. I will be as good a man as I can be."

Dimitráki was the second son of his widowed father's marriage to widow Kallíope Papanas. She brought her son, George with her into her new home and assumed the responsibility to raise three daughters and one son that Athanásios had fathered with his first wife.

Just as Athanásios and Kallíope shared their marriage bed, the bones of their dead spouses shared space on a shelf in the village churchyard ossuary.

George Papanas, the eldest of all the children, had no future in Mávrovo. His half-brothers were dismissive of his seniority in the family, because their father, who was his stepfather, focused all his attention on the products of his seed. George was unforgiving of his mother for having married and brought forth siblings whose competition he found unbearable. At fourteen, he became a shop helper and apprentice in the fur industry that had been established in Kastoria two hundred years before to exploit the lake's beaver population. At eighteen, he had sufficient skill as a furrier to immigrate to America's New York City.

Athanásios' son by his first marriage, Nikoláos, worked for his uncle Theodóros in Egypt. As a young man, Theodóros emigrated from Macedonia, became a successful member of the merchant class in Alexandria and benefactor of Mávrovo's school. He had married late, so welcomed Nikoláos as an able, hard-working apprentice to assure preservation of the wealth he had created. His own first son was only a baby when Nikoláos had arrived in Alexandria.

Dimitráki's older brother, Kóstas, a tall, introspective boy loved books and learning, not the exploits that Dimitráki pursued. Thomás and Aristédes, Dimitráki's younger brothers, too young to participate in his adventures, were of no interest to him. As women, except for the services that they provided to the household, his older half-sisters had no immediate place in Dimitráki's life.

The winter night that Dimitráki crossed over the ice from Mavriótissa to Mávrovo, the Great War in Europe had not much affected the lives of the people who lived in or close to Kastoria. Caravan merchants who traded goods in exchange for Kastoria's manufactured fur garments brought news about the conflict from Thessaloniki and Monastír. Dimitráki and his brother, Kóstas, would sit in a corner and listen to the village elders discuss Germany and Austria, and how those countries were allied with the Turks against far away England, France, and the great Orthodox Tsar of Russia. Rumor had it that King Constantine of Greece would not enter the war against the Turks because his sister was married to the king of Germany, and Turkey was Germany's ally.

"How could that be?" the boys asked each other. Greece had just fought the Turks to free Macedonia and Kastoria. The Turks were enemies; the Germans should be too.

Their father argued: "King Constantine should be fighting the Turks and taking back Constantinople before the Tsar takes it."

News arrived at the end of September 1915 that the Bulgarians had mobilized and joined in the war on the side of Germany, Austria, and Turkey. By December, the Serbian army had retreated south and had been pushed across the border into Greece by Austro-German forces. They established defensive positions to the south and southeast of Kastoria. The French Oriental Corps helped to block any German advance into Greece.

Meanwhile, Bulgarian divisions, eager to capture territory they had failed to annex in the Balkan Wars, threatened central Macedonia and Thessaloniki.

Greece continued to avoid entry into the war.

Late in the year, Athanásios received a letter from his brother in Egypt.

My Dear Brother Athanásios,

I write terrible news. Your beloved son Nikoláos, who was as a son to me, has left us. He was victim to one of the fevers that have plagued Egypt since British troops came here.

Thank God, he suffered little and died in peace. I provided him the funeral I would have given to my own son, and he rests among Orthodox Christians.

I ask that you send Kóstas to me to take Nikoláos' place.

I grieve with you and Kallíope. Life to us.

Your brother,

Theodóros

CHICAGO, ILLINOIS

In November, Eléni received a letter from Konstantínos.

19 October 1915

Dear Eléni,

Sofía and I send our prayers and kisses to you, and to our beloved niece, Evangelía.

You are a strong, capable, and brave woman. Be true to yourself in this difficult time. Have courage. The Panaghía will help you.

Things are going badly in Greece. There is political turmoil. The King and Venizelos are at odds, the French and English have landed troops in Thessaloniki, and the Austrians, Germans, and Bulgarians have invaded Serbia. Everyone expects the Bulgarians to attack Greece to take as much of Macedonia and eastern Thrace as they can.

The military may call Dimitrios to serve. Smarágda is sick with worry.

Hrístos is fifteen. He is safe for a little while. I have other plans for him than to fight for the politicians the way I did.

Zenóvios left Paris in August. He is in America, in New York. Things have been better in Paris, but the Germans are close. Who knows what will happen? I think that it is too dangerous for Stávros to stay. However, he will not leave because he is in love with a French girl named Marie-Yvonne. We worry for him.

Hrístos will sail for America to join Zenóvios within weeks. They will be in New York when you arrive there.

We received a letter from Chrysóula. She agreed to have Katína come to us. She is fourteen. We expected her days ago. She is traveling by land with another family because warships have closed the Hellespont. We pray that she is in Greece by now, and that she escaped the Bulgarians.

Do what you must, Eléni. Protect yourself and Evangelía. We hope that you write to us from New York soon.

Embraces and kisses from Sultána, Smarágda, and Dimitrios.

We kiss you and Evangelía,

Konstantínos and Sofía

One month later, Leonardo struggled through deep snow wearing a heavy coat, and gloves, with a long muffler wrapped over his hat and around his head. He stomped his shoes at the front steps, mounted the stairs, and opened the door to the apartment that he shared with Eléni. He found Evangelía in the parlor, snuggled on the floor next to a kerosene heater, reading. Eléni was in the kitchen preparing his dinner." It's freezing out there, Eléni."

"Take off your coat and shoes, *agápe mou*. I have hot soup on the stove. There's a letter from Italy."

Mána pays so much attention to Leonardo, Evangelía thought.

Leonardo changed into a warm sweater and slippers while Eléni served his dinner. He sat at the kitchen table and sampled a spoonful of bean soup, a little cheese, an olive, and a piece of warm, crusty Italian bread. Washing it all down with wine, Leonardo turned to the envelope and carefully opened it with a table knife. Between mouthfuls of food and sips of wine, he read the letter aloud in Italian, translating words and phrases into Greek or English when Eléni's facial features made it clear that she did not understand.

30 November 1915
Dear Brother,

Leonardo, I hope this letter finds you well. Kisses from mama, and Philomena.

The war goes badly. We have not heard from papa for months. He is somewhere in the north, in the mountains near Austria. In his last letter, he wrote to mama that I should take Philomena and come to you in America before the army takes me too. He says that mama will be safe here alone, and that we can send money to her from America.

Can we come? Can you send money for our tickets? We can leave on a Greek ship from Naples. They are safe.

Write soon, please.

Luigi

"Eat, Leonardo, eat," Eléni said. "Then write to your brother."

"What should I write?"

"That you'll send the money for tickets as soon as we have an address in New York. That we'll greet him and Philomena there."

Leonardo smiled, and with a sigh said, "Thank you, Eléni. When?"

"As soon as we can, *agápe mou*."

Evangelía had been listening intently. "Are we going to New York, *mána*? Do we have to go?"

"Yes, *hrisó mou*. We've talked about it for a long time."

Evangelía closed her book, rolled on to her back and stared at the ceiling. *I hope New York is nice*, she thought.

"Leonardo, what do you think?" Eléni asked. "How soon can we leave?"

Leonardo got up from the table and went into the bedroom. He retrieved a cigar box from its hiding place under the bed, brought it back to the table, and opened it. Eléni and Evangelía watched Leonardo count bills and coins. He looked up and said, "We can be in New York before the end of January. But first we must get married."

Eléni threw her arms around Leonardo, first hugging and then kissing him.

Evangelía turned her head to the wall, thinking, *Mána never let Spíros hold her*. She got up and left the room.

Later, when Evangelía crawled into bed, she heard noises from her mother's bedroom. *What are they doing?*

MÁVROVO, KASTORIA
THE KINGDOM OF GREECE

On the eve of Ághios Vasílis, the last day of 1915, Athanásios Mavrovitis worried about how he and his family would survive the Great War when it came to Greece.

Chapter Thirteen
1917
New York City

Dimitráki disembarked at Ellis Island on Easter morning. The night before he had served as chanter for a Resurrection service held in the third-class hold of the Greek ship, the King Constantine. The dark, cavernous space was proxy for Christ's tomb.

The priest was a gentle, middle-aged cleric on his way to serve a newly formed Greek congregation somewhere in the vast center of America. The immigrants needed a priest to make their lives complete — to marry them, baptize their children, bury their loved ones, and celebrate Orthodox feast days. The heavily cloaked *presvytéra*, the priest's wife, and her three children — two dark-eyed, black-haired girls who were approaching their teens, and a fidgety boy of five — stood near the improvised altar. The priest prompted Dimitráki and nodded approvingly at the boy's chanting. The worshipers' eyes reflected the flickering light of the few candles they shared when the priest proclaimed the miracle of the Resurrection.

Two days later, after a ferry ride from Ellis Island to Manhattan, Dimitráki made his way to an address scribbled on a tattered piece of paper that he held tightly in his hand. It was evening when he stood at the door of a building on West 17th Street. He gathered his courage, entered the front door, and climbed the stairs to the second floor. Dimitráki went from one apartment to the next until he found a number on a door that matched the one on the piece of paper. He smoothed his rumpled clothing as best he could, knocked on the door, waited, and knocked again. George Papanas opened the door with an annoyed look on his face. He dabbed his mouth with the loose end of the napkin that was tucked in his shirt collar under his chin. When he recognized his half-brother, his face showed disbelief. "Dimitráki? It's you? What are you doing here?"

"Who is it, George?" a woman's voice asked in English.

"You're supposed to be in Egypt."

Smiling broadly, Dimitráki proclaimed, "*Hristós Anésti.*"

By the look of surprise on George's face, Dimitráki's declaration of Christ's resurrection might just as well have been of his own.

"George, who is it?" the woman's voice asked again.

George called over his shoulder. "It's my brother. From Kastoria. From Mávrovo. My half-brother, Dimítrios." He turned back to Dimitráki. "*Alithós Anésti.*"

"Your what?" The woman's voice was a bit louder.

Dimitráki stood in the dark hallway. His brother neither hugged him nor kissed him. A slim young woman with long curly hair stepped in front of George. She smiled sweetly at Dimitráki, and while he did not understand her words, her warmth, and the hug and kiss she gave him on his cheek were clear messages of welcome.

"Come in, Dimitrios. George, help him with his bag. Dimitrios, I'm Mary."

"Mar--y?"

"Yes, that's right. Mary. Ask him if he has anywhere to stay, George."

194

"He doesn't know anyone, or anything about the city."

"Then he can stay here and sleep on the second bed in the children's room. Thomas isn't ready for it yet anyway. He likes his crib. Ask him to come in and sit down. Is he hungry?"

George gathered his wits and found his voice. "Dimitráki, give me your bag. Come in. Sit down — there, at the table. Mary will get you something to eat. We have lamb from Easter."

Dimitráki saw two little heads poke around a corner. They were Helen and Thomas, his niece and nephew. The moment they saw his eyes on them they vanished.

George peppered his brother with questions. "How is my mother? When did your ship reach New York? What was its name? How long did the voyage take? How did you find me?"

Dimitráki gave a short answer to each question while he devoured the food that Mary put before him. Slices of succulent lamb, steaming with the smell of lemon, garlic, and oregano, pan-roasted potatoes, vegetables, a basket of bread, and cheese, olives, and a half-full bottle of wine provided a feast for the famished teenager. Mary enjoyed watching the young man eat. She sat quietly and listened to the brothers, understanding almost nothing of their exchange. Her Greek was limited. "Is his name Dimitrios or Dimitráki?" she asked.

"Dimitrios," George responded. "We called him Dimitráki — little Dimitrios."

"He's not little anymore. Call him by his full name. Dimitrios."

Dimitráki looked up quizzically at Mary, and then at is brother.

"No more 'Dimitráki'," George said. "Mary says you're grown up. Dimitrios from now on."

George poured a second glass of wine for his brother and one for himself, sat back and watched the fifteen-year-old finish his meal. Dimitrios told his story between mouthfuls, and George translated for his American wife.

"Théo Theodóros wrote in December that Nikoláos died in Alexandria. He asked babás to send Kóstas in his place. But the military officers in Kastoria wouldn't allow him to leave because if Greece goes to war he's old enough for the army."

"Is he in the army now?" George asked.

"No, not when I left. I begged *babás* and *mána* to let me go to Egypt. First, *mána* said no. Then *babás* said that it would be better to get me out of Greece. I went to Ioánnina to apply for the papers. It took five days through the mountains in Épiros on the back of a mule to get there. It's beautiful. It has a large lake just like Kastoria. The officials gave me the papers because I am in my sixteenth year. I returned home and left in late February with others from Mávrovo. We traveled by mule to Kozáni and then by train to Athens. I saw the King's palace."

George looked incredulously at his brother. "But how did you get here? Why aren't you in Alexandria?"

"I had to come to America. I traveled to Piraeus with our cousin, Pantelís. He and his friends were all going to America. I wanted to come here too, not to Egypt."

"Your father and your uncle will be angry." George pondered the situation for a moment. "But you're here. I can't send you back."

"I have a ten-dollar gold piece. Is it enough to start?"

"For now, Dimitráki…Dimitrios. Get some sleep and we'll make plans tomorrow."

George's plan was to have his brother work as an assistant in his shop on West 28th Street. The boy was eager to become a furrier. He had seen fur shops in Kastoria, and their beautiful garments, and heard that furriers made a lot of money.

George put him off. "You have lots of time, Dimitráki. I'll teach you the trade. For now, you take care of errands, cleaning up, and deliveries. You can open skins, too."

"Open skins?"

"It's the first thing a furrier does — open the bellies of the skins so they lie flat. Then you cut off the tails, paws, and heads, and stretch the skin. It's easy." But the summer passed without George taking the time to teach his brother much of anything.

George was a well-dressed philanderer who went out of his way to meet and talk to young women. His work habits were casual. He bought more finished garments from other manufacturers than he made himself. These he sold to female clients at what he claimed as a wholesale price, sparing no opportunity to hold their shoulders as he helped them to try on a stole or cape, or brush his hands across their legs while he pinned a coat's hemline. One day he closed the front of a coat from behind a good-looking young woman and allowed his hands to linger at her waist. The woman twirled out of George's reach, laughing, "Don't be naughty, George."

When she left, George winked at Dimitrios. "Don't worry, Dimitráki, in a year or two you'll be old enough for women."

The implications of George's comment embarrassed Dimitrios even more than his behavior.

George would often disappear from the shop for an entire afternoon, leaving his brother to answer the door and take messages. On those days, he closed-up the shop in the evening and went home to a quiet dinner with Mary, Helen, and Thomas. Some days he stayed at home and watched his niece and nephew while Mary went shopping or visited friends.

On nights when George came home late, red-eyed and with liquor on his breath, he abused Mary and his children, yelling sarcastic comments. Once, Dimitrios found Mary crying in the kitchen. She tried to hide her face. "George was nice when I met him." When she looked up, there was a red welt across her cheek. "I even left my family in Chicago to marry him. They won't talk to me. They told me ..." Her voice trailed off and she began to sob. He sat with her quietly, not knowing what to say or do.

In the fall, Dimitrios enrolled in night school to learn English. George teased his brother and complained about his studies. "Do you think that you're a scholar? Books and paper cost money."

In the middle of December, Dimitrios decided that his work and living situations were intolerable. He had saved a little money and learned of a job opportunity from a teenager in his English class. He packed his few belongings and moved to Brooklyn to share a flat with friends that he had met at church. Mary told him that she was sad to see him leave. George was indifferent.

Dimitrios reported for his first day of work as a Western Union bicycle delivery boy on a morning that began with a light dusting of snow on the streets of midtown Manhattan and the promise of more to come.

"Dimitrios is no name," his Irish supervisor told him. "Greeks named Dimitrios all call themselves Jim or Jimmy in America."

"Jimmy," Dimitrios decided.

With telegrams stashed in the case he carried over his shoulder, Jimmy rode his bicycle and made a few deliveries until the increasingly heavy snowfall decreased visibility. The weather conditions compounded his basic problem — he did not know his way around the city. There was virtually no one on the street that he could ask for directions, even if his English had been good enough. By late afternoon, with more than ten inches of snow blocking sidewalks and streets, it was all he could do to carry the bicycle back to the Western Union office and return undelivered telegrams to his fuming supervisor.

"You're a lazy, stupid kid. What've you been doing all day?"

The derision in his supervisor's words humiliated Jimmy. He walked to his locker in the backroom, changed out of his uniform and left it on the floor.

Another delivery boy who had heard the exchange warned Jimmy, "You'd better hang up your uniform or the boss will fire you."

"Fire?" Jimmy questioned.

"Make you go. You'd lose your job and have to leave."

"Leave mean go?"

"Yeah."

"I leave."

"Are you going to quit?"

"Quit mean leave?"

"Yes."

Jimmy walked out into the main office, turned to his supervisor, and said, "Quit." He went out the door without a job, but with a new first name and his pride intact.

On the following Sunday, Jimmy served as assistant *psáltis* at Brooklyn's Saints Constantine and Helen church on Schermerhorn Street. After the service, a chisel-faced, olive-skinned, dark-haired young man approached Jimmy in the church's small locker room and extended his hand saying, "I'm Panayiotis Stamatis. You have a wonderful voice."

Jimmy disentangled himself from his cassock and reached out to shake the stranger's hand. "Thank you. I'm Dimitrios Mavrovitis. They call me Jimmy."

"You're from Kastoria, aren't you?"

"Well, from Mávrovo. Near Kastoria."

"Good. I am from Macedonia too. Do you have plans for dinner? Perhaps you'd like to join me and my friends at a good Greek restaurant we know."

Jimmy paused for a moment. He had never been to a restaurant. Restaurants meant spending money. He had none to spare.

"Join us — as my guest," Panayiotis added warmly.

Jimmy hesitated again. However, there was something in Panayiotis' voice and smile that made him feel comfortable. And he was Macedonian.

"Yes, I will. Thank you."

"Brilliant. Call me Peter. I'll wait for you at the front door and we'll go on from there."

After they were seated at the restaurant, three other young men, each older than Jimmy, joined them at their table. Peter introduced them to Jimmy, who was pleased that all were from Kastoria, and all were furriers. He admired them, for they seemed successful and were well dressed and at ease.

The restaurant, named The Parthenon, was long and narrow, had several dark oak booths set along one wall, and rows of tables filling the rest of the space. Its blue-bordered white walls were crowded with framed prints of the Acropolis, Delphi, and other ancient sites, photographs of King George, and of Crown Prince Constantine with Sophie and their children. Posters of Prime Minister Venizelos and of Alexander the Great stood guard on either side of Pericles' bust, which sat on a corner shelf. There were replicas of ancient Greek amphora, plates, and platters decorated with mythological personages and the gods of Olympus hanging on the walls in irregular clusters. Greek and American flags decorated the far wall on either side of a serving table that held olives, several cheeses, fried eggplant and squash, roasted and skinned peppers in olive oil and vinegar, and plates of sardines and anchovy. Jimmy studied the wall decorations and noted what the restaurant's customers had on their plates: *dolmádes*, chicken and rice, gilled lamb chops, roast lamb, lamb stew with tomatoes, green beans and potatoes, dandelion greens, and baked fish, which Peter told him was *tsipoúra*, a snapper. Jimmy had no experience with salt-water fish; fresh-water carp and perch from the lake at home were the only fish he had ever eaten, except for the salted tuna and anchovy that had come to Kastoria by caravan from Thessaloniki.

Jimmy saw one woman in the restaurant — only one. She was middle-aged, and sat in a front booth with what he was sure must have been her husband or brother. He had not expected to find a woman, especially a Greek woman, in a place filled with men who were not members of her family.

The smell of food coming from the kitchen sharpened Jimmy's appetite. He ordered roast *tsipoúra* with potatoes and a plate of boiled dandelion greens drizzled with olive oil and lemon juice. In the time between ordering his dinner and it being served, Jimmy answered a few questions about his village, and how he had come to America. And he learned about his new friends.

"How do you like the fish, Jimmy?" Peter asked.

"Good, very good," he answered, meaning it. He reached for a slice of bread and helped himself to the *feta* cheese and olives that were on the table for everyone. During dinner, Peter and his friends talked about the fur market, new fashions, and business. They ate slowly, savoring every mouthful of food and sip of wine.

Just as they finished their meal, one of the men, Kosmas, spoke up. "The Greek newspaper says that French and British troops landed in Athens to get hold of munitions from Greek arsenals. The king's forces stopped them. But a mob backing Venizelos' provisional government helped the French and British."

Peter responded, "The Venizelos supporters shot at our countrymen, and the French ships anchored in Phaleron Bay fired their guns at the palace. The situation in northern Greece is getting worse."

Someone else offered, "That pro-Anglo-French bastard Venizelos and his crowd in Thessaloniki are going to destroy the country. He is against the King. He'll cause a civil war."

A bookish-looking, heavyset man at the next table blasted, "No. No. Venizelos is right. It's time for the Greeks to get rid of the king and his family of leeches and join the allies to fight Germany and Austria. Bulgaria will be at our throats."

Several men voiced oaths that they would go home to Greece to fight if the Bulgarians attacked.

They talked until they emptied the wine carafes, exhausted their information, and tired of politics, and then one by one they left with worry on their faces. Jimmy realized how little he knew about the world and politics. He felt anxious about his family in Macedonia. The only way he knew to help them was to earn and send money.

As they left the restaurant, Peter put his hand on Jimmy's shoulder. "Have coffee with us before you go home. There's a *kafeneío* down the street."

Jimmy was glad to accept. He welcomed the opportunity to spend a few minutes more with his host.

Once their coffee was served, Peter offered Jimmy a cigarette. He took one and held it clumsily to his lips. Peter lit a match. The first tentative puff made Jimmy cough.

"Don't smoke if it bothers you," Peter suggested.

"No, I want to try." Jimmy took another puff, grimaced, and rested the cigarette in the ashtray.

Peter waited for a moment and then asked Jimmy about where he worked and how he liked New York. Jimmy told Peter about his relationship with his brother George and how much he had wanted to become a furrier. He admitted to being unemployed and related his experience as a Western Union delivery boy.

Peter listened sympathetically and asked, "Do you know how to sew at a machine, Jimmy?"

"Just a little. My brother gave me some scraps to practice on."

"Are you willing to learn?'

"Yes — if I could find work."

"Listen. I know a man in Brooklyn who is in charge of a factory that makes stuffed toy animals. They are little bears - Teddy bears. Everyone is buying them for their children. His name is Schmidt, and he is fair and honest. He needs sewing machine operators. It isn't the fur business, but you'll learn skills that you can use later. What do you think?"

"I need work."

"Brilliant. I'll take you there tomorrow morning."

BROOKLYN, NEW YORK

Jimmy inhaled icy air through his muffler. When he exhaled, the moisture in his breath crystallized on the wool that protected his mouth. He stopped at the door of the factory and swept his shoulders with his gloved hands to remove epaulets of snow.

It was warmer inside. But not warm enough to make his sweater and jacket unnecessary.

Jimmy's goodhearted foreman greeted him. "*Guten Morgen. Hergekommen. Wärmen Sie sich.*" He gestured to him to come closer.

Jimmy understood the invitation more from the hand motions that he saw than from the German words he heard and decided to stand close to the kerosene heater for just a few minutes. He did not want to waste time. There was a mountain of Teddy bears to sew, and each of them put coins in his pocket. Jimmy had learned about the opportunities in piecework, and that the more productive he was, the more he earned. He took little part the banter that went on all day among the men at the sewing machines, for most were Germans, and he knew no German and little English. While he worked he was absorbed in thought — worried about his family in Macedonia. He remembered his village, and dreamt about his future.

GRAND CENTRAL STATION, NEW YORK CITY

Zenóvios and Hrístos Kapidaghlís met their aunt Eléni, her new husband Leonardo, and their cousin Evangelía on the platform at Grand Central Station just as they had arranged in an exchange of telegrams between New York and Chicago. They had taken new names. Zenóvios was now John, and Hrístos, Chris. For both, Kapidaghlís became 'Capidaglis'. Chris shortened it at work to 'Capi'.

After hurried hugs and kisses, Zenóvios and Hrístos gathered suitcases and trunks from the station's baggage room and swept the new arrivals by taxicab to the flat they had rented for their aunt in a neighborhood between 7th and 10th Avenues called Hell's Kitchen.

The next day, John and Chris' factory manager hired Leonardo and referred Eléni to a business friend who hired her to work in his dress factory on 7th Avenue. They became one of the thousands of immigrant families that crowded into cold-water flats stacked one on top of another in the tenements of Hell's Kitchen. Sewing machine operators, bus boys and waiters, dishwashers, slaughterhouse butchers and packers, street cleaners, garbage men, hotel workers, shoeshine boys, delivery boys, and store clerks lived and worked as neighbors, learning the ways of their new world.

Seeking relief on hot, humid summer nights, family groups gathered on rooftops to sleep. The music of accordions, mandolins, clarinets, and guitars accompanied multilingual songs. In winter, they took refuge in their small flats, heated against the cold with coal-fired kitchen ovens and portable kerosene heaters. Fire or asphyxiation united many souls with their Maker. Gaslight illuminated their rooms after dark. Few flats had flush toilets or bathtubs.

Leonardo's friends had been right about the opportunities in New York. Two-thirds of the clothing made in the United States originated in the eighteen-square-block garment district of Manhattan between Thirty-fourth34th and 40th Streets, and 6th and 9th Avenues. There was a demand for skilled workers, and the pay was good.

The fur market was nearby, just to the south between 27th and 33rd Streets. Further south, in lofts from 14th to 26th Streets, manufacture of men's clothing held sway.

To the west of 10th Avenue, slaughterhouses fouled the air of the city and the water of the Hudson River. Along the river, wharves accommodated the coming and going of merchant and passenger ships.

Eléni and Leonardo discovered lines of pushcart vendors, and vegetable, meat, poultry, and fish markets along 8th and 10th Avenues. "Look, Leonardo, he has *vourví*," Eléni exclaimed, pointing at a basket in a pushcart.

Leonardo picked a couple of little purple onions out of the basket. "Ah, wild onion — *cipolinni*."

"Come here, Leonardo. Look, *bakaliáros*." The salted, dried cod was stacked like cordwood at the entrance to a delicatessen.

"*Baccalá*," Leonardo smiled.

A clerk overheard Eléni speaking Greek and said "*Háiretai, Kyria*. My name is Zoë. May I help you?"

"You're Greek?" Eléni asked.

"Yes. My father owns this store. Look around. See what we have."

Zoë showed them stick-like dried fish on hooks above the counter. Eléni was overjoyed. "Look, Evangelía. *Réngha*." Next to the dried herring hung bouquets of dried herbs — oregano, bay leaves, dill, mint, and thyme, and below the herbs, containers on the floor held aromatic spices — cinnamon, nutmeg, coriander, and cumin. Displays of large open tins of anchovy, sardines, and *lakérda* were behind glass in the ice-filled cooler, and mountains of sesame-seed-covered loaves of bread crowned the counter top. Jars contained more herbs and spices, even the rare *mahlépi*, the kernel of the wild cherry used to scent traditional holiday breads.

"Where is a good place to buy meat and fish near here?" Leonardo asked.

Zoë laughed. "Just walk down the street and look at the shops in the middle of the block. They have everything." She was right. A pyramid of fresh lamb heads was in the butcher's shop window. Leonardo conjured their smell on his dinner table — split, bathed in olive oil and lemon juice, rubbed with salt, pepper, garlic, and oregano, and roasted crispy brown with potatoes. The butcher assured Eléni that he'd have pigs' heads, hocks, and feet at Christmas for her to make the winter soup, *patsá*, and lamb and goat at Easter.

At the fish store, Eléni purchased fresh fish livers and roe. "We'll take these and I'll show you how to prepare them, Evangelía. We'll buy enough to have for dinner tonight. Leonardo, look, fish heads, and *mídthia*." She picked up a mussel. It had a briny smell, and the shell did not budge when she tried to force it open with her fingers. "It's fresh," she said. "Next week I'll buy three or four dozen and stuff them."

Leonardo started to fill a bag. "I want some steamed, tonight."

Eléni, Leonardo, and Evangelía melded into the immigrant life of the West Side. Eléni began to feel secure, comforted by the availability of familiar foods and the company of Greek-speaking immigrants. Her spiritual support came from St. Elefthérios, the Greek Orthodox Church located near them on West 24th Street.

Eléni worked in a factory owned by Nathan Rosenbaum. Unlike the sweatshops that operated in New York's squalid lofts and brownstone apartments following the Triangle fire that killed over a hundred young women in a shirtwaist factory, his establishment had adequate fire exits, washrooms, ventilation, and good lighting. Filling an entire floor of a manufacturing building, it held four rows of worktables, with twenty sewing machine operators aligned on either side of each row, and a line of cutting tables set against its window wall. One hundred and sixty sewing machines droned in the space, while supervisors walked the aisles between the tables to observe work, assure a sufficient supply of raw material, and pick up baskets filled with finished goods.

Eléni did not like her supervisor, or the grim and overbearing forelady, Mrs. Catania, who derided workers who did not meet her expectations. Eléni easily out-produced anyone on the floor, and within a few days the forelady tapped her on the shoulder and grudgingly told her through Gus, a Greek cutter, who translated, "Mr. Rosenbaum wants to see you in his office."

"Mrs. Perna?" the meticulously groomed man behind the desk asked when Eléni appeared at his door.

"*Si*, yes."

"Come in, come in," he said, looking over his glasses.

Eléni waited at the door.

"Nothing to be afraid of. Come in. Have a seat." He motioned toward the chair in front of his desk.

Eléni noticed his long, slender hands and manicured fingernails. She felt self-conscious. "English no so good." she said, sitting upright on the edge of the seat as though ready to leave.

"Ah, yes. Are you Italian?"

"*Ellinída — Greca.*"

"Greek?"

"Yes."

"Mrs. Perna, we've been watching you. You sew very fast. Can you teach others to work like you do?"

"Me, teach?"

"Yes, girls and men. Can you teach them? Teach — it means show how to work."

"I teach? No sew?"

"No. I want to try something. I want you to be the supervisor for new operators. I'll pay you more than you've been earning." Rosenbaum saw bewilderment in Eléni's face.

"Wait. Sit, Mrs. Perna." He motioned with his hands for her to stay seated. "I'll be right back."

Rosenbaum returned with Gus, who once again served as translator. The man was a burly, stubble-faced Greek whose work was to cut bolts of cloth into a garment's component pieces. In a few moments, Eléni understood that she was going to be a supervisor, teach new employees how to sew efficiently, and build her own production line. For this, Rosenbaum would pay her more money. Gus's attitude toward Eléni changed as he translated and his respect for her became almost palpable.

Eléni left Rosenbaum's office excited. Gus followed her and in a few minutes spread word across the factory that this new woman, Mrs. Perna, was going to be one of the bosses.

With Rosenbaum's backing, Eléni set production quotas in meetings with her Jewish, Italian, and Greek workers, who managed to translate for each other. They respected her ability, the way she taught and encouraged them, and her fairness. As the weeks passed, they became the most productive workers in the factory, and she was making money for Mr. Rosenbaum.

Mrs. Catania was resentful of Eléni's success. She missed work, and when she did not show up for two consecutive days, Mr. Rosenbaum called Eléni into his office. He had come to another decision. "Mrs. Perna, I want you to be forelady in the shop. I'll pay you by the week, and give you bonuses for production. What do you say?"

Eléni stared at him." Forelady? You mean boss? What happen Catania?"

"Yes, well, I'm the boss. You'll be in charge of the factory. Don't worry about Mrs. Catania."

"Super too?"

"You won't have time. You'll train the supervisors, keep production going, work with the designers and cutters and coordinate with finishers."

The possibilities dawned on Eléni. She was going to run a big part of this man's business. He needed her.

Excitedly mixing languages, she pressed him. "*Signomi, 'scusa* — you give *sposo kai kori* — *e figlia* work? Leonardo good tailor, dressmaker. Evangelía good finisher."

"Who? Mrs. Perna, Eléni — no, you must change your name. Eléni is the same as Helen, isn't it? We'll call you Madame Helen. Everyone will respect you more."

"Leonardo *e* Evangelía?"

"Who is Leonardo?"

"*Sposa* – husband."

"And Evan, Evangel?"

"Evangelía. *Ónoma, nome,* daughter."

"Okay, you can hire them. But they have to produce."

"Thanks you."

"You know, your daughter should have a modern name — an American name. How about Violet? Camille is popular. And Lily. Americans love flowers."

"Lily?"

"Yes. And maybe Louie for your husband."

When she went home from work that night Eléni stopped at the grocery store. She knew that the twenty-year-old daughter of the proprietor spoke English perfectly. Zoë, tall, dark-haired and smiling, was behind the counter.

"*Chairetai*, Kyria Eléni."

"Zoë, *Chairetai. Pes mou,* Zoë, *ti ínai* — what means Lily?"

"Lily? Lily is a flower, the same as *chrínos.*"

Eléni left the store as fast as she had entered it. Zoë was puzzled. However, in a few days, she understood and learned the names Eléni's husband and daughter had assumed. Evangelía became Lily; Leonardo, Louie; and Eléni, Madame Helen — though her Greek workers respectfully called her Kyria Eléni.

EIGHTH AVENUE, MANHATTAN

Lily struck the pose she thought best showed off her exotic harem costume. A white, flower-embroidered veil covered her head and flowed down over her shoulders to her waist. Her long-sleeved dress reached to mid-calf. Deeply split in front it revealed full, billowy pantaloons that ended in ruffled lace just above her ankles. Black, patent leather dancing shoes with inch-high heels held her feet.

Mr. Klentzos, the skinny photographer and studio owner, hurried to finish the session. The gray afternoon, with the potential for a stormy March night, made him eager to get home to his dinner before it started to rain, or perhaps even snow. He stroked his goatee after he focused his camera, and then again after putting the film in place. "Head a little higher, Lily."

Lily had to struggle not to grin. She loved her new name, and although her mother still called her Evangelía, Leonardo – now Louie – used Lily when he spoke English and Evangelía in Greek or Italian. Sometimes she gave people the American version of her name, Evangeline.

The photographer adjusted the flash pan. "Tilt your head up. Good, good."

The camera clicked, there was a dazzling flash, and a billow of white smoke belched from the flash pan and clung to the ceiling of the room like a cloud layer.

"Bravo, Lily. We're done."

Lily relaxed and moved toward the coat rack. Her cousin, Thomás Thomá, took her silk-lined coat from a hanger and held it while she slipped her arms gracefully into its sleeves, wrapped it about her and tied its belt securely at her waist.

Thomás had arrived in New York from Piraeus at the start of the year. His cousins John and Chris, now old-timers in the city, took him in hand and rapidly produced an eighteen-year-old man-about-town. Thomás had learned enough of dressmaking from his Uncle Konstantínos in Athens to be valued at the factory that employed John.

"When will my photographs be ready, Mr. Klentzos?" Lily asked.

"Come on Friday. The proofs will be ready late in the afternoon. Once you choose the ones you like, I'll have finished copies ready in three or four days."

The studio was on 8th Avenue, convenient for immigrant families, and not far from the large two-bedroom, third-floor flat that Lily, Louie, and Eléni occupied. After their first year in New York, they had moved from their smaller apartment on West 21st to West 38th Street. While the first flat was closer to the church, this one was newer, larger, and near their places of work, and to the shops.

The photographer, the Greek who owned Central Studio, had recently taken a formal photograph of Eléni and Louie. In it, Eléni, a full two inches taller, and twenty pounds heavier than Louie, had stood next to her husband with her arm through his. Her black satin dress and the gauzy veil that covered the upper half of her face made her look severe. Louie had worn a black three-piece suit with a high-collared white shirt and a smallish hat. He looked like a schoolboy accompanied by an elder sister. They sent copies of the photographs to their relatives in Italy, Greece, and Bulgaria.

Lily enjoyed the attention she received posing for her photograph and decided that she would have others taken. She looked more mature than her thirteen years. Her legs had taken shape, and her breasts were starting to show their roundness. Earlier in the day, she had noticed admiring glances from men as she walked to the studio, her arm through her cousin Thomás' as if he were her suitor, not a chaperone.

Glances were the extent of the attention she received from men. Her mother, Louie, or a relative accompanied her when she left the apartment, except when she went to shop at the stores immediately around the corner on 8th Avenue. In that respect, she was protected as she would have been in Greece or Bulgaria.

Her mother and Louie had designed and sewn the costume Lily wore under her coat. She would wear it at the dance celebrating the end of the pre-Lent carnival season. Lily was sure that it would be the most beautiful costume there. No one had a family more skilled with a needle and thread than she.

"*Mána, mána,*" Lily called, rushing up the stairs with Thomás.

Eléni came to the door in time for Lily to throw her arms around her mother's neck.

"Kyrie Klentzos said that I should be a model."

"Don't mess your costume, Evangelía. You want to be pretty at the dance tonight." She held Thomás at arms length and admired him. "Come in, Thomás. Your mother should see you. How handsome."

Lily swept into the parlor, where Louie was sitting with an Italian newspaper in one hand and a glass of wine in the other.

"Louie," she called. "Thank you for the costume. It's beautiful."

"I'm glad you like. Thomás, take a glass of wine to warm you."

"Stay for dinner, Thomás," offered Eléni.

"Thank you, Théa, but I can't. My friends are waiting for me."

"You were good to chaperone Lily. Are you going to the costume dance?"

"Yes, Théa, and I'll be happy to take Lily. Zenóvios, Hrístos, and I will escort her, and Katina and Haríklea. We'll be here at nine o'clock."

"Thank you, Thomás. You're a good boy. We'll be there too. You won't have to spend all of your time watching the girls."

Thomás smiled, hugged and kissed his aunt and cousin, and said, "*Buona sera*," to Louie as he went out the door.

"*Buona sera*," Louie responded absentmindedly.

Louie opened his Italian language newspaper. It contained difficult news. The Italian army had suffered hundreds of thousands of killed, wounded, or captured in attacks on the Austrians along the Isonzo River, and in defense at Asiago. While battle casualties had abated in the winter, reports promised more slaughter in the spring.

Louie sipped his wine.

Luigi and Philomena were safe in New York. They lived with an Italian family just a few city blocks away, worked for a shirt manufacturer, and were able to contribute to supporting their mother, who wrote that she had heard nothing from her husband for months. Louie held little hope for his father, whose remains might never be found in the artillery-devastated landscape of the Alps. His mother had been told that he was missing. That was all.

KALITHÉA, ATHENS, GREECE

"Sofía. Where are you? Sofía."

Konstantínos shut the door behind him, and then went to the window and looked out cautiously. Seeing no one, he pulled the curtains closed and then put the sack he carried on the kitchen table and opened it. From it he took a bag of lentils, two bottles of olive oil and three onions. He rinsed three handfuls of lentils, put them in a bowl, and covered them with water.

"Sofía can cook these when she gets home," he murmured to himself. "Where is she?"

In exchange for the food, Konstantínos had fitted a dull-witted son of a prominent politician with a new military tunic. He was a vain young officer, eager to impress palace dignitaries. Even after the Anglo-French navies had imposed a blockade in an attempt to force King Constantine into the war against Germany and Austria, Konstantínos and his brother-in-law, Dimitrios, had managed to feed Sofía, Smarágda, Sultána, and their children.

One morning before the blockade began, Dimitrios recognized a man talking to the foreman of his work gang at the wharfs.

"Costas, Costas Zelios," he cried.

Costas looked at Dimitrios with disbelief.

"Dimitrios?"

"Yes, it's me."

Costas grasped Dimitrios's hand and gave him a hug before he turned to the young officer who accompanied him. "Leonárdos, this is Dimitrios Parousis. He's from Sozópolis. He worked with me at the salt flats at Anchíalos. Dimitrios, meet by brother-in-law, Leonárdos Panteliás."

"*Chairetai, kapetánios,*" Dimitrios said, doffing his cap in a show of respect.

"*Chairetai, Dimitrios.*"

The foreman's shrieking whistle called the men to work, ending the brief introduction.

"You. The new man. You go with Dimitrios since you know him. He'll show you the work."

"Thank you, Leonárdos," Costas said as he followed Dimitrios. "I'll see you tonight."

At their lunch break, Costas told Dimitrios the story of his escape from Bulgaria in 1912. "When my wife, Anastasía, her sisters, and I got to Volos, we snuck away from the soldiers at the dock and stayed there instead of going to one of the camps. No one came after us."

"You were lucky," Dimitrios told him. "Eléni and Evangelía were taken to Efxinoúpolis."

"What we heard bad things about that place and Nea Anchíalos. I found work as a stevedore, and met Leonárdos when he needed help to carry his bags off a ship I was unloading. That day Anastasia and her sisters brought my lunch to me, and Leonárdos met Dómna."

"How did Moschánthi meet her husband?" Dimitrios asked.

"Through Leonárdos. He and Demosthénes are good friends. He made the introduction, and Demosthénes — Helmis is his last name — married Moschánthi. After they were promoted, they decided that Piraeus would be a better location. They came here, and Anastasia and I followed."

It was only a matter of days before the six sisters from Sozópolis, three from each of two families, found themselves and their husbands together in Konstantínos' home, fast becoming close-knit expatriates.

With Dimitrios and Costas working at the port, and the positions Demosthénes and Leonárdos held as ship's officers, the families were able to barter Greek liquor and wine for food and British and French currency.

Konstantínos decided to reward himself for his efforts with a cup of coffee and a cigarette, and to write to Eléni. He prepared the coffee, lit a cigarette, and sat at the table with pen and paper.

April 6, 1917

My dear Eléni, Leonardo, and Evangelía, we kiss you, and pray that this letter finds you well.

Dimitrios will give this letter to a French sailor to mail for us. He sees many French and British sailors every day at the port. The French and English navies blockaded us, trying to force the king to enter the war. There is no food coming into Athens. The people are having a difficult time and there is hunger. Some talk of starvation.

We are fortunate. Do you remember the Zelios family? Their son, Costas, surprised Dimitrios when he appeared at the port to work. He married Anastasía Criticós. Her sisters are both married to ship's officers and are here in Piraeus. With their help, we are able to barter for and buy food.

By the time this letter reaches you, Easter will be long past. The day after tomorrow will be Palm Sunday and the start of Holy Week. It is hard for us to concentrate on Christ for we are once again in the middle of a war and thinking of survival. Will this land ever see peace?

Athens is in turmoil. Venizelos formed another government in Thessaloniki. He wants to go to war against Germany. The Bulgarians are at our frontiers waiting like vultures to eat Greek land.

We received a letter from Stávros. The Germans are only one hundred kilometers away from Paris. He had a surprise for us. He married a French girl named Marie-Yvonne. That was why he did not go to America with Zenóvios. Stávros wrote us there is a girl in Paris that Zenóvios wants to marry, a girl from Belgium named Leonie. She is trying to leave for Argentina with her parents. How will they ever get together?

God has his plan, they say. What can it be for us?

We have heard nothing from your mother. But don't worry. Sozópolis is out of the way of the war. Write to us when you can. I do not know when mail from America will be delivered again. This war will end one day. God willing, we will join you then.

With our love and many kisses,
Konstantínos and Sofía

MÁVROVO, KASTORIA, GREECE

Kallíope, her daughters, and women of the village followed behind Athanásios, his sons, and the men. They walked slowly out of the cemetery toward their home. The orchards were green, apple and pear blossoms had set their fruit well for summer maturation, and the grain fields were ready for harvest. Life was bearable here in the mountains in spite of the turmoil that the politicians were causing in Thessaloniki and Athens. The villagers would carefully hide this year's harvest and store it against the probability of war and scavenging armies.

Relatives and village friends joined Athanásios and his family at their home for the *makaría*. Kallíope and her daughters had prepared a light meal of fried lake perch, boiled greens, and bread that morning. Neighbors provided *paximádia*, the hard, twice-baked pastry.

Athanásios and Kallíope were in shock. It had happened so fast. No illness, no warning — just a scream from the stable when his sister, Polixéni, had gone to fetch Thomás. The thirteen-year-old boy had been sent to bring the mule to carry lunch to the men in the fields and was slow in returning to the house.

"Polixéni, what's wrong?" her mother called, running to the stable.

"It's Thomás. His head. It's bleeding. He isn't moving."

216

Kallíope rushed into the stable and saw her son lying face up, his eyes glazed and staring. She knew immediately that he was dead. She fell to her knees and wailing, took the lifeless body in her arms. Polixéni ran to the fields for her father.

The blow to Thomás's head had torn the flesh of his scalp and exposed shattered bone. Athanásios' mule, tethered in its stall, was munching fodder, its rear hoofs just clear of the boy's body. The usually placid mule had kicked Thomás's head.

After the *makaría*, Athanásios sat on the divan in the parlor of his home, surrounded by his sons, Kóstas and Aristédes, his brother Michaelis, and several village friends. They drank their coffee in silence until Michaelis asked, "Athanásios, what do you hear from Dimitráki?"

"We received a letter last week. He sews bear dolls in a German factory."

A neighbor, Evángelos asked incredulously, "He is working for Germans? Does he know that Germans are at our border?"

"He knows. America is in the war now. In America, Germans own doll factories while Americans get ready to fight their relatives. And soon, we'll fight the Germans too."

Michaelis turned to his nephew. "Have you heard anything from the officers in Kastoria, Kóstas?"

"No, Théo, not yet. I was told to stay in Mávrovo with the rest of the young men until I'm called."

Michaelis leaned forward. "I heard an officer in Kastoria complain about us because we are royalists. He does not remember that King Konstantínos freed us from the Turks and saved Thessaloniki from the Bulgarians in 1912. The Greek troops in the army to the north of us, between Prespa and Salonika, are with Venizelos, and with the British army. If King Konstantínos leaves, Venizelos will have us in the war against Germany."

Athanásios sighed. "Enough talk. Let me mourn my son. I have lost two now. I pray God will protect Kóstas and Aristédes here, and Dimitráki in America."

SEVENTH AVENUE, MANHATTAN

Peter pushed the door open and stood aside. "Go in, Jimmy."

Jimmy stepped into the shop and found a smiling man standing before him. "You want to be a furrier, eh? Good. Come in, come in." A few wispy gray hairs were combed back over the top of the man's balding head. Jimmy noticed that he had several conspicuous gold-clad teeth.

Peter made the introductions. "Kyrie Psáltis, this is my good friend, Dimitrios Mavrovitis. He calls himself Jimmy."

Psáltis took chairs from behind sewing machines and set them out for Jimmy, Peter, and himself. "Come, sit down for a minute." When he sat down, his stomach folded over his belt.

"Jimmy, I'm going to give you the chance to learn the fur business because Peter vouched for you. Besides, you're from Kastoria." Psáltis slapped his thigh with his hand to accentuate his pleasure at his last statement.

Jimmy stammered. "I was born in Mávrovo."

"All the same. Kastoria, Mávrovo, Krepení, and the other villages around the lake. All Romiói. All Macedonian. Do you have any questions?"

"No. But thank you for this opportunity."

"Well then, go with Panayiotis. He'll introduce you to Vasílis. Work hard and between us we'll teach you the trade."

Peter led Jimmy to the back of the shop, where another young man was putting on a white smock. He was in his early twenties, athletic-looking, with the shock of thick, straight-combed, black hair and a broad smile.

Peter introduced them to each other. "Jimmy Mavrovitis, this is Vasílis Rusuli. Everyone calls him Bill."

The two shook hands.

"Are you from Kastoria?" Bill asked.

"Yes, from Mávrovo."

"It's a small village across the lake, isn't it?"

218

Jimmy was about to take offense to the slight. Everyone in Kastoria knew and honored Mávrovo.

"It has been a long time," Bill added. "I haven't been home for over ten years."

"You came to America as a baby?"

"No, my father sent me to Russia when I was six — to St. Petersburg — to be raised by one of his cousins and apprentice in his fur business. I haven't been in Kastoria or seen my family since then."

Peter handed Jimmy a fresh white smock. "Here, Jimmy, take off your suit coat and put this on. We change them once each week."

Jimmy followed Peter's directions. The wrap-around cotton smock reached to his knees.

"Welcome to the Market," Peter said. "Now. Let's get to work."

Dingy high-rise buildings were the fur market's home. There was heat to warm the spaces in the winter, but not a lot of it. During New York summers, the shops were hot, humid spaces relieved only a bit when the wind blew fresh from the north and west, finding its way through open windows to restore the workers.

Two ethnic groups dominated the Market. Kastorians from Macedonia, including men from villages close to Lake Kastoria, like Jimmy's Mávrovo, and Jews from Eastern Europe and Russia who were the two-thirds majority. The two disparate groups conducted business with ethical standards rooted in their strong religious and cultural heritages. The Market worked on a system of honor and trust, and a man's word was his bond.

"Vasílis — Bill," called Psáltis. "Start Jimmy opening the new bundle of skins. Show him how to cut off the heads, paws and tails, and how to stretch them."

By noon, when the whirring of Bill's sewing machine stopped, Jimmy felt comfortable using a razor-blade knife on the precious furs that passed through his hands. Jimmy watched Bill get up to clear a small table in the corner of the shop.

"Time for lunch," Peter called.

Psáltis, Peter, and Bill washed their hands and opened packages of bread, cheese, olives, and slices of what looked like meat.

"Wash your hands and join us, Jimmy. There's plenty," said Peter. "Don't worry, you can contribute tomorrow."

"What's the meat?" Jimmy asked.

"Salami. It's Italian. Taste it. It's good," Bill promised.

Jimmy imitated Peter, sliced off a six-inch piece of bread, and tore it open. He heaped on cheese and salami and took a bite of the sandwich.

Peter smiled at Jimmy. "Do you like it?"

"Yes. It's good. So is the cheese. It's different."

"It's Provolone. Italian," Peter explained. "Bill, have you heard anything from the army?"

"Not yet. They'll probably call me in January. Have you registered for the draft, Jimmy?"

Peter answered for his friend. "Jimmy just turned seventeen in September."

"How does it work?" Psáltis asked. "Aren't they going to draft everyone?"

"No," Peter answered. "It's not that simple. This time they're only drafting men that were between twenty-one and thirty-one in June."

"Are you registered, Peter?" Bill asked.

"No. I wasn't old enough in June. My twenty-first birthday was in July."

"They make it too complicated," said Psáltis. "I don't think that you'll be gone long, Bill. Peter may never be called. Jimmy is too young. I think we will all be together this time next year. We'll train Jimmy to fill in for you until you get back."

They finished their sandwiches and talked about the fur season, what styles were selling, and which of them the best retail stores in

New York were ordering. Psáltis wiped his mouth with his napkin and offered toothpicks to his young employees from the box that he kept on a nearby shelf. Jimmy watched the men use the toothpicks. "Use one, Jimmy," Peter advised. "It will save your teeth."

Psáltis stood. "Let's clean up and get back to work."

CHAPTER FOURTEEN
1918
FIFTH AVENUE, MANHATTAN

Arm in arm with her cousins Hariclea and Katina, Lily turned left at the corner of 57th Street and 5th Avenue and strolled north towards Central Park. The girls, born in a world alien to 5th Avenue, had transformed themselves. Their appearance was indistinguishable from that of other well-dressed young women. Only their speech would have identified them as immigrants. Of the three, Lily's English was the most fluent and natural in pronunciation. Even her new name fit in. Hariclea had anglicized the spelling of hers — she substituted a 'c' for the 'k' in Haríklea, and dropped the accent in its written form. Katina remained Katina.

"It's wonderful to walk 5th Avenue without *mána*, or one of the boys." Lily said. "We shouldn't have to have chaperones all the time, especially during the day."

"What do you think I am?" Hariclea asked. "I'm a married woman. Your mother trusts me to look after you and Katina."

"Oh, please," protested Katina. "Just because you're twenty-three and have been married for six weeks. That makes you a chaperone, does it?"

Hariclea's husband, Fotios, had arrived in New York the previous June to claim his bride. He had escaped Greece just before the country entered the war against Germany. Prior to his leaving, Konstantínos Kapidaghlís gave him permission to marry his daughter with the stipulation, "You may marry Haríklea when her Théa Eléni approves."

Eléni made the timing of a wedding clear: "Fotios, you and Haríklea may marry when you have work and have saved a few dollars. And she has to have a proper place to live."

Eléni managed the process artfully. She had rented a one-room apartment next to her own for Hariclea and Katina when they arrived in the summer of 1916, and she had notified the landlord that she wanted the two bedroom apartment directly beneath hers for Fotios Demas and his bride. While it was large for a newly married couple, Eléni knew that Fotios' mother would join her son one day. By the time the apartment was vacant, Fotios had worked long enough, and earned and saved enough, for Eléni to give her consent.

Though sixteen, Katina was the most youthful and naive of the three 5th Avenue strollers. Hariclea had been an older sister to her on the trip across the sea and continued in the role while they lived next door to their Théa Eléni. Lily, Katina's junior by two years, behaved more like Hariclea. Katina was a child when compared to precocious Lily, who was learning the ways of women.

They stood for a moment at the corner of 59th Street. Katina pointed toward the motorcars that were pulling up to the entrance of the Park Plaza Hotel. Two women had just stepped out of a limousine. "Look at them. There."

"Don't point like that, Katina," Lily ordered, in a whisper. "*Mána* says it's not ladylike."

Bellboys carrying sets of matching leather luggage followed the women into the hotel lobby. The cousins were in awe of such luxury.

"They are so glamorous," Katina gushed.

Turning away, they crossed 5th Avenue to its east side and continued walking north. Taxicabs honked their way past chauffeur driven limousines. People walking into Central Park vanished behind groves of leafing trees.

Lily carried a gray hatbox whose lid, which was tied in place with a black satin ribbon, had an elegantly engraved label on top. She could easily have been taken for a young woman who had been shopping with friends at the stores along 57th Street or on 5th Avenue. But Lily had not been shopping — she was making a delivery from the milliners where she had worked since the previous fall.

Lily had tired of being a finisher under her mother's constant supervision; she wanted more independence. So, Eléni had arranged for her to apprentice to Madame Poulos, a milliner who provided custom hats to specialty stores like Bruck-Weiss and Rhea Brummerand, in addition to a few private clients. Lily had a natural talent for the work. She quickly learned to design and make hats from the myriad colors and textures of felts, ribbons, jewelry, veils, and feathers that surrounded her at Madame Poulos' shop.

"Why are the Americans having Easter this Sunday, Hariclea?" Katina asked. "Lent just started. Our Easter won't be until May."

"They aren't Greek. Our church is different."

"But why?"

"I don't know, Katina. I remember *babás* saying that Christians who were not Orthodox were barbarians." Hariclea thought for a moment. "Or maybe he said that the Orthodox Christians in Greece were barbarians." She paused as they reached a street corner. "They may have a different calendar."

They had walked a bit further, when Lily gestured toward a number chiseled into a stone block at the front of a building opposite Central Park. "This is the address." She climbed the granite steps to the front door of an imposing residence and pushed the doorbell. A tall, straight-backed, balding man dressed in formal black clothing and wearing white gloves opened the door. Lily thought he was the resident.

"Yes?" the man asked.

"I bring Madame's hat."

The man's lips pursed. He jerked his balding head backward. "Make your delivery at the servant's entrance."

"Where?"

"In back." He stepped forward on to the doorsill and pointed stiffly with his glove-encased thumb to a small gate at the side of the house. "Through there." He then turned and closed the door.

Hariclea and Katina, who stood at the curb, giggled as Lily turned toward them and shrugged her shoulders. She stepped to the wrought-iron gate, opened its latch, and walked down a long, narrow concrete path that led to the rear of the house. There was an entrance there, a door with a large brass doorknocker and a doorbell. Before she was able to use either, the door opened.

The same tall, straight-backed, balding man was standing in front of her. "Follow me," he ordered. Lily trailed the somber man through a vestibule, and then through a pantry whose shelves she thought were as fully stocked as a grocery store on 10th Avenue. She entered a hallway. To her right was a large kitchen, and directly in front of her was an oval space with hallways branching off in two directions. She heard another command: "Wait here."

In a moment, an elderly woman wearing an ankle-length black dress appeared at the end of the hallway directly in front of Lily. Long sleeves covered the woman's arms, and white lace surrounded her wrists and neck. Light falling from a window high behind her filtered through her white hair and gave her the appearance of an icon, a nimbus-crowned saint. Her face was pale

— wrinkled but not withered — and she had bright eyes and a sweet smile. She held her hands together in front of her, as if in prayer, and looked at Lily critically.

"You dress well, young lady."

Lily smiled at the complement. "Thank you, Madame."

"Let me see what you brought for me to wear at Easter, my dear."

Lily held the box forward. The woman untied the ribbon and took off the lid, handing it and the tissue that covered the hat to her butler. Lifting the hat from the box, she turned it in her hands and inspected it carefully.

"Lovely, lovely," she said and smiled. "Follow me."

The woman led Lily down the hallway to a grand foyer. A long, narrow, marble-topped table, shaped to fit against the curved wall, stood opposite the front door. On either side of the table were stairs that swept upward to the building's second story. An oval mirror suspended above the table reflected fresh flowers that had been arranged in the vase directly before it.

The gentle woman tried on her hat and turned her head from left to right in front of the mirror to make her assessment. "Yes, yes," she murmured. A shiny satin band encircled the navy hat. At its side, a trio of white feathers rose from the center of a delicate bow that couched a miniature mother-of-pearl brooch. The feathers swept gracefully over the hat's crown.

The woman looked at Lily's reflection in the mirror. "What do you think, my dear?"

"Pretty, Madame."

"Did Madame Poulos make this for me herself?"

"No. Me."

"You made this hat?"

"Yes, Madame."

"Very good. Excellent." The woman turned from the mirror and beamed at Lily. "Please tell Madame Poulos that I am pleased."

"Yes, Madame."

The woman touched Lily's face with her slender fingers. Lily was charmed. She raised her hand to touch the woman, but then stopped when the aged face moved back slightly, signaling a limit to the moment of familiarity.

"John, please give this girl twenty-five cents on her way out."

"What happened?" Katina asked when Lily came through the side gate.

"I've never seen … it's a dream. Look. Look what the lady gave me," she said as she held out her twenty-five-cent piece.

The cousins joined arms and retraced their steps toward the west side and its world of immigrants. Their dresses, coats, hats, and gloves — products of the skills honed by their family to serve the well-to-do — and their self-assurance made them inconspicuous on 5th Avenue. They thought themselves attractive and chic; and they were.

KALITHÉA, ATHENS, GREECE

Konstantínos and his family attended the Resurrection service and returned home in the early morning hours carrying lighted candles. Before entering the house, he fulfilled a tradition. He held his candle high and with it made the sign of the cross at the top of the doorframe.

Waking at dawn, Konstantínos rose from his bed to make coffee and roll his first cigarette of the day. He enjoyed both while reading a newspaper. The five women of the house were all asleep.

With her husband Ioánnis' death on Mt. Kitka, Sultána Thomá and her daughter Ioánna had joined Konstantínos and Sofía in Kalithéa, and had therefore become Konstantínos's responsibility. Sultána's son, Thomás Thomá, helped the financial situation by sending money to his mother from New York.

Konstantínos raised his eyes from the newspaper at the sound of his brother-in-law entering the kitchen. "*Hristós Anésti*, Dimitrios. You're early. Do you want some coffee?"

"*Alithós*. No. Thank you. No coffee." Dimitrios set down a large package. "Smarágda told me to bring the lamb to the bakery to be cooked. I stopped to borrow Sofía's large roasting pan."

"Where did you get it?"

"I traded with a farmer who was bringing his lambs into Athens. The baker will take some of the meat in exchange for the use of his oven."

"Will it fit in the pan?

"It's half a young lamb, about eight kilos. It will fit."

Konstantínos got up and rummaged in the closet that held the household pots, pans, and sundry other cooking implements. He pulled out the pan and set it on the counter. "It's bigger than I thought. Put the lamb in it at the baker's."

Dimitrios picked up the pan and the package and started toward the door. "Smarágda, the boys, and I will be back mid-afternoon. Sofía said that we'll have dinner before evening."

Konstantínos returned to his cigarette, coffee, and newspaper. He read an editor's opinion that with America in the war it would be over soon. *Well, he thought, at least when Prince Alexander became King, and Greece's policies came in line with the Allies, they lifted the blockade and food began to flow back into Piraeus. Venizelos outwitted poor King Constantine.*

He got up to empty what was left in the *ibríki* into his cup and thought for a moment about his brother and sister, Sofía's mother, and her father's brothers and their families in Bulgaria. He worried. *But what can I do? There is nothing I can do. They are out of the way of the war and probably safe.* He did not expect to receive any letters that would tell him about the conditions in Pyrgos or Sozópolis.

In the last letter he received from Paris, Stávros had written optimistically about the future.

> When peace comes there will be a huge demand
> for luxury clothing in America and Europe. Now,

even while the Germans are battering us with their new giant cannon, and flying airplanes over Paris to drop bombs, our firm manages to send beautiful collections to America's finest stores. Think what they will do when the war is over.

Don't worry about us here. The Parisians have grown used to war and its dangers. The cafés and restaurants are busy. The newspaper writes that the Ritz has some American guests who complain about the Boche cannonading and bombing Paris, and ruining their vacations.

While Konstantínos pondered his son's words, Calypso entered the kitchen. Yawning, she put her arms around her father's neck, her blond curls hiding her face. Theanó followed her younger sister into the room.

"*Hristós Anésti, hrisá mou.*" Konstantínos hugged and kissed his daughters.

"*Alithós Anésti, babás.*"

CENTRAL PARK, NEW YORK

Louie walked briskly from the subway station at Columbus Circle toward the mall at the south end of Central Park to attend a War Bond music festival held in honor of Italy, America's ally. That morning, men and women at Rosenbaum's factory had dropped money into Louie's hat for the Relief to Italy Fund. Mr. Rosenbaum exchanged the bills and change for his personal check and mailed it with a note from the workers to the Fund's banker, J. P. Morgan & Co., on Wall Street.

Once in the park, he join a throng of Italian men and women who waved small Italian and American flags and applauded enthusiastically at the orchestra's performance of *The Star Spangled Banner*. They exploded into cheers when the great tenor, Enrico

Caruso, entered the park and led his wife to the stage. People shouted their approval at his performance with bravos after each of the operatic arias he sang and were disappointed when he took a seat on stage to rest for a moment. There was a short pause, the conductor raised his baton, and the orchestra began to play the opening bars to *Va' pensiero*, the chorus that Italians had adopted as their national anthem. Every voice in the mall joined to sing the words of the Hebrew slaves longing for freedom in Verdi's opera, *Nabucco*. Emotions overflowed and tears streamed down cheeks.

Finally, in a bow to the United State's roll in the Great War, Caruso sang George M. Cohan's *Over There*, America's call to arms.

Jimmy, walking west along Central Park South after delivering a fox coat to a customer on 5th Avenue, heard an orchestra playing and a voice singing *Over There*. He stopped for a moment to listen and then went on toward the subway station at Columbus Circle.

The next evening after dinner, Jimmy sat at a reading desk of the new library on 40th Street and opened the pages of *The New York Times*. The elegant room, with its book-lined walls, marble floors, and hushed, reverent atmosphere, made Jimmy feel that he was in a cathedral of learning. Jimmy's English teacher at night school had advised him, "Read the *Times* every day, as much of it as you can, Jimmy. And carry a pocket dictionary. You'll learn English, and a lot about the world. It's an education."

Jimmy read the war news first, especially the reports of the September offensive near Monastir, north of Kastoria. The French and the British were attacking the Bulgarians in force. There was little news of the Greek army, which was fighting on the Macedonian-Thracian border. His brother, Kóstas, was there in the middle of the battle. Jimmy felt guilty — he would have been there too had he not come to America. But even in America Jimmy had been lucky. He missed having to register for the draft by one day. His eighteenth birthday was on thirteenth of September. The draft law in 1918 required men who were eighteen on the twelfth of September or before to register.

Jimmy turned the page of the newspaper and read the words:

CARUSO CHEERED BY 50,000 IN CENTRAL PARK
Sings 'Over There' and other War Songs

So that's his name. What a voice, he thought. He read on: Enrico Caruso – opera star

Jimmy got up from his chair and walked to a lectern that held a massive dictionary. "Opera — opera," he repeated to himself. He turned to a page with entries starting in l, and then m, n, and o. His fingers ran down the page until he came to the words: Onyx. Oodles. Oophore. Ooze. Opelet. *Funny words,* he thought. *Ah, opera.* He read: "A dramatic performance in which music forms an essential part ..." He stopped and looked up dramatic, and then performance, and finally, essential. *It must be like Greek drama. Aeschylus and Euripides,* he thought. *What a voice.*

The following Monday morning, Kyrie Psáltis took Peter and Jimmy to their first fur auction. The *Times* advertisement for the auction listed wolverine, fisher, fox, mole, house cat, badger, squirrel, lynx, and opossums of several types, polar bear, raccoon, skunk, marten, stone marten, weasel, muskrat, fitch, broadtail, seal, caraculs, and even water mice. *What would water mice be made into?* Jimmy wondered.

They walked from the shop to the Masonic Temple at West 23rd Street early in order to scrutinize the furs before the auction began. "Boys, we'll come to the auctions on Tuesday, Wednesday, and Thursday mornings. I am going to bid on blue and gray fox, marten, stone marten, and skunk. That's what we'll work on for next season." Each morning, before the auction began, Jimmy followed Psáltis from one bundle of pelts to another. Psáltis encouraged his apprentices. "Look at as many skins as you can, boys. I will show you what is important in the ones I know about. No one is an expert at everything."

Psáltis instructed his students with a running commentary during each visit to the auction. "See the uneven hair heights on the fisher? — Look at the different colors in this bundle of silver fox. — Think about how you would match these marten skins. — Can you see how light the veiling is on these chinchilla? — Look at the *grotzen* on the mink in this bundle. The hair along the back is heavier and darker than usual."

Jimmy witnessed thousands of skins change hands during the four days of the auction. On Thursday, he asked Peter, "Do you know who bought that last bundle of Russian sable? They had a rich color and sheen."

"I think Lefkowitz got them, but I'm not sure."

"No, boys," Psáltis interjected. "It was the Manolis brothers, and they were beautiful."

Psáltis bought stone marten on Monday, blue fox on Tuesday, gray fox on Wednesday, and skunk on Thursday. The larger, more prestigious manufacturers bid on the higher-end furs — Russian sable, chinchilla, and mink.

When they left the auction in the early afternoon on Thursday, Psáltis, pleased with his purchases, motioned to his boys to follow him. "Come on, boys. I'll buy you lunch at the Acropolis." Psáltis led them to a second-floor restaurant on 7th Avenue run by a Greek from Kastoria who knew the cuisine his furrier customers enjoyed.

At lunch, Psáltis explained how furriers risked everything on their choice of fur types. "That's the gamble, boys," Psáltis told them. "That and designs. If you don't pick the furs and designs that women want next season, you end up with a storeroom full of fur jackets and coats with no one to buy them, and no way to pay your bills. Read the fashion sections of the newspapers. Read fashion magazines. Keep up or go boom."

MÁVROVO, KASTORIA, GREECE

Athanásios came through the door calling to his wife, "Kallíope, we have a letter from Kóstas."

In moments Kallíope appeared. She sat next to her husband and waited anxiously for him to read the letter.

> My Dear Parents, I kiss you.
> I am sorry for the dirt on this letter. I write from a trench. I am not allowed to tell you where I am.
> The rest of the boys from Mávrovo are together with me. We look out for each other.
> No one from Mávrovo has been hurt. We expect to fight the Bulgarians tomorrow.

Athanásios paused for a moment. His voice trembled.

> Pray that we all come home safely, soon.
> Zíto Ellás. Zíto Vasiléfs.
> With kisses,
> Kóstas

"Is that all?" Kallíope asked.

"Yes. Thank God that we heard from him and that he's alive."

"Is there any more news in Kastoria?"

"The French officer told us that there's fighting between Florina and Monastir. The Bulgarians are retreating."

Kallíope stood, started toward the door and turned.

"Do you think that Dimitráki will have to fight in the American Army? Is he old enough now?"

"Maybe, if this war doesn't end soon. He is of age."

"Dear God," she said, crossing herself. "Protect Kóstas and end the war before the Americans make Dimitráki a soldier, and Aristédes is old enough to fight."

"*Amín*," Athanásios prayed, as he made the sign of the cross.

MANHATTAN'S WEST SIDE

Eléni and Louie sat exhausted in their small parlor after four days of anticipation and celebration. Their apartment, the one next door that Katina now shared with Lily, and Fotios and Hariclea's on the floor below, had been enlisted to handle the coming and going of family, friends and co-workers who had been invited to the party.

It had started on the Friday before when an erroneous report of the end of the war brought thousands of deliriously happy people into the streets of New York City. Many still wore gauze masks to protect themselves from influenza. Hearing and seeing a tumult in the street below, Mr. Rosenbaum called Eléni into his office. "Helen, close the factory. No one is going to do any work with this news. Celebrate."

Later in the day, they learned that the report had been wrong. New Yorkers' joyous bubble burst, and Louie and Eléni's party ended. That Sunday, at St. Elefthérios, they gave thanks for having survived the influenza epidemic and prayed for peace, and for the welfare of their families in Europe.

Before dawn on Monday morning, the eleventh of November, the sounds of horns and sirens woke Louie and Eléni. It was certain. The War was over. They and all New Yorkers resumed the celebration that had come to a standstill on the Friday before, this time with even greater enthusiasm. The city's streets filled with American born and immigrants. They climbed on top of the trolley cars and waved flags. Even the fresh memories of the influenza pandemic and the deaths it had caused could not prevent strangers from hugging and kissing.

Lily and her cousins hurried to shop and prepare platters of *tirópites*, *loukánika*, *taramasaláta*, cold lamb and chicken, cheeses, bread, salads, and olives. Wine bottles stood at both ends of a food-laden table. Family and friends gathered to celebrate in Eléni and Louie's apartment. They ate, drank, and gave thanks that the war had spared them and their families.

Early in the evening, Chris Capi arrived at his aunt's front door with a young woman on his arm. Eléni welcomed her nephew with a hug, a kiss, and a question in Greek: "Who is this girl?"

"Théa, this is Marion Gates," he answered in English. "She's in the Oratorio Society that I sing in."

Eléni hugged the round-faced, freckled, foreign-looking girl. "Marion. Come in." Eléni took Marion by her arm and led her into the room. "Come, Marion. Eat, drink."

Seventh Avenue, New York

Jimmy went to work on the morning the war ended. He and Peter waited at the door for Kyrie Psáltis, who arrived half an hour late.

The older man exclaimed, "It's over. What a morning."

Psáltis entered the shop, went directly to the cupboard and took out three glasses and a bottle of brandy.

"Come, boys. We'll drink to the end of the war, and you'll take the day off. Meet your friends and have a good time. I am going home. Where is Achilléas?" Psáltis had hired Achilléas to do uncomplicated beginner's work in the shop when the army had drafted Bill. Both Peter and Jimmy shrugged their shoulders to indicate that they did not know.

Peter drank the brandy down in one gulp. Jimmy, not used to hard liquor, coughed a bit. The drink made his throat burn.

"I heard from Bill," Kyrie Psáltis reported. "He's fine, and enjoying his training in New Jersey. That boy loves physical work. He won medals in the army's running and jumping contests."

"Do you think he'll be back soon?" asked Jimmy.

"Yes. The government will send him home as quickly as they can. New Jersey isn't far from 7th Avenue."

Psáltis saw Jimmy frown. "Don't worry, Jimmy. Business has been good. I will keep Achilléas. You won't have to go back to opening and stretching skins. Where is that boy?" He closed the shop and left for home. Peter and Jimmy went out on 7th Avenue and were soon among friends.

The following day Jimmy arrived at the shop to find Peter alone and asked, "Where is Kyrie Psáltis? And Achilléas?"

"Kyrie Psáltis was here a few minutes ago. He looked terrible. He thinks that he has the Spanish Flu. Achilléas is sick."

"What will we do today?"

"Kyrie Psáltis told me to match and cut the marten coat and work on the fox stoles. You have enough sewing to keep you busy for today, and I'll have more for you tomorrow."

They worked through that day, and most of Wednesday, each performing secondary tasks of opening and stretching skins, and nailing. On Wednesday afternoon, Peter complained that he had a headache and felt weak-kneed. When he failed to show up at the shop on Thursday morning, Jimmy went to Peter's one room apartment on West 23rd Street to find him in bed with a high fever.

Peter told Jimmy, "I thought the epidemic was over. Kyrie Psáltis, Achilléas, and I must be the last. You've been spared. Take today and tomorrow off. On Monday we should all be back at work."

On Thursday afternoon, Jimmy walked though Central Park and enjoyed its open space and serenity. Crossing the park and turning north on 5th Avenue, he came to the broad steps of the Metropolitan Museum of Art. Entering it for the first time, he wandered its vast galleries, and was overwhelmed by the number and beauty of Greek and Roman statues, oil paintings from Western Europe, and modern sculptures. Before this, most of the art he had experienced was the iconography of the Eastern Orthodox Church — dramatically angular, expressionistic, and vividly colored depictions of Jesus, Mary, and the saints.

On Friday, Jimmy lunched at the Acropolis restaurant on 7th Avenue with several friends who worked in the fur market. Afterward, he walked across 28thStreet to 5th Avenue and then north. He stopped at stores to look at their furs. Franklin Simon showed Scotch mole capes, Hudson seal coats, and broadtail wraps from Avioty in Paris. Bonwit Teller also featured Parisian designs in a variety of furs. Jimmy drifted from store to store, evaluating the quality of the fur pelts and the workmanship that had gone into the garments he studied.

When he reached 57th Street, he walked west to Broadway, and then south, passing restaurants that would soon empty as patrons left to make the curtain at one of many Broadway shows. He had never been in a theater and wondered what those entertainments were like.

Automobiles filled the streets surrounding Times Square. Honking horns and the voices of happy people confirmed that this first weekend after the end of the war was one for celebration. Jimmy passed the Astor Hotel, whose lobby was crowded with visitors arriving for the weekend. He continued down Broadway. Just past 40th Street, he saw an entrance to a big theater and recognized the name on the poster at the door: Enrico Caruso — the man whose voice he had heard weeks before in Central Park.

There was a queue at a ticket window counter immediately inside the entrance. Jimmy stepped into the lobby and got in line. In a few minutes, he reached the ticket window.

"How much?"

The clerk looked at him. "One dollar."

Jimmy frowned.

"It costs less to stand," he advised.

"Good. I stand."

Jimmy entered the Metropolitan Opera at the cost of the coins in his pocket. Before taking the place the usher showed him, he walked down the center aisle to look back at the ornately appointed house. Five tiers of seating rose up into the darkness. Elegantly dressed men and women entered what seemed to be separate little spaces in the first tier. He stood aside for equally smart couples that walked down the orchestra's aisle. Intimidated, he hurried back to stand at the wall behind the orchestra seats.

The audience applauded when the lights dimmed, and moments later an orchestra in the pit in front of the stage started to play. The curtain rose, and from the first scene to the end of first act, Jimmy responded emotionally to the orchestra's music and the artists' voices.

At the first intermission, the man standing next to Jimmy asked, "How you like?" He was short, rotund, and smelled of garlic. Thick gray hair fell to his shoulders. He squinted when he listened to Jimmy's answer.

"I like very much Caruso, and the lady."

"You like opera? You come a lot?" the man asked.

"First time. I like very much."

"You know story this opera?"

"No."

"Buy libretto." The man reached into his pocket and pulled out a folded pamphlet-like publication. "Like this. Tell story. Italian, English. Look."

Jimmy read several of the English words. "Tell story?"

"Yes. Buy outside."

The houselights darkened and the performance resumed.

Jimmy had recognized Caruso's voice immediately. The woman who sang with him was young and beautiful. He had never heard a woman sing in public, and had been taught that women who performed on stage were fallen, like prostitutes. But this woman sang with such beauty. *She can't be a bad woman,* he thought. When her character died in the last scene he was devastated.

After the curtain fell, Caruso and the woman came on stage repeatedly to enthusiastic ovations and applause.

On his way out of the Opera House Jimmy found the table with librettos for sale. They were expensive, thirty-five cents, but he bought one. That night he struggled to read as much of the story as he could before closing his eyes.

On Saturday, at the top of a page in *The New York Times*, Jimmy read the name of the opera he had seen: 'La Forza Del Destino'. Four lines below the opera's name he read: 'Rosa Ponselle Captivates ... brilliant debut ...,' and, 'There is one word with which to characterize Caruso's singing — glorious.' Jimmy opened his dictionary. He looked up 'captivates', 'brilliant', 'debut', 'characterize', and 'glorious'.

CHAPTER FIFTEEN
1919
MANHATTAN'S WEST SIDE

John Capidaglis led Chris up the stairs to Eléni's door. He waited for a moment before knocking and cautioned his half-brother, "Tell Théa Eléni everything. If you don't, I will." He knocked on the door.

In a moment, Eléni stood before them with her arms open wide in welcome. She had put on a few pounds since arriving in New York. That, and her stature and confident manner made her an imposing woman. "Come in, come in. What handsome boys. Your parents would be proud of you." She hugged and kissed them, hung their coats and hats in the entry closet and led them into the parlor.

Louie looked up from his letter writing. "*Kali spéra* Zenóvios, Hrístos," he said, using the young men's Greek names. Neither Louie nor Eléni used the brother's newly assumed American names, John and Chris.

"Sit," Eléni urged them. "Would you like coffee?"

They sat on an overstuffed sofa while Eléni went out into the hallway and knocked on the neighboring apartment door.

"Evangelía, Katina." she called. "Come into the parlor, your cousins are visiting. But first fix coffee, and make some for Leonardo, too."

Louie looked at John, and then at Chris. They both leaned forward and looked down. Chris' shoulders folded forward and he fidgeted, twisting one hand around the other.

"Is it getting colder?" Louie asked, breaking the awkward silence. Without raising his head, John answered, "Yes, I think it's warming up."

Louie's face showed surprise at John's incongruous response.

Eléni entered the room smiling. "Evangelía and Katina will be right in. Coffee is on the stove."

"Théa," John looked directly at Chris and not at his aunt. "Hrístos has something to tell you."

"Yes?" Eléni sat in a chair that faced the sofa and leaned forward. "What is it?"

Chris looked up. Perspiration formed on his brow.

Eléni's voice was impatient. "Hrístos, speak up. Tell me what the problem is."

He said nothing. Lily and Katina came through the door and broke the tension. "My handsome cousins," Lily cried. The young men rose to greet the girls.

Eléni saw that Chris was embarrassed. "Evangelía, take Katina into the kitchen and prepare some *paximádia*. Close the door. Zenóvios and Hrístos have some business to talk to me about."

With quizzical expressions on their faces, Lily and Katina obediently left the room. Louie sat back. Eléni was in control.

Chris looked down and twisted his fingers together.

"Go ahead," prompted John.

Finally, with his head down and staring at the floor, Chris murmured, "Théa."

"Yes?"

"Théa, do you remember the girl I brought to the party when the war ended?"

"Yes. The *Amerikanáda*. What about her?"

He looked up. "She sings in the Oratorio Society with me. We're close friends."

"Good. That's nice. What else?"

"I...she...she's in trouble."

"What kind of trouble?"

Chris' lips trembled. He choked out: "She's...ah...she's going to have a baby."

Eléni collected her thoughts for a few seconds. "What does that have to do with you, Hrístos? Or me?"

"Théa," he whispered. "What should she do?" He stared down at his shoes.

"Do? Have the baby. But that's not the question you're asking, is it? You're asking, 'What should I do?' Because it's your baby, isn't it, Hrístos?"

Lily entered the room carrying steaming demitasse cups on a tray. Katina followed behind her with a dish of *paximádia*.

"Put everything down, *korítsia*, and go to your rooms. I'll call you when your cousins are leaving."

"We want to stay and visit too," said Lily.

"Do as I tell you." Eléni's voice was stern. "Now."

They girls looked at each other, shrugged, and left the room. Once in the hallway, their curiosity prevailed. They left the door open a crack and held their heads close together to listen.

"Well, Hrístos? Answer my question. Is it your baby?"

Chris looked at his brother for help. He sighed and said, "Yes. It's mine." He looked up at Eléni and asked, "Is there anything we can do to get rid of the baby?"

Eléni rose from her chair and stood looking down at Chris. "Get rid the baby?" she said with disbelief. "Get rid of the baby?" she shouted. She raised her arm and brought her hand down fast and hard, slapping Chris across his face. He fell to his knees in front of the sofa. She hit him again.

Louie and John froze in shock. At each phrase that exploded from her mouth, Eléni slapped Chris' head with her open hand.

"Get rid of the baby? *Paliópaido*. Get rid of the baby? Weakling. You took your pleasure and now you want to run? You say 'To hell with the woman and the baby.'"

Louie snapped out of his daze, got up and stood behind Eléni, grasping her shoulders. "Enough, Eléni. Stop."

Chris sat on the floor and covered his head with his arms. There were welts on his face. Not a sound came out of him, not even evidence of breathing.

John looked stunned.

Eléni pulled free of Louie and knelt before Chris. "Hrístos, listen to me," she said softly. "Look at me. Listen to me."

Chris lowered one arm slowly.

"I won't hit you again. Hrístos. Look at me."

He lowered his other arm and lifted his head toward Eléni, who took it in her hands and kissed his forehead and cheeks. He was crying.

"Hrístos," she said gently. "You've behaved like a greedy boy, not like a man. You will take responsibility like a man. Bring your girl here tomorrow. What's her name?"

"Marion," he sobbed.

"Yes, Marion. Bring her here tomorrow morning at ten o'clock. We are all going downtown. You are going to be married. Your baby will have a name and a father."

"But Théa, I don't ..."

Eléni raised her voice. "Don't tell me that you don't anything. You be here with her at ten o'clock tomorrow. You liked her well enough to go to bed with her. You'll learn to like her as your wife."

Chris was silent. Louie was silent. John was silent.

"Sit on the sofa, Hrístos," Eléni ordered. "The three of you have your coffee. I am going to get some ice for Hrístos' face. But first I'll tell Evangelía and Katina to go to bed."

As Eléni approached the front door, she heard it close.

"Evangelía. Get in here."

The door opened and Lily and Katina stood there sheepishly.

"I know you were listening. You heard nothing. Go to bed. This is my family business. Now. Go to bed."

SOZÓPOLIS, BULGARIA

Olga knelt on the floor next to the bed, held her husband's limp right hand, and prayed. Her hair was no longer fine and gold. Age had coarsened it and changed its color to gray mixed with brownish yellow strands. Her eyes were deeper blue than they had been. The Russian accent she had brought to Sozópolis from the Ukraine was gone.

The evening before, her daughter Chrysóula had pounded on Vasilikí's door, calling, "Théa, Théa, something is wrong with *babás*. Please come."

While they hurried to Décimos' home, Chrysóula told Vasilikí that her father had felt faint during dinner. He had set aside his plate, saying that he was not hungry, and talked with her husband, Ángelos, for a few minutes. Suddenly, he slumped unconscious in his chair and fell forward onto the table.

After they carried Décimos to his bed, Olga sent Ángelos for the priest, and Chrysóula for Vasilikí.

Before Pater Elefthérios arrived, Olga prepared the small bedroom table according to custom. On it, she placed an icon of the Panaghía holding her infant Son, a Bible, and several unlit candles set in a bowl of sand. She then lit the oil-fed wick of a votive lamp and set it before the icon. A few minutes after Olga's preparations were complete, the priest entered the room with Chrysóula.

Pater Elefthérios' beard was full and white and fell to the middle of his chest. It hid sunken cheeks. The self-important priest was gone. In his place stood a weary, humble man with deeply set eyes and a furrowed brow. He was lean, more accustomed now to fasting than to feasting.

"Décimos, can you hear me?" the priest asked.

Décimos moaned and nodded almost imperceptibly. Pater Elefthérios opened the satchel he carried and set its contents on the table Olga had prepared.

Vasilikí entered the dimly lit bedroom with Chrysóula. At the sight of the priest standing over Décimos, she crossed herself and knelt on the floor before the icon, behind Olga. Ángelos stood in the corner of the room.

Pater Elefthérios' voice chanted, "Holy Father, physician of our souls and bodies ..." When he finished the petitions and prayers, he asked Décimos, "Can you talk?"

Décimos uttered a soft murmur. His head moved.

"It's all right, Décimos. Have you sinned?"

Again, a slight nod.

"Do you regret and repent your sins?"

A nod.

Pater Elefthérios absolved Décimos of his sins, recited the prayer of Holy Communion, took a small chalice and spoon from the table and said, "Open your mouth, Décimos. Open. Try." Nothing happened. The priest pried open Décimos's mouth with the fingers of one hand and emptied the communion spoon into it with the other.

"Pater, what is wrong with him?" Vasilikí whispered.

"Look."

The right side of Décimos' face sagged, without expression, in sharp contrast to the opposite side of his face, which continued to reveal his emotions. He was unable to move his left arm or leg.

"Apoplexy," the priest said.

Vasilikí crossed herself and took her sister-in-law in her arms.

"Courage, Olga," Pater Elefthérios said. "Panaghía will help you." They kissed Pater Elefthérios's hand as he prepared to leave. "I'll come tomorrow, Olga."

"Ángelos, please walk with Pater to his home," Olga asked.

Chrysóula remained with her father until dawn, mourning the man who now lay helpless in his bed. She remembered him waving to her from a ship as it left Sozópolis' harbor to sail south toward Constantinople, or north to Varna and Odessa. How tall and strong he had been, his form moving with the ship as it passed the breakwater, sure of his every move. When he returned, weeks later, he would burst through the door with the energy of a great wave, encompassing his family in his arms and distributing gifts from far-off ports.

In the morning, Vasilikí joined Olga in prayer at Décimos' bedside. She raised her head and said, "His brother should know, Olga. Have you heard anything of Ioánnis and Rhodóstama and their children?"

"No. Nothing. Konstantínos or Eléni may have. They shouldn't have left during the war," Olga fretted. "I hope they get through to Greece. Who knows where they are? I'm waiting for a letter from Katina. Thank God Chrysóula and Ángelos sent her to America before the war."

"Eléni will take good care of her," Vasilikí agreed, comforting her sister-in-law and friend.

"We're the only ones left. Chrysóula misses Katina. But she won't leave because of me. Will you go to America to be close to your girls?"

"I don't know. It is so far away. I miss my daughters and grandchildren, but I want my bones next to Hrístos. How will he find me if I die in America?"

Décimos moaned.

Olga struggled to make her husband comfortable. "Help me, Vasilikí. I'll lift his head. You put another pillow under it."

As strong as their peasant life had made them, the women found it difficult to arrange Décimos more comfortably. It mattered little. Décimos was past sensing discomfort.

Pater Elefthérios, who had visited in the morning, returned late in the afternoon.

"Is there any change, Olga?"

"No, none."

"Can Vasilikí and Chrysóula stay with you?"

"Yes, of course we will, Pater," Vasilikí answered.

"Ángelos is here when we need him," Chrysóula said. "He'll stay here with me tonight."

The women kept their vigil for three days. Décimos remained unconscious. He could not swallow water, and, as the hours passed, his breathing became labored.

It was the time of the summer solstice. The days were long, and the evenings soft, with gentle winds from the sea. At the end, they heard a final, peaceful whisper of breath. Vasilikí said that it was his soul leaving.

MANHATTAN'S WEST SIDE

Jimmy posed in front of the camera sitting, standing, full-faced, and in profile. Bill waited his turn to be the center of attention at Central Studio. The young men, carefully groomed and dressed in their best suits, were having portrait photographs taken to send to their families in Kastoria and Mávrovo as evidence of their good health and prosperity.

"Your mother won't recognize you," Bill teased.

Bill had returned from his army service in March and, for six months, he and Jimmy had worked for Kyrie Psáltis side by side with Peter and Achilléas, who had chosen Archie as his American name. Psáltis was fond and proud of his boys. They were hard working, honest, and eager to learn. Like most of their friends from Kastoria and its surrounding villages, they resolved to bring honor to their families and their origins. *Philótimi* was the word Psáltis used to describe them — young men with honor, dignity, a sense of right and wrong, and a commitment to duty.

The fur business boomed in New York City. It put enough money into Jimmy and Bill's pockets for them to buy fashionable clothing, experience Manhattan's nightlife and send funds to their families. They exchanged their timidity and uncertainty as poor, uneducated immigrants, for the confidence of independent, self-supporting young men, and they learned the language of society and business in America.

Although they were friends, Jimmy and Bill had different interests. Bill spent most of his free time at the Y.M.C.A., competing as a short to mid-distance runner and in other track and field events. Jimmy attended the opera once or twice each week during the season, standing at the rear of the orchestra with his libretto and opera glasses in hand. He attended English classes with Bill and Peter once a week.

Peter, who was on the parish board of St. Constantine and Helen's church in Brooklyn, nominated Jimmy to fill a vacant position; a responsibility in addition to his role an assistant chanter.

Jimmy, who took pleasure in chanting the responses and ancient hymns of the church, secretly wished he were able to sing the arias that he heard at the opera and knew by heart from listening to them on his Victrola. The thick, heavy, one-side only RCA Victor Red Seal discs that he purchased were a luxury, as was his habit of protecting his recordings by using a steel needle only three or four times. He would read the words of an aria from a libretto and sing along with Enrico Caruso and Beniamino Gigli in the privacy of his room.

On Sundays in the summer, he, Peter, and Bill went to the beach at Coney Island, parading their masculinity in fashionable solid navy tank top bathing suits with white belts.

Life was good in America.

PIER ON THE HUDSON RIVER SHORE, MANHATTAN

On a cold, late December day, in long winter shadows on a wharf at the shore of the Hudson River, Eléni embraced Zenóvios and his bride, Leonie. They had just arrived on a ship from Argentina. Lily, Louie, Hariclea and her husband, and Katina were there to welcome the young couple.

Immediately after the Armistice, Leonie had sent a wire from Buenos Aires to Zenóvios, addressed in care of Stávros in Paris. Stávros forwarded the wire to Zenóvios in New York, and Zenóvios immediately wired Leonie. Her response settled matters, and Zenóvios sailed on the first available ship for Buenos Aires. They booked passage on the next ship back to New York, and by the time the couple arrived, Leonie had grown accustomed to Zenóvios's new name, John, and to being Mrs. John Capidaglis.

"Where is Chris?" John asked, looking for his half-brother.

"At the hospital with Marion," Lily told him. "She is having her baby."

One hour later, Eléni led the group up the stairs to her apartment on 38th Street where everything was ready to celebrate Zenóvios and Leonie's marriage and arrival.

Chris waited at her door.

"Théa, it is a boy. I have a son," he announced proudly.

"*Na mas zísi*," the family cheered.

"Our first born in America," Eléni declared. "How is Marion?"

"She's fine, Théa."

"Did you bring her flowers?"

"Well, no."

"*Haíde*. Do it now. We'll all go to see her and your son tonight."

CHAPTER SIXTEEN
1920
MANHATTAN'S WEST SIDE

Each of three men carried a heavy case in his arms. One by one, they moved carefully up several slippery steps and entered the apartment building. This was their fourth trip from 10th Avenue. The first nine cases they had lugged contained wine.

"Louie, my back hurts." Fotios looked for a foothold on the ice-covered concrete.

Louie took Fotios' arm. "Here, steady yourself on the railing." Then he encouraged his second helper. "This is the last of it, Zenóvios. We're almost done."

Louie paused in the vestibule to catch his breath and asked Zenóvios, "Can you celebrate without whiskey? Without brandy? Can you eat *stefádo* without wine on the table?"

The final three cases that they carried down to the storage room contained bottles of the whiskey and brandy that Louie and Eléni found indispensable for entertaining, and for the treatment of colds and toothaches. In anticipation of the start of Prohibition,

Louie had paid a premium for the hoard even though the storeowner was a compatriot from Calabria.

"Let's have a little brandy to warm up and celebrate our good work," Louie suggested, taking a bottle out of a case. He locked the storage room door and led his helpers up the stairs to his apartment.

After they drank their brandy, they joined Hariclea, Leonie, Katina, Eléni, and Lily for dinner at a happily crowded table. The steaming *stefádo*, redolent with cinnamon, contained the rabbits that Lily had purchased on 10th Avenue, dozens of pearl onions swimming in a tomato and wine-based sauce flavored with bay leaves, cumin, several sticks of cinnamon, salt and pepper, and a dash of wine vinegar. It was accompanied by rice, chunks of feta cheese, olives, and warm sesame-covered bread.

While sopping up gravy with a large crust, Louie again posed the question he had asked earlier. "How can you eat dinner without wine on the table?" He filled his mouth with the bread, chewed and swallowed, and reached for his wine glass. The red liquid passed through his lips, leaving him with an impish smile on his face. "Bravo, Evangelía. *Stefádo, magnifico*." Everyone at the table joined in praise of Lily's cooking.

PARIS, FRANCE

Konstantínos re-read the letter he had just written before sealing it.

March 15, 1920

My Dear Eléni and Louie, I kiss you and Evangelía.

I am in Paris working on next fall's fashions. Stávros and Marie-Yvonne expect their first child in the early fall and are very happy.

Sofía, Theanó, and Calypso, and Smarágda, Dimitrios and their sons were all well when I left them in Greece two weeks ago.

We finally had news from Ioánnis and Rhodóstama. After they left Sozópolis, they were trapped for several months in a village in southern Bulgaria. Because the fighting made it too dangerous to travel south into Greece by land, Ioánnis decided to go north to Romania. They are in Constanza, and are happy living there in a Greek community. They will stay in Romania. Their sons found work with a Greek shipping company.

When I left Greece, Venizelos and the king were at each other's throats. Nothing has changed since 1915. With Greek troops in Smyrna, I think that the situation with Turkey will get worse.

The idea of a new empire is blinding Greece. Reality has left our people. Their hearts are in Constantinople, and I am afraid that their hearts are going to be broken. We will never have our capital there again. Greeks will have to be satisfied with Athens.

It is time for us to leave Greece. My plan is to return to Athens in the summer and then to go to Bulgaria before fall to bring your mother back to Kalithéa with me. If I can convince them, I will bring Olga, Ángelos, and Chrysóula as well. I do not think that they will come. Even your mother may not want to leave Sozópolis. It has been her whole life.

Dimitrios and Smarágda will stay in Athens with their sons. Dimitrios is crazy with his political and labor associations here, and is excited about the revolution in Russia. I have tried to persuade him to be less at the front of his group, and pleaded with him to think of his family first. There is no talking to him.

I wrote to Zenóvios yesterday. He will tell Hrístos and Haríklea of my plan.

God willing, your mother will be with you next year, and we will follow after I settle our business in Athens. I expect that Stávros and Marie-Yvonne will be in America as soon as they can travel with their baby.

As for Sultána, your sister has not made up her mind. She will send Ioánna to New York, either with us or before. Sultána may return to Sozópolis.

Costas and Anastasía Zelios will leave for America in a few days, and bring Moschánthi and Dómna with them. I gave them your address. They will be on the King Alexander with Anastasía's brother-in-law, Leonárdos Panteliás. He is one of the ship's officers.

I kiss you all,
Konstantínos

OYSTER BAY, LONG ISLAND

Eléni had longed for a day by the sea, so Louie, and his brother, Luigi, organized an outing for her. At dawn on a clear, pleasantly warm Sunday in June, four automobiles loaded with family, friends, and picnic baskets full of food and drink, left the West Side of Manhattan. The caravan crossed over the East River on the Queensboro Bridge and motored to the shore of Long Island Sound's Oyster Bay.

By mid-morning, Louie, Luigi, Chris Capi, Costas Zelios, Fotios Demas, Thomás Thomá, and John and Stávros Capidaglis were gathering mussels and clams, and fishing for flounder, while the women prepared the picnic site, took walks along the beach and chatted about their lives. Lily, Louie's sister, Philomena, Katina, Hariclea, and Marion were busy with Chris Capi's son, little Robert, whom they called Bobby. His was the first Anglo-Saxon name in the family — an early sign of a strained relationship between Marion and Chris. By insisting on a non-Greek name, Marion had demonstrated that her cultural identity was not going to be overwhelmed by Chris's. She relented when Chris demanded that Robert's middle name be Constantinos in honor of his father.

Dómna and Moschánthi were there with their sister Anastasía and her husband, Costas, who took the role of cook. He built a fireplace of rock, gathered firewood, and prepared kettles for steaming and a grill for broiling. From the time they had bonded with Konstantínos and Sofía's family in Kalithéa, Dómna and Moschánthi frequently attended family gatherings without their husbands. They had become accustomed to the lonely times when their men were at sea. Their friends made sure that they were always included in holiday and party gatherings.

In the afternoon, Costas steamed mussels and clams, and grilled fresh fish over driftwood embers. Cold chicken, lamb, and *dolmádes*, were set out on blankets and sheets with salads, bread, cheese, olives, and cold cuts. The company ate and drank the beer and wine they had chilled in the water of the bay. They talked about their families, their lives in New York, their work, and their dreams. When the afternoon flowed into evening, they added fuel to the fire and circled round it. As they listened to the snap and hiss of the burning wood, the wind, and the recurring sounds of the gentle surf, a whispering, haunting melody rose from within Anastasía. Plaintive words that expressed loss of place and identity joined her florid vocal line. Anastasía's lament, and the *amanés* that followed, awakened in them bittersweet memories. When her voice stilled, they gathered their belongings, loaded the automobiles, and in the twilight returned in silence to the West Side of Manhattan Island. Their thoughts were of homes and lives they had left far behind, and of twilights over a distant sea.

Sozópolis, Bulgaria

Holding her embroidery, Vasilikí sat in the late summer afternoon sunlight that streamed through her parlor window. Her eyes were sharp enough to thread a needle and follow a pattern. The sound of footsteps warned her that someone was mounting the stairs to her front door. There was a knock.

"Kyria Vasilikí?"

"Yes, who is it?"

"Konstantínos."

"Konstantínos?"

Vasilikí was on her feet and at the door in an instant. She opened the door and her arms to her son-in-law. "Konstantínos. Konstantínos, it's you," she said pulling his head down to kiss him.

"Yes, it's me." His hug lifted her little body off the floor. "Kisses from Sofía, Smarágda, and Sultána, Dimitrios and all the children."

"Are you hungry? What can I get you?"

"Nothing. I stopped to see Chrysóula before I came here and had something to eat with Ángelos."

"I can't believe my eyes. How is Sofía? The children? What have you heard from Eléni?"

For the better part of the two days that followed, surrounded by Vasilikí, Chrysóula, and Ángelos, relatives, and friends, Konstantínos told stories about Kalithéa and Athens, Sofía and her sisters and the children, and about his sons in Paris and his trips there. They listened to how Eléni had found them in Kalithéa, and what he knew of her life and success in America.

On the third morning after his arrival, Konstantínos sat quietly with Vasilikí drinking the coffee she had prepared for him, and said: "It's time for us to talk about America. I came here to bring you to Greece, and then to send you to Eléni."

"How can I leave Hrístos and my father and mother? They are here. I visit and pray for them almost every day. What will I do in America?"

"You'll be with Eléni and Evangelía. Sofía and I will follow. Most of your grandchildren will be there. The Panaghía will listen to your prayers for Hrístos in America as well as here."

Within two days, she resolved her conflict. She gave most of what she owned to Chrysóula, embraced her and Ángelos for the last time and, with two cloth cases that contained her clothing, left the city she and generations before her had called their home.

Her last image of Sozópolis was its small harbor, its anchored caïques bobbing up and down in gentle swells, and seagulls rising from the water, circling the bay, and becoming pinpoints in the sky.

BAY RIDGE, BROOKLYN

The real-estate agent had given Eléni directions on the phone and had assured her that she could not get lost. "Just get off the train at 69th Street. It's that easy."

Climbing out of the subway station's darkness at 69th Street and 4th Avenue, Eléni and Lily saw a man's dark shape against the sky at the top of the stairs. A voice asked, "Kyria Perna?"

Eléni shielded her eyes from the bright October sun, and answered with a question. "Kyrie Pappas?"

"*Chairetai*," he said. "Welcome to Bay Ridge."

As they shook hands, Pappas said, "This young lady must be your daughter?"

"Yes, my daughter, Evangelía."

"Lovely girl. Did you have any problem getting here?"

"No, but the ride was a little longer than I'd expected."

"But look where you are. Clean air. Bright blue sky. Peace and quiet. Come, we'll go to the house." Eléni and Lily followed Pappas down 69th Street in a direction that led toward New York Bay.

Eléni liked the slim and vigorous agent. Businesslike, Pappas wore a wing-collared shirt and bow tie, and carried his fifty years lightly. He mixed English with Greek as he told them about this neighborhood in Brooklyn called Bay Ridge.

A few days before, Eléni had received a wire from Konstantínos informing her that her mother was in Athens. He reported that Olga, Ángelos, and Chrysóula remained in Sozópolis just as he thought they would, and that her mother would be on her way to

America within weeks with Fotios Demas's mother and Ioánna Thomá. At seventeen, Ioánna would look after her grandmother and her cousin Hariclea's mother-in-law on the ship. "Smarágda and Dimitrios have decided to stay in Piraeus with their sons," he wrote. "But Sofía, our girls, and I will be with you in America in a few months."

"Louie," Eléni said the night she received the wire, "I'm going to buy a house."

Louie put down his newspaper. "How much cash will we need?"

"No, Louie. I am going to buy the house with my money, what I saved. You keep your money. I want the house to be in my name only."

"But we're married, Eléni. I want to help you with this."

"I know you do, and I'm grateful. But I want to know that Evangelía, my mother, and I will be secure, no matter what happens to me, or to you."

When Eléni asked friends and people at work about buying a home, Kyria Poulos, who owned the millinery business that employed Lily, suggested, "Come where my husband and I bought a house. It's a good neighborhood," she said, "and the subway makes it easy to travel back and forth to work. I'll call Kyrie Pappas for you. He helped us."

Pappas turned left at the corner of 3rd Avenue. Eléni and Lily followed.

"There's the apothecary, and there, a store for newspapers and cigars. Here, this is Cosentino's Fish Market. Look at the fish in the window. Beautiful, yes?"

Before turning right at the next street, Ovington Avenue, Pappas stopped for a moment at the corner and pointed down 3rd Avenue saying, "Right there, in the middle of the block, a bakery, and a grocery store. Across the street, the meat market, and a little further down a good delicatessen. The German owner even sells olives, and *féta* and *kasséri*."

He led them along Ovington Avenue. Giant elm trees stood in front of a long line of brownstone houses. Pappas stopped at the third one.

"This is it," he said, turning into the small courtyard. "There's no one at home. I have a key. Come in."

Eléni inspected the house from its basement to the third floor. Electric fixtures had replaced gaslights on the walls, and there were electric outlets in every room. The living and dining rooms boasted elegant, decoratively painted molded ceilings, and rich, dark oak wainscot.

In the basement, Eléni found a hatch that opened into the front courtyard. From it, a chute led to the cellar's coal bins. There was ample storage space, a coal furnace with a hot-water heater, and a room outfitted as a small second kitchen with two deep sinks for washing clothes. A stairway led from the basement to the garden.

Lily ran up and down the stairs, opening closets and inspecting the bathrooms.

"It is beautiful, *mána*. Can we buy it?"

Eléni turned to the realtor. "Kyrie Pappas, I would like to look at the garden."

"Certainly, Kyria. This way."

Pappas led Eléni and Lily through a large kitchen and a small vestibule that opened into the garden. She walked to the rear of the space and looked back at the house. The brownstones attached on either side of it had far nicer gardens, with trees that offered shade and paved areas that accommodated garden tables and chairs. Except for a magnolia tree at the back and a few rose bushes placed at random, the plot that she stood on had nothing but uncultivated soil and weeds. In her mind's eye, she saw fruit trees, flowers, and roses surrounding her family at a long table laden with food. As she started back toward the house, with Lily and Pappas following closely behind her, the thorns of a rose bush snagged her sleeve. Eléni smiled. "Ah, the rose bush wants me."

Pappas accompanied his client to the subway station. His parting words were: "It's a wonderful house, Kyria Perna. And there's a school for your grandchildren, when they come, just two blocks away."

The next day, Eléni telephoned Pappas. "I want to buy the house. Ask the owner if he will accept nine thousand five hundred dollars. You said that he would lend money to me. Ask him if he'll lend six thousand." Pappas was not used to doing business with a woman and worried about the owner's response. The seller had no qualms. He accepted three thousand five hundred in cash and gave Eléni a mortgage loan in her name for the balance.

On the Monday before Christmas, Eléni moved into her brownstone on Ovington Avenue with Louie, Lily, and Katina. Fotios and Hariclea stayed on West 38th Street, taking over Eléni's larger apartment and preparing it for the arrival of Fotios's mother.

Offering a modest rent, and giving him the assurance of help for Marion, Eléni persuaded Chris Capidaglis to take the third floor of the house for his new family. With them upstairs, she thought, she would be better able to help Marion control her handsome husband.

A few days after Eléni moved her family into their new home, Costas and Anastasía Zelios gave thanks for the delivery of their first child, Dimitrios. Eléni and Lily lost no time in visiting Anastasía.

Rocking Anastasía's newborn, contented baby in her arms, Lily asked Anastasía, "Have you decided on anyone to be his godmother?"

"No, not yet."

"May I? I promise I'd be a good godmother."

"I'd like that, Evangelía. Let me talk to Costas."

Eléni was happy when Anastasía and Costas told Lily that they wanted her to be their son's godmother and christen the boy

Dimitrios. The new relationship firmly cemented the bond between the families from Sozópolis.

A gnawing worry from the past plagued Eléni. In a quiet moment, she took Anastasía aside. "Anastasía, we are like sisters." She hesitated, looking down for a moment, and then resumed. "I want no one to know about Spíros Stamatiou — about how I came to America."

"I've never talked about him."

"I know. I have asked the same thing of everyone in my family. Will you help me?"

"Yes, of course."

"Will you ask Costas never to mention Spíros?"

"Yes. Don't worry. Costas never respected him. He thought Spíros was weak."

Eléni and Anastasía had an understanding.

CHAPTER SEVENTEEN
1921
CHELSEA PIERS, MANHATTAN

An unusually warm early January day allowed two petite, elderly women in ankle-length wool dresses to huddle next to each other on the ship's deck from the time it entered New York Bay. Behind them, seventeen-year-old Ioánna Thomá stood ready to help the women; her grandmother, Vasilikí, and Sofía Demas, the mother of the man who had married her cousin Hariclea. The three had shared a second-class cabin for the trip across the Atlantic.

A gigantic statue of a woman wearing a crown and holding a torch towered in the middle of the great bay. It amazed them. And they were awed at the sight of buildings that reached to the sky above America, taller and greater in number than they ever could have imagined.

The ship eased into its berth at the shore of Manhattan's Hudson River. A multitude on the wharf looked up to the ship's rail, waving and calling to passengers above them. Vasilikí looked down in bewilderment, not recognizing anyone.

Ioánna shepherded her wards down the gangway and into the crowd on the pier. She sought a friendly face until she heard: "Ioánna. Ioánna. Here. It's me. Thomás."

She turned to see her brother's round, red face smiling the great grin he had had from childhood. From behind him, an excited family rushed to encircle her, her *yiayiá* Vasilikí, and Sofía Demas.

Eléni stepped forward. She took her mother in her arms, cried and murmured tenderly, "*Mána mou, mána mou.*"

SEVENTH AVENUE, MANHATTAN

Bill whispered, "Look. That's the girl I told you about." He was at the sewing machine directly behind Jimmy.

They watched Kyrie Psáltis greet a young woman and usher her into his small office area. She removed her hat and gloves, and then her coat to reveal a slender figure clothed in a dark gray wool suit. The multicolored silk scarf around her neck brightened her appearance. Her face was oval — her hair, curly and black — her complexion, clear and fair — and her eyes, bright blue. She spoke to Psáltis for a moment, then sat at his desk and turned her attention purposefully to the papers and ledger before her.

"She's the bookkeeper, Jimmy."

Jimmy turned his head and whispered over his shoulder. "She is beautiful. Kyrie Psáltis must think a lot of her to let her sit at his desk. Are you going to greet her?"

"Yes, in a few minutes."

Bill had talked about nothing but this woman since he met her four weeks before at the Kastorian Furriers' Christmas dinner dance. Kyrie Lagounis, one of her clients, had escorted her to Psáltis' table and made introductions. "Kyrie Psáltis, this is the wonderful bookkeeper I told you about, Rose Dimitroff."

"*Chairetai*, Kyrie Psáltis," she smiled. "*Kalá Hristoúgena.*"

"Merry Christmas," Psáltis responded, visibly enjoying his use of the American greeting.

Bill gazed at the young woman while Lagounis praised her abilities and Psáltis succumbed both to his need for her services and her charm. Within minutes, she had agreed to keep Psáltis's books in the New Year. Before she left the table, Bill stood and bowed, saying, *"Kalá Hristoúgena.* My name is Vasílis Rusuli. I work for Kyrie Psáltis."

Rose smiled at Bill. "Perhaps I'll see you at Kyrie Psáltis' then. Excuse me, I must return to my table. Merry Christmas."

The following Monday morning Bill was waiting for Kyrie Psáltis at the door of the shop. "Is Rose Dimitroff going to keep your books?" he asked before Psáltis had a chance to get his coat off.

"Rose? Dimitroff? Oh, yes. Yes, she is."

"Will she start soon?"

Psáltis turned to Bill. "Are you interested in bookkeeping?" He saw the earnestness in Bill's face. "Yes. She'll start soon. She is a bright young woman. Good-looking too, eh?"

"Do you know if she's spoken for? Does she have a family?"

"She lives with her mother and her brother. They are refugees from the war in 1913. Bulgarian father, killed in the fighting. Their mother is Greek."

"Is her brother the head of the family?"

"He's the head all right. Louis Dimitroff is smart and successful," said Psáltis. "He sells life insurance and goes to school at night."

Bill counted the days until Rose appeared at the shop. Now that she was here, his stomach churned and his palms sweat at the thought of speaking to her.

Jimmy prodded him. "Go ahead. Talk to her. She seems nice."

Bill summoned all his courage, got up from his sewing machine, smoothed his hair with his hand and took the few steps to where Rose sat working. "Good morning, Miss Dimitroff."

She looked up and stunned him with her smile. "Good morning — Vasílis, isn't it?"

"Or, Bill."

One timid word between them followed another until somehow they arranged that they would see one another at a dance at the McAlpin Hotel the first Saturday in February. "I'll be there early," Bill said. He hesitated for a moment, and then added, "I would like to meet your brother at the door."

Rose smiled. "That's good. He is stricter than most fathers."

BAY RIDGE, BROOKLYN

Vasiliki sat in the sunlight that entered the kitchen through the frost-framed window and looked out to the garden. Snow covered the ground, and mounded over azaleas and pruned rosebushes. Her eyes brightened when she saw sparrows peck at the suet Lily had tied to the top of the wire fence, which had a ridge of snow running its length. Each time they approached the treat, their beating wings created little clouds of the powdery stuff.

Her large, upholstered rocking chair surrounded Vasiliki's small form. It had been the last of the purchases Eléni had made to assure her mother's comfort. She furnished a small room next to the kitchen for her mother with a bed and nightstand, a set of drawers, a mirror, and a shelf built into its corner to hold icons of the Virgin and Child, and of Sozópolis' patron saints. An oil-filled votive lamp suspended from the ceiling by three linked brass chains hung above the icons. Its flickering wick created a soft, red glow in the corner of the room, reassuring Vasiliki as she lay in her bed.

Vasiliki fell in love with her Italian son-in-law. He was as attentive and caring as he would have been to his own mother. And she adored Evangelía — Vasiliki had difficulty with her granddaughter's new name, Lily — though she worried and fussed about Evangelía's short dresses, immodest behavior, and even boldness. No man in Sozópolis would want such a woman. For her part, Lily tried to dissuade her grandmother's disapproval by showering her with care and affection. Vasilikí came to recognize how similar Evangelía was to Eléni. Both were strong and independent.

After her grandmother's arrival in America, Lily left her job as a milliner to become full-time housekeeper for the family. While Eléni and Louie worked, Lily cared for her grandmother, shopped, prepared meals, and did laundry. She was happy at home, serving her family. Her cousins often visited her and their grandmother during the day, stayed for lunch and occasionally went shopping with her in downtown Brooklyn. *Yiayiá* Vasilikí encouraged Evangelía's homemaking and made frequent, straightforward suggestions about how she might best prepare for marriage.

Lily did not need coaxing. She already anticipated having a husband, children, and a home of her own.

Anastasía and Costas Zelios moved into an apartment just three blocks away from Eléni. Dómna and Moschánthi followed Anastasía, and took apartments next door to each other, near to their sister. Lily visited with them every few days, especially to see her godson. She held Dimitrios and played with him at every opportunity.

Eléni was aware of her daughter's growing interest in marriage and family. As much as she wanted Lily close to her, she wanted to keep her daughter safe from the excesses of American life. The best way to accomplish that was to see her married and settled. When Eléni heard that the Kastorian Furriers Association was sponsoring a Greek dance at the McAlpin Hotel in February, she decided that it was time to present Lily as a marriageable young woman.

THE MCALPIN HOTEL
BROADWAY AT 34TH STREET

Bill, Peter, and Jimmy entered the McAlpin Hotel's lobby at eight-thirty, half an hour early, and a full hour and one half before any significant number of people would arrive. Located within walking distance of the West Side, where many Greek immigrants lived, the McAlpin was a center for their social occasions.

After they checked their coats and hats, Bill led his friends to the restroom. He inspected himself carefully in the mirror, adjusted his tie and combed his hair.

Jimmy reassured him. "Bill, relax. You look fine – handsome. She'll be impressed."

"I wonder what her brother is like," Bill worried aloud. "Kyrie Psáltis told me that he is three or four years older than Rose. That must make him about my age." He frowned. "He's very successful."

Bill had repeated the same concerns to Jimmy and Peter every day, several times a day, for two weeks.

"Come on, Bill," Peter suggested. "Let's find a table where we can see the ballroom's entrance, order mixers and have a drink. I have a flask of scotch. You'll be able to watch for her."

Louie, Eléni, Lily, and her cousin Thomás climbed the stairs at the 34th Street subway station and walked to the McAlpin. Silk stockings, high heels, and a short, bare shouldered formal dress under a wrap cloak were not good choices for a cold winter night with ice and snow on the ground. But neither weather nor street conditions fazed Lily. She was young, and excited at the prospect of dancing the night away.

"Is that the way you're going to go?" Vasilikí had asked when Lily entered the large kitchen and twirled around in front of her flabbergasted grandmother. "Bare shoulders? Legs showing? What are you?"

"This is America, *yiayiá*. This is how we dress here." She kissed her grandmother's cheek. Smiling exuberantly she said, "I'm going to dance all night."

"Eléni, Eléni, where are you?" Vasilikí called.

Eléni hurried down the hallway into the kitchen. Her mother's disapproving look criticized Eléni's appearance too. "Are you going to let Evangelía go out like that?"

"Yes, *mána*," Eléni answered soothingly. "She'll be fine. No one will think badly of her. Louie and I will be there."

"And she'll dance with a man's arms around her waist, like she did here with Thomás?"

"It's all right, *mána*. We'll watch her."

"Have ten eyes," Vasilikí cautioned. "Ten eyes." She shook her head sadly and murmured, "It's sinful." She clicked her tongue and repeated, "Sinful."

Once inside the McAlpin, Thomás waited in the lobby while Lily went to the powder room. She and several other young women admired themselves in the mirrors and made last-minute adjustments to their hair and make-up. Lily stood next to a young woman who asked, "Are my seams straight?"

"Turn around. Lift your skirt a bit. Your right stocking needs to be straightened."

"Thank you." She worked on her right stocking. "My name is Rose, Rose Dimitroff. Is that enough?"

"Yes, it's straight. I'm Lily Athenas."

Lily liked the sound of her name, Athenas. She had used it for only a few months. Eléni had decided long before that Evangelía would never use Stamatiou as her last name, and that it should be different from Perna. "Not Atanasov," she told her daughter. "It makes you a Bulgarian. Your father's name was fine in Pyrgos, but not here. I used Athanasiou in Greece. Athanas is close enough, and it's Greek."

Lily mulled it over for a minute. "May I use Athenas? We came from Athens, and it sounds like Athanas."

"Yes, yes, that's fine. Evangelía Athenas. I like that."

Rose brought Lily back to the present with a question. "Have you been inside, Lily?"

"No, have you?"

269

"Not yet. My brother is waiting for me at the door."

"My cousin is with me. I hope someone asks me to dance."

"Sure they will." Rose smiled at her. "I'll see you later."

Lily looked at herself in the mirror one more time, and, satisfied, glided out of the powder room, took Thomás' arm and entered the ballroom. Inside, families sat with their daughters, keeping them in sight every moment they were on the dance floor. Mothers accompanied their daughters to the powder room. Single men sat together at tables, or stood in small groups at the side of the room.

Lily made her way toward Eléni and Louie, who were sitting at a table close to the dance floor. She saw Rose standing with two young men. They were shaking hands.

Jimmy, who sat next to Peter, saw Lily walk into the room. "Peter, do you know that girl? The one that just walked in. The fair one — with black hair."

"No, I don't think so. The people at the table she went to must be her parents. I don't recognize them from the market."

Jimmy's voice was urgent. "How can I meet her, Peter?"

"You, too?"

"Don't make fun of me."

Peter raised his eyebrows and shrugged. "All right," he said. "Walk up to the table and introduce yourself to her parents. Then ask them for permission to ask her to dance. But be sure she's not wearing a wedding ring. I don't think she's married. The man with her acts more like a brother or cousin than a husband."

"I don't know how to dance," Jimmy said.

Peter was incredulous. "Well then, ask them if you can introduce yourself to her. No, that won't work." He thought for a moment, and said, "I'll go to meet her, and introduce you to her on the way to the dance floor."

Bill returned to the table as Peter got up. "Her brother invited me to join them at his table."

"Bravo, Bill," said Peter. "Now let's see what I can do for Jimmy."

"Jimmy? Where are you going, Peter?"

"Just watch."

Later that evening Peter introduced Lily to Jimmy and Bill. She and Jimmy spent a few seconds in a casual exchange. Then he watched her dance with other young men and tried not to make his interest in her too obvious.

Whether the young people danced to Greek or American music, chaperoning fathers, mothers, aunts, uncles, godparents, and cousins monitored their every movement to assure that good names and reputations stayed intact.

Bill danced with Rose twice.

Peter, secure, and at ease in the social situation, became Jimmy's role model. Leaving the lobby of the McAlpin Peter advised Jimmy: "Take dancing lessons. Soon."

Eléni turned to her daughter on the subway ride to Bay Ridge. "Did you like Peter, the tall young man you danced with? The one that introduced you to his friends."

"Yes, mána. He is elegant."

"You'll meet more young men," Eléni said. "There's no rush."

Louie, who sat on the other side of Eléni, listened to the conversation without comment. The rumble of the train had almost lulled him to sleep when Eléni nudged him. "We're at 59th Street, Louie. Next stop, 69th Street."

Walking home holding her mother's arm, Lily thought about how wonderful the evening had been. She had met young men, been admired, and danced almost every dance. She was thrilled when Peter Stamatis asked her to dance. He was mature, tall and good-looking — really a man. The boy he had introduced her to, Jimmy, was handsome, but so shy. He didn't even ask her to dance. *Oh, well.*

271

ST. CONSTANTINE AND HELEN GREEK ORTHODOX CHURCH
SCHERMERHORN STREET, BROOKLYN

Little Dimitrios Zelios splashed the water in the baptismal font with both of his hands while Anastasía beamed at him. Lifted from the font, wrapped in a towel, anointed, tonsured, and dressed in his baptismal clothing, his Théa Dómna handed him to his proud *nouná*, Lily, to receive communion.

Louie stood as godfather to the baby. The baby's parents and the priest overlooked Louie's Italian Roman Catholicism.

Costas and Anastasía held a reception for family and friends in the church basement. Lily could not let go of her godson.

BAY RIDGE, BROOKLYN

On the first day of September 1921, Eléni's family filled the house on Ovington Avenue to welcome Konstantínos and Sofía, whose immigration papers had anglicized his name to Constantinos Capidaglis. "We did it, Eléni," he said. "We're here, all who wanted to be and could be, all here in America, and in your home." He took her hands and kissed both her cheeks.

"I wish Sultána and Smarágda were here with their families," Eléni said.

"Sultána did not want to come to America without a husband. She knew that Chrysóula and Ángelos would take care of her in Sozópolis."

"I think that Dimitrios had to stay in Kalithéa," Eléni mused. "He would miss the politics on Piraeus's docks and Athens' streets too much. As long as Smarágda is content with him and with their life together — that is all that matters. Someday we'll visit them."

272

MANHATTAN'S GARMENT DISTRICT

Mr. Rosenbaum's secretary waited for Eléni at the front door of the factory. "Madame Helen," she said. "Mr. Rosenbaum wants to see you right away."

"I take off hat and coat and come."

Eléni hurried through the factory, acknowledging the workers who had already arrived, and wondering what was so urgent. Mr. Rosenbaum's door was open. She knocked on its frame, entered without waiting, and found two men sitting across from him. He looked up from his desk and smiled at her.

Her employer and business teacher had aged in the five years she had known him. She guessed that he was about sixty. He had had a little gray hair when she first met him. Now it was nearly white, and he had put on several pounds.

"Madame Helen, come in. Let me get you a chair." He rose, moved a chair from the corner of the room to the side of his desk and positioned it to face the two men who stood up to greet her.

"Madame Helen — Mrs. Perna, I'd like to introduce you to Mr. Kurzrok and Mr. Helitzer."

Each of the men stood, said good morning, and extended a hand to Eléni. She had learned business courtesies by watching Rosenbaum, so she gave them a firmer handshake than they expected from a woman.

Kurzrok had a ruddy complexion, thick eyebrows, and green eyes. He smiled easily when he shook Eléni's hand. Helitzer was the more timid of the two. His face was thin and white, his smile a little forced.

"We have news for you, Mrs. Perna," Rosenbaum said. "Please, have a seat."

Eléni sat down and listened. Rosenbaum continued. "Mr. Kurzrok and Mr. Helitzer are business partners. They own a large factory on 36thStreet. It's twice as big as ours. And they manufacture a similar line."

Eléni had not yet heard anything of importance to her. She turned toward Rosenbaum.

"Well, the news is they are buying my business. You'll start working for them next Monday."

"I work for Mr....ah?"

"Kurzrok," Rosenbaum said slowly and clearly, "and Helitzer."

Eléni turned toward the men. "Kur-zrok," she said. "I keep job? *Sposa*, Louie, too?"

Kurzrok leaned forward in his chair.

"Mrs. Perna, my partner and I want you to run this factory for us, the whole factory. If you stay, we will increase your salary and bonus."

"I stay. Louie too?"

"Louie Perna is Madame Helen's husband," Rosenbaum explained.

"Of course your husband can stay," Kurzrok assured her. "You will move into Mr. Rosenbaum's office on Monday. His secretary...what's her name?"

"Marta — Marta Feinman," Rosenbaum replied.

"His secretary, Marta, will work for you," Kurzrok said.

"You leave, Mr. Rosenbaum?"

"Yes, Helen. I sold my business to these men. My wife and I are going to retire to Florida, where it's warm all winter."

"Madame Helen — I'd like to call you that," said Mr. Helitzer. "You are one of the reasons that we bought this business. We look forward to working together."

"You'll see more of me than you will of Mr. Helitzer," Kurzrok said. "He takes care of the money part of the business. I will work with you on the product line with the designers, and handle the shows and buyers. You will be the factory manager here and coordinate with Saul, our factory manager on 36th Street. Do you understand?"

Eléni understood enough to know that she was going to run the factory herself and earn more money. She also realized that she would be in a position to hire whomever she wanted. This fellow, Kurzrok, seemed like a good man. She thought she could work for him.

"Yes."

"Good. I'll be here on Monday to see that you're settled in and that everyone in the factory knows that you're in charge. Don't tell anyone now. Understand?"

"Yes."

EIGHTH AVENUE, MID-TOWN MANHATTAN

Jimmy was embarrassed. The feelings he had as he held the red-haired Irish dance instructress were new to him: shortness of breath, tremors, and a physical sensation below his waist that he tried desperately to control.

"Relax, Jimmy," she cooed. "Count. One, two, three — one, two, three. Good."

The waltz was the least discomfiting of the dances he was learning. There was safety in twirling around and keeping one's partner at arm's length. The foxtrot gave him the most anxiety. Irene, his teacher, would often come close enough for him to feel her breasts brush against his chest, and their bodies would touch below the waist. Irene was in her mid-twenties, slender, graceful, and casual about physical contact with him.

When the waltz was over, Irene put a foxtrot on the wind-up Victrola. The piece had a slow tempo, and Irene made the most of the opportunity to be close to Jimmy.

"Has anyone told you that you look like Valentino?" she whispered.

Jimmy wanted to run. He had seen Valentino in *Camille*, a story that appealed to his romantic nature, and more recently in *The Sheik*. Older women in the market had complemented him on his good looks, and more than one had mentioned Valentino.

"Did you see him dance the tango in *The Four Horsemen*? You have the same posture — straight back, and a great profile. Let me teach you to tango."

Jimmy signed up for more dance lessons that night, not knowing with whom he would ever dance the tango.

THE BRONX

Mrs. Rentas, a middle-aged woman with clown-like circles of rouge on her cheeks, accompanied a lean, mustached young man across the parlor of her apartment to where Lily and her cousins Ioánna and Theanó sat chatting on a sofa.

"Girls, I'd like you to meet James Tsavalas. His sister, Kyria Drivas, and I work together."

The girls introduced themselves to James under Eléni's watchful eyes. She and Louie were sitting in the dining room with their hosts, and Mr. and Mrs. Drivas. Other guests watched their sons and daughters meet and talk in this safe environment.

Maria Rentas had been sent to Eléni from Kurzrok's 36thStreet factory to be trained at his newly acquired plant. It took only a few conversations for them to build a friendly relationship, and not long after that for Eléni to receive an invitation to this party, planned as a social event for marriageable young people to meet.

James was attentive and complimentary to Lily. "Your dress is pretty."

She was flirtatious. "I'm glad I was invited to this party."

Eléni watched with a hopeful eye. "Maybe there is something there?"

THE METROPOLITAN OPERA HOUSE

Jimmy choked with emotion in response to the pathos of the last act of *La Traviata*.

It was the eve of Thanksgiving, and opening night. The week before the performance, Jimmy had approached an Opera House ticket agent that knew him well. "Hello, Harry."

"Good to see you, Jimmy. Are you set with tickets for the new season?"

Jimmy had to listen to Harry closely, for the blond, middle-aged man behind the counter had a severe lisp.

"I would be ... if I had a ticket for opening night."

Harry took off his glasses and cleaned the lenses with his handkerchief. "Galli-Curci as Violetta, and Gigli singing Alfredo. Have you ever seen *La Traviata*?"

"No. But I read Dumas' *Lady of the Camellias,* and saw Valentino in the film."

"You've never seen anything like this. Galli-Curci was fabulous in rehearsal. I snuck in."

"Is there a chance, Harry?"

"For you?" He put his glasses on, reached into the open drawer at his waist, and passed a ticket across the counter. "You'll love it, Jimmy."

In the first act, Galli-Curci had stepped on stage wearing a stunning sequined gown. Camellias were set in her hair, one over each ear. "She's beautiful," Jimmy said softly. He held his opera glasses to his eyes until she started to sing.

At the end of the opera, he watched Violetta, the tragic fallen woman in Verdi's operatic version of *Camille* die in Alfredo's arms. He felt as though his own heart was breaking.

THE BRONX

After their first meeting, Lily expressed sufficient interest in James Tsavalas for Eléni to talk to Mrs. Rentas, who spoke to James's sister, Kyria Drivas. Another party was arranged, and

Eléni and Louie once again accompanied Lily, Ioánna, and Theanó on the long subway ride to the Bronx.

The party was much like the first. Several sets of parents escorted their children to a family get-together whose subplot was to pair young people for marriage.

James maneuvered Lily to the corner of the dining room to talk to her privately. "Lily," he said in an earnest voice, "I'll be out of town on business for a few weeks and won't return until after New Year's Day."

"That's a long time. I thought I might see you at another party."

"There's a Greek Society dance at the McAlpin in mid-January. If you go, I'll be there."

"I'll ask *mána*. Where are you going?"

"Detroit," he said. His voice took on a serious tone. "I'm negotiating to open a new business there."

"Where is Detroit?"

"Just a few hours by train. Not too far from New York."

"Oh, good," she exclaimed, looking down immediately to hide her blush.

Vasilikí was sitting in her rocking chair, sipping hot water with lemon and honey when the family returned from the party. Lily entered the kitchen with her cousin Ioánna in tow. Her grandmother asked, "Evangelía, did you meet any nice young men?"

"I think so, *yiayiá*." Lily turned quickly to her mother. "*Mána*, can we go to the Greek Society dance in January?"

"Is there a reason to go?"

Lily shrugged. "It would be fun." She yawned elaborately. "I'm tired. Come on, Ioánna, let's go to bed."

Whispering and giggling, the girls hurried upstairs. Eléni turned to her mother. "*Mána*, I think that Evangelía is attracted to a young man. This is the second time she has met him, and they talked a lot."

"Good," Vasilikí said firmly. "The sooner she's married, the less trouble you'll have."

SEVENTH AVENUE, NEW YORK

Psáltis raised his glass in a toast. "*Kalá Hristoúgena, paidiá.*" He had moved his shop to larger quarters on the next floor up in the building; and there were nine more employees. The nailing table, covered with tablecloths, held trays of cold cuts and salads. A small army of bottles at one end of the table proved that Prohibition had not yet exhausted Psáltis' inventory of liquor and wine.

Jimmy struck his glass against Bill's. "Merry Christmas."

"Merry Christmas, Jimmy. Can you come to a party on my name day?"

"*Ághios Vasílis?* Of course. Where?"

"Rose and Louis Dimitroff are hosting an open house for me at their apartment."

"Really?" Uncharacteristically, he asked his friend a personal question. "What's going on?"

"I talked to Louis and Rose's mother yesterday. I couldn't say anything until Rose's brother and mother approved."

"You're getting married?"

"We'll announce our engagement on my name day."

"Congratulations. Do Peter and Kyrie Psáltis know?"

"Not yet. I'll tell them later, when everyone has left."

The two friends returned to the party. By late afternoon, when only Psáltis, Peter, Bill, and Jimmy were in the shop, Bill told Psáltis about his engagement.

Psáltis turned to the other two bachelors. "Well, how about you boys? Or at least you, Peter. It's time that you thought of settling down. Jimmy is young. He can wait four or five years."

Maybe, Jimmy thought. *Or maybe not.*

CHAPTER EIGHTEEN
1922
BAY RIDGE, BROOKLYN

L ouie set his coffee cup on the kitchen table and shuffled down the hallway in his robe and slippers to answer the relentless ring of the doorbell. When he opened the door, he found Constantinos shivering in the courtyard, his arms hugging his body. Frozen wax held his twisted, white mustache in sharp points on either side of his mouth. He had squeezed his eyelids into slits to protect his bright blue eyes from the cold.

Louie gasped when he took a breath of the frigid air. "What are you doing out here? Come in. Fast. It's freezing."

"Louie. Open the coal chute to the basement and I'll have the truck driver lower everything down to you."

"What driver? What things?"

"It's a surprise. " Constantinos pointed toward the street, where a burly, heavily dressed man untied the straps of a canvas that covered the back of a delivery truck. He grunted at each exertion and the moisture in his breath condensed into little clouds in front of his face.

Louie stopped asking questions. He lifted the snow-blanketed hatch cover in the courtyard, and then, shaking snow from his slippers and trembling from the cold, hurried into the house and down the cellar steps to unlock the grated security screen. He pushed the coal chute out of the way. He heard Constantinos ordering the deliveryman in Greek. "Easy. Easy, man. Don't drop it." A crate appeared directly above Louie's head and then slowly descended. Louie guided it to the floor. "What's in this?" he asked. He untied the rope and moved the crate out of the way. He heard Constantinos chuckle as the rope was pulled back up to the courtyard.

They repeated the routine several times. "This is the last one," Constantinos called. "I'll put the wood cover back on and come down. Lock the grate." In minutes, he appeared at the bottom of the cellar stairs holding a brown paper-wrapped package, which he put on top of one of the crates. After removing his hat, gloves, muffler, and coat, he walked to the glowing coal furnace at the far end of the basement. "I'm turning myself like a lamb on a spit," he told Louie. "Open the big crate. I'll warm myself for a few minutes."

It took some effort with a small crowbar before Louie cracked open the largest crate. In it, he glimpsed shiny copper. Constantinos stepped up. "It's a still," he said gleefully. When they finished taking apart the crate and removing the packing material, a cylindrically shaped, kerosene burning, and copper-clad boiler stood on the floor. A long spiral condensing tube and a cooling tank lay alongside it.

A slightly smaller but heavier crate contained a grape press. Centered at its top was a V-shaped trough. On either side of the V, opposing interlaced spiked rollers linked to a long-handled manual crank. "Look, Louie. The grapes go into the rollers. They crush the grapes, and the juice, grape skins, and pulp — all of it falls into the barrel."

Another small crate contained a leather case. It held a graceful, hand-blown, eighteen-inch long glass hydrometer, couched in green velvet.

"These other crates — oak barrels — two fifty-gallon, and five smaller," Constantinos boasted.

Louis' eyes darted from the press to the still, then to the hydrometer, back to the still, and then to the barrels. "Where did you find these things?"

"First a glass of brandy and a cigarette," Constantinos demanded.

There were voices on the floor above. Eléni called, "Leonardo, what's going on down there? Is that Constantinos?"

"Yes, he's here. I'll be right up."

Louie set up the card table that leaned against the wall, unfolded two chairs, and ran up the stairs. He returned with a bottle and two glasses. "Sit. Sit down. Eléni, Vasilikí, and Lily are having breakfast. Would you like something?"

"A little coffee, but later."

Leonardo sat down opposite his friend and poured brandy into each of their glasses. "Now – where did you get these things?"

"It's a good surprise, isn't it?" Constantinos reached for the paper-wrapped package he had set on a crate and put it on the card table. "This is for Eléni. *Tsíri* and *réngha*."

"Yes. But where did it all come from?"

"Ha!" Constantinos took a sip of brandy and snuffed out his cigarette. "I wrote to my brother-in-law, Dimitrios, in Athens," he said at last. "Leonárdos Panteliás took the letter and money to Dimitrios on his last trip. Dimitrios brought all these treasures to Panteliás on the *King Alexander*. I have been watching the newspapers for the ship's arrival and hired the delivery truck to meet it when it docked this morning. Next fall, Louie — we will make *krasí*. And *rakí*. Prohibition — bah! They can go to the devil."

THE MCALPIN HOTEL
THIRTY-FOURTH STREET AND BROADWAY

Jimmy entered the ballroom at the McAlpin thinking, *It was easier to shoot at the Kaimakan.*

At the end of his last lesson two nights before, Irene had tried to boost his confidence with a pep talk. She raised herself up on her toes, gave Jimmy a more than affectionate peck on the corner of his mouth, intentionally missing his cheek, and said, "Don't worry, Jimmy, you're good enough to teach here. With your looks — well, don't break too many hearts at your Greek dances."

Jimmy looked around the ballroom. He spotted Louis and Rose Dimitroff, and Bill Rusuli, at a table, but there was no sign of the girl he had come to dance with. He sat with his friends, fidgeted, and searched the room with his eyes until Rose could take it no more. "Bill," she said, "I'm going to dance with Jimmy and calm him down a little." Louis smiled. Bill helped Rose to her feet, held her chair and gave her hand a squeeze before Jimmy led her to the dance floor.

White haired and sporting a boutonnière, Louis Dimitroff looked more mature than his twenty-seven years, and was granted the deference of an older more experienced man. He attended Greek social functions for two reasons. Even he did not know which of the two was more important — assuring his sister's good reputation by being her constant chaperone, or working the room for clients. Since his sister was under the protection of her fiancé, and dancing with a good friend, he left the table to pursue the second objective.

The band played a popular foxtrot, and on the dance floor Jimmy guided Rose into a promenade walk. "Bill told me that you just learned how to dance. You lead wonderfully."

"It's not hard to lead someone as graceful as you." The words Irene had taught him came easily.

Rose smiled.

When the foxtrot was over, Jimmy escorted his partner back to their table and sat down to watch the doorway that opened into the ballroom.

At ten o'clock, the room was nearly full. Jimmy looked at his wristwatch and watched the seconds tick by for a moment, preparing himself for disappointment. When he looked up, the young woman he was waiting for entered the room with her parents, guided by the same man who had escorted her to the dance the previous fall. Jimmy's stomach churned while he watched them edge through the crowd to join two middle-aged couples and two young women at a table. *They're probably the other couples' daughters,* he thought.

After a few minutes, Bill prodded Jimmy, "Are you going to go or not?"

Louis overheard Bill's question as he came up to the table and was about to offer Jimmy encouragement when Rose asked, "Jimmy, it's the girl wearing the flower in her hair, isn't it?"

"Yes." His eyes looked at Rose as if he were pleading for help.

"Go ahead, ask her to dance. I met her here last year. She seemed nice, and as nervous as the rest of us."

Rose watched Jimmy's slim figure approach the girl's table. He bowed slightly and spoke to her parents. A moment later, he led the young woman to the dance floor, put his arm around her waist, and seemed transformed.

Timidity gone, Jimmy danced Lily out to the middle of the floor. "Do you dance a lot?" she asked.

"Why?"

"Well, you seem to enjoy it."

"Only when I have a partner, like you."

Lily smiled. "Are you a furrier?"

"Yes. I've been with Kyrie Psáltis for three years. Do you know him?"

"No. My family is in dressmaking."

The orchestra finished the number and put down their instruments to take a break. Jimmy escorted Lily to her table and asked with some assurance, "May I have another dance later?"

Lily gave him a generous smile. "Yes. Thank you. That was nice."

Jimmy returned to his table feeling triumphant. But after the band returned from their break, and a man led Lily to the dance floor, his spirit sank. He sat glumly, taking some comfort from his judgment that Lily's new partner was not a good dancer.

He was too late for the next waltz; someone else got to her first. It was forty minutes before he had a chance to dance with her again.

"Do you like to waltz, Lily?"

"It's a little old-fashioned."

Jimmy put his arm around her waist and nearly lifted her on to the floor.

They danced first clockwise, then counterclockwise. He twirled her under his upraised arm. She found it easy to follow him; his hands gently pressured her to move in the right directions. Some couples actually cleared a path for them as they circled the floor. She smiled at the attention. "Oh, Jimmy. What fun."

Eléni and Louie watched them dance. Eléni whispered, "The Rentas and Drivas families have their eyes on Lily like hawks in a tree."

"He's a good-looking young man, Eléni," Louie commented. "They dance well together."

Eléni shrugged. "Young," she answered. "Not ready for marriage yet."

"I was young when we were married."

"That's was different. You were a little older than he is."

"James is coming," Louie said.

James walked up to the table and waited for Lily.

"That was wonderful," Lily said as Jimmy returned her to her parents. "Did you see people watching us dance, *mána*?"

Showing a little irritation, James ignored Jimmy and pulled out Lily's chair for her. She took her seat, turned from James and looked up over her shoulder at Jimmy.

He smiled. "I hope to see you at the next dance. I'll look for you."

Eléni saw Lily return the smile.

Jimmy proceeded to his table, sat down and looked at Bill and Rose. "Do you know that man? The one that sat next to her?"

Bill looked toward Lily's table for a moment. "No. I don't think he's a furrier."

The stranger led Lily to the floor when the orchestra started to play the last dance. Jimmy scowled. "I have to find out who he is. I don't like his look. Should I talk to her mother, Bill? Rose?"

"About what?" Rose asked. "Don't rush into anything."

"I'm not rushing. But I ..." He stopped, turning his head away. *There's time*, he thought. *She's young*.

THE BRONX, NEW YORK

"It's really important," James Tsavalas told his brother, pleading for the favor. "If you and Christina invite Lily and her parents to dinner, it will show them that we're a close family. They'll have more confidence in me."

Niko paced the floor, arguing with his brother. "It's just weeks since Christina gave birth to Aristotelis, and you want her to have a party for you? They've already been to our sister's place."

"I'm not the only one interested in this girl, brother. She seems to like me. Christina can really help me with her."

Christina overheard the conversation from the kitchen and stuck her head into the room. "All right. Just this once, Niko. It won't be anything fancy. I'm exhausted."

James issued the invitation, and Eléni accepted for her family. "I want to see what his brother is like," she told Louie. "I can't make James out."

A week later, Eléni, Louie, and Lily drove to the Bronx with James. "Can you see the street sign, Lily?" James asked.

It had taken Louie several weeks to learn how to drive. He steered the new Nash closer to the curb and slowed down. Lily read the sign. "It's Caldwell Avenue."

"Good. Look for building numbers."

Lily sat in the front seat next to Louie. Eléni was in the backseat with James, who sat back comfortably; pleased that Eléni and her husband could afford such luxury. Her year-end bonus from Kurzrok and Helitzer had paid for the Nash and provided money for her to invest in the booming economy. "There, there's the address," cried Lily.

James leaned forward. "Yes, that's it."

Louie parked the Nash a few feet from the entrance to the apartment building. He was relieved that there was ample space – he had trouble with parallel parking. They left the car, entered the building, and took its elevator to the fourth floor. James led them to an apartment and knocked at its door. They heard a baby crying.

James laughed. "That's my nephew, Aristotelis. He's six weeks old."

A tall man opened the door. About thirty, he was heavier-set than James, with thick brown hair, a short, straight nose and a wide jaw. He wore a white shirt, tie, and open vest without a suit coat. Smiling, he hugged James.

"Brother," James said. "I want you to meet Kyrie and Kyria Perna, and their daughter, Evangelía. She calls herself Lily." He turned to Eléni and Louie. "This is my brother, Nikoláos."

"Bring them in, Niko," a voice called from inside.

"That's my wife, Christina. Come in. Let me take your coats."

Two little boys were playing on the floor of the parlor. Christina waited there with an infant in her arms. She wore an apron over her housedress. Her long, fine brown hair was twisted up on top of her head, and she wore no make-up.

"What a beautiful baby," Lily said.

Christina smiled a welcome.

"*Na sas zísi*," said Eléni.

"Thank you. Niko, take the boys to the bedroom to play. I'll put Aristotelis in his crib."

Christina quickly returned to the parlor, saying, "I have to finish dinner. Please excuse me for a little while."

"Can I do something to help?" Lily asked. Before Christina could answer, Lily followed her into the kitchen, put on an apron that hung from a pantry doorknob and went to work composing a salad from the vegetables that were in a cauldron by the sink. Christina accepted her assistance without a word.

The company spent a pleasant evening eating, sipping wine, drinking coffee, and talking about unimportant things. Lily helped put the children to bed and stayed with Christina while she nursed Aristotelis.

When the evening ended, James told Lily and her parents, "I'm not going back to Brooklyn with you. Tomorrow is a busy day for me, and I have some business to discuss with my brother. May I call this week to arrange to visit next Sunday? I have something important to ask."

Lily turned to her mother.

Eléni responded: "We'll expect to hear from you, James."

James squeezed Lily's hand for a moment as she left. "I'll see you next Sunday."

The door had barely closed when James asked, "Well, what do you think?"

"I really like Lily," Christina offered. "You'd be lucky to have her."

Annoyed, James turned to his brother. "Niko, what do you think?"

"You don't deserve her," his brother said with a frown. "What are you going to do in Detroit? Can you support her? What have you told her parents?"

"I told them that I'm in the confectionery business, and that I'm buying a factory and wholesale operation in Detroit."

"How? You don't have the money. You've never run a business. What do you know about candy and cake?"

"Don't worry. I have plans. Once I'm in Detroit I think that I can make it happen, especially if Lily is my wife. Her mother has money."

Christina shook her head and left the men. She went into her bedroom and sat in the dark at the corner of her bed. Later, when her husband entered the room she looked up and said sadly, "Niko, James will not make that girl happy."

SEVENTH AVENUE, NEW YORK

Bill burst into the shop through a buzzing security door and set two wet brown bags on the nailing board. Archie tore open one bag. "What did you bring for lunch? I'm starving."

Bill took off his hat and turned down his wet collar. While he hung his coat and muffler on the coat rack in the corner he complained, "It's a cold rain — miserable. You're lucky that I'm not having lunch with Rose today. You'd have had to get your own sandwiches."

Peter laughed. "Don't see too much of Rose before your wedding. The June Rose may lose her blush."

"What does that mean?" Bill was annoyed.

"Nothing," Jimmy said to calm his friend. "He is just showing off that he did his English lesson. It comes from a poem or a book."

Peter continued teasing. "Three more months, Bill. Then you'll be home every night."

"Enough," Psáltis said, pulling up a chair. "You should be thinking of marriage, too, Peter. You're not getting any younger. Being alone in a bachelor's room is no way to live."

As they ate their sandwiches, Bill took a Greek newspaper from one of the bags and opened it on the table. "Look," he said. "Greece and Turkey may agree to an armistice."

The men huddled over the article. "We could have had Constantinople," lamented Psáltis.

"What happened?" asked Jimmy. "The Greek army was winning. They almost had Ankara."

Peter scoffed. "Venizelos and his Big Idea. A nightmare for Greece. Our little country didn't have enough money, or men for war ... and the English left us. None of the great powers wanted us to destroy Turkey and take the City."

The conversation went back and forth while they ate, resolving nothing. When they had finished, Bill and Archie cleared the table, Peter took a bundle of skins to his worktable to match, and Jimmy sat sipping the last drops of his coffee. He turned a page of the newspaper and cried out, "No. It can't be. No!"

Startled, Bill asked, "What? What can't be?"

Jimmy rushed to the bathroom, gagging.

Bill looked picked up the newspaper, read the announcement, and called: "Peter, come here."

"What?"

"Read this."

"Is Jimmy sick?"

"Read this."

Peter took the newspaper and read:

Mr. and Mrs. Louie Perna announce the engagement of their daughter, Evangelía Athenas, to Mr. James Tsavalas. A civil ceremony in April will be followed in June by a wedding at St. Elefthérios Church in Manhattan.

"Isn't that the girl Jimmy learned to dance for?" Peter asked.

"Yes."

They stood silently for a moment, and then, not knowing what to say or do, they turned to their work.

In June, Jimmy attended two weddings. The first was a happy event. It joined Vasílis Rusuli and Rose Dimitroff. Louis Dimitroff spared no expense for his sister's wedding. His mother looked uncomfortable in the finery that he had chosen for her to wear. She seemed in awe of her son, once a ten-year-old dishwasher in Hell's Kitchen, and now a successful and respected businessman.

The catered reception that followed the wedding ceremony featured a five-piece Greek-American orchestra. Louis had invited family, friends, Rose's clients, and Bill's friends and co-workers. Playing the debonair host, he went from table to table, chatting with his guests, seeing to their needs, and making sure all knew that he was in the insurance business.

In his happiness for his friend and out of respect for Rose, Jimmy did his best to enjoy the wedding and reception. He sat with Kyrie Psáltis and his family, and with Peter. Jimmy and Peter took it as their obligation to make Bill's wedding a success. They danced with as many young women as they could, sitting down only when the musicians took a break.

The second marriage ceremony Jimmy attended took place late on the following Sunday afternoon. He had waited down the street from St. Elefthérios until he saw a white-gowned bride and her family enter the front door of the church. After the sacrament began, Jimmy crept into the church, lit a candle, and sat in back out of view.

During the sacrament, ten-year-old Calypso Capidaglis squeezed past her mother and father to go to the bathroom. Stepping softly along the side aisle of the church, she noticed a man, half-hidden in a rear pew. He was wiping away tears with a handkerchief. Their eyes met. When she returned a few minutes later, he was gone.

A TRAIN FROM DETROIT

"*Mána*, what am I going to do? What's going to happen to me?"

Eléni held her sobbing daughter's trembling body close to her. Lily buried her face in the fur that covered her mother's shoulder. The train, somewhere in Pennsylvania, raced eastward, thumping along the tracks toward New York. It was early Saturday evening. The coach was half-empty, giving Eléni and Lily a measure of privacy. The conductor, a kind-faced man, was concerned for the young woman. He gave Eléni an understanding smile. "Is there anything I can get for you? For the young lady?"

"No. Wait – water? Glass water?"

"Yes, I'll bring it."

Later, as the conductor passed Eléni she asked, "How soon New York?"

"In about an hour, Madame. Can I get you anything?"

"No, thank you." She had been perfecting her use of English phrases.

Earlier, in the midst of her sobbing, Lily had fallen asleep on her mother's shoulder. Eléni shook her lightly.

"Evangelía — Lily — wake up. Wake up, *hrisó mou*."

Lily opened her eyes, realized where she was, and remembered. The memory brought sobs and she crumpled again on Eléni's shoulder.

"Evangelía, stop. Stop crying. There will be time for that later. Listen to me. Listen."

Lily sat up in her seat and dried her eyes. "Are we almost there? What will people say? What am I going to do?"

"Ssh. Listen. Your family loves you. We all love you, and you are coming home to us. The family won't say anything. It will be just as it was before all this happened. You'll live at home and take care of *yiayiá*."

"I don't want to see anyone."

"No one will see you but us, in our home. You will have to be patient — for a time you won't be able to go to dances or parties. Later?" She sighed. "Well, later - I don't know. We'll see what happens."

Louie was waiting for them on the platform when the train pulled into Pennsylvania Station. He gave Lily a hug and kissed his wife. In a few minutes, Louie had Eléni and Lily in the back of the Nash. Driving them home, he said nothing and asked no questions. They were silent.

BAY RIDGE, BROOKLYN

Constantinos siphoned the last of the fermented grape juice from an oak barrel into another, aging barrel. "Save half of the second barrel for the still," Louie said as he hammered a large cork stopper into place. Several weeks before, Eléni had yelled at them both when they had burned sulfur in the barrels to kill fungus spores and bacteria. "The house stinks like Hades," she had complained to them innumerable times in the days that followed.

At the far end of the basement, long, cable-like links of *loukánika* hung drying from clothesline, their fat dripping onto newspapers set out below them. Eléni and Lily had made the sausage the week before, under Vasilikí's supervision. "Don't grind the meat too much," she had ordered.

Lily turned the handle of the meat grinder slowly and caught a handful as the meat squeezed through the cutter. "Is this all right, *yiayiá?*"

Vasilikí poked at the meat with her finger and wrinkled her nose. "Yes, that's just about right. Don't forget to chop the onions finely. And grate lots of orange rind." She continued giving directions to be sure that they used enough wine, added salt, pepper, and thyme to her taste, and filled and tied the casings properly. "Now hang them in the basement to dry," she ordered. "Put lots of paper under them to catch the fat."

A lot of fat had dripped from the sausages in the days that had passed, and now, nearby, Costas Zelios labored over a cutting stone. He carried torpedo-shaped tuna from the washtub in the little basement kitchen to a cutting stone, where he disposed of their heads and fins, and sliced their bodies into inch-thick steaks. These he layered with salt in two large stone crocks. They were the making of *lakérda*. The family prized the delicately flavored salted fish when it appeared on the dinner table.

Tsíri, strips of dried, smoked mackerel were marinating in vinegar, olive oil and dill in jars on the basement shelves. Clusters of *réngha* hung on hooks along the walls. Eléni broiled these fatty dried herring in the garden over charcoal until their oil dripped and sputtered in the flames. She stripped the flesh from their bones and steeped the morsels in an onion, olive oil, and lemon juice marinade.

The crocks Costas filled joined others on the covered steps that led to the garden. In this cool, dark space, isolated from the house, earthenware crocks and glass jars contained brine-preserved cabbage, green tomatoes, carrots, celery, cauliflower, and peppers. Pungent, fermented cabbage odors vented out to the garden through cracks in the cellar doors. On winter days, Lily would stuff pickled cabbage leaves with spiced, minced pork, and bake the rolls in tomato sauce. The delicacy was one of her Balkan specialties.

Louie set up the bright copper still on a makeshift wooden bench next to a card table that was surrounded by several chairs. He and Constantinos puzzled over how to empty the mash into the still. Costas stepped up. "Look," he said, "let's tip the barrel, pour the mash into the bucket, and then empty it into the still."

Costas held the bucket while his partners lifted the barrel and poured the mash, and then filled the still with it. Finished, he lit one of the cigarettes that seemed to always hang from the left corner of his mouth and returned to slicing tuna. Smoke filtered through the left side of his mustache adding to its already yellow-brown stain.

Constantinos and Louie sealed the boiler and screwed the condensing tube into place. It spiraled downward through a cooling container, out its bottom and into a clear glass gallon jug. While Constantinos poured kerosene into the base of the boiler, Louie filled the cooling tank with cold water and took a box of matches from his trouser pocket. "Ready? Shall I light it?"

Constantinos inspected the setup. "Go ahead. I think we've got it right."

Louie struck a match and lit the kerosene burner. It gave off a smell sure to cause trouble with Eléni. He ran to open the cellar door that led to the garden a crack, and then went upstairs and out to the front courtyard to move the chute cover an inch or two. Cross-ventilation solved the problem.

Returning to the basement, Louie instructed, "Constantinos, you watch the still, I'll fix some lunch for us. Mitso and Stelios are coming in a little while. We can eat down here, play cards and keep the still filled with mash."

Louie brought food and drink from the first-floor kitchen to the basement just as Costas completed his work. Constantinos, Louie, and Costas congratulated themselves on the apparent success of their effort. They agreed that in forty days, the *lakérda* would be ready to sample, and in two or three months, the wine would be too. Mitso and Stelios, Louie's friends from the garment district, arrived in time to see the still deliver the first drops of clear liquid into the jug. They all thought they should test the *rakí*, so while they played pinochle in the light of a single hanging light bulb, they took turns holding a one-ounce whiskey glass under the condensing tube, and sipped at small amounts of the ferociously strong, raw alcohol.

In mid-afternoon, Lily came down the cellar stairs carrying five demitasse of coffee on a tray. Eléni followed directly behind with a platter of *kouloúrakia*. The last of the visitors was Vasilikí, who held on to the railing and leaned against Louie as she descended the stairs. "I want to see. Where is the wine?"

Louie led his mother-in-law around the basement to inspect the wine barrels, the *loukánika*, *réngha*, *tsíri*, and *lakérda*. Lily followed close behind. She took two pickled green tomatoes from a crock of *toursí* and put them on a plate. "Here, *yiayiá*, we'll take these upstairs for you to have later with your salad."

"Thank you, Evangelía." She looked at her granddaughter. Earlier she had told Eléni, "Evangelía should be in her own home with a husband. What will happen to her?"

Lily saw the look in Vasilikí's eyes and knew its meaning. "What do you think, *yiayiá*? Have we prepared enough for winter?"

"Oh, yes," she sighed. "It makes me remember Sozópolis. It even smells like our storage room. I love you all, but I miss my home, the storeroom, and Hrístos' tools and nets."

"I know. I know, Vasilikí," Louie said. He put his arm around her shoulders and tried to comfort her. "We have our memories."

The men stayed in the basement until midnight, tending the still until it dripped the last of its precious liquid.

The next morning Louie and Constantinos removed the artful, hand-blown hydrometer from its case and used it to measure the liquor's alcohol content. They added distilled water to dilute the *rakí* – or *grappa*, as Louie would call it in an Italian moment – to ninety-proof, and then filled small casks to age the liquor.

In the days that followed, Louie worked without help. He added flavorings to turn the liquor in one of the casks into brandy, checked the brined *toursí* and cabbage, and replaced the fat soaked newspapers that lay under the *loukánika*.

Lily spent October and November sheltered and protected by her family.

"Time," Eléni told her. "Time will solve the problem, darling."

SEVENTH AVENUE, MANHATTAN

On a November evening, Kyrie Psáltis pulled a chair from one of the sewing machines, set it where there was enough space and called, "Come on, boys. Let's have the talk you wanted." Jimmy, Bill, and Peter pulled chairs up in a semi-circle close to Psáltis. That morning they had asked him for a few minutes after work to discuss business.

Psáltis saw that they were nervous and guessed why. He smiled. "All right, boys, who's leaving?"

"Kyrie Psáltis," Jimmy began, "you know we respect you and appreciate what you've taught us and done for us." He paused.

"Yes? Go on," Psáltis said, encouraging Jimmy with a smile and hand motions.

"Well, Bill and I, we — we're good friends, and we think that we could have our own business."

"And Peter?"

Peter laughed. "I'm not going anywhere. These two are eager to start out on their own. I'm not. Besides, a partnership between two people is difficult — between three, impossible."

298

"Bill, what do you have to say?"

"I think that Jimmy and I could be good partners. He likes the manufacturing side of the business. I like selling — dealing with people."

"Kyrie Psáltis," Jimmy began, "we hope you … "

"Enough, boys." He held up his hand and his smile broadened. "I'm proud of you. You want to be in your own business. Good. You are young and ambitious. Have no worries. Wait a minute."

Psáltis went to the cupboard and took out a brandy bottle and four glasses. He filled the glasses and passed them around.

"Congratulations and good luck to you both. I know that you'll succeed."

"We won't leave until you bring in one or two operators to take our place. Is that all right?"

"All right? What more could I ask?"

The next day Jimmy and Bill met Rose for lunch and they each gave her two thousand dollars to open their partnership account. She agreed to be their bookkeeper. The next day they started looking for space to rent.

St. Constantine and Helen Church, Brooklyn

Lily held Anésti in her arms and cried — partly in happiness at having been asked to baptize Anastasia's second son in spite of her predicament, and partly from the pain of not knowing whether she would ever have a child of her own. She was relieved that there were so few people present. Moschánthi, Dómna, Anastasia, Costas, Eléni, and Louie were there with two-year-old Dimitrios. Moschánthi and Dómna's merchant marine husbands were at sea, now both first officers.

On her return from Detroit with her mother, Lily's family and their close friends had embraced her without questions about her marriage or reference to her husband. For a time, she received reminders of James. Letters and telegrams arrived from him and his brother with threats and entreaties. Some she read. Others she gave to her mother without reading. All were destroyed. Having left her husband, she had broken acceptable Greek social norms and was the subject of gossip and rumor. Her social life was restricted to contact with her family.

Lily was in prison.

THE GARMENT DISTRICT, MANHATTAN

Marta Feinman knocked on Madame Helen's office door and opened it.

"Madame Helen, Mr. Kurzrok and Mr. Helitzer are here to see you."

"Yes, bring in, Marta."

Eléni relied on Marta and treated her like family. For Marta, it was a miracle to work for a competent, caring woman. She felt appreciated, and with Eléni in charge gained dignity and respect for the first time in her working life. Mr. Rosenbaum had been a good employer, but he had not paid attention to the abusive behavior many men in the plant imposed on its women.

Eléni spent little time in her office. She made her greatest impact on the factory floor. Her office was a place to hang her coat, talk to an employee in private, make telephone calls for business, and to her home and family, and occasionally to eat lunch. Marta read everything that came in the mail, reporting its contents to Eléni, who told Marta what to write in response. Marta even signed Eléni's correspondence for her. Eléni seemed simply too busy for that kind of detail.

Eléni rose from her desk to greet the two men.

"Happy holidays, Madame Helen," Kurzrok began. "Mr. Helitzer has something for you." The partners were smiling.

Helitzer handed an envelope to Eléni. "Happy holidays," he said with a bow. "You've helped us make a record year. We hope that this shows you how much we appreciate it."

Eléni took the envelope and started to put it into her purse. "Thank you, Mr. Kurzrok, Mr. Helitzer," she said in her halting English. "Very much thank you."

"No, Helen," said Kurzrok. "We want you to open it now. There's a reason."

Eléni retrieved the envelope from her purse and opened it. There was money inside. She thanked God that it was not a letter of some kind. She had learned to read numbers, but she was able only to recognize the written form of her name, and the names of her husband and daughter. The men smiled at her and at each other as she took two one thousand dollar bills from the envelope. They saw her eyes open wide. She looked up. "But, but so much?"

"A two-thousand-dollar bonus is what you deserve, Madame Helen. You increased our production and profit way above our expectations." Kurzrok went on, "There's more, Madame Helen. We have a business proposition for you."

Eléni was confused. "What proposition is?"

"I'll tell you, Madame Helen," Helitzer said, not realizing that Eléni was unsure of what the term meant. "We want you to open a factory in Glens Falls, just three or four hours north of New York by train. Land and buildings are cheap, and the labor cost is lower."

"Glens Falls? Me?"

"Please think about it. Ask me any questions you want," Kurzrok urged her. "We want you to go to Glens Falls on a one-year contract. If you are happy, and we are making the money we expect, we will renew the contract every year. You can hire whoever you want, pick your equipment, run the show. We will raise your salary. If things go well, you can look forward to bonuses bigger than this one."

Eléni heard four things: 'Glens Falls, more money, more bonus, hire anyone.' For almost two hours they talked about how large the new plant would be, how many workers might be employed and production details. "Thank you," she said finally. "I talk to Louie. Decide tomorrow."

"Fine. Fine, Madame Helen. We'll wait for your call."

They were walking out of her office door when she called after them. "Take Marta, too?"

Kurzrok turned and shrugged. "Yes, sure. If she'll go."

Lily and Louie's reaction to Eléni's announcement of Kurzrok and Helitzer's offer was shock. "How can we leave our home?" Louie asked. "What about your mother?"

"Where is Glens Falls, *mána*? Is it far? Will I be able to see my cousins?"

"Look, this a great opportunity," Eléni insisted. "Evangelía will be far away from gossip, and we can make a lot of money."

"And your mother?" Louie asked. "Will we take her with us?"

"No. It's too much for her to move that far again. She'll have Constantinos, Sofía and Theanó here. I think Moschánthi and Dómna would be happy to move into our house and take care of her. I will be in New York every few weeks on business and I can check on things. You can come sometimes too, Louie."

The next morning she took Marta into her office and closed the door. "Sit, Marta, sit," Eléni said in a soft voice. Marta sat forward in her chair with her stenographer's pad and pencil, ready for work.

Eléni held up her hand. "No, Marta — I want ask question."

Eléni told Marta about Glens Falls. Marta was frightened at what Eléni was saying until she heard: "Marta, I go — and you too? You come?"

Marta smiled broadly, got up and gave Eléni a big hug. "Yes, I'll go with you Madame Helen."

302

Eléni hugged Marta back.

GLENS FALLS, NEW YORK

It took less than one month for Eléni to organize her family. She offered Anastasia Zelios' sisters, Moschánthi and Dómna, the use of her house if they would care for her mother. Sofía and her daughter Theanó, who lived one block away, agreed to help. In late-January of 1923, Eléni and Louie boarded a train at Grand Central Station. Kurzrok had already commissioned a realtor to help them find a house in Glens Falls, and to locate several possible factory sites. With her native intelligence, initiative, and organizational skills, leasing a house on Elm Street and deciding on the factory's location took only three days.

Two weeks later Eléni, Louie, and Lily moved into their white, Victorian, modestly furnished Glens Falls home, and a week after that, Marta Feinman arrived and took a room on the second story of a boarding house a few doors away from them.

Glens Falls, a thriving community at the gateway to the Adirondack Mountains, was two hundred miles from New York City, on the north and west banks of the Hudson River, just past the point where the river turns west. The falls that gave the city its name — the largest on the river —had as its source a small lake located far up in the Adirondacks. Lumber, limestone, black marble, paper, the shirt-and-collar industry, and manufacture of other goods were the sources of the community's prosperity. Millionaire capitalists located dozens of factories on Warren, Ridge, Maple, and Glen Streets, and built their mansions on Warren and Ridge Streets, within walking distance of downtown. Financial service companies, hotels, and shops grew in number with the city's industries and its population.

When the winter of 1922-23 melted into spring, Kurzrok and Helitzer's new factory was in production. Eléni was its general manager, Louie the production foreman, and Lily was the supervisor of the workers who sewed linings and labels into garments and performed final detailing and pressing.

In April, Louie asked his brother Luigi and his sister Philomena to join him in Glens Falls. They jumped at the chance to leave Manhattan, and to be close to their brother and to Eléni, who they thought of as mother, sister, and guardian angel. Eléni put them to work training immigrant Italian men and women who flocked to the new factory when they heard there was an Italian speaking and sympathetic management.

Lily enjoyed her days at work with Louie and her mother, but was lonely. Thrilled when her cousin Katina arrived from New York to visit, she cried at the train station when Katina left, pleading, "Come back soon. Tell Ioanna, Theano, and Calypso, and the boys to come. Come together."

Next to come north to Glens Falls were Constantinos, Sofia, and their children, wanting to visit their family and find relief from the summer heat of Brooklyn. Thereafter, hardly a month went by without visitors. All of Lily's cousins came, singly, in pairs, and as a group. They spent leisurely days along the river, went to movies at the Rialto, and walked home in the evening with Hall's ice cream cones. Louie and Eléni took them on excursions to Lake George and Fort Ticonderoga. They picnicked at Cooper's Cave. "I read about this cave in *The Last of the Mohicans*," Lily told her cousins. Reading became important to her during Glens Falls' long winters.

In March of 1924, Theano arrived with exciting news. Stepping off the train into Lily's hug she announced, "I'm engaged!" Lily's personal situation did not dampen her enthusiasm for her cousin.

"What's his name?"

"Giorgios Pierides."

"Is he handsome?"

"Yes. And good."

When Eléni heard of the engagement, she showed the concern and suspicion that had grown out of her daughter's misfortune.

"Where's he from? What does he do? Has your father asked about him?"

"Cyprus," Theanó answered. "He's a baker. *Babás* visited him at the bakery where he works."

"When will you marry?"

"In June," Theanó answered nervously. "We're going to have a civil marriage in New York. Then, Giorgios is taking me to Cyprus to meet his family and have the wedding there." She was on the brink of tears.

Eléni, realizing that she had been behaving like an inquisitor, softened her tone. "Good. Good, Theanó. He sounds wonderful."

As happy as she was for her cousin, Theanó's news tortured Lily. It seemed inevitable that Theanó and Hariclea, Katina, and even her youngest cousin, Calypso, would be married with children while she would have neither home nor family. Distance from New York, separation from the gossip of Greek society, and hard work had made it possible for her to live each day without allowing self-pity and regret to consume her. However, Theanó's happy news reminded Lily that she was captive in an empty marriage, destined to be alone and without children.

The years passed — 1923 — 1924 — 1925. Eléni, Louie, and Lily visited Brooklyn; Eléni more frequently than the others. Her trips to Manhattan were to meet with the factory's owners, and the firm's designers and suppliers. Marta always accompanied Eléni. She would read the dining car menu aloud to Madame Helen, and order their meals and pay the check in the dining car of the train. Eléni had countless reasons for not reading a menu or a letter: her glasses were misplaced, or the bridge of her nose hurt, or she had a sty, or it was easier for her to listen and think when Marta read to her. "I can't read as fast in English as I do in Greek," she would explain. Marta was pleased that her manager and friend needed her. She never gave the matter any thought, attended all of Eléni's meetings to take notes and read them to Eléni during their return train ride to Glens Falls. It was how they worked together.

Once, Eléni confided her fear about being illiterate to Louie. "What will I do if they find out? Maybe they won't keep me in my job?"

"Don't worry. No one will care if you can read or not. Besides, how will they find out as long as you have Marta?"

Louie looked forward to his trips to Brooklyn — especially on early fall weekends for the annual grape crush with Constantinos. In Glens Falls, he found a new outlet, a passion for vegetable gardening. He laid claim to a plot in the town's large communal garden and planted tomatoes, lettuce, radishes, and cucumbers for the family's summer table.

On her infrequent visits to Bay Ridge, Lily, always conscious of herself as an outcast from Greek society, spent time at home with her grandmother and relatives, and visited only her cousins and godsons.

For the most part, their lives focused on work and on making the factory a success. In the boom years of the 1920s, Kurzrok and Helitzer were making more money than even they had thought possible, and they rewarded Eléni handsomely. She shared part of her bonuses with her secretary, right hand, and friend, Marta.

Marta's life changed when Renaldo Mazola came to work for Louie. Slender, and black-haired, he spent his days judging how best to cut bolts of cloth into pattern-shaped pieces. Eléni loved his boyish 'See what I did?' smile when he found a particularly efficient way to utilize cloth. One day, the middle-aged Italian bachelor, who was balding and timid, stammered, red-faced to Louie, "Signore Perna, would you introduce me to Signora's secretary?"

Louie smiled. "Sure. I'll call you when I find a good excuse."

Louie made the introduction, and after several hellos, good mornings, and goodnights, Renaldo offered to walk Marta home from work. Then he asked her to have an ice cream, and finally he asked if he could take her home to dinner to meet his family. Marta bloomed under the attention she received and married Renaldo, blessing Eléni for having brought her to Glens Falls.

Eléni's savings grew. She caught the fever that spread through America, and with the help of a Greek broker in New York, bought foreign currencies and speculative shares in companies that she knew nothing about. The financial reports she received from her broker indicated that she was on the road to independent wealth. It was an unprecedented time.

CHAPTER NINETEEN

1926

BAY RIDGE, BROOKLYN

At the end of 1925, having turned the factory at Glens Falls over to a manager that she had trained, Eléni boarded a train for New York City with Louie and Lily. It was a few days before the Christmas holidays. They looked forward to the New Year — 1926 — in their home, close to family and friends. Before he left Glens Falls, Louie had stood in Herkimer County Superior Court and taken the oath of allegiance to the United States of America. "We belong here now, Eléni," Louie told Eléni with as much relief as pride. "We are Americans."

Within minutes of walking through the door of their home in Brooklyn, Lily said, "*Mána*, let's get a Christmas tree and have a party."

"Yes, pick a big tree at the grocer's on 3rd Avenue and have it delivered. We have ornaments in a box somewhere in the basement. We can buy more. We'll have everyone here for Christmas."

Louie set the tree in front of the bay windows in the second-floor parlor, and Lily decorated it under *yiayiá* Vasilikí's critical eye. The family assembled on Christmas Day, crowding the extended dining room and kitchen tables while Lily served *patsá*, a lip-sticky soup made of pigs' heads and feet, flavored with garlic, paprika and vinegar. She had prepared platters of roast pork and *sarmárdes*, and bowls of winter delicacies. At the end of the Christmas dinner, Eléni raised her wine glass to toast, "We're here for good. From now on I'll be working in New York."

"I'm so glad to be back in Brooklyn," Lily told her cousins. She hugged her grandmother who responded with, "Glory to Him. Finally you're home."

Once the holidays were over, Eléni, Lily, and Louie settled in to their new routine. Winter passed before they knew it. When there was no longer any snow on the ground, Louie started to work on garden projects. He took time off from work to supervise paving of a walk that led around the garden and bordered the areas that he marked off for raised flowerbeds and a vegetable patch — a miniature of the one he'd planted in Glens Falls. He had a grape arbor installed, and then, in early spring, in defiance of New York's climate, he planted a fig tree. By mid-summer, Louie's vines had climbed up the posts of the arbor and covered most of the overhead area, providing shade for the table and chairs that were set under it.

Later in the summer, on warm, clear evenings, the men played cards in the light provided by a single incandescent bulb. It dangled above them, suspended on an extension cord that ran over the arbor and through the window of the kitchen to the nearest electrical outlet. Moths circled the light, scorching themselves on the incandescent glass. The thickening canopy of vine leaves mostly hid Louie, Constantinos, Costas, and their friends from the neighbors' view. The women sat to the side, unseen in the dark. They talked animatedly and rose from time to time to serve refreshments to the men. Fireflies lit up like showering sparks in the dark space that surrounded the card table and its players. A jug of dark red wine, half-filled glasses, servings of melon, and cups of half-drunk coffee, bets of pennies and nickels, and expletives that announced the luck of the moment filled the scene.

Vasilikí was content. Lying in bed, she listened to the talk and laughter that came through her bedroom window.

Earlier that day when she had been in the garden with Eléni, Sofía, and Constantinos, she had closed her eyes and said softly in an audible meditation, "I hope Chrysóula goes to the cemetery for me and prays for Hrístos, and tells him about us." Sofía held her mother's hand and comforted her. "Of course she does. *Babás* knows where we are. He knows, and he is happy for us."

Inevitably, Eléni's thoughts drifted to Andrei and the little town on the sea. She sighed and thought, *I'm forgetting Andrei's face, and how Sozópolis looked, except for the sea.* Her immediate worry about Evangelía brought her back to the garden and summer afternoon. She turned to Sofía and Constantinos. "What can I do about Evangelía? What can I do for her?"

Constantinos had little to offer. "I wish I could help, Eléni. Time. Time will tell us." Unhappy with his vague response and frustrated at his impotence, Constantinos stood, walked slowly around the garden and stopped to admire a rose.

Vasilikí listened to the happy sounds of her family in the garden. Crossing herself, she looked at the icons in the corner of her room and prayed, "Thank you, Panaghía. Thank you, God. My children are safe here and have a good life. Please help Evangelía."

SEVENTH AVENUE, NEW YORK

"Elegant, Mrs. Barnhardt," Bill said, looking over the woman's shoulder and seeing both his and her reflection in the showroom mirror. "If you turn a little to your left, Mrs. Lancaster can see how the tip of the collar comes to your chin. It's perfect for her profile, isn't it Mrs. Lancaster."

The second woman nodded approvingly. "It is very becoming, Cynthia."

Jimmy listened with half an ear to the flattery Bill paid the two women. They took turns admiring themselves in the three-paneled mirror of the small showroom. It was actually a space, not a room — nothing more than a foyer created by ceiling-high partitions that separated it from the shop. Bill's charm, however, turned it into a place where women fulfilled their fantasies.

He had grown more handsome and self-assured as he approached thirty. It did not hurt that he had an athlete's body, sculpted at the expense of a lot of sweat at the Y.M.C.A. He was quick to smile, and women loved the chivalrous attention he gave them as they tried on one coat, stole, or jacket after another.

Archie had joined Bill and Jimmy soon after they opened their business, and had graduated to the position of sewing machine operator. Bill worked at the machine too, when he was not busy in the showroom selling. They paid a man by the hour to nail sewn garments to patterns, and they contracted out linings and monograms to the finishers on the floor below them. Jimmy concentrated on buying skins, matching, and cutting, and occasionally helped Bill with a sale by fitting a client for special alterations.

Louis Dimitroff referred Mrs. Barnhardt and Mrs. Lancaster to Mavrovitis & Rusuli after meeting them at a business event they had attended with their husbands. The impressive Mr. Dimitroff took every opportunity to refer the wives of wealthy executives, whether clients or in his company, to Jimmy and Bill.

Bill helped Mrs. Barnhardt out of the fox coat. "A wonderful choice," he said. Bill's English had improved steadily. He learned from his brother-in-law and Rose, listening carefully to them and to their many American-born contacts. "This coat was meant for you."

Mrs. Cynthia Barnhardt beamed. "When can I have it?"

"I'll take it to the finishers to have them sew in your monogram as soon as you leave. Would you like me to drop it off at your husband's office tomorrow? Or I can deliver it to your home by late afternoon."

"The office will be fine. I'm coming in to meet John for dinner and the theater." She stroked the soft fur of the fox. "I'll be able to wear it tomorrow night. Perfect timing. Fall evenings are chilly."

"Nice women," Bill said after he saw his customers out and went back into the shop. "I think they'll send us more business."

Jimmy blew on the hair of a damaged skin to disclose a fault. He thought for a moment about how to repair it and then made the necessary cuts. "Is Rose coming to work on the books today?" he asked.

"A little later. She says that the year looks good."

"You sold a lot more private accounts this year, Bill."

"It's your craftsmanship, Jimmy. Our garments are beautiful."

That night Jimmy read a letter from his mother, who wrote that his brother, Kóstas, was going to marry Ekaterina Badavia. Jimmy remembered being in a school play with her when he was eight or nine years old. He stopped reading the letter for a moment and hummed the song they had sung together until the words came back to him. He was homesick and lonely.

His relationship with Bill and Rose, and her brother, Louis, provided him with a sense of family. Rose tried matchmaking for Jimmy, introducing him to young women at dinner-dances and parties. He was always attentive, but nothing came of the introductions. Even Kastorian fathers who thought that he would be a good catch for their daughters and promised him handsome dowries gave up.

Jimmy and Peter Stamatis spent most of their free time with a dwindling number of bachelor friends. They enjoyed summer Sunday afternoons at the beach in Coney Island, or as far away as Long Beach or Atlantic City. In the fall, they walked in Central

Park, or sat on one of its lawns observing the scene, dapper in their three-piece suits and straw hats.

While he had stopped attending English classes, Jimmy read widely. Books by Dumas, Hugo, de Maupassant, Dostoyevsky, and Mark Twain found their way into his bookcase and challenged him late into the night. His passion for opera was unabated. He attended virtually every opera during the Metropolitan's season – and now sat in the balcony. His library of recordings and libretti had expanded, and he treated himself to a pair of elegant mother-of-pearl opera glasses imported from France.

On the last weekend of October in 1926, Jimmy went hunting for the first time with Louis Dimitroff and Bill at a farm in the Catskill Mountains. He was reminded of the mountains that surrounded the lake at Kastoria, and of hunting birds with his slingshot. The three men were natural companions, enjoying each other's company and sharing a love of the outdoors. They shot rabbits, pheasant, and grouse, relaxed in the evening with drinks after a dinner of salad and grilled steak, and on the drive home the next day, made a pact that they would go hunting together often in the future.

In December, Mavrovitis & Rusuli moved their business to a larger shop, where Bill had a real showroom with two sets of three-way mirrors, comfortable seating, and a coffee table on which to serve drinks and coffee to his clients. There was space for another matcher and cutter, and four sewing machine operators. Their production, sales, and profits grew.

Work, church activities, weekends at the beach, Kastorian social events, the opera, museums, and reading filled Jimmy's time, but not his life.

As the fifth anniversary of his partnership approached, Jimmy found that he thought more often about marriage and a home, and the emotional security that a wife would give him. But the girl he had danced with at the McAlpin haunted him. Bill spoke to him about it only once. It was late on Thursday, the 30th of December, their last day of work before New Year's Eve. They were closing up the shop when Bill took a bottle of Metaxa from the cabinet in the showroom and poured two drinks.

"Jimmy, toast our partnership, a good year, and an even better one coming."

Jimmy finished putting on his suit jacket and took the glass from Bill. "Happy New Year."

They both downed the drink in one gulp.

"Will you meet Rose before going home?" Jimmy asked.

"Yes, she's at Vlastis' shop. I'll pick her up on the way. You're coming to visit us on my name day, aren't you?"

"Sure."

Bill hesitated for a moment and then said, "We worry about you, Jimmy. When are you going to find a wife?"

"When the time is right, Bill." The look on Jimmy's face closed the subject.

BAY RIDGE, BROOKLYN

Lily and Eléni were setting the table for their New Year's Eve dinner party. They set the fourteen-inch-round, golden *Vasilópita* that Anastasia Zelios had baked as the centerpiece. She prepared the traditional St. Basil's Bread for her children's godmother and her family. It filled the dining room with the aroma of the *mahlépi* and *masticha* that she had used to flavor it.

"I'm afraid, *mána*," Lily said. "What will happen after we meet with the lawyer?"

Eléni put a fork at a setting on the table and sighed. "I don't know, *hrisó mou*. Kyrie Psaki will tell us when you sign the papers on Monday."

"Kyrie Psaki said that it would take months for me to be free. Why — if everything is like he said?"

"I don't know. Have patience. The New Year may bring you a new life."

Lily grimaced, turned, and walked down the hallway to the kitchen where Louie was pouring wine into decanters. *Yiayiá* Vasilikí was tending to her embroidery. Lily bent to kiss her cheek, and her grandmother smiled up at her. Smells of *sarmádes* and roast pork nestled in pickled cabbage filled the kitchen, and soon would overwhelm the delicate scent of *mahlépi* in the dining room.

Lily went up the stairs to her room to primp, though she knew she did it only for herself and her family. She fought to keep up her spirits. *I won't cry. It's New Year's, and maybe, if what the lawyer told mána is true, maybe things will be better in 1927.*

On an October morning two months before, Eléni had approached the door of a third-floor office on West 47thStreet. Black lettering on the door's glass pane read:

Nicholas G. Psaki
Attorney at Law

Eléni knocked on the door and entered. Dressed in a conservative suit, a secretary with a straight hairstyle that culminated in a tight bun at the back of her head greeted her in Greek and immediately ushered her into an office. The man who had been sitting behind a desk rose and came around it with his hand extended. "Kyria Perna?" he asked.

"Yes. You are Kyrie Psaki?"

"I am. Please have a seat. Would you like some coffee? Tea?"

"A little water?"

"Of course." He went to his office door.

"Mika, would you please bring Kyria Perna a glass of water?"

They were seated and comfortable, and a glass of water was in front of Eléni on Psaki's desk when he commented, "Perna is not a usual Greek name."

"No. My husband is Italian."

"Ah, I see. Well, what brings you to see me?"

Eléni explained that she had the money to pay-off the loan on her home and wanted an attorney to handle the matter for her. She also wanted him to prepare her will. Psaki gave the mortgage papers Eléni placed on his desk a cursory examination. "It's a small matter to pay your loan and have the title to the house changed, Kyria Perna," he told her.

"Title?"

"The papers that show who owns the house."

"Me."

"I need more information before I can prepare your will. Let me ask you some questions."

"Ask."

With each of Eléni's answers to his questions, Psaki's interest grew.

"Let me be sure I understand," he said, frowning. "Your daughter was married before her eighteenth birthday — she was seventeen?"

"Yes, seventeen."

"And her husband told her, and you, when he asked to marry her, that he was in business in Detroit, a confectionery manufacturer? That he employed workers?"

"Yes."

"And after they were married you actually saw him in Detroit begging in the street and pretending to be blind?"

"Yes."

Psaki sat back in his chair and was silent for a moment. Eléni studied him. She liked this man. Psaki was in his late forties, of medium height and build, and brown-eyed. He had a smooth, olive complexion, and deep laughter lines on both sides of his mouth. With horn-rimmed glasses, gray hair at his temples, and dressed in a navy suit, white shirt, and striped tie, Eléni thought him distinguished. He was like a rich American, and yet, in spite of his distinction and his great education, he was easy to talk to.

"Kyria Perna," he began. "If we can prove what you told me, I'm sure your daughter's marriage can be annulled."

"Annulled? What does that mean?"

"It means that the court — that is the government... Well, it means that the marriage never happened."

Eléni shook her head in confusion. "But Lily got married. There was a ceremony. Everyone was there."

"Yes, but under the law, a marriage is like a contract. Only people eighteen or older can enter into a contract. When Lily filled out the Marriage License, she wrote that she was 'eighteen' because that is the Greek way – she was in her eighteenth year. But under American law she was only seventeen, which means she could not enter into a contract, therefore the marriage is null and void."

The idea took form in Eléni's mind. She felt a surge of hope. "Lily isn't married?"

The lawyer shrugged. "We have to prove it in court."

"How?"

"I can file papers declaring that she was only seventeen, and that Tsavalas committed fraud to induce her to marry him."

"Fraud?"

"It means that he lied to you and to her about his business. You gave your approval to the marriage and Lily agreed because he said he was a successful confectionery manufacturer."

"Yes, that's right."

"Kyria Perna, do you want me to represent Lily and file for the annulment?"

"How long will it take?"

"It's hard to tell. Six months. Maybe a year. Bring Lily in to see me and I'll have a better idea."

"When?"

"Make the appointment with Mika on your way out. By the time we meet again, I'll have all the papers ready to pay off the mortgage, and we can finish your will."

"And the annulment?"

"I'll interview your daughter. Then I'll prepare the papers for the court. I'll try to have everything ready to file by the first week in January."

Eléni left Psaki's office in a state of elation. "Annulment. Annulment," she repeated to herself. *Evangelía not married? Free?* The information was too good to believe. *Hurry, train. Hurry,* she thought as the subway took her to Brooklyn. *I have to tell Evangelía.* Happy tears welled in her eyes. *Hurry.*

Chapter Twenty
1927
Supreme Court Building, Brooklyn

In spite of August's heat and humidity, Lily wore a high-necked white dress with sleeves. Her lawyer had warned her to dress modestly. Louie left Eléni and Lily at the curb in front of the building to be sure they would be fresh in court, and then he drove off to find a place to park. The two women climbed the steps of the intimidating edifice and were relieved to find Nicholas Psaki waiting for them in the granite-cool hallway.

As he had promised, Psaki filed Lily's complaint against James Tsavalas on the court's first business day in January. The seemingly endless procedural processes that followed confounded Eléni and Lily. Because neither Psaki nor his process servers could find Tsavalas, the court required that letters be sent to Greek attorneys in Detroit requesting information about Tsavalas's whereabouts. In addition, the court ordered Psaki to contact Greek Orthodox priests in both New York and Detroit to attempt to have the complaint served at Tsavalas's last known address, and to publish notices in Brooklyn and Detroit newspapers asking

Tsavalas to contact the court. None of the measures produced him. Tsavalas had vanished.

Finally, satisfied that every attempt had been made to give Tsavalas the opportunity to defend himself, the court set the date for an inquest. Seven months had passed.

Psaki scrutinized his client in the dark, hushed hallway and whispered, "Perfect, Lily. You look just right."

Louie, his brow dripping from the effort of parking the car and hurrying into the courthouse, listened to the lawyer rehearse Lily and Eléni for the final time. "This isn't a trial. There will be no jury, only a justice. His name is Druhan. Answer the questions I ask you just the way you did last week in my office. Justice Druhan wants to hear your testimony so he can judge whether you're telling the truth."

"How will he know?" Eléni asked.

"He's an experienced justice and a good man. He will know. Besides, we can't find Tsavalas. He won't be here to challenge anything you say."

They stood when Justice Druhan entered the courtroom from his chambers. The only people present other than Lily, her family, and her attorney were a small group of men sitting in the back of the court holding pencils and notepads. The clerk called the matter of the petition of Lily Tsavalas for the annulment of her marriage to James Tsavalas.

"Is the attorney for the petitioner ready?" asked the Justice.

"I am your honor."

"I take judicial notice of the fact that the defendant, James Tsavalas, is not in court and is not represented."

Psaki made a brief opening statement summarizing the facts of Lily's case. When he finished, the Justice looked up from the papers before him and said, "You may call your first witness, counselor."

"Thank you, your honor. I call Mrs. Lily Tsavalas."

Psaki motioned to Lily to come forward and guided her to the witness chair. The clerk administered the oath.

"Are you the plaintiff in this action?" Psaki asked Lily. His voice was gentle.

When she glanced up at Justice Druhan, she heard, "Just look at me, Mrs. Tsavalas. Answer the question." She turned to the voice and saw Psaki smiling at her.

"Yes."

"You are suing the defendant, James Tsavalas, for annulment of your marriage to him."

"Yes."

"What was the date you married him?"

"April twentieth, nineteen twenty-two."

"Where?"

"In the Borough of Brooklyn."

"Where were you born?"

"Pyrgos, Bulgaria."

Psaki turned to the judge. "That city is now named Burgas, your Honor."

"Noted," said the Justice. "Go on."

"What was the date of your birth?"

"November eighth, nineteen four."

Psaki looked at her expectantly and motioned at her, as if to draw her forward.

"Old calendar," she added.

The judge leaned forward. "Old calendar? What does that mean?"

"Your Honor, the plaintiff was born in the Balkans where the Greek Orthodox Church adhered to the Julian calendar. It is thirteen days behind the Western Gregorian calendar. Under the new calendar, recently adopted by Greece for civil purposes, the plaintiff's birth date is on October twenty-sixth."

"Interesting. You may proceed."

Psaki took up his questioning again. "What was your exact age at the time of your marriage to Mr. Tsavalas?"

"Seventeen years and five months."

"Your Honor, that would be six months under the Gregorian calendar."

The justice nodded. "Proceed."

"When did you meet Mr. Tsavalas, your husband, for the first time? What date and year was it?"

"I met him toward the end of February, 1922." Lily's voice squeezed through her throat. She listened to the questions carefully.

"And how many months before you married him?"

"About three or four months."

"Where did you first meet him?"

"First time — at a friend's house, at a party."

"And then?"

"At a Greek dance — the McAlpin Hotel."

"Did he ask you for your home address?"

"Yes."

"And did you let him have it?"

"Yes."

Psaki saw his client tightening up, her eyes staring forward. He asked his next question in a conversational voice. "How soon after that did you see him again?"

Lily responded to Psaki's tone. She relaxed. Her voice softened. "He called at the house about a week after that."

"Where?"

"At my mother's house. In Brooklyn."

"How many times did you see him before he proposed marriage to you?"

"About four times."

"The first time he asked you to marry him, did you accept his proposal or refuse?"

"Refuse."

"Why?"

Lily twisted in the witness chair. She glanced at the justice, then at the men in the back of the room and found her voice. "Because I didn't know his business or who he was, and I wanted him to speak to mother before I accepted him."

Justice Druhan interrupted. "Did you feel any affection toward Mr. Tsavalas? Did you love him?"

"Oh. I liked him."

"Liked?" The justice looked up at the ceiling with a quizzical expression, and then directed, "Continue, counselor."

Psaki waited for a moment. He turned to Lily brusquely. "What did he — Tsavalas — say about himself?"

Lily composed herself. "He told me that he was a wealthy man with a confectionery store and a wholesale business in Detroit."

The justice interrupted, asking, "And you relied on that?"

"Yes, sir."

"And then you married him?"

"Yes."

The justice sighed. "You may continue, counselor."

Psaki looked at his notes for a moment, and then, accelerating his pace asked. "Did you talk to him about the same subject after that?"

Lily answered more rapidly. "Yes, I spoke to him with my mother, and with my mother and grandmother."

"That was before you married him?"

"Yes."

"Did you see him outside of your home?"

"Yes."

"Where?"

"At dances and at his brother's house for dinner."

"Were you ever alone with him?"

"No. My mother and stepfather were with me all the time."

In her responses to Psaki's questions, Lily explained that she married James Tsavalas in a civil ceremony and did not live with him until after they were married in church. Soon after, he left for Detroit. Lily remained behind in Brooklyn to complete her trousseau. He returned and they left for Detroit together in late July.

Psaki's questioning went on. "After you arrived in Detroit, Michigan, where did you and your husband go?"

"He took me to a rooming house run by a woman."

"Is that what you expected?"

"No. I thought that we were going to his house. A big house."

"And what did Mr. Tsavalas do the day after your arrival?"

"He left for his business."

Psaki checked his notes. "Was your landlady a Miss Johnson? Did she tell you anything that surprised you?"

"Yes," Lily said in a firm voice. "On the thirty-first of August, a Thursday, she said to me, 'Lily, I have something to tell you.' I said, 'What is it?' She said 'I think it is right for me to tell you that I see your husband down on the main street of Detroit wearing a shabby Palm Beach suit, with a pair of glasses on his eyes, a cane, and a basket around his neck.'" Lily looked at the justice. "He was selling things on the street out of the basket," she said contemptuously. Nervous perspiration darkened the underarms of her dress.

Psaki coughed to get Lily's attention. "Did you and Miss Johnson go the following day to see where he was?"

"We went and saw him there. When I went back home I felt sick, and I stayed in Miss Johnson's apartment that night. The following day I asked her to call up my mother, long distance, and I talked to my mother and told her to come for me because I was very sick. She came on Saturday morning, September second, nineteen-twenty-two."

"After your mother arrived there, did you and Miss Johnson go out on the street again?"

"Yes. Miss Johnson took her down to the same street where she took me the day before, and showed my mother, and my mother

326

said, 'I will walk ahead and you stay with Miss Johnson.' She walked ahead. I saw her pull his glasses off his eyes. She yelled at him and he ran."

"Where did you go after that?"

"We went home. My mother brought me back home."

"Did you ever see Mr. Tsavalas again?"

She sat up straight. "No, I never saw him."

"And you have been living at home?"

"Yes. I live with my mother."

"I have no further questions, your Honor."

Psaki smiled at Lily, took her arm and led her to her seat. "You did very well," he whispered.

He called Eléni to the stand next. The preliminary questions Psaki asked her elicited support for Lily's testimony about her age and the history of her relationship with Tsavalas. Then he asked, "Did James Tsavalas come to you and ask you to consent to his marrying his daughter?"

"Yes."

"What did he tell you at that time?"

"He said, 'I love very much your daughter and I like marry your daughter.' I said, 'All right, if my daughter love you, all right. What kind of business you got?' He said, 'I got a candy confectionery in Detroit, Michigan, I got five or six employees, I am very wealthy man,' and I said, 'All right.'"

"And how many times did he tell you about this?"

"Two, three times."

"Did you receive a call from Lily in Detroit at the end of August?"

"The first day September, Friday. Eight o'clock at night. Just when I come back from business I had telephone call, and Miss Johnson talked on the telephone and she say, 'Your daughter like to talk to you,' and my daughter come to phone and she can't talk, she is so weak and sick and crying. She say, 'Mana, come over, because I am die,' and I take train ten o'clock Friday night and I arrive Detroit, eleven o'clock Saturday."

Justice Druhan asked, "Was your daughter actually sick?"

"She sick heart. Feel like die."

"You mean she was depressed?"

"Sad. Feel like die."

"Thank you, Mrs. Perna. Continue, counselor."

"Mrs. Perna, what happened then?" Miss Johnson say, 'Sit down. Take rest.' I drink cup of coffee, and after Miss Johnson take me and my daughter – I don't know the street, the place – and say, 'Mrs. Perna, you know this man?' I say 'No.'"

"She say, 'You don't know this man? That is Mr. Tsavalas, Lily's husband.'"

"I say, 'Miss Johnson, don't talk to me like that.'"

"She say, 'Yes, Mrs. Perna, that your daughter's husband,' and I say, 'Please ...'"

Justice Druhan interrupted with, "What was he doing?"

"He has a bad suit, old suit and black glasses, and cane, and do this way."

Eléni demonstrated, moving her hand from side to side and up and down.

"As if he were blind?"

"As if blind."

"I say to Miss Johnson, 'Please keep my daughter close to you,' and I go there and I take glasses and I say, 'Are you man that marry my daughter?' He run."

"Was he begging on the street?"

"He beg on the street."

"Do you have any more questions, counselor?"

"No, your Honor."

"Mrs. Perna, you may step down."

"Mr. Psaki, do you have any more witnesses?"

"No, your Honor. We have no further witnesses or evidence."

Justice Druhan thumbed through the papers on his desk for a moment. He looked up at Psaki and said, "The court reserves judgment in this case. Court is adjourned."

Psaki looked at the men in the back of the room and then motioned to his client to follow him out of the court. But the men rushed forward, blocked the aisle, and fired questions.

"Mrs. Tsavalas, how do you feel about your husband now?"

"Mrs. Perna, does Lily have any boyfriends?"

Psaki turned to Louie: "Hold on to your wife and Lily, and follow me, quick." He pushed past the men.

"Hey, wait," one yelled after them. "Don't you want to tell your story to the papers?"

Psaki led the way out of the court, down the hallway and into a small conference room, slamming the door behind them.

"Who those men ask questions?" Louie asked.

"Newspaper reporters. They love these stories."

Lily blanched. She trembled. "Will they write about me?"

"I think so, Lily. Newspapers love scandals. People like to read about them."

"What happen, Kyrie Psaki?" Eléni asked in English. "Lily annulment?"

"Yes," he replied. "But he won't write his decision for two or three weeks."

"*Mána*, what's going to happen to me?" Lily burst out crying. "Everyone will know what happened."

Psaki took charge again. "Mr. Perna, bring your car to the front of the courthouse. When I see you, I'll bring Lily and your wife and keep the reporters away."

Twenty minutes later Lily and Eléni were in the backseat of the car. Lily sobbed and trembled. Louie drove. No one spoke. Eléni put her arm around her daughter and pulled her close. Lily rested her head on her mother's shoulder. Exhausted, they stared out the windows at blurs of people — trees — buildings — shrubs — homes. Louie sped them home.

The doorbell's insistent ring woke Louie. It was just light. He had planned to sleep late and stay at home with Eléni to recover from their day in court. The bell rang again. Eléni raised her head from her pillow and looked at the clock.

"Louie, you awake?"

"Yes."

"Who is ringing the doorbell?"

"I don't know. I'll go down and look."

Louie hurried down to the first floor in his pajamas. He looked through the window to see one man at the front door and two others in the courtyard. The man at the door spotted him and yelled. "Hey, mister. We want to talk to Lily Tsavalas."

"Who you?"

"I'm from the *Mirror*."

"Newspaper?"

"Yeah. We want to interview Lily."

"Go away," Louie growled, shooing the man away with his hand and pulling down the shade.

He was halfway up the stairs when the telephone rang. He hurried back down, went into the kitchen, and lifted the earphone from the telephone's cradle. "Hello?"

"Louie?"

"Constantinos?"

"Louie, Hrístos called me. He said get *New York Times*. They write about Lily."

"What?"

"There is a story about Lily."

"Oh, God. I'll get it."

Eléni came down the stairs. "Leonardo, who's at the door? Who called?"

"There are newspaper men outside. Don't open the door. Don't talk to them. Keep Evangelía away from the windows. Constantinos called." Louie pushed past her. "I'm going to dress and go to the newspaper stand."

Within half an hour, Louie had dressed, gone out and returned home, elbowing his way past the reporters both coming and going. He came through the front door with the *Times* in his hand and made for the kitchen. Lily, who had been pacing the floor, was waiting for Louie with her mother and grandmother. "What's in it?" she asked.

"I don't know," he said, handing her the paper. "I didn't read it."

Lily opened the *Times* on the kitchen table, turned its pages and moved her fingers up and down the columns. "There," she gasped. Her finger pointed to a byline. She read for a moment.

Eléni put her arm around Lily's shoulders. "What does it say? Read. Read it out loud."

"I can't. It tells everything. Everyone will see it."

Crying, Lily ran down the hallway and up the stairs. Eléni followed her. Louie looked at the paper.

'CANDY MAN' A BEGGAR
BROOKLYN BRIDE FINDS

— — — — — — — — — — — — — — — — — —

She Sees Him in Detroit Street,
Posing as Blind — Marriage
Is Annulled for Fraud

Frightened by the commotion, Vasilikí reached for Louie's arm. "What is it, Louie? What's wrong?"

"Evangelía's story is in newspaper. All about her and Tsavalas. Everything."

Vasilikí crossed herself. "Poor Evangelía. God help us. Tell her it will pass. People forget."

SEVENTH AVENUE, MANHATTAN

Bill pushed the security button in response to the loud buzzing noise that announced that there was someone at the shop door. When it opened, Rose stepped into the showroom. She was agitated. Bill stared at her. "This is a surprise. Is something wrong?"

She stepped toward him, her fingers at her lips. She whispered, "Have you read the paper?"

"No.

"Is Jimmy inside?"

"Yes. What's going on?"

"Read this."

She opened the paper and pointed at the article. "It's about that girl he's been mooning over; Lily."

Bill sat down, quickly read the article, and then looked up at Rose. "Should we tell him?"

Rose put her hand on his shoulder. "Let me."

She went into the factory with the *Times* in her hand. Jimmy was in the middle of cutting a skin.

"Hello, Jimmy."

He turned his head toward her. "Good morning. Is everything all right with our books?"

"Everything's fine. I have something for you to read. I wanted you to see it before you heard the news anywhere."

She put the paper on the cutting table in front of him and pointed to the article. She started to leave, but turned and said, "We love you, Jimmy."

He sat on his high stool at the cutting table and read.

BAY RIDGE, BROOKLYN

For the week following the hearing, Lily and her family hid from the reporters that cordoned their home. Several times Louie called the police pleading, "Please. Help. Newspapermen in front of house. Tell them go away."

"It's a free country, mister," the police responded. "Newspapermen are tough to handle. Don't worry. Ignore them. They'll be gone in a day or two."

Lily spent hours sitting in the kitchen with her grandmother, out of sight of the front windows. She drank coffee, read, and re-read newspaper articles. The *Times, Journal, American,* and *Daily Mirror* printed stories about the annulment proceedings. Even the Greek language newspaper, *The National Herald,* managed an article that included all the lurid details. She shuddered thinking, *Everyone knows about me. All the Greeks know about me.*

The most humiliating piece was a full-page feature in the *American Weekly,* a tabloid that relished scandal. She stared at its headline.

Her 'Millionaire' Husband a 'Blind Beggar'

Somehow, the *Weekly* obtained a copy of her portrait. They published it with photographs of Eléni's home, an artist's conception of James Tsavalas, and a large, cartoon-like representation of her mother pulling Tsavalas's dark eyeglasses off his face when she discovered him begging on the streets of Detroit.

On the following Saturday, the reporters were gone. Lily's story was old news. They had found fresh grief to exploit. Freed from the siege, Eléni decided to liven up the house and boost Lily's morale. She took to the telephone to invite as many family and friends as she was able to contact to come to dinner a week later, on Sunday.

Lily's mind turned immediately from her shame to what to prepare for the party. Midweek she baked *tirópites* and *spanakópites,* prepared *taramasaláta* and *dolmádes,* and wrote out a shopping list for Louie. On Friday, he brought home a large net bag full of fresh mussels from Cosentino's Market, two legs of lamb, cheese, olives, salads, greens, and loaves of fresh bread from the bakery. Lily lost herself in cooking. She stuffed the mussels with rice, currants, dill, and pignoli nuts, and marinated the two legs of lamb.

Eléni and Vasilikí used the small kitchen in the basement to make deserts: *baklavá*, *karidópita*, and *galatomboúreko*. Vasilikí drove Eléni crazy giving her detailed directions and correcting her at every step.

Cooking proved therapeutic for Lily. As the guests arrived on Sunday, she greeted each one cheerfully with a hug and kiss. Some quietly congratulated her, telling her to forget the past. They applauded the dinner that she served to them. She came alive, leading everyone through the garden dancing to Greek music played on a portable Victrola. Even *yiayiá* Vasilikí got up to lead a dance, holding a white handkerchief belonging to her grandson Chris in her hand. As evening came, the men set up a card table under the arbor and the women served dessert and coffee. Later, they gathered around Anastasia, whose singing transported them to places in their memories.

Louie was in the kitchen getting a pitcher of ice water when the telephone rang. He answered it, and came to the garden door.

"Eléni, telephone."

"Who is it?"

"I don't know. A man."

Eléni came into the kitchen and went to the phone.

"Hello?"

"Kyria Perna?"

"Yes."

"My name is Jimmy — Dimitrios Mavrovitis. I met you once at a dance five years ago. I danced with your daughter."

"Yes?"

"I read about her in the paper. May I come to visit you, and her?"

Eléni's maternal defenses were aroused. "Why?"

334

"I was disappointed when she married. Now she is not married. I would like to visit her."

Eléni was cautious. "Kyrie Mavro ... what's your name?"

"Mavrovitis."

"Kyrie Mavrovitis, I'll talk to my daughter. Call again in a few days."

"Kyria Perna, tell her that I'm the Jimmy she waltzed with at the McAlpin Hotel, the night the dancers moved aside for us."

"All right, I will."

"Thank you. Good night."

Eléni vaguely remembered the young man and asked Louie, "Do you remember anyone named Dimitrios or Jimmy dancing with Evangelía when people made room for them on the floor? At the McAlpin?"

"Not his name," he said with a grin. "But I remember I said something about a nice young man she was dancing with. You said he was too young."

"Ah, him." Eléni nodded, allowing herself a small smile. "Well, he's older now. I'll talk to Evangelía after everyone leaves."

Lily did remember dancing with Jimmy. Everyone had watched them waltz around the floor. At seventeen, she had been flattered that James was jealous when she returned to the table.

"Do you want me to let him visit?" Eléni asked.

Lily's thoughts were as confused as her emotions.

Eléni took her daughter by her shoulders. "Well, what do you think? Are you ready to meet someone? You don't have to."

"Yes," Lily said decisively. Then her courage wavered. "When? What will I say?"

"I think we'll wait a few weeks. Just be you. He already likes you or he wouldn't ask to come."

Jimmy's call on the following Wednesday resulted in temporary disappointment. It was the last day of August and Eléni invited him to come on the last Sunday in September, almost four weeks away. "We are very busy for the next three weeks," she explained.

Jimmy carried a nosegay of violets to the brownstone on Ovington Avenue. They were the first, early blooms of the new season, and expensive. Louie greeted Jimmy at the front door and ushered him through the house and into the garden. Eléni and Vasilikí sat waiting under the arbor. Its vines showed signs of fall — their vibrant green summer leaves had faded and were brown at the edges. It was pleasant in the garden and comfortable in the shade. Eléni got up from her chair. "I am Eléni Perna, Evangelía's mother."

"*Chairetai*, Kyria Perna."

"And this is Evangelía's grandmother, Vasilikí Zissis."

"*Chairetai*, Kyria Zissis."

Jimmy stood awkwardly for a moment, clinging to the violets. Eléni sat down.

Louie, sitting in a garden chair facing Eléni, pointed to the empty one next to him. "Have a seat, Dimitrios." Jimmy sat down and waited, holding the violets in his lap with both hands.

Eléni broke the silence. "Where are you from, Dimitrios? Do you work in the city?"

"I was born in Mávrovo. It's a village near Kastoria in Macedonia. I'm a furrier. In Manhattan. On 7th Avenue."

"Is Kastoria Greek?" Vasilikí asked.

"Yes. In the mountains. In the north."

Vasilikí leaned forward in her chair to see the nosegay more clearly.

"Violetta? Beautiful."

"Violets? Yes. They're for ..."

"Where do you work?" Eléni interrupted, pursuing information. Louis got up and started to deadhead roses on the bushes that bordered the sitting area. He left Eléni to conduct her interview.

"I have my own business, with a partner, Vasílis Rusuli. We've been in business for five years."

Eléni hid her initial reaction, skepticism. *I've heard this before*, she thought. She promised herself, *I'll make some calls and check on him.*

Vasilikí asked, "Are your parents living?"

"Yes. In Mávrovo with my brothers and sisters."

"Do they depend on you? Do you help them?" Vasilikí leaned forward.

"Well, they ..." Before he could go on, Lily stepped into the garden. She was wearing a light, bare shouldered summer dress that showed off her figure and slender legs. Her face was no longer that of a teenage girl. She had become a graceful woman. Jimmy stood to greet her.

"I'm Jimmy. Do you remember me from the time we danced together?"

"Yes." Lily smiled. "We waltzed."

She sat down next to her mother. Jimmy took his seat opposite them, not sure what to say next.

"Are those for me?" Lily asked with a little smile, pointing to the violets.

"Yes." He held them out to her.

"They're beautiful." She learned to love violets at the end of the Great War, just as they were going out of fashion in New York. Jimmy thought of violets in terms of romantic heroines in opera: Violetta in *La Traviata*, and Mimi, who sold them on Paris' street corners in *La Bohème*.

Their talk was of work, family, and origins. Jimmy told them about his activities at church. He was courteous and quiet, careful with his choice of words. Lily, usually outgoing, was subdued, responding to Jimmy's reserve.

Eléni warmed to the young man, asked Louie to bring brandy and went in to the kitchen herself to prepare coffee and pastry. A little more than an hour had passed when Jimmy thanked them for their hospitality and rose to leave. He said goodbye to Louie, shook his hand firmly, bowed to Vasilikí, and turned to Lily.

"It was very nice to see you again."

"Thank you for the violets. I love them."

Lily's words encouraged him. "Kyria Perna, may I speak to you for a moment?"

"Yes, come with me."

Eléni led him through the house to the front room.

Jimmy looked at her earnestly. "Kyria Perna, I'd like to see Lily again. Often, if you permit."

"Dimitrios, you – are you sure?" Eléni thought that she might as well get the worst in the open. "You know that Evangelía was married?"

"Yes."

"And you read the newspapers? And what they said?"

"Yes, I know. Please do not mention it again. That's the only thing I ask."

Eléni nodded her head.

"May I come again next week? I would like to bring my friend, Vasílis Rusuli, with his wife, Rose. Perhaps you'd allow Lily and me go for a walk with them, nearby."

"I'll ask Evangelía. Call me tomorrow."

Eléni saw Jimmy to the door and paused after he left. She thought well of him. *He is a gentleman, not a bragging type like Tsavalas. His friend is married — his wife would be a good chaperone. But Evangelía had been married. Does she need a chaperone?*

Eléni found Lily in the kitchen. She was putting the violets in a glass. "Tell me," she asked. Her tone was urgent. "What did he say?"

"He wants to see you again next week."

"Does he know everything about me?"

"He does, and he doesn't care. He said he never wants to hear about it again. Do you want to see him?"

"Yes. Yes, I do."

Rose and Bill accompanied Jimmy to Brooklyn the next Sunday afternoon. Eléni's telephone inquiries had confirmed that Vasílis and Dimitrios, who she learned were called Bill and Jimmy, were long-term friends and successful partners. Jimmy introduced his friends to Eléni, and then to Lily. Rose smiled. "Do you remember me, Lily? At the McAlpin Hotel?" She whispered, "Remember? You helped me to straighten the seams of my stockings."

"Yes," Lily exclaimed. She relaxed. "I was nervous."

Eléni's positive estimation of Jimmy grew on meeting his friends. Their dress and manners were refined. They were warm toward Lily and thoughtful in their exchanges with her, and with Vasilikí and Louie. Eléni encouraged the two couples to go for a walk together and return for coffee and pastries.

Jimmy visited Lily every weekend in October, coming alone or with Rose and Bill. The last Sunday afternoon of the month, Calypso, and her parents, Constantinos and Sofía, were visiting Eléni when Jimmy arrived. Calypso recognized him immediately. She found Théa Eléni and Lily alone in the kitchen, closed the door and drew close to them. "That's the man I saw crying in the back of the church when you got married, Lily," she whispered. "That's him, your Jimmy."

"Are you sure?"

"It's him."

Eléni took her niece by her shoulders. "Never repeat this, Toto. Never."

On the first Sunday in November, Peter Stamatis and his wife of three months joined Jimmy and Lily for an afternoon in Manhattan and an early dinner. Eléni had resolved the issue of Lily going out alone with Jimmy and his friends. Her daughter was a grown woman.

Lily laughed when Peter told her the story of Jimmy's surprise when he announced that he was going to marry Athena. Peter had kept the fact that he had been courting a secret until they set the wedding date.

"Jimmy's the only bachelor left," Peter said as he finished his story. There was an awkward silence.

The following week, Rose, Bill, Athena, and Peter went dinner dancing with Lily and Jimmy in New York. It was a first for Lily. Jimmy was confident and sure. He led her to the dance floor and made her the center of attention. When the orchestra started to play a tango, she demurred. "I've never tangoed with a man. Only with my cousins."

"Just follow me." Other dancers moved aside to watch them.

Later, walking from the train station, he was telling her about the new line of fox jackets that he and Bill were manufacturing when he stopped in the light of the entrance to a drugstore. Customers stepped around them. "I want to talk to your mother about us. Is it all right?"

"About what?"

"Marriage. Will you marry me, Lily?"

She threw her arms around his neck. "Yes," she said. "Yes. Ask mother tonight."

SEVENTH AVENUE, MANHATTAN

Thoughtful of his mother's feelings, Jimmy had maintained minimal contact with his half-brother, George, seeing him in the market, visiting him briefly on his name day, and at times like Christmas, and on his niece and nephew's birthdays. He knew that Mary continued to suffer George's abuse and neglect. Once, in a moment of anguish, she confided to Jimmy that she was a Jewess. "My parents held a funeral service for me when I married George. I gave up my family for a bum," she sobbed. "At least I have my children. I'll leave him as soon as Tom is eighteen."

Both Jimmy and George received letters from their mother after she learned about Jimmy's engagement. She wrote that it was sinful and a disgrace to the family that her Dimitráki was going to marry a woman who had left her husband. Jimmy arranged to meet his brother George for lunch. They ate slowly, exchanged small talk about the fur market and avoided any mention of their mother's letters until Jimmy pushed his coffee cup and its saucer toward the center of the table, and asked, "George, how did *mána* learn about Lily. Did you send a telegram to her?"

"Not me. Gossip spreads fast, even across the ocean. Mother doesn't understand. Neither do I. You have your pick of women. Why one that left her husband?"

"Not another word, George, or we'll never speak again. I am going to marry her, and I'd like someone from my family to be there. Will you be my witness?"

"But, Jimmy ..."

"But nothing. Yes or no. Will you be my witness and treat Lily as a member of our family?"

"Will you have a church wedding?"

"We can't. Lily never applied for a divorce or annulment from the church. I asked Pater Kazakos. He told me that without her husband's cooperation it is impossible."

"And you don't care that you won't be married by a priest?"

"Did you care about the church when you married Mary? Did you think about mother when you married a Jewess? I am going to marry Lily. Let God be my judge."

Three days after Justice Druhan signed the final judgment granting Lily's annulment, George stood next to his brother in the court building as his witness. Jimmy and Lily took their vows in front of the Clerk of the Court. When the clerk finished the short ceremony with, "I declare you man and wife," Jimmy kissed Lily lightly on her lips and accepted his brother's good wishes. Half an hour after the ceremony, they entered Eléni's home to shouts of congratulations. Lily's family and friends filled the house. Bill and Rose, Peter and Athena, and Kyrie Psáltis and his family were there.

He stepped forward and kissed Jimmy and Lily. "Now I'm happy," he told them. "My boys are all married."

Mid-afternoon, while Louie drove the newlyweds to Manhattan to board their train for an Atlantic City honeymoon, Jimmy opened a box that contained a sumptuous three-quarter-length silver fox coat with a monogram sewn into the lining that read: *Lily Mavrovitis.* Lily removed her wool coat, put on the fox and snuggled close to Jimmy. Reaching into her purse, she took out a jewelry box and handed it to her husband. It contained a gold ring with a solitary diamond. Jimmy put it on the fourth finger of his left hand, drew Lily even closer and kissed her for a long time.

Embarrassed, Louie kept his eyes on the road and traffic, avoided looking in the rear-view mirror and focused on driving. Driving up to the curb of the railroad station he stammered his goodbyes, called a porter to take the couple's suitcases, and then watched them pass through the station's doors, arm in arm. They were aware only of each other.

CHAPTER TWENTY-ONE
1928
BAY RIDGE, BROOKLYN

Jimmy and Lily returned from their honeymoon with no thought of living anywhere but with Lily's parents. Eléni was elated. Her new son-in-law adored Lily, doted on Vasilikí, was good company for Louie, and showed her love and respect. He melded into the family's routine, worked hard, eagerly came home to Lily each night, and enthusiastically joined in Eléni's family gatherings. Once, he reminded Eléni of their agreement. They were in the kitchen waiting for Louie and Lily to finish dressing before they all left to attend a wedding.

"Have you told everyone never to talk about Lily's first marriage?"

She took his face in her hands and answered, "Yes. They know," and kissed his cheek.

On the first Sunday of March, Jimmy took Lily to church at St. Constantine and Helen's on Schermerhorn Street. Having fasted they went forward to receive communion. When Lily accepted the red chalice cloth from Jimmy's hand and placed it under her chin, the priest hesitated for a moment. He saw that Lily was with Jimmy, and that she wore a wedding ring. Finally, he uttered the words: "The Servant of God, Evangelía ...," and placed the spoon that contained the body and blood of Christ into Lily's mouth.

The next morning, Eléni, Louie, and Jimmy walked to the subway station to board the subway to Manhattan. Meanwhile, Lily made her grandmother comfortable in the rocking chair and then busied herself clearing the kitchen table, doing dishes, and making beds. She bathed and dressed, and was about to put on her make-up when the doorbell rang. She applied her lipstick quickly and went to the front door.

"Lily?" asked the man standing at the door. "Lily Tsavalas?"

Her face darkened. "Mavrovitis."

He handed her an envelope. "You don't remember me, do you?"

"What is this?" she asked, taking the envelope. "Who are you?"

"I'm James's brother, Niko."

"No!" Lily slammed the door and hurried down the hall to the kitchen. By the time she got there, she was shaking, and oblivious to the envelope that she dropped on the kitchen table.

"What is it, Evangelía?" Vasilikí asked. "What happened?"

Lily sank to the floor at her grandmother's knees. She was frightened and bewildered. "Why did he come here? Why?"

Vasilikí tried to comfort her. "Shh, shh, my child. Tell me. What is it?"

The telephone rang several times. Each ring was more demanding. "Answer the telephone, Evangelía. Please. Answer the telephone."

Lily got to her feet and picked up the receiver. "Hello."

"Lily, is that you?"

"Yes. Who is this?"

"Nicholas Psaki. Your lawyer."

"Yes?" Her voice was flat.

"Are you well? You don't sound all right."

She choked. "James's brother was here."

"James Tsavalas' brother?"

"Yes. Niko."

"What did he say?"

"Nothing. He just told me who he was."

"What did you do?"

"I closed the door."

"Is that all?"

"Yes. No. Wait — he gave me an envelope."

"I thought so. Lily, can you come to my office this afternoon?"

"Yes. Why?"

"James is back. He is going to cause trouble. Can you be here at two o'clock?"

"Yes," she whispered.

"Good. Bring the envelope. I'll call your mother and Jimmy and ask them to be here too. I will explain everything then. Don't worry. I'll see you at two."

"Yes. Two." When he hung up, she stared into space, holding the phone in her hand.

Eléni and Jimmy were waiting in Psaki's office when Lily arrived. Psaki looked up from his desk. "Ah, Lily. Please take a seat."

Jimmy gave her a kiss and held her chair. "When did you see Tsavalas?" he asked angrily.

"He came to the house this morning."

"James?" cried Eléni. "That devil. I'll kill him."

"No. It was his brother, Niko."

"Lily, did you bring the envelope Tsavalas gave you?" Psaki asked.

Lily took the unopened envelope from her purse and dropped it on the desk.

"Please be patient for a moment." Psaki understood his clients' alarm and the need for calm. Psaki opened the envelope and scanned its contents. Lily took Jimmy's hand. Eléni, twisting the straps of her purse, leaned forward, waiting for Psaki to speak.

"Let me explain what's happening. James Tsavalas retained — hired — a lawyer, named Yarchover, to file an action to quash your annulment."

"What does quash mean?" asked Eléni.

"Quash means to vacate or null an action." Psaki saw that there was no understanding in his clients' faces. "He wants a judge to say there was no annulment, and that Lily is still married to James Tsavalas."

Lily started to cry.

"Can he do that?" Jimmy asked.

"Please, just listen for now. The deposition — the statement — that James signed is full of nasty allegations. He says bad things about your character, Lily, and that you lied about everything."

Lily gasped. "He is lying."

Psaki smiled grimly. "His lawyer says some bad things about me too."

Eléni got up from her chair and raised her arm. Her face was contorted. She growled, "I'll kill him."

"Please calm down, Kyria Perna. Let me finish."

Eléni took her seat and contained her anger.

Psaki went on. "Yarchover doesn't include any depositions — statements — that support Tsavalas's claims, not one. And he says nothing about the fact that Lily was underage at the time of the marriage."

Jimmy stood up and stepped behind Lily, his hands on her shoulders. "Why would Tsavalas do this?"

"Who knows? Maybe he wants to get even for the bad press he got in the papers last August. Maybe he wants to save his reputation. Or maybe he wants some money to drop the matter and go away. I'm sorry to say this Lily, but it looks like that's why he married you in the first place. Money. He may want a payoff."

"Payoff?" Eléni asked.

"Yes, to be paid money to go away. Not to bother Lily any more. Kyria Perna, do you want me to ask Tsavalas' lawyer about a financial settlement? About giving him money?"

"You mean me give him money?"

Psaki shrugged. "You could try it."

"What else can we do?"

"A hearing is set for the fifteenth of March. I would have to submit written responses to the court by the fourteenth. That's nine days. I can do it. The justice will make a decision on whether to quash the annulment, send the matter to trial, or dismiss Tsavalas's petition."

Eléni turned to her daughter and Jimmy. "*Paidiá*, I don't want to give that *paliánthropos* even a nickel. We fight. All right?"

Jimmy knelt next to his wife and looked into her face. "We have to fight, Lily. We can't let him get away with the terrible things he said about you."

"Yes," Lily said. "No money."

Psaki smiled. "That's what I hoped you'd say. Lily, can you stay and work with me?"

"Yes."

"Good. You can leave now, Kyria Perna, but I will need to see you in a day or two to prepare your deposition. I'll call you. Jimmy, you can stay if you'd like, but you don't have to."

"Go, Jimmy," Lily said. "Go back to the shop. I'm all right."

Jimmy hugged Lily and kissed her. As he left he heard Psaki say, "All right, Lily – let's get to work."

SUPERIOR COURT, BROOKLYN

Psaki, their attorney, filed depositions for Lily, Eléni, and Louis, and for himself, countering every allegation made by Tsavalas, who claimed that Lily had an 'easy way' with men, and attempted suicide when Tsavalas said he would not marry her. He attacked her character, asserting that she had pursued him in 'salacious ways' unknown to her mother, and that he had not told her, or them, that he was a business owner and wealthy. He argued that the family had induced him to marry Lily by giving him money to 'tide him over' when he first went to Detroit. He insisted that he had never posed as a blind beggar, and that Lily had attempted to obtain a divorce by asking him fraudulently to admit to having committed adultery. Finally, he declared that she had destroyed his reputation in the annulment proceedings without giving him the opportunity to defend himself.

At the time of the hearing, Justice Cropsey, a no-nonsense, stone-faced jurist with a massive head of long gray hair sat at his desk in chambers with the opposing attorneys sitting across from him. "Gentlemen," he said, looking over his reading glasses, "I've read the file — all the depositions filed last year, the transcript of the inquest, the depositions in support of quashing the annulment, the depositions in opposition, and your arguments. Do you have anything to add?"

Yarchover and Psaki simultaneously said, "No, your Honor."

Yarchover sat back in his chair with a smug look on his face. His thin-line mustache, multicolored paisley bowtie, matching pocket-square, and overpowering cologne gave the impression of a Broadway producer.

"Mr. Yarchover, can you tell me anything more about why your client might not have heard anything about — ah, where is it?" he said shuffling through the papers on his desk. "Yes, the action for annulment by Lily Tsavalas, now Mavrovitis?"

"Well, your Honor, the deposition I submitted shows clearly that the plaintiff and Mr. Psaki did everything they could to avoid getting my client's address, or finding his whereabouts."

The justice interrupted Yarchover. "His relatives live in New York. Correct?"

348

"Yes, your Honor."

"They read Greek or English. Perhaps both. Correct?"

"Yes, your Honor."

"I assume that the relatives have friends that read newspapers too. No response is necessary."

The justice grimaced, looked at a sheet of paper on his desk, and leaned forward toward Yarchover, turning his open hands palm upward in a questioning gesture. "Now, five and one-half years after his wife left him, and seven months after the inquest, your client wants to quash the annulment of a marriage to a woman he does not want to be married to, in order to save his reputation by having a trial in open court on the merits? Is that right?"

"Yes, your Honor."

"Really?"

Psaki sat quietly.

Justice Cropsey picked up a paper from his desk, read for a moment and then asked, "Tsavalas claims that he moved to New York in November of nineteen twenty-four. Correct?"

"Yes, your Honor."

"I note that he claims not to have been aware of the annulment proceedings, or Justice Druhan's decision until late in November of last year, nineteen twenty-seven. Mr. Yarchover, can you show me any evidence that the plaintiff's attorney did not comply fully with Justice Carswell's order regarding the service of the summons by publication?"

"No, your Honor." Yarchover squirmed in his seat. "But he was not contacted."

"Neither you nor your client challenge the plaintiff's testimony that she was seventeen at the time of her marriage. Correct?"

"Yes, your Honor."

"Mr. Psaki, do you have anything to add?"

"No, your Honor. My clients' depositions stand on their merit."

"Thank you, counselors. That will be all. You will have my decision in three to four weeks."

Good to his word, Justice Cropsey's decision was delivered to Psaki in three and one half weeks, mid-morning on the ninth of April. Psaki read the decision, picked up his telephone, and dialed. He heard the phone ringing on the other end of the line.

Lily picked up the receiver of the ringing telephone and answered. "Hello?"

"Lily? This is Nicholas Psaki."

Lily listened.

"Lily? Are you there?"

"Tell me. What's happened?"

"I received the decision. Listen to what the justice wrote." Psaki read excitedly. "Now, on the motion of Nicholas C. Psaki, attorney for the plaintiff, it is ordered that the motion of the defendant be and the same is in all respects denied."

Lily's voice rose. "What does that mean?"

"Congratulations, Mrs. Mavrovitis." He emphasized her name. "You're rid of Tsavalas. You won."

Lily cried and laughed. She thanked Psaki repeatedly. After she put down the phone, she sat quietly for a few minutes, breathed slowly, and forced herself to the realization that it was over. Moments later, Lily telephoned Jimmy, and then Eléni, telling them about the decision in just a few words. And then Lily went into the kitchen, knelt by the rocking chair, and put her head on her grandmother's lap.

Yiayiá Vasilikí had heard everything — she had heard Evangelía telling her mother the news in Greek. "Evangelía," she said, stroking her granddaughter's hair, "thank the Panaghía and God."

THE METROPOLITAN OPERA HOUSE

The conductor silenced the orchestra and vocalists with a sweep of his baton, the curtain fell, and the audience rose to its feet.

"Bravi. Bravi." Jimmy called from his orchestra seat. He stood, and Lily stood next to him, applauding Puccini's powerful score and the Oriental splendor of the final scene of *Turandot*.

It was the tenth of December, their first anniversary. Jimmy decided that they would celebrate with a suite at the Astor Hotel, dinner in its best dining room, and orchestra seats at the Metropolitan Opera. He had carried a suitcase containing his tuxedo to work, and walked with it in hand to the Astor at the end of the day in time to register just before Lily arrived. He watched her step out of a cab, and then into the lobby. She was followed by a bellman. He carried her formal gown and her suitcase. Jimmy kissed her, took her arm, and guided her into an elevator. Rewarded with a handsome tip, the bellman left the couple in their corner suite, where they rushed to make love before dressing for the evening.

An intimate dinner, hurried because of curtain time, preceded their short walk to the opera house. Her three-quarter-length silver fox coat kept Lily warm against the December chill.

Jimmy's precious recordings had not prepared Lily for Laura-Volpe's performance of *Nessun Dorma*. His soaring high notes, ending in *'Vincerò. Vincerò.'* astounded her.

Yes, thought Jimmy, *victory*.

They ended the evening with dancing at the Astor and a passionate return to their suite. In the morning, after breakfast, Jimmy accompanied Lily out of the hotel's lobby to Broadway, where a bellman opened the door of the cab that would take her to Brooklyn. She was aglow. Jimmy kissed her, shut the cab door, and in an uncharacteristic display, waved goodbye to her from the curb. Smiling, he turned down 7th Avenue and walked toward the market.

CHAPTER TWENTY-TWO
1929
BEAR MOUNTAIN, NEW YORK

Eléni had clapped her hands rhythmically for almost an hour, keeping time with a clarinetist and a mandolin player who were enraptured by their own music. Content sitting at a table in a green-canopied mountain glen with her family and friends, she listened to Lily and her cousins sing familiar Greek songs and watched them dance hand-in-hand in a small circle. Eléni would like to have brought her mother with her on this outing. But at eighty-eight, Vasilikí was no longer able to leave the house for any length of time. She spent her days sitting in the kitchen observing and commenting on what was happening around her or drifting into sleep. Her embroidery was in her hands, but she used less and less thread each day.

Louie, Constantinos, and Jimmy finished their picnic lunch with fruit, cheese, and wine. They had taken off their linen coats and vests in deference to the warm afternoon and informal environment, but they maintained their dignity by wearing their ties. The young women wore flowing summer dresses and had flowers in their hair. No cosmetic could have improved their youthful glow.

At eight o'clock that morning, the picnickers had met at the Day Line's steamboat, the Alexander Hamilton, for the trip north on the Hudson River to Bear Mountain. Carrying food-filled wicker baskets and laughing at his imitation of Charlie Chaplin's comic walk, they followed Louie up the gangway and onto the open deck. Once settled on board, Louie, the trip's organizer and promoter, was quick to put his new Kodak camera to work.

When they arrived at Bear Mountain, they found their own special place, a quiet glen. They took walks or lay on blankets allowing their eyes to follow the yellow-white, gray-fringed clouds that passed far above the lacy cover of the forest. Early in the afternoon, they gathered for their picnic lunch, music, singing, and dancing.

Louie took photographs at every opportunity. After the music ended, he captured Lily and her cousins in a gentle composition of smiling young women, and later snapped one of Jimmy and Lily. He sat against a tree with his arm around Lily's shoulders. She rested her head on his chest with her eyes closed. The click of Louie's camera woke Lily from her reverie. She looked up at Jimmy. "Let's take a walk to the lake."

Jimmy took Lily's hand to help her to her feet, and holding hands, they wandered away from the glen. Eléni watched them until the path they followed led them out of sight. *Life is good*, Eléni thought. *Glory to God. All is well.*

Sofía walked up to Eléni, sat next to her and prodded her arm, saying, "Look at Calypso."

Calypso, who was now more often called by her pet name, Toto, stood close to her husband, Petros. Indifferent to her presence, he focused on a game of *távli*. Handsome, tall, and broad shouldered, he behaved with conceit and arrogance. Eléni watched her niece hover about him. He had drunk too much wine and showed no evidence of having had enough. When Toto put her arm around his shoulders, he shrugged and pushed her away.

Her son-in-law embarrassed Sofía. "Eléni, I'm worried about them."

"Do you want me to talk to him?"

"No. He'll only sulk. Constantinos says it was a bad match. Petros didn't even talk to Constantinos before announcing that he was going to marry Toto."

Eléni distracted Sofía by drawing her attention to her daughter, Theanó, and to her grandchildren. "Theanó looks wonderful. Look at Ralis with his sister on the blanket. He protects Alexandra."

Sofía smiled at her grandchildren, then frowned and looked again at Petros.

Late in the afternoon, the women packed the wicker baskets with plates, silverware, glasses, and what remained of the picnic feast and called the men to take up their burdens. They left the glen quietly, making their way to the waiting steamboat. Sped by the river's current, it carried them south past New Jersey's Palisades.

As the Alexander Hamilton reached the northern tip of Manhattan and twilight faded into darkness, the steamboat's passengers could just make out the steel towers that grew from the river like giant trees. They would soon hold the span of the George Washington Bridge, linking Manhattan to New Jersey. Lights in the windows of the grand houses and apartments that lined Riverside Drive twinkled like distant stars.

Lily pressed close to Jimmy. "I'm going to tell *mána* now."

They walked from the rail where they had been standing to where Eléni sat with Louie. Lily took her mother's hand. "We have news."

Eléni smiled. "I think I know."

"I'm pregnant. I told Jimmy this afternoon."

Eléni hugged her daughter. "I knew it. You've looked different for two or three weeks. *Yiayiá* said so too."

Louie jumped to his feet and shook Jimmy's hand. "Congratulations."

Jimmy, who was getting used to the idea, smiled, thinking about the moment that afternoon at the lakeside when Lily had said simply, "Jimmy, you're going to be a father."

SEVENTH AVENUE, MANHATTAN

Jimmy took off his white smock, reached for his suit coat and said, "I'm going out for an hour, Bill. The jeweler promised to have Lily's ring ready this morning."

Bill looked up from the paperwork he had spread out on their showroom coffee table. "Rose is coming before lunch. Will you show it to us?"

"Sure," Jimmy answered, hurrying out the front door.

Bill continued to work on a list of garments to retrieve from storage in the afternoon. It was Friday and he planned make deliveries to a few of his best clients on Saturday. He had followed the same routine all through October. He brought coats, jackets, capes, and stoles out of storage to the shop for customers to pick up, and personally delivered a few items on Saturdays. In the spring, he reversed the process. In addition to fees for storage, alterations, and repairs, he gained two opportunities each year to make contact with his customers and promote new business.

A little before noon Rose rang the security bell. Bill let her in and greeted her with a kiss. "Where's Jimmy?" she asked.

"He'll be right back."

Rose took off her coat and hung it up before going to the desk. She started to open the mail. After working for a while she said, "I saw Lily yesterday, she's really filling out. She loves being pregnant."

356

Bill frowned. "I'm sorry, Rose. I wish that there were something the doctor could ..."

"No, Bill. I'm sorry I said anything to worry you. We don't have to have children. I'm happy as we are."

Just as Bill stepped close to hug her, they heard the front door lock open. Jimmy smiled at Rose. "I'm glad you're here. You have to see the ring I bought Lily for her birthday."

He opened the box and handed the ring to Rose, who immediately put it on her own finger. It was a three-carat diamond set in platinum and surrounded by little diamonds. "Oh my. Lily is going to love it. It's gorgeous."

Jimmy grinned. "Can I afford it?"

"Well, business hasn't been as good as last year. But it's good enough for now." Her face darkened and she hesitated for a moment. "Has our broker called, Bill?"

"No. He said yesterday not to worry — the market is ... ah ... correcting. He says it'll go back up."

"I'm going to call him." She went to the phone.

Jimmy put the ring back into its box and dropped the box into a drawstring sack that displayed the jeweler's emblem. He hid it under his jacket on the coat rack.

Rose held the phone to her ear and grumbled. "Busy, busy, busy." She dialed again. "I wish he had more lines."

The security bell rang. Bill opened the door and took delivery of their lunch. He prepared the table while Jimmy filled the teapot with water and set it on the hotplate.

"Ben? Finally," Rose exclaimed. "I thought I'd never get through to you. How's the market?"

Bill turned toward her and waited.

"How far?" she asked. Her face turned ashen. "But you said ... but ... well ... I know you don't control it, but you ..."

She stopped talking, listened, and then slammed down the phone. "It's worse," she said. "The market is falling."

BAY RIDGE, BROOKLYN

Eléni had been anxious all through the weekend. Her broker had called her on Friday to tell her that she had to sell stock to cover her account. She had never asked what it meant to buy on margin.

On Saturday, October twenty-sixth, Lily's birthday party had taken Eléni's mind off her financial fears. Her daughter's healthy pregnancy, and the beautiful ring that was Jimmy's present to Lily, gave Eléni much to be thankful for. Besides, the broker told her that the market would improve after the scare passed.

On Monday, the stock market traded more than nine million shares, a record. Everyone was trying to sell, and as prices tumbled much of Eléni's wealth evaporated.

On Tuesday, her broker's telephone call left Eléni numb. "The market crashed, Madame Helen. All you have left is some cash."

"Where my money?"

"You owned shares in companies and foreign currency. I had to sell to pay your loans. You're lucky that you had enough in your account to cover. Listen — you are better off than most. You have more than twenty thousand left. Some people lost their homes, everything."

Eléni and her family put aside their worries for the Christmas holidays. In spite of her swollen belly and aching back, Lily spent the better part of two days preparing the feast, cooking all the foods that her Macedonian husband and relatives from Sozópolis would enjoy. Jimmy contributed by making *kadaífi*, the layered, shredded-wheat-like version of *baklavá* that was favored in Kastoria. Everything was kept fresh in the modern two-door GE refrigerator Eléni had purchased earlier in the year to replace the icebox.

"What's there to worry about?" Eléni asked everyone around her dinner table. "I've only lost money. I have my family — health — the house. We have each other. We've survived worse."

After dinner, the family gathered in the parlor in front of Eléni's Christmas gift to them. The open doors of a cherry wood cabinet revealed the dials of a radio. Heat from its mammoth transformers and glowing tubes warmed the room. *Yiayiá* Vasilikí leaned forward in her chair when she heard the voice of an announcer introduce a program of Christmas music. "Come out of there," *yiayiá* Vasilikí ordered, pointing at the magical box. "I know you're inside. Come out, I want to see you."

"There's no one in there, *yiayiá*," Lily explained. "The voice comes through the air, and this box brings it into the house for us to hear it."

"America has devils everywhere," Vasilikí complained. "A box that makes ice. A box that talks. Does the priest know we have these things?"

"Yes, *yiayiá*. The priest knows. He says that they're not evil."

"God protect us," Vasilikí said as she crossed herself.

I'm glad I bought the refrigerator and radio before I lost all that money, Eléni thought. She looked at Jimmy and then at Lily, who, in spite of carrying an almost full-term baby and having cooked and served all day, was energetic and enjoying the holiday.

Louie sat next to Eléni on the sofa and pressed against her. "*Kalá Hristoúgena*," he said, and kissed her cheek. She hugged his arm, comforted by him and the scene of her family. *The worst is over*, she thought. *We have a good life and a baby coming. Everything will be fine.*

CHAPTER TWENTY-THREE
1930
SHORE ROAD HOSPITAL, BAY RIDGE

In the hospital nursery, Eléni held her grandchild in her arms and said, "The child of my child is twice my child." She kissed Athanásios's hand. He made a little whine, puckered his lips, and sank back into a peaceful sleep.

A nurse took Athanásios from Eléni, who gave him up reluctantly. Jimmy watched Louie gently pinch the baby's toe. "Is my wife awake?" he asked the nurse.

"Yes. She is waiting for you. It's almost time for her to nurse your son."

He smiled and walked from the nursery to Lily's private room. Its window faced west, overlooking windswept Lower New York Bay, and across its expanse, the low hills of Staten Island. Snow and ice on Shore Road and its sidewalks sparkled in the bright winter sun, whose rays filled Lily's room with a golden glow. There was a bouquet of violets in a small vase on the nightstand next to her bed. She smiled when Jimmy entered her room. "Thank you for the violets, Jimmy," she said, opening her arms to him.

He bent to kiss her. "I love you. Our son is beautiful."

Eléni and Louie followed Jimmy into the room. He stepped aside to allow Eléni to kiss her daughter. "How do you feel, darling?" she asked.

Lily whispered. "I'm sore. And the baby's sucking — that hurts a little, too."

"You'll be fine. We have everything ready at home — a crib, diapers, baby clothes, blankets."

"Did the doctor see you this morning?" Jimmy asked.

"He was here earlier. He said I can go home the day after tomorrow."

The ever-thoughtful Louie spoke up. "I'll have the car checked and keep the heat on before you get in. The house will be nice and warm, too."

"Thank you, Louie."

Louie smiled. Lily looked at him and in a flash of recognition realized that Louie had always been there to help her. He never interfered or criticized her. He loved her. She softened toward him. "You're a *pappoú* now, Louie. How does it feel?"

Louie beamed. "Good, Evangelía. Very good."

"Your son is hungry," the nurse announced coming through the door with Athanásios in her arms. He uttered short, demanding cries.

"I'll be back tonight," Jimmy said. He kissed Lily and his son. "Listen to him. He's strong."

Jimmy and her parents left her room and Lily put her eager baby to her breast.

Lily relaxed, fully happy as her son sucked sustenance from her body.

MÁVROVO, KASTORIA, GREECE

"Kallíope," Athanásios called from the barn. He closed the stall gate behind his horse and walked across the yard toward the back door of the house. His boots sank ankle deep in the spring thaw's mud. "Kallíope," he called again, peeking inside his vest to be sure the letter was there. He pulled his lambskin cape up around his neck to protect it from the chill, raw dampness. The bottom of his coarse wool skirt was soggy and patterned by embedded lumps of mud that splashed on him each time his horse plunged a hoof into a black puddle on the road. He stopped at the side door of the house to scrape muck from his boots.

His horse was named Bucephalus, after Alexander's legendary beast, who the old man said had carried the Macedonian king through the mountains past Kastoria on his way to subjugate Thebes. Bucephalus was at an age equivalent to his master's eighty-one years. "I'll stop riding when Bucephalus dies," he promised Kallíope. The old man had built a little platform to help him mount and dismount his horse. Athanásios' arthritis was painful.

"Kallíope." Athanásios stepped into his house, and closing the door behind him called again. "Kallíope. We have a letter from Dimitráki. He sent the money for Kóstas. Kallíope."

"Yes, yes, I'm here," she said as she walked down the hallway toward him. "Stop shouting. Take off those boots and your wet cape." She approached her husband with a rag. "Let me wipe that mud off you." At fifty-nine, Kallíope had the unvarying, dour appearance of a middle-aged, black-draped woman of the Balkans. Her face was thin, and her nose pointed. She brushed the last piece of mud off her husband and wiped her hands clean on a towel. "Now, tell me," she said. "What's the news?"

"Dimitráki sent the money for Kóstas. He was out of jail before I left Kastoria. Tonight he'll be home with Ekaterini and the children."

"God bless Dimitráki," she said, making the sign of the cross. "He answered my letter quickly. I hope Kóstas learned his lesson. He has no head for business — only for reading books and talking politics."

"He meant well trying to build a building for merchants. He just didn't know the laws about building and paying workers. Now, the letter."

Kallíope followed her husband into the parlor, where they sat close together on a divan. Athanásios warmed his hands over the glowing coals that were heaped in the center of the brazier before them, and then carefully sliced open the envelope with the knife that he carried in a scabbard at his waist. He began to read.

> 25 February 1930
> My Beloved Parents, I kiss you.
> Evangelía gave me a son. He was born five days ago, and is strong and healthy. His name, dear father, is Athanásios.

"Glory to Him." Kallíope crossed herself.

There were tears in the old man's eyes. "Athanásios. *Na mas zísi.* You must write to Evangelía. She is our daughter, and she has given us a grandson. Put your feelings aside."

Kallíope pouted. She could not accept that her Dimitráki had taken such a woman. "Write? Maybe. Read more or give the letter to me."

Her husband continued.

> The money you asked me for to help Kóstas should have already arrived at the post office in Kastoria. I sent it to the authorities to pay Kóstas' fine and debt. I am glad I was able to help this time. Please tell Kóstas not to build anything else. Times are getting hard even in America. Business is not good.

George visited my shop this morning to congratulate me about my son. He is having business worries too. His children and Mary are well.

We will have a photograph taken of Athanásios in a few weeks, and I will mail his image to you.

I must hurry now. With many kisses, and love from Evangelía and me,

Dimitrios

"This is the first time Dimitráki has written about business problems," Kallíope said worriedly. "What do they do in America when they don't have money?"

Athanásios sat back on the divan and took a deep breath. He thought about the gold liras he had saved, and how they had found their way into the hands of the Kaimakan. "I don't know," he said. "We have land and animals, grow grain for bread, and vegetables, and catch fish from the lake. What do people do in a city like the one Dimitráki lives in? No land. No animals. They have to buy everything with money. That must be hard in bad times."

SOZOPOL, BULGARIA

A motor-driven boat crossed the bay, plowing through choppy swells. It was cloudy and cool, and mist lying low on the water swirled upward in mysterious patterns. Constantinos clung to the mast with his arm and strained his eyes, searching to see his birthplace. Here and there, Constantinos caught a glimpse of Sozópolis. He called back to the *kapetánios*, "Why don't you use sails?"

"We only hoist sails when the engine fails, Kyrie."

Constantinos shook his head, thinking, *Sails are more beautiful.* Then he shouted over the engine's noise. "Is the quay the same?"

"Yes. You'll see it soon." The boat's captain and owner, a Romiós even older than his passenger, had refused to leave Bulgaria in the troubled times thirty years before. A cigarette hung from his lips. In spite of the irritating smoke that made him half close his left eye, he guided his boat into the harbor with ease. Constantinos noticed how tanned and weathered the captain's face was. *Mine is white,* he thought. *Like a wrinkled shirt.*

"Does everyone call the city Sozopol now?" Constantinos spat out the Bulgarian name for his city.

"No. The Romiói still call it Sozópolis. But Anchíalos is gone forever. The Bulgarians renamed it Pomorie. And Mesembría is Nesebar. They are getting rid of everything Greek. Just like the Turks did."

"Sozopol," he said it again to himself, and then thought about how the Greeks were doing the same thing. They had changed the names of villages in the Peloponnesos and even Macedonia from Slavic to ancient Greek names. *But this is different,* he thought. *It is wrong for Bulgarians to give Bulgarian names to cities that have been Greek from their beginning. From ancient times.*

"There, — there it is," the *kapetánios* called. His extended arm and fingers pointed to starboard.

Constantinos looked. He saw the quay that he remembered.

It had been a long trip from New York to Piraeus, and then on to Constantinople and Burgas. When Sofía had told them how much their father wanted to walk Sozópolis' streets once more, his sons Chris, John, and Steve, who had Americanized his name from Stávros, decided to send him. They expected Sofía to take the trip with her husband. "No, I don't think so. There's nothing there for me anymore," she told them.

They approached Eléni, asking whether she and Louie would like to take the trip with their father. Her response was unequivocal. "Me? Go to Sozópolis and Pyrgos? To Bulgaria? Never."

They did not have to ask why, and Constantinos traveled alone.

Konstantínos did not recognize Chrysóula when she opened the door to the house where he and his brothers had been born. His niece – Décimos' lithe, blond little girl – was now a middle-aged woman, rotund, and gray.

"Théo Konstantínos?"

He smiled and held out his arms.

"Plátonas, Plátonas, come," she called as she gave herself to her uncle's embrace.

For ten days, he wandered the streets of Sozópolis, walked along its shore, watched gulls search the surf for smelt, and drank coffee with men at the *kafeneío*. He sat for hours with his niece and her husband and told them about Katina's life in America. They could not hear enough about her, or about the man that she was soon to marry. "Eléni is watching over her," he told them. "And she approved the engagement."

Konstantínos recounted his experiences and listened to them tell of how times had changed, and of how much Chrysóula missed her mother, Olga. "She died peacefully," Chrysóula said, "in her bed. She thought she saw *babás* in the room and closed her eyes."

For the most part, he was sad and disappointed. He had returned to Sozópolis with the romantic illusion that he could step back into the past, to his youth, and to the days when he had marched north with Bulgarian volunteers to join the Russian forces that swept through the mountains to annihilate the Turks. Konstantínos expressed his feelings to an elderly Greek fisherman who sat with him one afternoon sipping coffee. "Listen," the man said, "you are old enough to know better. What is over is over. Carry what is good to remember in your heart. Forget the rest. Live today."

The night before he left Sozópolis, Chrysóula gave her uncle a large envelope. It contained a black-and-white photograph of the city taken from its southern beach, from a place where their house on the bluff was visible. Konstantínos carefully set the photograph on the parlor table and inscribed in Greek:

SOZÓPOLIS, ANATOLIA ROMYLIA (BULGARIA 1930) BIRTHPLACE OF KAPIDAGHLÍS (TSVETKOV)

Directly over the house he wrote:

KAPIDAGHLÍS HOME

He carried the photograph on the long ocean voyage to Brooklyn and hung it in his bedroom where he could see it when he closed his eyes at night and opened them in the morning.

Sofía disliked the stark black-and-white image. It was not the Sozópolis of her childhood. But in his mind's eye, he saw blue water and sky, the green of trees that were no longer there, sun-drenched, warm, red tile roofs that sheltered the people of Sozópolis, and gulls that swooped up from the sea, circled, and glided back to the surf.

BAY RIDGE, BROOKLYN

Doctor Falkowitz led Jimmy and Louie out of the room. Eléni and Lily remained behind and stood silent by Athanásios's crib. The elderly neighborhood doctor was rumpled and tired. "I'm going home to have dinner and rest a bit. I'll be back to check on your son in two or three hours." At the front door, he took a deep breath of the September evening air, turned to Jimmy and spoke in a hushed voice. "Mr. Mavrovitis, your son is very ill. You might want to call a priest."

Louie heard the doctor's warning. "You call the priest, Jimmy. Tell him I'll pick him up in twenty minutes."

Lily and Eléni took turns holding the feverish baby until Louie returned. They stood close to the crib to witness Athanásios's baptism and to pray with the priest for God's help and mercy. Three days later Lily, Jimmy, Eléni, and Louie watched

Athanásios' small coffin lowered into a grave. Pneumonia had taken him, and had left the family devastated.

Only they accompanied Athanásios to Mount Olivet Cemetery in Maspeth, Long Island. Anastasia Zelios cared for Vasilikí and sat with the old woman before icons and a flickering candle, praying with her for the baby and his family.

After the burial service, Jimmy relinquished Lily to her mother's arms in the back of the Nash. Louie drove them home.

"Listen, Evangelía," her mother whispered, doing everything she could to contain her own grief. "Athanásios has no pain now — he is an angel — he is not suffering. You'll have another baby."

Lily could not respond. She shuddered, her body heaved with each of the spasms that accompanied her moans. They held each other and cried together. Jimmy choked back his own grief, while Louie, who had bonded to the grandchild that was not of his blood, forced his attention on driving in spite of his pain.

SEVENTH AVENUE, MANHATTAN

On the Monday following Thanksgiving, Rose sat at the desk in Jimmy and Bill's shop. She closed the ledger and put her pencil down. Looking first at Bill and then at Jimmy she said, "That's it. I paid your lease through December. You have enough left to cover the telephone bill, garbage, and incidentals. That's all. You can each leave with about three thousand dollars to carry you over, and your bank account will be zero."

"How much do we owe?" Bill asked. "What happens?"

"You go boom," she responded, using the fur market's colloquial term for going bust — bankrupt. "You owe almost forty thousand dollars to fur dealers, finishers, and storage. Most of that is to Kaufmann for the skins you bought in the past two years. Lily owns your house, Jimmy. Doesn't she?"

"No, her mother does."

"Good. Then it's safe. You can go bankrupt and walk away from the debt."

He shook his head. "What do you think, Bill? I don't like the idea."

Bill reached for the package of Chesterfields that were on the desk, took a cigarette, and lit it. "One of the reasons we're friends and partners is that we think the same way about our obligations. We pay our debts."

"Good." Jimmy smiled grimly. "Fifty-fifty?"

"We're partners. Aren't we?"

"Rose, will you prepare the papers for us?"

"They're promissory notes, Jimmy."

"Promissory notes, then."

"What terms do you want to offer?"

"Just write that I will pay as fast as I can, with interest — ask him how much — no more than three percent. It may take years. I'll tell Kaufmann that myself."

"The same for us," Bill said. "Figure the total we owe and split it. Then make up the notes for each of us."

"I'm so proud of you both. You're real men."

They spent the afternoon cleaning up the shop and arranging to sell their equipment. When they left that night, they stood in the hall to look at their names on the door for the last time: *Mavrovitis & Rusuli*. Jimmy extended his hand. Bill pulled his friend into his arms and hugged him, saying, "There'll be better days."

Jimmy walked home from the subway station on 69th Street worrying about how to tell Lily. *Have courage*, he told himself. *Have faith. Have courage. Persevere.*

BAY RIDGE, BROOKLYN

Christmas dinner was simple and quiet. There was no party. There were no guests. Eléni, Louie, Vasilikí, Lily, and Jimmy sat

370

together at the kitchen table. Lily had prepared traditional Balkan dishes. They ate little, and without relish.

After they finished, Jimmy and Louie sat in the front room reading newspapers while Eléni and Lily cleaned up. Vasilikí watched her daughter and granddaughter from her rocker through half-closed eyes.

"Evangelía," Eléni said. "Louie and I are going to spend some of the money I have left and take a trip to Italy and Greece next year. Business is slow. They won't miss me."

"You have to be here in the summer and fall."

"Why?"

Vasilikí brightened and spoke up. "Can't you see anything, Eléni?"

"What?"

Vasilikí smiled. "You're pregnant, aren't you, darling?"

"Are you?" Eléni asked.

"Yes, I'm sure."

"Glory to God." She crossed herself. "Does Jimmy know?"

"No, I was going to tell him tonight."

"Now. It's wonderful news at Christmas."

"Jimmy. Louie. Come in for coffee," Lily called.

Her news eased the aching memories of the past year.

CHAPTER TWENTY-FOUR
1931
MID-TOWN MANHATTAN

Eléni and Lily stepped into Nicholas Psaki's reception room. Rose Rusuli followed. Mika greeted them, and after being introduced to Rose, opened Psaki's office door and announced, "Kyrie Psaki, Kyria Perna is here."

Psaki came out immediately, smiling at Eléni and Lily. "Kyria Perna, it's nice to see you again. Hello Lily, how are you?"

"Hello, Mr. Psaki," Lily responded. Stepping aside she said, "Mr. Psaki, I'd like you to meet our friend Rose Rusuli."

After exchanging courtesies, Psaki guided the women to their chairs. "Would you like some coffee or tea?"

They declined his offer.

"I have the papers all ready for you to sign, Kyria Perna. But first let me be sure I understood what you want to do. Would you like to meet with me privately in the next room to talk about the details?"

"No. This isn't secret."

"Fine. Let's see — ah — you want to have Lily's name with yours on the deed to your house. Is that right?"

"Yes."

"And not her husband?"

"No. Just Evangelía. Can I do that?"

"Yes. You want Lily to own the house with you, and own it all if you die. And in your will — everything goes to Lily. Correct?"

"Everything to Evangelía."

"And Kyrie Perna?"

"Everything to Evangelía."

"I'll be back in a minute."

While Rose told Lily about an upcoming holiday at Lake Placid, Eléni thought about why it had been urgent for her to finish her business with Psaki.

In the weeks following her grandson's death, Eléni had experienced shortness of breath when she walked up stairs. She had to pause to gasp for air. Sometimes it happened to her in bed. She found that two or three pillows under her head and shoulders helped. One day, on the subway steps, a pain stabbed through her chest and she clutched the handrail to support herself. "Are you all right, lady?" a teenaged boy had asked her. "Do you need help?"

"No. Thanks you. Thanks you." She recovered and walked home fearfully, as if she expected someone or something to attack her. Along the way, she decided to go to the doctor — alone.

Dr. Falkowitz had been gentle when he cared for little Athanásios, and Eléni felt safe with the soft-spoken physician when she told him, "Sometimes hurt, doctor, and hard breathe."

"Hurt where, Mrs. Perna?"

"Here," she said, pointing to her chest, "and arm."

"Is it hard for you to breathe when you walk up stairs?"

"Yes."

"And when you lie down to sleep?"

"Yes. What means?"

"We'll see." He called his nurse. "Edna, please take Mrs. Perna into the examining room and help her into a gown."

When she had changed, Falkowitz came into the room and gently took Eléni's blood pressure. "This won't hurt. It will feel like your arm is being squeezed." Once he recorded the reading, he moved the stethoscope from place to place on her chest and back, asking her to breathe deeply, and then normally. His concentrated facial expression troubled her.

"This is a stethoscope, Mrs. Perna. In Greek, *stethos* means chest. Doesn't it?"

"Yes. Chest."

"Hold your breath for a moment. Good."

"And scope is Greek too. I think I remember it means aiming."

"*Skopi*, mean like look." The doctor looked up. "Is breathing becoming more difficult? Is it harder for you to breathe now than last month?"

"Yes. What means?"

Doctor Falkowitz palpated her abdomen, placed his stethoscope on the inside of her thighs, near her groin, and pressed her ankles and lower legs with his finger. "You may get dressed, Mrs. Perna. We'll talk in my office."

A few minutes later, Eléni stepped through the door from the examination room into the doctor's office.

"Have a chair, Mrs. Perna. I'll be just a minute."

Doctor Falkowitz scribbled on a sheet of paper. When he finished writing, he folded the sheet, put it into an envelope, and sealed and addressed it, adding a telephone number below the address.

"Mrs. Perna, I want to you to see another doctor. He is a specialist."

"Specialist?"

"He is a doctor who knows more than I do about the heart and lungs. His name is Dr. Dunseith. His office is on Park Avenue in New York."

"What I have?"

"You have a problem in your heart. And you have high blood pressure. Would you like me to call Dr. Dunseith now and make an appointment for you?"

"Yes. Call."

Unsure of what Dr. Falkowitz's words about her condition meant, Eléni left his office with an envelope that contained his findings and an appointment.

A few days later, she was in Dr. Dunseith's office. Rose Rusuli, who had promised to keep the matter secret from Eléni's family, accompanied her. It fell on Rose to translate.

"Kyria Eléni," she said, after listening intently to the doctor. "Dr. Dunseith says that your heart is not working right. There is something wrong with it. Because your heart doesn't work well, you can't breathe easily. Your heart hurts because it's not getting enough air."

Eléni looked at the dignified, gray-haired doctor. "You fix? Give medicine?"

Rose took Eléni's hands in hers. "Dr. Dunseith can't fix your heart. He says you must rest, and maybe stop working. You should eat less, lose weight, and not eat salt. Use two or three pillows when you go to bed. And he'll give you some medicine."

Eléni was stunned. *Stop working? No salt?* She turned to the doctor.

"Doctor, I die?"

Rose asked the doctor, "What is the answer?"

"Tell her that if she does everything I tell her she may live for a long time. But her condition is serious. She needs to be followed regularly by a physician. Dr. Falkowitz told me that he is going to retire. Does she want me to suggest someone?"

Rose explained the doctor's comments and question to Eléni.

"Who should she see, Doctor?"

"There is a young doctor in Brooklyn I recommend highly — a student of mine. Dr. DeTata, Ettore J. DeTata."

Dr. Dunseith wrote Dr. DeTata's name, address, and telephone number on a prescription slip for Eléni.

"I'll telephone Dr. DeTata and send a report to him. You should see him soon."

Rose walked Eléni to the subway station. "Are you all right? Can you get home alone?"

"Yes. I'll go right home."

"You should tell Louie and Lily."

"Not now. I have to think."

Psaki entered the room, saying, "The documents reflect exactly what you want to accomplish." Mika followed him and placed sets of papers on his conference table. Eléni scratched her name where Psaki indicated. Rose signed the same pages as witness.

"That's it, Kyria Perna," Psaki said as he gathered up the documents. "My assistant will take the papers to the county this afternoon to record the change in deed."

"If I die now, Evangelía will own the house, just Evangelía?"

"Yes."

"And everything else?"

"Yes."

"Thank you, *mána*." Lily hugged and kissed her mother. Eléni looked at Rose over Lily's shoulder and held a finger to her lips.

Rose nodded her head to acknowledge the secret between them.

ITALY AND GREECE

The trip had been difficult for Eléni even in the comfort of a second-class stateroom. She had lost a few pounds, but found climbing the stairs on board ship difficult. Louie believed her exhausted from many years of hard work and worry, and in need of rest.

He noticed that her ankles swelled during the day. She told him that it was her shoes, and that she needed better support.

He heard her get up at night, stand at the porthole, and breathe with difficulty. She told him she needed fresh air.

Their ship took them to Naples, where they rested for a few days and visited Capri and the ruins at Pompeii. Louie decided that a trip to his birthplace would be too difficult for his wife. Besides, everything there would have changed just as the name had changed: Monteleone di Calabria was now Vibo Valentia — it now celebrated its Roman past and had severed its link to the Norman conquest.

They went on to Corfu. The island and its surrounding sea charmed Eléni. Today's sunny walk at the seashore flowed into tomorrow's rest under the quiet green cover of ancient, gnarled olive trees at the center of the island. At dinner, she and Louie enjoyed fish, mussels, and lobster brought directly from the sea and prepared for their table. On their last afternoon on the island, they took an excursion to Panaghía Paleokastrítsa, the ancient, white-walled monastery that overlooked the Ionian Sea. From its small garden Eléni gazed toward the horizon, and Italy. She heard the soft rush of wind in the pines that bordered the garden and the song of a bird. For an instant, time was suspended and she found peace. She slept well, breathed more easily, felt less fatigue, and gained hope that the doctor was wrong and that she had just been overtired.

Eléni came alive when their shipped docked at Piraeus and she saw Smarágda and Dimitrios standing on the wharf. Their eyes looked up and searched the faces of the passengers who lined the ship's rail. Eléni waved at them and shouted. "Smarágda. Here. Here I am. Smarágda." They were in each other's arms the moment Eléni's feet left the ship's gangway. Not long after, in Kalithéa, they sat in the garden where she and Constantinos had first talked about America and how they might get there.

Louie enjoyed the shade of the great tree and listened while Eléni and her sister condensed twenty years of their lives into two hours of dialogue. Louie's knowledge of Greek was too limited to understand Dimitrios' analyses of the politics of Greece, the labor movement, and the human tragedy brought about by the worldwide depression. He did his best to listen and to learn about the family that had decided to stay in Athens.

The excitement and the late afternoon heat overcame Eléni, and she once again had difficulty breathing. "I'm tired, Smarágda," she said, waving aside her sister's concern. "Dimitrios, can you help Louie find a carriage or taxi for us?"

Within a few minutes of their arrival and check-in at the Grand Bretagne Hotel, Eléni was asleep on her bed. She had not even looked at the square she had circumvented twenty-years before when she walked to and from the palace.

The next day she was better. In the morning, she inquired after Kyria Anthoula and took a taxi to the place where she had once worked with her partner. The little shop showed no evidence of dressmaking. It was a hardware store. She learned from its proprietor that Anthoula Mavromátis had returned to Bulgaria. *I wonder why?* thought Eléni. *Why would she go back?*

Their days in Athens passed with excursions to Hydra and Aegina, and a visit Sunion. They made their pilgrimage to the Acropolis, and even posed for photographs with the Evzones at the Tomb of the Unknown Soldier in Syntagma Square.

Both Eléni and Louie grew depressed over economic conditions in Greece and weary of Dimitrios' political and economic ranting. He parroted socialist and communist rhetoric with fierce invective and questioned how it was that Eléni and Louie were able to afford the luxurious accommodations of the Grande Bretagne.

After a few days, the warmth of the first hours of the sisters' reunion cooled. They exhausted their topics of conversation, and Smarágda was unable to hide her jealousy of Eléni. She argued the same points against power and wealth as Dimitrios did and finally let slip: "It must be nice to stay in a hotel and have your bed made, Eléni. You must do that a lot."

"No, sister. Only when we travel."

"But you do travel. You eat at restaurants often, too. Don't you?"

"Yes. Sometimes. Why?"

"Not everyone can do that. Dimitrios doesn't know how long he'll have work. The docks are slow."

Eléni did not know what to say. Smarágda's life had not changed from the time Eléni left for America. It seemed more precarious now that Dimitrios earned barely enough to support his family.

"Can I help you, Smarágda?" Eléni asked. "Do you need money?"

"No. We don't need your money."

Eléni left Athens with a gulf of envy and resentment separating her from her sister. A few days later, Eléni and Louie were at a restaurant outside of their hotel in Nauplion. They were there to visit the great theater at Epidaurus, and the ancient healing center, the Sanctuary of Asklepios. Eléni put down her fork – the grilled octopus was tough – and sighed.

Louie dabbed his lips with a napkin. "What is it?"

"I'm tired. I want to go home, to my home, to Evangelía and my mother. There is nothing for me here. I'm happier in New York."

As soon as Louie was able to arrange their passage, they boarded a ship at Piraeus. Watching the buildings that surrounded the harbor fade, Eléni dismissed her memories of her last departure from the port, the foul conditions she experienced in steerage, and the man who had waited for her in St. Paul.

Louie led her to their cabin with its private toilette and bath, ample bed, closet, and bureau. He encouraged her to lie down to rest while a maid unpacked her sea trunk. She closed her eyes and was asleep in moments. Louie gave the maid a gratuity and asked her to return later.

BAY RIDGE, BROOKLYN

Eléni held Elenítsa in Lily's private room in Shore Road Hospital, rocking her namesake and cooing, "Elenítsa, *agápe mou*," to the sleeping infant. Jimmy had insisted on naming his daughter after his mother-in-law.

Dr. DeTata stepped into the room with Lily's chart in his hand. "Lily, how do you feel? Ah, Signora Perna. *Buon giorno. Come stai?*"

"*Ettore, sta bene.*" Eléni had started calling Dr. DeTata by his first name on her second appointment with him, when she brought Louie to meet the young Italian doctor and learn about her condition. His practice increased as she referred her friends and relatives to him.

DeTata won Jimmy and Lily over the first time he examined her. He had a good sense of humor and a quick laugh that constantly animated his mustache at the corners of his mouth. It was not long before they met the doctor's wife, Anna, and by the time Elenítsa was born, Anna and Ettore – Lily and Jimmy called him Eddie – had become their good friends.

DeTata listened to Lily's heart and lungs. "Good. How do you feel?"

"Fine, Eddie."

He turned to Eléni. "Signora, let the nurse hold the baby for me." Eleni gave up her grandchild reluctantly.

DeTata felt the baby's tummy and listened to her heartbeat and lungs.

"You can take your baby home tomorrow, Lily."

Louie crept down to the cellar. Once he was in the little room that held the tools and sundry screws, nails, washers, and useless brass and copper fixtures that he treasured, he pulled out a shelf, put his hand down the empty space in the wall behind it and groped for a moment. A smile broadened on his face as he withdrew a dusty bottle with a blank label. He took a pen from his vest and carefully wrote: 'For Elenítsa Wedding.' Happy that he and Eléni had returned from Europe in time, he held his private celebration of the arrival of his granddaughter.

Five months later, in the depths of the New Year's winter, Lily knelt next to her baby's crib in fear as she watched Dr. DeTata examine her daughter. The baby cried weakly as DeTata listened to her heart and lungs. Jimmy and Louie waited for DeTata to speak. Eléni and Vasilikí sat together waiting in the kitchen.

"Open the window and keep the furnace hot," DeTata ordered.

"But it's February, Eddie," Lily said. "It's freezing."

"I want her to get fresh air."

Louie nodded to Jimmy. "You open window. I shovel coal."

Lily moaned. "Eddie. Not Elenítsa too."

Dr. DeTata put his stethoscope into his medical bag as he spoke. "She has pneumonia. Give her a couple of drops of whiskey with lemon and honey every four hours. Try to get her to drink water."

"Eddie, will she live?"

Lily's voice was virtually gone. Fatigue and worry had overcome her. Jimmy was in no better condition. Months of unemployment had taken their toll. Fortunately, Louie and Eléni were working, and Eléni had her savings.

"She's fighting, Lily," DeTata said. "Keep the room warm and the window open. Hold her as much as you can. I'll be back later."

For three sleepless days, Jimmy and Louie took turns going to the basement to shovel coal into the furnace. They kept its walls cherry red. Eléni and Lily sat by Elenítsa's crib. They changed her, held her, and used their fingers to pry open her mouth and drip water between her lips. Heat radiating from the hissing, silver-painted radiator beneath the windowsill tempered the cold air that passed over it through the window. Dr. DeTata visited twice each day. His presence and the way he touched Elenítsa gave them comfort and hope.

On the morning of the third day, Anna asked her husband, "Isn't there anything you can do, Eddie?"

"No. We'll know in a few hours."

That afternoon, Dr. DeTata examined the baby and smiled. "The fever has broken, Lily." He bent over the baby and uttered, "Elenítsa, it's time to eat."

"Is she going to be all right?"

"Yes, she's going to live. Give her lots of fluid."

After Dr. DeTata left, Eléni sat next to her granddaughter, and Louie tended the furnace while the Lily and Jimmy slept. In a few hours, Lily and Jimmy took their turn, exchanging roles with Eléni and Louie. Three days later, Elenítsa seemed never to have been ill, and the family's bond with Ettore DeTata was permanently forged.

CHAPTER TWENTY-FIVE
1933
BAY RIDGE, BROOKLYN

Eléni made the sign of the cross over the *Vasilópita* before cutting pieces in the traditional order: for Christ, the Virgin Mary, St. Basil, the poor, and each member of the family in order of age. Anastasia Zelios had delivered the fourteen-inch round, almond decorated, sesame-sprinkled, golden-brown loaf on New Year's Eve — her annual tribute to her children's godparents. The fragrances of *mahlépi* and *mastícha* filled the warm kitchen.

Louie admired four generations of women in the room: Vasilikí, Eléni, Lily, and little Elenítsa. Lily held her baby on her lap at the kitchen table. She turned to her grandmother and said, "Here, *yiayiá* let me butter the *Vasilópita* for you. Take Elenítsa."

In her favorite chair, the one that looked out to the stark winter garden, Vasilikí rocked the baby, murmuring, *"Agápe mou. Hrisó mou."* Elenítsa grasped at her great-grandmother's finger.

Eléni took a small bite of *Vasilópita*. She had put on weight, and her eyes, deeply set in their sockets, showed fatigue. Earlier that morning she had gone to the basement with Louie to cut links of *loukánika* for their breakfast. He followed her up the stairs carrying a bottle of wine. "Eléni, you're breathing hard. Are you all right?"

"Yes, sure," she gasped, pausing for a moment to catch her breath. "I'm getting old."

Jimmy read his newspaper at the kitchen table. Gaunt, he had just recovered from pneumonia, and suffered abdominal pain from ulcers. DeTata told him to go to a warm climate — Florida or Cuba — for two or three weeks. "I can't, Eddie. I can't afford it," Jimmy had confessed. He put down his newspaper and asked, "What time do you want to be at Bill and Rose's, Lily?"

"Let's get there about three. Can we make it if we leave at one-thirty?"

"I think so. The streets are clear."

"Wear a flannel undershirt. Dress warmly."

Lily looked forward to the drive across the Brooklyn Bridge and up the West Side to 157th Street. The afternoon would be happy, without reference to the dark days of the Depression that brought suffering to the world and the country, and made life difficult for her, and uncertain for her family.

Rose, Bill, and Louis lived well in spite of the state of the world economy. They wore fine clothing, enjoyed a new Buick, and attended Broadway shows. Bill struggled in the faltering fur market. But he was more successful than most furriers. A well-paid executive, Louis referred business associates and wealthy clients to him. And furriers who survived the bad times continued to need Rose's bookkeeping skills.

Jimmy and Lily had asked Rose if she and Bill would baptize Elenítsa. Rose was excited at becoming a godmother, and Bill encouraged it. "I can't give you children, Rose, but we can have godchildren."

"Don't put it that way. Maybe I couldn't have carried a baby. We don't know. We can be good godparents to Elenítsa."

Jimmy drove over the Brooklyn Bridge to Manhattan, up Broadway, and continued north from Columbus Circle. Lily sat in the passenger seat wearing a broadtail coat with a blanket over her legs. She stared at decorations and blinking lights in the small shops along Broadway. They were tawdry in the gray light of a post-Christmas winter afternoon. "I miss Peter and Athena," she said. "This is the first time they won't be with us for Bill's name day."

"I miss them too," Jimmy answered. "But I'm happy for them. Peter will do well in Montreal. It's not that far. They'll visit. Someday we can visit them."

"I'd like that. I never went to Canada, even when we were in Glens Falls. *Mána* was worried that they wouldn't let us back into America."

When they arrived at their destination, a liveried doorman opened the car door and then the building's front door for Lily. She stepped into the lobby while Jimmy drove to a nearby garage where Louis had arranged for Jimmy to park for the afternoon and evening.

Tiled with large black and white squares, the lobby had a plush red carpet that led thirty feet, from the front door to the three elevators that served the building. French doors to the left side of the lobby opened onto a small garden, deep in snow. On the right, snow-blocked doors barred access to a walkway and Riverside Drive. Lily waited for Jimmy near the lobby's glowing fireplace. It and a twinkling Christmas tree warmed her hands, feet, and spirits.

In a few minutes, Jimmy arrived carrying a box of two-dozen tight-budded red roses that he had stored in the trunk of their car the previous afternoon. The elevator operator ushered them into the elevator for their trip to the twelfth floor, where they found Bill, waiting at his apartment's front door and smiling. Lily planted a kiss on his cheek. "Happy name day, Bill."

"Happy New Year," he answered, and gave Lily a hug. "How are you feeling, Jimmy? How is my goddaughter? Come in. Get warm."

Bill led them from the front door into a circular foyer whose focal point was a portrait of Louis Dimitroff, white-haired and resplendent, wearing his constant accessory, a white boutonnière. Rose appeared from behind Bill, hugged and kissed her friends and accepted the roses from Jimmy. She handed them to a maid. "Please put these in the crystal vase on the grand piano." Another maid took their coats and hats. They stepped into the midst of bustling guests who filled the parlor and dining room. Bill and Louis both wore deep maroon, velvet house-jackets with silk navy lapels. Rose was in a black, low cut, bead and sequin decorated cocktail dress and wore a three-stranded pearl necklace.

Dominated by a Christmas tree whose lights, shaped like trees, houses, sleighs, and Santa Clauses blinked on and off, the spacious living room had French doors leading to a small terrace with a view of the George Washington Bridge and New Jersey's Palisades. Down a hallway to the left of the foyer were three large bedrooms, two bathrooms, a kitchen with its service entrance, and an adjoining maid's room and bathroom.

Rose had set a buffet on a festively decorated table in the dining room. It signaled that the hosts had separated themselves from the world of immigrants. There were no Greek delicacies, not even an olive. Roast beef, smoked turkey, Virginia ham, cured salmon, and American casseroles and salads prevailed.

A beverage-serving cart in the corner of the room held all the accessories and liquor a sophisticated household required: silver cocktail shaker, crystal carbonated water dispenser, and highball and old-fashioned glasses. Dimitroff had purchased the bottles of scotch, whiskey, and gin through his contacts in Canada and had them smuggled across the border to his hunting camp in Maine, where he took delivery during the deer season. Prohibition's repeal was months away. A waiter and two maids served drinks and canapés, and cleared glasses and plates. The hosts were free to entertain their guests.

Through the afternoon, the conversation, laughter, and ample food and drink in the twelfth-floor apartment overlooking the river denied the existence of the hungry and homeless in the streets below.

At Louis' request, Lily and Jimmy stayed after all the other guests had left. Rose served coffee, wishing desperately that she could light a cigarette – she and Lily had had one secretly in the bathroom earlier. Louis was a man-about-town who kept his bachelor life and his rumored mistresses private. Publicly, he disapproved of women drinking or smoking. He lit a custom made cigar. Bill took a cigarette from the package of Chesterfields on the table next to his chair. They talked about the holidays, the recent election, and family news until a long lull in their conversation ended the party mood. It was as if a bright light had dimmed. Jimmy leaned forward. "How much longer do you think business will be bad, Louis?"

"Who knows? I don't think Roosevelt has the answers. It'll be six more weeks before he takes office, and months before he organizes his government."

Rose filled Lily's cup. "How is your mother?"

"I'm worried about her. She uses Elenítsa and my grandmother as excuses to stay home. She doesn't have the strength she had."

"She'll feel better when spring comes."

"I hope so."

BAY RIDGE, BROOKLYN

Affirming that May had arrived, the magnolia tree in the back of the garden bloomed, daffodils and tulips swayed like dancers in the breeze, Louie's grapevines budded out, and his fig tree, with its protective carpet and leaf-filled insulation removed, had defied the ravages of another winter and boasted tiny new leaves.

Eléni and her family were finishing dinner — one of her favorite meals — mussels stuffed with rice, pignoli nuts, and currants.

"Remember how your father loved these?" asked Vasilikí.

Eléni smiled. "I remember him bringing them home in a sack, dripping water through the house. He'd steam and eat two dozen before you could stuff them." A moment later, she collapsed on the kitchen floor, her face ashen.

Lily screamed, "*Mána, mána!*"

Louie knelt on the floor next to Eléni. "Jimmy, help me lift her. We'll put her in *yiayiá's* bed."

"Call Eddie, Lily," Jimmy ordered.

She caught DeTata at home having dinner. Within twenty minutes, he was examining Eléni, who groaned with pain.

"It's not good, Lily. Your mother had a heart attack." He handed her a hypodermic syringe. "Boil this and bring it to me in the water. I'll give your mother morphine to help with the pain."

"She'll be all right – won't she?"

"I don't know," he answered. "Call your priest just in case. I'll be back after I finish my house calls."

The priest arrived. Chris and Marion came down from their third floor apartment and sat silently in the kitchen. They sent their son, Bobby, for his grandparents, Sofía and Constantinos, who arrived in minutes. The priest chanted psalms and prayers. Lily, Jimmy, and Louie watched him administer Holy Unction. He made small crosses with the holy oil on Eléni's forehead, cheeks, chin, and hands.

Vasilikí sat in the corner of the room. She held a cross in her hands. Except for the movement of her lips, she was motionless. Constantinos stood next to her whispering, "I was there when she was born." Sofía prayed at the foot of the bed. Hours passed.

Dr. DeTata returned just before midnight. He took Eléni's hand, and as if she had been waiting for him, her eyes opened, she looked at him, sighed, and her eyes closed. DeTata took his stethoscope, placed it on her chest, and listened.

"She's gone."

DOWNTOWN, BROOKLYN

A five-foot-long floral spray of white orchids and roses covered Eléni's coffin. It was from Rose — just Rose. She had designed it herself with the help of her florist in Manhattan.

George Constantinides was overwhelmed. The funeral director's chapel at South Oxford Street in Brooklyn was crowded with mourners. They came from the garment district and the fur market, from Glens Falls, from Brooklyn and Manhattan, their neighboring communities, and from as far away as Montreal. Flowers spilled out of the chapel into the lobby. It was difficult for Constantinides to arrange them in an orderly way.

Lily and Sofía sat next to each other close to Eléni's casket on the two afternoons and evenings it was open for viewing. Constantinos, Jimmy, and Louie greeted people in the lobby and brought them into the chapel. Eléni's nephews and nieces, Jimmy's brother George and his family, Peter and Athena Stamatis, and Rose, Bill, and Louis were there endless hours. Amidst their tears, they all told stories — stories of Eléni — of her strength, grace, and commitment to the family.

On the second afternoon, a middle-aged woman dressed in a tailored black suit, and wearing a black hat and veil, entered the chapel and walked slowly to the casket.

"Madame Helen," she whispered. She lifted her veil to kiss Eléni's forehead, and then turned and knelt before Lily.

"Lily, it's me, Marta."

"Marta Feinman?" Lily could barely see through her red, swollen eyes.

"Yes. It's not Feinman anymore. Remember? I married Renaldo Mazola, the cutter, in Glens Falls. I am so sorry about your mother … my friend …" Her voice broke and she started to cry.

Lily got up from her chair and hugged Eléni's loyal secretary. Then she took her arm and led her into the lobby. "I do remember Renaldo. My mother was happy for you. I can't think. I don't see people. I can't believe ..." Lily sobbed, "*Mána*."

"God bless her. Without her...without her I don't know what my life would be."

"She loved you."

"I wish she had written to me, just a little."

"How?" Lily stopped crying. She smiled unexpectedly at Marta and announced, "She couldn't read or write."

"What? Of course she could."

"No." Lily smiled again at the memory of her mother making everyone believe that she could read. "Only her name. She fooled everyone. Even you."

Louie walked about dazed, and at times sat in the foyer staring at a stained-glass window. His lips quivered. Constantinos came to his side. "Louie, are you all right? Is there anything you need?"

Louie scoffed. "Need? Yes, I need my life. Eléni was my life." He paused. "I'm sorry, Constantinos. I didn't mean to attack you."

"It's all right, Louie. I know. Have you seen Dr. DeTata and Anna?"

"No, they won't be here or at the funeral. I spoke to Anna and she asked forgiveness. Ettore never goes to funerals. I don't know why."

Jimmy felt as though he had lost his own mother. He struggled to maintain his composure while he attended to all the details for the funeral.

The next day, a hearse carried Eléni under the high gate of the cemetery. Gold letters set into the ornamental black wrought iron arch read: Mount Olivet Cemetery. A procession of limousines and private automobiles followed the hearse. The last three carried floral tributes.

At the grave, one that she would share with her grandson Athanásios, Constantinos stood behind Sofía, next to Louie, Lily, and Jimmy. The priest chanted the *Trisághion*: "*Ághios O Theós, Ághios Eeskhirós, Ághios Athanátos, Eléison Imás*; Holy God, Holy Mighty, Holy and Immortal, have mercy on us."

As he listened to the prayer, Constantinos looked up and saw a flock of gulls land on the hill just above the gravesite. His imagination raced back in time to a window overlooking the Black Sea, when he had heard the cry of a baby join the cry of gulls.

The *makaría* concluded at the St. George Hotel in downtown Brooklyn, with mourners raising their brandy glasses. They chorused, *Zoí Se Emás*.

Lily was inconsolable. When she entered the house on Ovington Avenue, she found her *yiayiá* sitting in the rocking chair by the window. Anastasia was at her side. "Did you kiss Eléni for me? Did you kiss my baby for me?"

"Yes *yiayiá*. I did." Lily fell to her knees and put her head on her grandmother's lap as she had done so many times before. She cried and Vasilikí stroked her hair. Louie and Jimmy sat quietly at the kitchen table.

Chapter Twenty-Six
1935
Seventh Avenue, Manhattan

FIERSTEIN & FIERSTEIN
FINE FURS

Jimmy stared at the names painted on the door. He hesitated for a moment, smoothed his hair, and self-consciously adjusted the knot of his tie. It was nine in the morning, and for mid-September, the outdoor temperature was comfortable. He wore a light summer suit. But even in the relatively cool hallway, perspiration glistened on his brow. He gathered his nerve, and rang the doorbell. A buzzer sounded. Simultaneously, he heard the click of the lock opening. He entered.

Inside, a woman guarded a second entry door. When she stood, her white silk blouse and tight skirt advertised her figure. That, and her derisive smile, upswept hair, and blazing red fingernails and lipstick made him think of a cocktail hostess. Her voice was dismissive. "Whad'ya want?"

"I have an appointment with Mr. Fierstein."

Her voice softened a bit. "Abe or Joe?"

"I don't know."

"What's your name?"

"Mavrovitis. Jimmy Mavrovitis."

The woman pressed a button on a large brown box that sat next to the telephone on her desk. A voice grumbled, "Yeah? What is it, Marge?"

"Joe, there's a Jimmy Mavrovitz here to see you."

"Mavrovitis," Jimmy corrected.

She spat the name out in a sarcastic staccato. "Mavrovitis, he says."

"Wait." Jimmy heard an unintelligible exchange of words come through the box, and then, "Yeah, he's here ta'see Abe first. Send'm in."

Marge buzzed the security lock and Jimmy went through the second door. He was excited and nervous. Three words repeated themselves in his mind. *Faith. Courage. Persevere.*

A short, pleasant-looking man stepped out of an office and extended his hand.

"Jimmy? Jimmy Mavrovitis?"

"Yes."

"I'm Abe Fierstein. Come in. Have a seat."

Jimmy liked the man. His face was round, topped with a receding mat of thin black hair. His image, established by a crisp white shirt, fashionable tie, polished shoes, and sharply creased trousers, corresponded with what Jimmy had learned about him and his role.

"Jimmy, my brother and me are doing okay even though there's a depression. Not great. Okay. I'm the outside man. I sell to department store buyers, 5th Avenue specialty stores and private clients. My brother, Joe — you'll meet him — he's the moneyman. He works with the bank, the factors, the union — all that crap. Clear?"

"Yes. I understand, Mr. Fierstein."

"Call me Abe."

"Yes, Mr. Fierstein."

"Abe. Okay?"

"Abe."

"Okay. Look. We have a good business in foxes. Our foreman dropped dead last week and there's no one to take over. Psáltis says you can handle the job. I checked you out in the market. They say you got a good eye for skins and are a great matcher and cutter. Whad'ya think? You like to give this a try?"

"How many operators do you have?"

"Six full-time now. And two matchers and cutters. They're pretty good, but no foremen."

"Nailers? Finishers?"

"Yeah. Everything. We do everything here."

Jimmy overcame his modesty. "Can I see the shop?"

"Sure, come on."

Abe led Jimmy through a mirror-lined showroom into a space in front of the combination-lock door that protected the fur vault. They went into the shop. It was large. Twelve sewing machines were set in a line parallel to a long matching and cutting table that abutted the ceiling-high windows.

Close to where Jimmy and Abe stood, three women with fur garments and silk linings in various stages of assembly in hand looked up from their work. They stared at Jimmy. His face reddened when he heard an increase in the undecipherable chatter among the women who were looking him over.

"Come on. You gotta meet Joe."

Joe's appearance — open-collared, rumpled shirt with a limp tie, creaseless suit pants, and disheveled graying hair — was in sharp contrast to Abe's. He greeted Jimmy gruffly, never taking the chewed-end of a cigar from his mouth.

"The market says you signed notes in '30. Didn't go boom. Right?"

"Yes."

"You pay off?"

"Not yet. Some. I will pay it all when there's work."

"That's what I heard. You're paying a little bit, now and then. That's okay. That's good. Whad'ya think, Abe?"

"Looks good to me."

"Wanna work here, Jimmy? Wanna be foreman?"

"What will it pay?"

"We'll start you off at sixty a week. Bonus at Christmas if things are good. Whad'ya say?"

"When can I start, Mr. Fierstein?"

"Call me Joe. Monday, eight o'clock. OK?"

"I'll be here."

BAY RIDGE, BROOKLYN

Lily heard the front entry door open, and then Jimmy's voice: "Lily. Lily." She was sitting in the kitchen with her grandmother, holding Jason while he sucked eagerly at his bottle, and reached for his feet with his hands.

"I'm in the kitchen feeding Jason."

Jimmy came in, lifted Elenítsa from the floor where she had been playing with a doll, hugged and kissed her, and then kissed Lily and his eighteen-month-old son.

Vasilikí, rocked slowly in her chair by the window, raised her arm toward Jimmy. "Come close to me, Dimitráki. Let me kiss you. Bless you. You're a good boy. A good husband and father. I love you, my child." She had not left the house since Eléni's death, and, even before that, had ventured out only rarely for a church service or an excursion to the bay to look at the water.

Jimmy kissed *yiayiá* and then turned back to his wife. "I found work, Lily — steady work."

Lily put Jason in his highchair and threw her arms around Jimmy's neck. "Where? How?"

"Kyrie Psáltis. One of his Jewish friends in the market asked him about a good fox man. Psáltis arranged for me to meet him."

"When do you start?"

"Right away. Full-time."

"Oh God, that's wonderful. Go, change, and I'll get dinner ready."

As Lily busied herself with dinner, she thought about the five years that she had watched Jimmy leave every morning to walk the streets of the fur market searching for whatever work he could find. *It wore him down*, she thought. *But he never complained.*

To save on grocery money, Lily had replaced loin lamb chops with riblets at their table, and served fried lamb liver and kidneys, roast lamb heads, *fasoúlia* and *fakí*, and fish chowders made from giant bass and cod heads.

Lily looked at her children and grandmother, and thought; *Thank you for our house, mána. You saved me. You saved us.*

Louie sucked at the end of a rubber tube. "Here it comes." He stuffed the tube into the open hole in the cask Constantinos held between his legs.

The wine siphoned from the large barrel, through the rubber tube and into the smaller cask. Constantinos reached into his pocket for cigarette paper and a pouch of tobacco. His nimble fingers deftly formed a cigarette, packing the tobacco to assure slow, even burning.

Louie went into the little storeroom for a moment. Constantinos heard sounds of boxes being moved about and then saw Louie appear with a bottle in hand. He smiled impishly. "Let's taste this," he said. "Hold the bottle for a minute." He went to the small kitchen at the end of the basement and returned with two small glasses.

Louie took the bottle from Constantinos, opened it, and poured amber liquor into the glasses he had set on top of the large wine barrel. The electric bulb hanging above them shot its yellow light through the shimmering liquor.

"What will we drink to?" Constantinos asked.

"Let's drink to a good wine."

They clinked their glasses. Constantinos smacked his lips after taking a sip. "Bravo. Outstanding." He drained his glass and held it out. "A little more for good health," he said, grinning.

Louie's face became serious. "I don't think that I'll be making wine with you here much longer."

"Why? We'll make wine for years."

"No. Not here. Jimmy and Lily, and the children need more room. With Eléni gone, and Vasilikí – you know she is failing."

"Yes. I know. But you can live here with Evangelía and Jimmy. You're the children's *pappoú*."

"I am. I really am. They are not my blood. They are Eléni's. But they are my grandchildren too."

"Blood goes just so far. Love goes further."

"I'm only forty-five. I need more in my life than being a widower. I miss Eléni. It's been two years."

"A woman?"

"Yes. And my own place."

"Have you found someone?"

"No. Not yet. But there are women at work, Italian women. I can tell they'd be interested."

"Have you talked to Evangelía?"

"No. She is good to me. I love her like my own daughter. But without Eléni, it's different. Lily always wanted her mother just for herself. While Eléni was here — well, what's the difference? This coming year or next, things will change."

They went about filling smaller casks with the young wine.

The next morning they and their friends ate, drank, and played cards at the table in the basement, relishing the aroma of dried sausage and herbs, and tending the still as it did its work.

Thanksgiving was the best they had celebrated in years. Jimmy had been working for two months and the weekly paychecks changed their lives — not only because of the money. They had regained a sense of security and the promise of a future.

The Sunday before Jimmy and Lily had gone to church for the second-year memorial of his father's death. Jimmy's brother, Kóstas, had sent him a telegram: "Father died yesterday in his sleep. He was eighty-five. Mother is well and strong."

Jimmy mourned his father. He wished that he had been able to take a trip to see his family. Marriage, children, illness, and the Depression had made any thought of travel impossible. He hoped that he would be able take Lily and the children to Macedonia in four or five years to visit his mother. First, he had to pay his debts.

In early December, Vasilikí asked Lily, "When will you baptize Íason?" Her voice was weak.

"In the spring, *yiayiá*." Lily helped her grandmother put on her nightgown, and get into her bed. She kissed the old woman's forehead, pulling the blanket up under her chin.

Vasilikí had grown frail. She held her embroidery in her hands all day long, but the needle did not pass through the material. She seemed distant, as if in a dream.

For three years, Lily had tenderly undressed, bathed, dressed, and groomed her grandmother. It never occurred to her to do otherwise.

"I won't be here in the spring, my child."

"Yes, you will, *yiayiá*. We have to wait until the weather is warm before we baptize Jason. We'll do it at home. I don't want ..." Her voice trailed off as she thought about Athanásios and pneumonia.

"That's all right, my child. He will have my blessing before I go."

"Don't say that, *yiayiá*."

Vasilikí smiled and laid her head back onto her pillow. "We all most go, my child." Smiling she closed her eyes and drifted into sleep.

Later, while she was cleaning, Lily looked at the icons of Saints Constantine and Helen, and the Virgin and Child that rested on the shelf in her children's bedroom. A soft red electric bulb illuminated them. It was safer than the wick of an oil lamp. She turned the icon of Constantine and Helen around to inspect the little leather bag held in place by a tack. Lily revered it. Eléni had told her, "The amulet and coin come from where you were born, Evangelía, gifts from my father and mother, and from my cousin Chrysóula. We may never go back, but you must remember them."

Lily had not opened the bag since her childhood. *I'll wait until Elenítsa and Jason are old enough to understand*, she thought when she tacked the little bag to the icon. *Then I'll open it and tell them its story.*

A few days later, Constantinos sat next to Vasilikí and basked in the warm morning sun that came through the kitchen windows. He was lean and smartly dressed, with a winged collar, cravat, and vest. His back was straight, and his mustache thin, white, and well trimmed. Anyone who had known him fifty years before, in Pyrgos, would have recognized him.

"Are you warm enough?" Vasilikí asked.

"I'm fine. The sun and hot coffee took the chill from me."

Vasilikí's eyes glistened. "I miss Sozópolis. I could see the sea from my kitchen window."

Sofía overheard her as she entered the room. "Evangelía and I will take you to the shore tomorrow, *mána*."

Vasilikí looked up. "Is the baby sleeping? Where is Elenítsa?"

"She's playing by his crib. She'll watch him."

Sofía, patient with her mother's often-repeated questions, answered each fully, no matter how frequently she asked them.

Lily and her cousins reacted the same way, always ready to calm their *yiayiá's* fears.

"When will Evangelía come home?"

"In an hour or two. Would you like something? Water? A sweet?"

"No."

Sofía pulled a chair up close to her mother. "We have a letter from Theanó," she said, taking folded papers from her apron pocket. "And from Chrysóula too."

Vasilikí leaned forward a little. "Tell me. Tell me."

"Theanó writes that they found a house in Cyprus and moved in. Giorgios bought a bakery."

"Why did they go so far away?"

"There was no work for him here. He knew he could support his family in Cyprus."

"And the children?"

"Ralis and Alexandra are in school. They send you their kisses."

"Will they visit us soon?"

"They are far away. Perhaps in two or three years they'll be able to come."

"Two — three years? I'll be gone."

"No, you won't. You are strong."

"I am tired."

Sofía looked at Constantinos questioningly.

"Vasilikí," he said, "there's other news from Sozópolis. Chrysóula sent a letter."

"Sozópolis," Vasilikí said plaintively. "I hope they take care of Hrístos' bones. Where will you put mine?"

They ignored her question.

"It's sad news. Do you remember Pater Elefthérios?"

"Yes. He baptized Sofía, and he married you. Is he gone?"

"Yes. He was quite old."

"May God forgive him his sins. My age, I think."

"No. Older," Sofía stammered.

"Is there a new priest?"

Constantinos smiled, remembering Aleksiev and Pater Elefthérios and their talks about Bulgarians and Greeks. "There is a new priest. He chanted the *Trisághion* in Bulgarian for Pater Elefthérios, and buried him. Pater Plamen is his name."

Vasilikí did not smile. A moment passed before she said, in disbelief, "Do you believe it? A Bulgarian priest in Sozópolis."

In the mid-afternoon, Lily returned from Christmas shopping to find Vasilikí sleeping in her rocker with her head resting on an embroidered pillow. Anastasia Zelios sat in the kitchen drinking coffee and listening to a soap opera on the radio. The children napped on the sofa next to her.

"When did Constantinos and Sofía leave?" Lily asked.

"Just after lunch. I came for coffee and told them I would stay until you came home.

"What happened on 'Our Gal Sunday' today?" Lily asked.

"I'm not sure. I think the lady ran away with the other man." Anastasia's English comprehension remained limited. She depended on Lily to make sure that she understood the stories of the soap opera radio shows. "Were the stores busy?"

"Namms' was crowded. Everyone is Christmas shopping."

Anastasia stood up. "It's time for me to go home. The boys will be starving."

Vasilikí opened her eyes and reached out with her hand. "Anastasia, are you leaving?" She grasped Anastasia's hand and kissed her face. "You have my blessing."

Later, after Lily served dinner, cleaned the kitchen, and put Elenítsa and Jason to bed, she took Vasilikí into the little bedroom off the kitchen to prepare her for bed.

"Bathe me, Evangelía. Take me upstairs and bathe me. Then dress me in my white nightgown. I am leaving tonight."

"Leaving?"

"Yes. I want to sleep forever and go to Hristós and Eléni."

Lily took her grandmother upstairs and bathed her in the tub. She combed and braided her hair, dressed her in the long white gown she wanted to wear, took her to her bedroom and tucked her in. Vasilikí kissed Evangelía. "Bless you, my child. Tell Dimitráki that I bless him and your children too. Now let me fall asleep and go." She closed her eyes.

Lily looked in on the children and then on her way to the kitchen to prepare coffee for Jimmy and Louie, she stopped at her grandmother's bedroom door. Vasilikí's chest was immobile, neither rising nor falling.

"Jimmy, call DeTata. Tell him to come. It's *yiayiá*."

Lily knelt at Vasilikí's bedside and put her arm under her grandmother's shoulders, lifting her. "*Yiayiá, yiayiá*, wake up. Don't go."

Vasilikí's eyes opened, and she gasped for breath, heaving, "What do you want? Leave me. Let me go."

Both Louie and Jimmy were in the room now. Jimmy said, "Eddie's on his way."

Vasilikí looked at them with sadness in her eyes. Lily brought water and offered it to her grandmother. She would not open her lips. Minutes passed. Jimmy, Louie, and Lily exchanged hushed whispers and encouraged Vasilikí to look forward to watching her great-grandchildren grow.

When he arrived, Dr. DeTata examined Vasilikí quickly, listened to her heart and lungs and asked, "Lily, what's wrong? She's fine."

"She said that she wanted to go, Eddie. She asked me to bathe her and prepare her for her funeral. Then she went to sleep and stopped breathing."

"*Yiayiá*, did you try to die?" DeTata asked.

Holding Louie's hand, Vasilikí told him to tell Jimmy and Lily to leave the room. She asked Louie in Greek, "What does the doctor say?"

Louie spoke gently to his mother-in-law. "The doctor wants to know if you wanted to die — if you tried to die."

"Tell him I want to sleep forever. I want to go to Hristós and Eléni. I was almost there when Evangelía woke me."

Louie translated what she had said into Italian for DeTata and he understood, responding in Italian: "Tell her she can go if she wants to. I'll tell Lily to leave her in peace."

Louie translated for Vasilikí, who smiled at the doctor. "Bless you."

DeTata straightened Vasilikí's blankets, touched her face, and left the room, signaling to Louie to follow. He closed the door behind them.

"How is she, Eddie?" Lily asked.

"Sometimes old people grow tired of life, Lily. We don't know how, but they go to sleep and stop breathing. Your grandmother was almost gone when you woke her. Leave her alone tonight. What happens is between her and God."

Two days before Christmas a hearse carried Vasilikí to Mount Olivet Cemetery to join her daughter and grandson.

CHAPTER TWENTY-SEVEN
1936
BAY RIDGE, BROOKLYN

The priest swirled the *thimiatíri*, filling the crowded room with the smell of sweet incense and the sound of tinkling bells. To make space for family and friends at the baptismal service, Louie and Jimmy had taken the dining room table apart and moved it and the dining room chairs to the basement.

Jason alternatively cried and laughed. He splashed the water in the baptismal font as though he were in a bathtub. The priest found it difficult to control the chubby two-year-old.

Elenítsa stood in front of the onlookers, sometimes clinging to the top of the baptismal font to look over its edge and watch her brother's ordeal. She was tall for her age; thin, and bright eyed, with an intelligence that had already surprised her parents. When not focused on her brother, or the bearded priest and his ornate vestments, she held her *pappoú's* hand or rested against her *nouno's* legs and sang along with the priest and the chanter.

Louie and Bill Rusuli stood on one side of the font, Lily, Jimmy and Rose Rusuli on the other. Rose and Bill, already godparents to Elenítsa, were now assuming the same role for Jason, whom they christened Constantine. Brother and sister would have the same name day.

Pater Ioánnis lifted Jason Constantine and wrapped him in the new white cotton blanket that Rose held ready.

"He's good and warm, Lily," Rose assured her friend.

Lily had set aside her memories of the pneumonia that took Athanásios after his baptism, and threatened Elenítsa after hers. Jason was strong, and spring was coming.

The priest anointed Jason Constantine, snipped three locks of hair from his head, and blessed the new shirt that he would wear. Anastasia took him from Rose's arms to the kitchen. She and her sister Moschánthi dressed the boy in his white baptismal clothing and returned him to the dining room. Pater put a gold necklace with a small baptismal cross about Jason Constantine's neck, lit the baptismal candle held by Rose, and, carrying him in his arms, led Rose, Bill, and Elenítsa around the font in a symbolic dance.

Bill held Jason Constantine while Pater administered communion to him. He liked the taste and reached for the baptismal spoon.

Rose and Bill presented Jason Constantine to Lily and Jimmy, declaring the baptism and Chrismation of their son, and his dedication to God.

"*Na sas zísi*," said Pater Ioánnis.

Eléni's portrait rested on the dark oak shelf that circled the room above her family and friends. Her face smiled down on them.

"She is here, Sofía. Eléni is here," Constantinos whispered to his wife. "Look at her face." He motioned with his head up, toward the photograph.

Sofía gripped her husband's arm. "I miss her so much."

"Now we all look to Evangelía — to Lily," Constantinos said. "Everyone turns to her. Even me."

"Without Eléni ..." Sofía's voice faltered.

"She is here — in Lily, and her children. We are here. Our children, their children, and their children's children will be here. That is what we dreamed — our family — safe in America."

GLOSSARY

agápe	Love. The agápe service referred to in the novel is usually conducted on the afternoon of Easter Sunday. It is a service of forgiveness and reconciliation at which the gospel of the Resurrection is read in as many languages as there are readers.
agápe mou	my love
Ághios Vasílis	Saint Basil — the name day of the Saint, January 1st. Ághios translates as saint.
agizlik	The mouthpiece used in smoking a narghilé. Often of carved amber.
alamánes	A rowed fishing boat. The name is a corruption from the Italian.
Alithós Anésti	Truly He is Risen. It is the response to Hristós

	Anésti (see below).
amané	Mournful songs or laments, known as amané from the characteristic ritual refrain of aman–aman (roughly, mercy–mercy)
Amerikanáda	American woman
amin	amen
anástasi	resurrection
andártes	Greek guerrilla fighters
antídoron	A consecrated piece of bread. Literally, instead of the Gift, or communion — the Body and Blood of Christ.
antío	Farewell, goodbye — a corruption of the French *adieu*, or Italian *addio*.
apo	from
babás	Informal for father.
bakeesh	bribe, tip
baklavá	Ground walnuts, almonds, or pistachios, mixed with cinnamon, sugar, and allspice, layered in buttered sheets of phyllo, and soaked with an orange or lemon zest, honey, and brandy sauce
bekrís	drunkard
bétheros	Father-in-law
buon giorno	Italian — hello, good day
caïque	From the French *caïque*, Italian *caicco*, and Turkish *kayık*.
City, the	Constantinople (Istanbul)
comatadjis	Bulgarian guerrilla fighters
con sposo	Italian — with spouse
dolmádes	Stuffed grape leaves — with herbed and seasoned rice only, or with a ground meat/rice combination — often served with an egg-lemon sauce.
Eastern Romylia	An autonomous province of the Ottoman Empire established in 1878. Unified with

	Bulgaria in 1885.
eféndis	master
énosis	union
éros	erotic, passionate love
fakí	lentils
fasoúlia	beans
féta	Soft, white cheese made from sheep's or goat's milk, cured and preserved in brine
fez	A red felt hat in the shape of a truncated cone; a black tassel hangs from the crown. The fez was popular in the Ottoman Empire in the 19th century.
galatomboúreko	Semolina custard layered into phyllo dough, and soaked with a simple lemon syrup
generális	general
grappa	Alcoholic beverage distilled from pomace, the residue mash from the fermentation of grapes into wine — in Greek, rakí
grotzen	The prominent, often darker line of hair that runs down the middle of the back of a fur skin
haíde	Adopted from Turkish for: 'Come on,' 'hurry,' 'go ahead,' 'do it,' etc.
háiretai	formal greeting
hrisó mou	my treasure — literally, my gold
Hristós	Christ
Hrístos	Short for Hristodoúlos
Hristós Anésti	Christ is Risen – an affirmation and greeting used on Easter and for forty days thereafter.
ibríki	Adopted from Turkish *ibrik*, a long-handled, small, copper-coated pot used to make coffee.
ikonostásion	The panel of icons that separates the sanctuary from the nave.
Il Natale	Italian — Christmas
kafé	coffee

kafeneío, kafeneía	coffee house, coffee houses
Kala Christoúgena	Merry Christmas
kali méra	good day
kali spéra	good evening
kalimáfion	A clerical hat adopted by Orthodox clergy at the end of the 18th century when it was worn by attorneys and judges. It is black and cylindrical.
kapetánios	captain
karadópita	walnut cake
kasséri	Medium hard yellow cheese made of sheep's or goat's milk
keftédes	Meatballs made with onion, garlic, mint, oregano, egg, parsley, tomatoes, etc. These meatballs are called kefta in the middle-east.
kléftis	thief
kokorétsi	A delicacy made from a lambs organ meats, highly seasoned, and tied together with the lamb's intestines.
kombolói	Worry beads — an odd number, preferably of amber or coral like the Catholic Rosary, but with no religious significance. Used to relax.
kóri, korítsi, koritsia	daughter, young girl, girls
koulourákia	A butter cookie in the shape of a twist, or braid
krasí	wine
lakérda	salted tuna
lambrópsomo	Literally, bread of the light. The terms Páscha and Lambrí (light) are both used for Easter.
loukánika	dried sausage (pork, orange zest, onion, wine, salt, pepper, oregano)
macháira	Macháiri is a knife — macháira is a knife wielding woman.

mahlépi	The ground kernel of the pit of the Persian wild cherry
makaría	The meal that follows a funeral. Literally a 'blessing.'
mána	mother — affectionate, informal
mastícha	Mastic resin from the mastic tree found on the island of Chios
Mavrothálassa	Black Sea
Megali Idhea	The 'Big Idea' formulated in the late nineteenth century. It represented the Greek Kingdom's desire to recover all Greek -speaking lands in the Balkans and Anatolia.
mezedáki	A little appetizer.
mezés	appetizer, hors d'oeuvre
mille grazie	Italian — a thousand thanks
mitéra	mother — formal
na sas (mas) zísi	May he (or she) live for you (us)— a phrase used as a prayer for life, and to welcome the newborn
narghilé, narghilés (plural)	water pipe, hooka
Nessun Dorma	Italian — the aria Calaf sings at the beginning of Act Three of Puccini's opera, *Turandot* — literally, 'No one sleeps'
nouná	godmother
nounó	godfather
paidiá	children
paliánthropos	bad man
palikári	manly, swashbuckling young man
paliópaido	bad boy
Panaghía	Virgin Mary
pappoú	grandfather
Pasás	Pasha — a governor or general in the Ottoman

	Empire. In this case, the pet name of a rooster.
Páscha	Easter
Pater	Father, as in speaking to or about a priest.
Pater Imon	Our Father — the Lord's Prayer
patéra	father — formal
patsá	A Balkan soup of pig's head, hocks, and feet, flavored with garlic, paprika, and vinegar. Jells when chilled into headcheese. Called *pichtí* is some regions of Greece.
paximádia	Twice baked bread or pastry sometimes flavored with orange, almond, vanilla, or anise
philótimos	One who has a sense of honor, dignity, and duty
Pontos Eúxeinos	The welcoming sea (Black Sea)
pórni	prostitutes
presvytéra	a priest's wife
prieka	dowry
psáltis	chanter, cantor
rakí	Turkish. An alcoholic beverage distilled from pomace, the mash remaining after fermented grape juice is drawn from the barrel for aging or bottling. Also known as grappa by Italians, and tsipoúra in Crete and Greece, where it is also the base for ouzo.
ráso	Like a cassock. A long black garment worn by clerics.
retsína	Pine resin infused white wine
Romiá	Roman female
Romiói	Romans — the way Greek speakers in the Balkans identified themselves as Romans, full citizens of the Easter Roman Empire (identified as 'Byzantium' by nineteenth century western scholars starting with Sir George Finlay, in 1851).

Romiós	Roman male
Romylia	uivalent to 'Eastern Romylia,' above
sarmádes	Stuffed cabbage leaves — in the Balkans, often pickled cabbage stuffed with an herbed and spiced pork and rice mixture
spanakópita (es)	Spinach, egg, feta filling, baked in layers of buttered phyllo dough
stefádo	A stew traditionally of rabbit (beef can be use) with onions, tomato sauce, cinnamon, wine, and vinegar as primary ingredients.
stéfana	Marriage crowns. Delicate, circular crowns woven with white wax flowers, beads, and leaves. The crowns, which worn by the couple being married, are joined by a white ribbon.
symbéthera	Mother of one's son-in-law, or daughter- in-law.
symbétheri	Parents related to each other through their children's marriage.
symbétheros	Father of one's son-in-law, or daughter- in-law.
taramasaláta	A spread made of the roe (taramá) of the red mullet (or carp), olive oil, lemon juice, garlic, onion, and bread.
tavérna (s)	tavern, taverns
távli	backgammon
thimiatíri	An incense burning censer used in religious ceremonies
tirópites	Feta cheese and egg filling, baked in layers of buttered phyllo dough
Tis Panaghías	The feast of the 'falling asleep,' or death of the Virgin Mary, and her assumption into heaven.
toursí	Vegetables (green tomatoes, cucumbers, carrots, celery, cauliflower, etc.) pickled in brine.
tsíri	Dried, salted young mackerel. Stripped from the bone, the flesh is marinated in vinegar, olive oil, and dill.

tuféki	Adopted from Turkish 'tufek' — gun or rifle.
tzamí	mosque
Vasilópita	Saint Basil's Bread — a sweet bread made especially for New Year's Day
Vinceró	Italian — I shall conquer
yiá sou	Informal greeting — hello, to your health
yiayiá	grandmother
Zíto Ellás	Long live Hellas (Greece)
Zíto Vasiléfs	Long live the King
zoí se emás	Life to us

Jason C. Mavrovitis

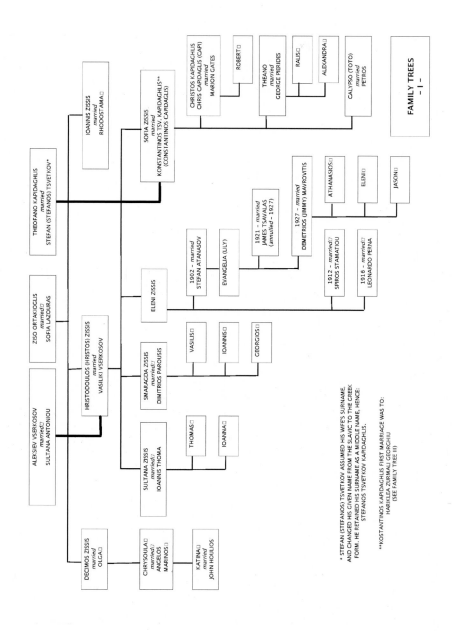

FAMILY TREES
- I -

ALEKSIEV VSERKOSOV
married
SULTANA ANTONIOU

ZISO ORTAKIOGLIS
married
SOFIA LAZOURAS

THEOFANO KAPIDAGHLIS
married
STEFAN (STEFANOS) TSVETKOV*

IOANNIS ZISSIS
married
RHODOSTAMA

SOFIA ZISSIS
married
KONSTANTINOS TSV. KAPIDAGHLIS**
(CONSTANTINOS CAPIDAGLIS)

HRISTODOULOS (HRISTOS) ZISSIS
married
VASILIKI VSERKOSOV

CHRISTOS KAPIDAGHLIS
CHRIS CAPIDAGLIS (CAP)
married
MARION GATES

ROBERT

THEANO
married
GEORGE PERIDES

RALIS

ALEXANDRA

CALYPSO (TOTO)
married
PETROS

SULTANA ZISSIS
married
IOANNIS THOMA

SMARAGDA ZISSIS
married
DIMITRIOS PAROUSIS

ELENI ZISSIS

THOMAS

IOANNA

VASILIS

IOANNIS

GEORGIOS

1902 – *married*
STEFAN ATANASOV

EVANGELIA (LILY)

1921 – *married*
JAMES TSAVALAS
(annulled – 1927)

1927 – *married*
DEMETRIOS (JIMMY) MAVROVITIS

ATHANASIOS

ELENI

JASON

1912 – *married*
SPIROS STAMATIOU

1916 – *married*
LEONARDO PERNA

DECIMOS ZISSIS
married
OLGA

CHRYSOULA
married
ANGELOS MARINOS

KATINA
married
JOHN HOULIOS

* STEFAN (STEFANOS) TSVETKOV ASSUMED HIS WIFE'S SURNAME,
AND CHANGED HIS GIVEN NAME FROM THE SLAVIC TO THE GREEK
FORM. HE RETAINED HIS SURNAME AS A MIDDLE NAME, HENCE:
STEFANOS TSVETKOV KAPIDAGHLIS.

**KOSTANTINOS KAPIDAGHLIS FIRST MARRIAGE WAS TO:
HARIKLEA ZURMALI GEORGHIU
(SEE FAMILY TREE III)

419

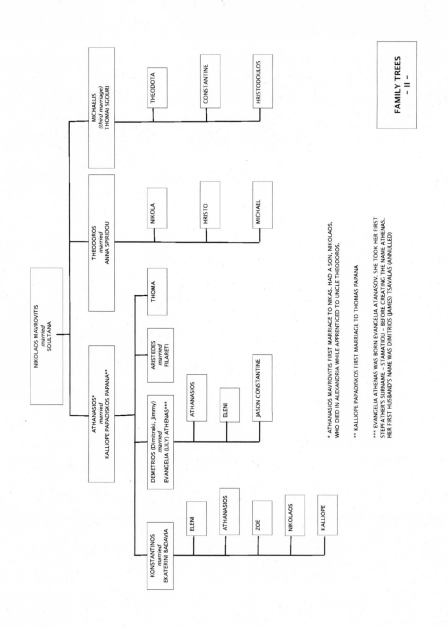

FAMILY TREES
– II –

NIKOLAOS MAVROVITIS
married
SOULTANA

ATHANASIOS*
married
KALLIOPE PAPADISKOS PAPANA**

THEODOROS
married
ANNA SPIRIDOU

MICHAELIS
(third marriage)
THOMAI SGOURI

THEODOTA

CONSTANTINE

HRISTODOULOS

NIKOLA

HRISTO

MICHAEL

ARISTEDES
married
FILARETI

THOMA

DEMETRIOS (Dimitraki, Jimmy)
married
EVANGELIA (LILY) ATHENAS***

KONSTANTINOS
married
EKATERINI BADAVIA

ATHANASIOS

ELENI

JASON CONSTANTINE

ELENI

ATHANASIOS

ZOE

NIKOLAOS

KALLIOPE

* ATHANASIOS MAVROVITIS FIRST MARRIAGE TO NIKAS, HAD A SON, NIKOLAOS, WHO DIED IN ALEXANDRIA WHILE APPRENTICED TO UNCLE THEODOROS.

** KALLIOPE PAPADISKOS FIRST MARRIAGE TO THOMAS PAPANA

*** EVANGELIA ATHENAS WAS BORN EVANGELIA ATANASOV. SHE TOOK HER FIRST STEPFATHER'S SURNAME – STAMATIOU – BEFORE CREATING THE NAME ATHENAS. HER FIRST HUSBAND'S NAME WAS DIMITRIOS (JAMES) TSAVALAS (ANNULLED)

JASON C. MAVROVITIS

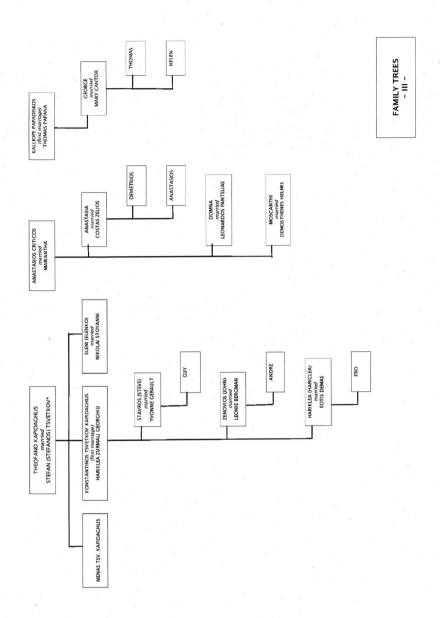